Absolution

Absolution

Patrick Flanery

W F HOWES LTD

This large print edition published in 2013 by
W F Howes Ltd
Unit 4, Rearsby Business Park, Gaddesby Lane,
Rearsby, Leicester LE7 4YH

1 3 5 7 9 10 8 6 4 2

First published in the United Kingdom in 2011
by Atlantic Books Ltd.

A CIP catalogue record for this book is available
from the British Library

ISBN 978 1 47122 197 2

Typeset by Palimpsest Book Production Limited,
Falkirk, Stirlingshire
Printed and bound in Great Britain
by MPG Books Ltd, Bodmin, Cornwall

MIX
Paper from
responsible sources
FSC
www.fsc.org   FSC® C018575

For
G.L.F. *and* A.E.V.

PART I

SAM

'I'm told we met in London, Mr Leroux, but I don't remember you,' she says, trying to draw her body upright, making it straight where it refuses to be.

'That's right. We did meet. Just briefly, though.' In fact it wasn't London but Amsterdam. She remembers an award ceremony in London where I wasn't. I remember the conference in Amsterdam where I spoke, invited as a promising young expert on her work. She took my hand charmingly then. She was laughing and girlish and a little drunk. I can see no trace of intoxication this time. I've never met her in London.

There was the other time, too, of course.

'Please, call me Sam,' I say.

'My editor says nice things about you. I don't like your looks, though. You look fashionable.' She draws her lips back on the final syllable, her teeth apart. There's a flicker of grey tongue.

'I wouldn't know about that,' I say, and can't help blushing.

'*Are* you fashionable?' She spreads her lips again,

flashes her teeth. If it's supposed to be a smile it doesn't look like one.

'I don't think so.'

'I have no memory of your face. Nor of your voice. I'd certainly remember that voice. That accent. I don't think we can possibly have met. Not in this lifetime, as they say.'

'It was a very brief meeting.' I almost remind her that she was drunk at the time. She's affecting to look uninterested in the present meeting, but there's too much energy in the boredom.

'You must know I've agreed to the project under duress. I'm a very old woman, but that doesn't mean I intend dying any time soon. You, for instance, might well die before me, and no one is rushing to write your biography. You might be killed in an accident this afternoon. Run down in the street. Carjacked.'

'I'm not important.'

'Quite so.' There's a lick of a smirk on one side of the mouth. 'I've read your articles and I don't think you're an imbecile. Nonetheless, I'm really not optimistic about this.' She stares at me, shaking her head. Her hands rest on her hips and she looks a little clumsy, at least clumsier than I remember. 'I would've chosen my own biographer, but I don't know anyone who would agree to undertake the task. I'm a terror.' There's a hint of the girlishness I saw in Amsterdam, something akin to flirtation but not quite, like she's hoping a man will find her attractive simply because he's a man, and I have to admit she still has a kind of beauty.

'I'm sure lots of people would jump at the chance,' I say and she looks surprised. She thinks I'm flirting back and smiles in a way that looks almost genuine.

'None that I would choose.' She wags her head at me, a reprimanding schoolteacher, staring down the famous nose. I may be tall, but she's taller still, a giant. 'I'd write my autobiography, but I think it would be a waste of time. I've never written about my life. I don't entirely believe in the value of life writing. Who cares about the men I loved? Who cares about my sex life? Why does everyone want to know what a writer does in bed? I suppose you expect to sit down.'

'Whatever you prefer. I can stand.'

'You can't stand the whole time.'

'I could if that suited you,' I say, smiling, but the flirtatious mood has passed. She pouts, points to a straight-backed chair and waits until I sit, then chooses a chair for herself on the other side of the room, so that we're forced to shout. A cat wanders past and jumps on to her lap. She removes it, putting it back on the floor.

'Not my cat. My assistant's. Don't put in the book that I'm a cat lady. I'm not. I don't want people thinking I'm a mad old cat lady.' There's a picture on the back of her early books – the publicity shot used for the first ten years of her career – in which she holds a baby cheetah, its

5

mouth open, tongue sticking out as her tongue does now. It suggests the suckling toddler, or the stroke victim. 'My British publisher insisted on the stupid cheetah,' she'll tell me later, 'because that's what an African writer was supposed to have, the wild clutched to her bosom, suckling the continent, all those tired imperial fantasies.'

'What form do you anticipate this taking?' she asks now. 'Please don't imagine I'm going to give you access to my letters and diaries. I'll talk to you but I'm not going to dig out documents or family albums.'

'I thought a series of interviews to start.'

'A way of getting comfortable?' she asks. I nod, shrug my shoulders, produce a small digital recorder. She snorts. 'I hope you don't imagine that we're going to become friends over the course of this. I won't take walks with you in my garden or visit museums. I don't "do drinks". I won't impart the wisdom of the aged to you. I won't teach you how to live a better life. This is a professional arrangement, not a romance. I'm a busy person. I have a new book coming out next year, *Absolution*. I suppose I shall have to let you read it, in due course.'

'I defer to you.'

'I've read your articles, as I said. You don't get things entirely wrong.'

'Perhaps you'll be able to correct some of my mistakes.'

Clare did not answer her own door when I

arrived. Marie, the beetle-eyed assistant, delivered me into a reception room that overlooked the front garden and the long drive, the high beige periphery wall mounted with barbed wire shaped and painted to mimic trained ivy, and the electronic gate closing out the road. Security cameras monitor the property. Clare has chosen a cold room for our first interview. Maybe it's the only reception room. No – a house this size will have several. There must be another one, a better one, with a view of the back gardens and the mountain rising above the city. She'll take me there next time, or somehow I'll manage to find it on my own.

Her face is narrower than her pictures suggest. If there was a fullness in her cheeks five years ago in Amsterdam, the health has receded and now her face is wind-cracked, a lake bottom in drought. It looks nothing like any of the photographs. Her unruly squall of blonde hair has silvered, and though it's thin and brittle it still has some of the old lustre. Her abdomen has spread. She's almost a very old woman, but doesn't look her real age – more like sixty than whatever she really is. Her skin is tanned and the line of her jaw has a plastic tension. Despite the slight hump in her back, she tries to remain erect. I feel a flash of anger at her vanity. But it's not my place to judge that. She is who she is. I'm here for something else.

'I hope you've brought your own food and drink. I don't intend to feed you while you feed off me. You may use the facilities at the end of the corridor on the left. Please remember to lower the seat when you've finished. It will encourage my sympathy.' She narrows her eyes and seems to be smirking again, but I can't tell if she's joking or serious.

'Are you going to record these discussions?'

'Yes.'

'Take notes as well?'

'Yes.'

'Is it on?'

'Yes. It's recording.'

'Well?'

'I'm predictable. I'd like to start at the beginning,' I say.

'You'll find no clues in my childhood.'

'That's not really the point, if you'll forgive me. People want to know.' In fact, almost nothing is known about her life beyond the slim facts of public record, and the little she's condescended to admit in previous interviews. Her agent in London released a one-page official biography five years ago when requests for information became overwhelming. 'Both sets of grandparents were farmers.'

'No. My paternal grandfather was an ostrich farmer. The other was a butcher.'

'And your parents?'

'My father was a lawyer, an advocate. The first in his family to go to university. My mother was a linguist, an academic. I never saw much of them. There were women – girls – to look after me. A succession of them. I believe my father did a fair amount of *pro Deo* work.'

'Did that inform your own political stance?'

She sighs and looks disappointed, as though I've missed a joke.

'I don't have a political stance. I'm not political. My parents were liberals. It was to be expected that I would also be a liberal, but I think my parents were "liberals" in the reluctant way of so many of their generation. Better we should speak of left-wing and right-wing, or progressive and regressive, or even *opp*ressive. I am not an absolutist. Political orientation is an ellipse, not a continuum. Go far enough in one direction and you end up more or less in the place where you started. But this is politics. Politics is not the subject at hand is it?'

'Not necessarily. But is it difficult, do you find, to engage in a critique of the government, as a writer?'

She coughs and clears her throat. 'No, certainly not.'

'What I mean is, does being a writer make it more difficult to criticize the government?'

'More difficult than what?'

'Than if you were a private citizen, for instance.'

'But I am a private citizen, as you put it. In my experience, governments mostly take very little notice of what private citizens have to say, unless they say it in unison.'

'I guess what I'm trying to ask –'

'Then ask it.'

'What I'm trying to ask is whether you think it's more difficult to criticize the current government?'

'Certainly not. Just because it's democratically elected doesn't grant it immunity from criticism.'

'Do you think that fiction is essential to political opposition?' I regret the question as soon as it's out, but sitting in front of her all the carefully formulated questions I've spent months preparing seem impossible to ask.

She laughs and the laugh turns into another fit of coughing and throat-clearing. 'You have a very strange idea of what fiction is meant to do.'

I stall for time, feeling her stare at me as I study my maze of notes. I naively assumed it would all go so smoothly. I decide to ask her about the sister; there's no denying the importance of politics there. As I'm trying to frame the question in my head, she clears her throat again, as if to say, *Come along, you must do better*, and I rush into another question I didn't mean to ask.

'Did you have any siblings?'

'You know this, Mr Leroux. It was the climax of a turbulent period. It's a matter of public record. But I absolutely will not talk about my sister.'

'Not even the bare facts?'

'The known facts of the case are on file in the court records and countless press clippings. No doubt you've read them. Everyone has read them. A man acting alone, he said. The court found that he was not acting alone, though no one else was arrested. Like so many others, he died in police custody. Unlike so many others, he had actually committed a crime – at least he never denied doing it. I can add nothing else except the experience of the victimized family and that is not new material. We all know how people suffer over the unexpected, violent death of a family member. It is fundamentally no different for the family of a murdered innocent or the family of an executed criminal. It is vivisection. It is limb loss. No prosthetic can substitute. The family is crippled. That is all I wish to say.'

*

Though it's only supposed to be our second meeting, Clare can't or won't see me today. Instead I go to the Western Cape Archives, park on Roeland Street, and nod at the car guard who's sheltering in the shade of a truck. He gives me a subservient smile and makes some kind of sound of assent. I find myself always on edge, expecting the worst. At the airport I was a foreigner, but a week later, in the market yesterday, I was already a local again. Over a display of lettuces, a woman addressed me, expecting a reply. A decade ago I might have come up with the right words. I had to shake my head. I smiled and apologized, explaining that I didn't speak the language, didn't understand. *Ek is jammer. Ek praat nie Afrikaans nie. Ek verstaan jou nie.* I've lost too much of my Afrikaans to be able to answer. I didn't know what to say about the lettuce or the fish, the *vis*. She looked surprised, then shrugged and walked away,

11

mumbling sharply, assuming perhaps that I knew but was refusing to speak her language.

The Archives have been housed on the site of a former prison for nearly twenty years. The car guard watches as I walk up the steps and through the green grille of the old gate in the nineteenth-century outer wall. Inside there are shabby picnic tables and plantings, and the new structure, a building within a building. I sign the register, put my bag in a locker, and carry my equipment to the reading room. The woman behind the desk, a Mrs Stewart, is uncertain at first what it is I want. She looks vaguely alarmed when she understands, but nods and asks me to take a seat while she sends someone to look for the files. All her sentences rise at the end, in a tone that questions everything without questioning directly. A few years ago, the staff might have let me do my own digging in the stacks – friends had such luck, finding things they weren't supposed to find. Now everything is more organized and more professional, but also a little less hopeful.

The other people in the room all appear to be amateur genealogists working on family histories. When the stack of brown folders with bold red stamps appears on my table I feel the others staring, wondering what kind of files I might be consulting, no longer confidential but still bearing that mark. I take out my camera and tripod and photograph page after page throughout the morning.

At lunchtime, two women from the reading room approach me in the lobby.

'Are you working on family history?' one of them asks, her voice rising like Mrs Stewart's.

'No. It's for a book. I'm looking at the files of the Publications Control Board. The censors.'

'Ohhh,' the other one says, nodding. 'How verrrry interesting.'

We talk for a few moments. I ask about their research. They are sisters, investigating their ancestors, trying to track down the right Hermanus Stephanus or Gertruida Magdalena over centuries of people with the same names.

'Good luck with your researches,' the first one says as we part on the steps. 'I hope you find what it is you are looking for.'

I give the car guard what I think is proper. It always seems like too little or too much. Later, I ask Greg what he thinks. I trust his opinion because I've known him since we were students in New York, and because he's the most morally and socially engaged friend I still have in the country. When I told him I was coming back, and that my wife would be joining me later in the year to take up her new assignment in Johannesburg, Greg insisted I stay with him for as long as I needed to be in Cape Town.

'It can never be too much because they need it more than you,' he says, balancing his son on his knee. 'Just like if your hire car gets stolen or somebody takes the radio or the hubcaps – you have to tell yourself, whoever took it needs it more. It's the only way to live with yourself.'

'I don't ever want it to look like charity.'

'Think of all the fuckers who only give them fifty cents and can't be bothered. Money isn't an insult. There's nothing wrong with charity. Not everything has to be payment for services rendered, however informally. And if you're a tourist you owe them a little more.'

'I don't think of myself as a tourist any more. I'm back now.'

'You haven't been local for a long time, Sam, no matter what shirt you wear or the music you listen to. And who's to say you're going to stay in the long run? Sarah's post lasts for – how long? – only eighteen months?'

'Three years if she wants it.'

'But then you'll go somewhere else. That means you're a tourist. You don't have to feel bad about it. Just remember it.'

'And how much do you give?'

'No, see, the thing is, I give less than I expect you to give because I give every day and have been giving for years. I employ a nanny who comes six days a week, a gardener who comes twice a week, a domestic who comes three times a week, and I give soup packets to the old man who comes to my front gate every Friday. I give my domestic and my nanny money to put their kids through school. I buy the school uniforms. I pay for their medical aid. When I park in the city, I don't give the car guards as much as I'd expect you to give because I give so much already, and even that isn't enough, you know. And I don't give food to people who come to the house any more, except the old man, because he's never drunk. So I'm one of the fuckers I hate. But you tourists, you've got to give a little more.'

He speaks quickly, his son playing with the beads around his neck. 'Dylan, don't pull Daddy's beads.' He looks up at me, smiling. 'I was thinking, let's go to the Waterfront this afternoon. There's a new juice bar open and I feel like shopping. We'll leave Dylan with Nonyameko. We can see a movie afterward.'

*

Another day. Clare shows me into the same room as the one we used for our first interview. This time she has buzzed me in through the gate and opened her own front door. The assistant must have the day off. We sit again in the same chairs. The cat passes through the room, only this time it takes to my lap instead of hers. Purring, it drools on my jeans and digs its claws into my legs.

'Cats like fools,' Clare says, straight-faced.

'Can we go back to your sister?'

'I knew you weren't going to let Nora stay dead.' She looks weary, even more drawn than the first time. I know that her sister's story is a detour from

15

the main route. This is not the real story I want, but it might be a way of getting there in the long run.

'Was your sister always political?'

'I think she regarded herself as *apolitical*, like me. But, that's not quite fair. I'm not apolitical. I'm privately political. But if one chooses a public life – either by career or association or marriage – that's another matter. She chose a public life by marrying a public figure.'

'A writer's life is not a public life?'

'No,' she says, and smiles – either condescendingly or, I flatter myself, enjoying the parry. 'It was unconscionable to take an apolitical stance in *this* country at *that* time, as a public figure. She was a victim of her own naïveté. She should have known she was marking herself for death. But she was the firstborn. Our parents made mistakes. Perhaps they left her crying in the crib instead of comforting her. Or they were strict where they should have been trusting. She always resented that I was allowed to shave my legs and wear lipstick when I was thirteen, to have skirts above my knees, to bleach my schoolgirl moustache. It was obvious the same standards did not apply to me, and she saw that. Our parents held her under their thumbs until she was sixteen. She did not go to university. Marriage was an escape from authoritarian parenting into an even more authoritarian culture. I was luckier.'

'You were educated abroad.' I know all this. I'm

laying down the foundations. Everything else will rest on this.

'Yes. Boarding school here, then university in England. A period in Europe after that.'

'And then you returned home, at a time when many in the anti-apartheid movement – writers especially – were beginning to go into exile.'

'That's correct. It was before I had published. I wanted to come back, to be a part of the opposition, such as it was.'

'Do you resent those who emigrated?'

'No. Some had little choice. They were banned, they or their families were threatened, and some were imprisoned. Or they left for a brief while – to study overseas – and found that because of their political activities they could not return, or simply they realized it was easier in many ways to stay in England or America or Canada or France, and so much the better for them, I suppose, if that's what they wanted, if that is what they felt they needed to do for themselves. I was not threatened, for the most part, and so I stayed – or rather, I returned and stayed. Is this going anywhere, this line of questioning? What can it say about me?'

When we met in Amsterdam she was drunk on the adulation, and on quantities of champagne. As a result, she was effusive and open-handed then, or seemed so maybe only because she was away from home and being celebrated. She pretended it was her birthday and took a magnum of champagne from the conference reception. At the bland tourist hotel where she was staying, she pleaded in halting Afrikaans for the concierge to get some glasses from the restaurant so she could toast her birthday with her friends, old and new. The concierge tried not to laugh at her language, but it had the desired effect.

I was one of the group then, a new friend. Given the champagne, it shouldn't surprise me that she has forgotten our first meeting, or that she imagines it was in London, at an awards ceremony instead of a conference. She's an old woman. Her memory can't be perfect.

I find it difficult, though, to reconcile the writer I so esteem in print, who took my hand with such grace in Amsterdam, with the woman sitting across from me now. There is open mockery on her face. It triggers a flash of memory that I instantly suppress. I can't allow myself to think about the past, not yet.

ABSOLUTION

It was not the usual kind of slow waking in the middle of the night, from the bottom of sleep. Clare's bladder was not full, she had consumed no caffeine the previous day. Her window was open, but noises from outside did not, as a rule, ever bother her sleep. Instinctively, she knew something was wrong. She was hyperventilating when she woke and her heart was beating so loudly that if anyone had been in the room it would have betrayed her.

For years she had resisted an alarm, insisting that locks were adequate; anyone determined enough to break through deadbolts and safety glass and burglar bars was worthy of whatever bounty they might choose. But now, how she wished for the alarm, and the kind of bedside panic button that her friends and her son, her scattered cousins, had all chosen to install. She knew, too, that the sound could not have come from Marie, who would be asleep upstairs on the top floor. It had come from below. If Marie had gone downstairs, Clare would have heard her pass in the corridor.

Trying to slow her heart rate, she said to herself,

There is silence, there is only breeze, an old mantra she had learned as a girl. The curtains played around the security bars. It was not valuables that worried her. Anyone who wanted them could have the electronics, such as they were, even the silver, the crystal, if thieves cared about such things any more. It was confrontation that terrified her, the threat of guns, and of men with guns. *There is silence. There is only breeze. One, two, three, four, slow, six, seven.* She had nearly calmed herself back to sleep when she heard the unmistakable swing of a door on its hinge, metal rotating against unlubricated metal, and the bottom of the door catching and vibrating against the coir mats in the foyer downstairs. And above there was movement, a creaking floorboard. Marie had heard it, too.

Clare grabbed for the phone in the darkness but when she put the receiver to her ear there was only a hollow silence. Although she had no cellphone she could not answer for Marie, who might be trusted to have a solution. How long since the door against the mat? Seconds? Thirty seconds? Two minutes? A smell began to work its way upstairs, sharp and astringent, chemical, not a smell of her home. And then another sound, pressure on the first stair, a loose board, and a collective intake of breath, or was that her imagination? She could throw her door closed, but the key for the lock had been lost long ago; she would be unable to escape out the window, there was no space under the bed where she might hide, the wardrobe was too full, there was no closet in her bedroom. The courageous thing would be to sit up in bed, turn on the light and wait for them to come, or to shout, 'Take what you want, I don't care!', but she had lost her voice, and her body was paralyzed. She would have screamed if her throat had let her.

More seconds, a minute, silence, or perhaps she was too distracted to hear. There was a granite stone on the floor which she used as a doorstop, almost a small boulder, and she hoisted it from the floor and into the bed, thinking – what? That she would hurl it at her attackers? Could sticks and stones still repulse men, or did it take harder stuff? These were things she suddenly felt she ought to know.

As she adjusted the boulder in her arms, four hooded men appeared before her, their reflections in the glass of the framed photograph on the wall opposite her bed. They passed in single file down the corridor, carrying stunted guns in their gloved hands. The guns were in fact a sick relief, less intimate; death would be quick. She was no stranger to the power of guns.

The last of the four men turned, looked into the room, and sniffed the air. His nostrils were congested. She could hear it as she shut her eyes tight, pretending to sleep, hoping that consciousness had no odour. She could smell him, pungent and sharp, and the metallic reek of the gun and its oils. Her heartbeats were so loud, how could he not hear them? He did hear them, turned, looked into the corridor for his fellows, but they had gone upstairs already – a shuffle, a scuffle, Marie subdued.

His weight came down on her, gloved hands, balaclava over the face, and the sound of his congested breathing. All of a sudden the stone in her hands was on the floor in a single movement, and he pressed down against her, felt for her, felt his way into her with one hand, the other, the waxed leather glove of it, over her mouth, the suffocation, her nostrils almost blocked, her heart roaring.

No, she had imagined that.

But she *could* smell him and the metallic reek of the gun. Her heartbeats were so loud, how could he not hear them, standing there at the threshold? But then he withdrew from the doorway, rejoined the others, and crept further down the corridor.

They would have been watching the house, known that only two women lived there, two women unlikely to have guns. They would have known there was no alarm, no razor wire or electric fence and, crucially, no dogs.

Clare felt the boulder, pale and heavy in her arms, resting alongside her. It was wet with perspiration and smelled of earth. She had dug it out of the garden's old rockery to make way for a vegetable patch. If only the men would whisper to each other, just to let her know they were still there. She thought they were at the opposite end of the corridor, and then was certain of it when the board of the first stair leading to the top floor sighed under the pressure of an intruding foot. God! She must cry out and warn Marie! But she was choked, her throat swollen. Air would not come. The chords would not vibrate. Everything was thick and hard about her.

And then, deafeningly, four bright, explosive shots, low growls, and a fifth, deeper shot, a sixth, bright like the first, and then a rush of feet past her door. The wall opposite her bed exploded in a shower of plaster, knocking the framed photo to the floor, shattering glass across the wood and rugs. There was a final quick shot, a groan and feet pummelling down the stairs, doors slamming, and then silence.

It was not a dream, but she woke from it to find Marie standing next to her.

'They've gone. I chased them.'

'I didn't know you had a gun.'

'You wouldn't get an alarm,' Marie said.

'I will now.'

'I'm going to the neighbours, to phone the police.'

'Did you kill anyone?'

'No.'

'You missed?'

'No. I aimed for their firing arms.'

'You got them?' Clare asked

'Yes. One wouldn't give up. I shot him again. And then the others came at me, and I shot

23

another one of them again. That was all my ammunition.'

'You were lucky.'

'I'll be back in a few minutes.' Marie hovered near the door, assessing the glass on the floor, the mounds of plaster, the exposed beams in the wall, the outer stucco. The extent of the damage would only be evident in daylight.

'Are you sure they've gone?'

'They drove away. They were really very stupid. I wrote down their car registration before they came upstairs. They were parked just outside the house.'

'It was probably stolen.'

After she heard Marie leave, locking the door downstairs, Clare sat up in bed, her throat still dry and hot. How dare Marie keep a gun without telling her? How dare she fire shots in Clare's house? How dare she assume so much?

Clare had not been so close to firing guns for years, not since she had spent the holidays at her cousin Dorothy's farm in the Eastern Cape, and the foreman had been killed in an attack, Dorothy wounded. The two Great Danes had been killed, too, and it was only the next morning when they were certain the danger had passed that they went out and dug ditches for the dogs and buried those huge, sleek bodies inside the compound. Danes do not have long lives. They wrapped the body of the foreman in potato sacks and put it in the back of the truck. Dorothy sat next to the man's body, her leg stretched out and still bleeding. Clare had driven half an hour on dirt roads, then over the pass to the hospital in Grahamstown. Surely there had been others with them, perhaps her daughter? Her memory was only of the bleeding cousin, the dead foreman, the dead dogs, and the invisible attackers. Her daughter could not have been there. By then, Laura had already disappeared.

Clare did not have the stomach to see if there was blood in the corridor, though she knew there would have to be, blood like battery acid, burning into the rugs and floorboards, impossible ever to remove.

The police confirmed that the deadbolts and doors had not been forced, and Marie insisted that she had remembered, as she always did, to check the locks before going to bed; it was as much a part of her nightly habit as flossing her teeth. Besides, she had a mania about security, so she would not have had a lapse, even on a bad day. The telephone line had been cut at its point of entry to the house. Clare stood in the kitchen, her pyjamas covered with a white robe, hair pulled back into a severe knot. She was trying to listen to the policeman questioning Marie, but no one came to question her. It felt as though they were ashamed of Clare's presence. Women were not meant to be giants. Police flashes flared in the upstairs corridor, accompanied by the high electronic whine of cameras. Forensics experts were dusting and collecting samples. She felt a coward.

If the crime had been so professional in its execution, then perhaps petty criminality was not the explanation; petty criminals, even violent criminals, would not have the kind of equipment that would open a lock without any detectable signs of force. Apart from blood on the floor and gunshot wounds to the plaster of her bedroom wall, her house was untouched. The damage had been done in the 'gunfight', as she felt she must call it, in a half-ironic tone that would drive Marie mad in the following weeks. *During the gunfight,* she would begin a sentence, or *I feared that gunfight might be my last experience of the world and it seemed such a waste, such an aesthetic failure.*

Only one thing appeared to have been taken.

'There is something missing,' she told the uniformed officer who was leading the investigation.

'Missing?'

'My father's wig.'

'I don't understand.'

'The tin box containing my father's wig. He was a lawyer. I kept it on the hearth. It has been taken.'

'Why should someone wish to take your father's wig?'

'How should I know?'

'Can you describe it?'

'It was a painted black tin box with my father's wig inside. The wig he wore when he argued cases in London. Made from horsehair. I don't know

26

its value. There were more obviously valuable things they might have taken.'

'What colour was the wig?'

'White. Grey. It was completely ordinary, as barristers' wigs go. Like you see on television. Old movies. Costume dramas.'

'It is a part of a costume?'

'No. Yes. That isn't the point,' Clare said, trying to check her exasperation.

'Would you like it back?'

'Of course I want it back. It belongs to me. It can have no meaning for anyone but me.'

'Except maybe a bald person. You are not bald. Perhaps the person who took it is a bald man. A bald man would need a wig more than you.'

'That is a ridiculous thing to say. Should I not give a statement?'

The officer stared at her through pale jelly eyes.

'A statement? I was told you saw nothing.'

'Don't you think you should ask me whether I saw anything? I saw things. I saw the intruders, their reflections.'

Clare was told to go back to bed, to one of the guest rooms. Walking upstairs, she passed little plastic shrines, police evidence tents marking drops of blood, snaking all the way to her bedroom door. She could not remember coming downstairs, nor could she remember having seen blood, but the tents suggested this was impossible; there was blood everywhere, and the smell of the invaders came back to her: synthetic, chemical, a kind of

27

orange disinfectant, a bathroom cleaning fluid or deodorizer. Those men had cleaned themselves before they attacked; they knew what they were about. When they left, she was certain, they did not disappear into the waves of numberless shacks that stretched out beneath the mountain to the airport and beyond; they went to private hospitals where questions would not be asked, and then home to wives or girlfriends who would tend their dressings with quiet discretion.

Dawn burned visibly through a crack in the exterior wall, wood and plaster riven by the shotgun blast. Clare was allowed to retrieve the photograph from the floor; although its frame had been broken and the glass shattered, she found that by some miracle the antique print itself was intact, almost unharmed, except for a small scratch in one corner. In black and white her sister Nora stared, stern-mouthed, not at the camera, but into the distance, looking out, imperious, through horn-rimmed glasses, her forehead shaded by a ridiculous white hat, the fashion of many decades earlier. Though she was not middle-aged when the picture was taken, Nora wore a dress of white polka dots against a pale background – probably pink, Clare thought – with satin rosette buttons. It was not a young woman's cut, dowdy rather than demure. The polka dots of the dress matched her pearl earrings. Nora's shoulders rubbed against another woman in a light herringbone coat and black straw hat decorated with ostrich feathers. Both looked smug, chins jutting forward, jowls already forming. Clare did not recognize the other woman; they were all interchangeable, sitting in their reviewing booths at identical party rallies. That was how she liked to remember her sister, buttressed against history, in denial of the currents of history, firm-mouthed and frowning, a year or two before her assassination. It was comforting to think of her that way, to imagine her static and immobile.

Marie was beside her again, panting, smelling of wet grass. 'Of course now you will have to move. They know they can get at you here. It's too easy.'

'I will have an alarm. Better burglar bars,' Clare protested.

'You need walls. You cannot stay in this country without walls to protect you. Walls and razor wire, electrified. Guard dogs, too.'

There was no doubt that Marie was going to win this battle. Marie, after all, had risked everything. Marie, the assistant, the employed, the indispensable, must be allowed to determine their future domestic arrangements.

'Marie, what was the car?'

'I gave the police the registration number.'

'But what make? What model? Was it old or new?'

'New,' Marie hesitated. 'A Mercedes.'

'Yes. I thought it would be something like that. You will make appointments with estate agents, tomorrow, won't you?'

CLARE

You come out, across the plateau, running close to the ground, find the hole in the fence you cut on entry, scamper down to the road, peel out of the black jacket, the black slacks, shorts and T-shirt underneath; you are a backpacker, a student, a young woman hitch-hiking, a tourist, perhaps with a fake accent. Soon it will be dawn. But no, I fear this isn't right. Perhaps it wasn't there, not that town – not the one on the plateau, but the one further along the coast at the base of the mountains, and you have gone overland to hide your tracks, not through the centre of town, not where anyone will see you at night, men coming out of bars, remembering in days to come the young woman, taut and determined, hurrying alone in the night. You went overland, up the mountain, circling round the north side of town, up through the old indigenous forest. How many hours' walk? – twelve kilometres or more, and that's if you kept near the road. Run, roll, slide over and down the mountain through the forestry land, the planta-tion, the even rows of tall pines, a grid of growth, into farmland, wide fields, the mountains behind you, the sea in front, and come down to the cross-roads, where others linger in the streetlights, women and men, children, people waiting for a taxi or a relative. An old woman with a child tied to her back scrambles up over the rear fender of a vehicle, helped inside by the other passengers as it drives away, ghosting along the coast road on its innocent journey.

And yours – the flight that becomes flight as soon as the bombs detonate – what kind of journey is that? I understand that you were responsible, but how can I know with certainty? How can I know whether it was that particular explosion or another, whether the strangers who came to me later were protecting you from something or someone else, or protecting me?

I have tried to make sense of you in the past, Laura, but each time I try it comes out wrong. I write it but fail to see it. Call it a mother's blindness. I try again, imagining it another way, but still it seems incomplete.

This new attempt to reconstruct the last days before your disappearance is only for my own sake, because there was never an official account. I begin this diary again, a new final beginning, at the same hour as I have put the pieces in motion that will result in the writing of my own life. The biographer now comes, invading my home and my mind; unlike others, no less malign in their way, I cannot deny him entry.

I dream that someday you may read this and tell me where I've gone wrong, so we might enjoy the irony of the imagined and the real grating against each other. In the absence of your own version, I know there must be another, a competing one, which I may yet choose to summon. I speak, of course, of the boy. I know that his is not my story to tell. There are gaps in my knowledge of your final days, but in the story of the boy I have no source upon which to rely other than your own partial account. The boy, perhaps, will tell his own story, in a way that I cannot.

There are days when I think I should have filed whatever it was that one was supposed to file at the time – a statement, a 'Victim's Statement', 'Human Rights Violations Statement', whatever the Truth and Reconciliation Commission requested – but I could not come to think of myself as a 'Victim' in the way that others were victims. You were a victim, but I knew you were not a 'Victim'. Anyway, I do not like this word, *victim*, with all of its Latinate baggage. We were not sacrificial, and there was nothing about what happened to us that had anything to do with the supernatural. What would I have achieved by making my statement, apart from hoping that some shady and predictable character from the old government might admit what had happened to you? I did not, I still do not, need the meagre money the government would have settled on me in an official capacity. Let them spend it on those who have genuine need, and so much more besides. I did not need to see my or your name on that list of Official Victims. Your brother did not push for it – neither did your father – so what good would it have done? What is good for us anyway? I need to find something good. I need at least to imagine what might have happened, to begin to chart a way through the little I know.

So I bring you back to the crossroads, where the journey must have begun, more than a dozen other people standing in hazy sanctuaries of flickering orange light around you, shifting at your arrival. Perhaps you nodded to the woman nearest you, and the woman smiled once but then turned away in embarrassment or fear for what you might represent – the threat you might pose simply by being there among them, standing alone in the dark. A white woman like you would not be waiting at the crossroads on the old forest road, not in the middle of the night, at the height of summer, on foot, rubber-soled shoes on the sweating asphalt, two sticky chemical substances that merge into each other if you stand still long enough. Even the children knew instinctively to beware. Women like you did not go on foot after dark, not in those days, not even today – especially not today. How mad you must have appeared, come rolling down the mountain in your backpacker's disguise. (Should I have tried to stop you? If you had said, *Mother, I won't do it for your sake*, would I have said *Don't do it, my darling* or would I have said,

No, you must *do it, for the sake of us all* ? Can I speak of the greater good in the same breath as I summon the nature of your act?)

You would have had supplies because you were always so well prepared: water in a thermos, and Safari Dates, your favourite snack as a child. I can see you sip and chew, alternate between water and fruit, pausing to take steady breaths, to calm yourself as I calm myself, counting heartbeats and willing them to strike a less persistent time. These were old movements, ones you learned from me, which I learned from my mother and she learned from hers. And if there had been only men about at the crossroads, you would not have stopped. You would have kept yourself going for safety, not out of panic but out of caution, always seeing what might come next.

It would have been deepest night, past two, but your plan would have been clear, the car would be coming, you would recognize it, knowing by the dip and rise of its lights that it was meant for you. The plan would have been to spirit you back, somewhere you could not be found, hiding until they stopped looking so intently and then over the border to Botswana or Lesotho, and then more remote exile. But perhaps the traffic was too sparse, or something happened and your associate, the driver, was apprehended – one of the ones rounded up and detained until they ceased to exist.

The time appointed for the rendezvous passed. You checked your watch, knew enough not to wait until dawn would expose you, and began looking for the right kind of alternative. Drivers knew stories of hijackings and ambushes. Only the impecunious travelled without fear. With nothing there was nothing to lose but life.

After ten minutes a truck approached, and you edged out on to the pavement, thumb erect, hair vivid in the dark. The truck dipped its lights and slowed to an idle next to you, its gears clunking. The driver was a man, and beside him sat a dog and a young boy.

This man, I imagine him always eating – the kind of brute whose appetite for food reflects his appetite for consumption in general, for consuming everything it might be possible to put into his mouth, an appetite out of all control, that regards moderation not just as a foreign idea, but as an enemy concept: to moderate is to limit his experience of the world. So when the truck pulls over to meet you, Laura, I imagine this man covered in the detritus of a meal, food staining his clothes, while the boy is left to starve.

I see you at the truck, trying to play the role of whore to get a lift, knowing you would be capable of anything to get where you needed to go. It was a game you sometimes played with your brother: the little flirt, the sexually precocious younger child, teasing him, poking fun at his small adolescent prick in the pool, your premature development intimidating. You were before your time in all things. *Don't get stroppy with me, Laura!* I would bark, watching as you waited until the last moment to pack, to shower for school, and then sulk when I pushed you. (How can I call you wilful, whom I miss most?) I can see you there now, at night, amongst those people, hiking up your skirt – no, not a skirt – opening the top button on your shirt or knotting it at the waist to expose your midriff, an ivory sash in the darkness, talking your way into that truck.

'Where you heading?' the man asked, leaning out through an opened window. He had leathery skin and wiry hair; his upper arms sagged where they emerged from his sleeveless shirt, and at the armholes his pale chest flashed.

Perhaps you shook your head or came up with a plausible story. Or perhaps you simply told the truth.

'To Ladybrand.'

'I'm going to Port Elizabeth. I'll take you that far. Hop in.'

Climbing up into the cab, you flinched at the smell of urine and dog. The boy scooted closer to the dog and the driver, making room for you.

'I'm Bernard,' the man said, 'and this is Sam.'

In your last letter to me, and in the last of the notebooks you bequeathed me, you recount your time with Bernard and the boy, the boy called Sam. Would you have given your real name? I don't think so. You would have given a name to suit the moment, a name under which to travel, to draw attention or not – to draw attention away, perhaps, from what really mattered.

'I'm Lamia,' you said.

'Funny name for a girl,' said Bernard. 'This is Tiger.'

'Funny name for a dog.'

'He bites like a tiger.' Bernard put the truck back into gear, accelerating through the intersection. 'I'm driving through the night. Tomorrow morning I'll stop at a picnic place, sleep all day, then get going again. That suit you?'

'I might want to carry on.'

'You sleep now if you want.'

'Thank you for stopping.'

'Pleasure. When I saw you standing alone back there, I said to Sam, *Christ man, that girly looks like she needs a lift.*'

You were no girl, not by then, but that's what a man like him would have seen, a girl alone and stranded, even a girl playing the whore.

'Hell of a place to be hitchhiking. All kinds of men out this time of night,' he said.

All kinds of men, and some in trucks. You were not the kind to take rides with men, but perhaps the child, the boy, reassured you, because he was a child. *Men with children are less likely to do things that might shame them in the eyes of a child.* I wrote that once, naively. But no, the concern would have been secondary; you were prepared for anything, ready to meet any threat, to go out fighting.

1989

The boy woke before Bernard that morning because the phone was ringing but this was nothing new because he was always awake before Bernard who was still passed out from the night before, next to the sink. Sometimes Bernard slept there by the sink and sometimes on the floor of the lounge by the couch, keeping the boy awake with talk in his sleep. One morning the boy found him with his head resting on the toilet, vomit sheeting the bathroom. He'd had chicken for dinner, and peas, and then something sweet. The boy could count the peas: thirty-seven whole ones and parts of others.

He answered the phone. It was the man with the funny voice again.

Listen kid is Bernard there?

He's asleep.

Fuck wake him up man.

The boy jabbed at Bernard's ribs with his bare foot. *Bernard. Bernard. There's a phone call.* But the man didn't move.

He won't wake up.

Fuck throw some water on him man this is important business.

He'll hit me.

He'll kill you if he hears he missed this call.

So the boy poured some water in a glass and splashed it in Bernard's flushed grey face, but the first glass didn't do anything and the boy had to do it again, but this didn't do anything either so he got a beer from the refrigerator, popped the lid, and poured it in Bernard's eyes and then the man snapped upright and wrapped one of those hard hands around the boy's throat and the other around the hand the boy was holding the beer can with and he looked like he would snap the boy's head off and eat it. But the boy put out his other hand, the one holding the phone, and said, *He told me to wake you up.* Bernard kept holding on to the boy's neck and his chest was going up and down but he took the phone and the boy dropped the beer can on the floor and the two of them were looking at each other for a long time.

No man. Give me half an hour rather. I'm in no fit state for public consumption. Can't be that urgent. They're already dead, hey?

Bernard hung up the phone and shook his head and stared again at the boy for a long time and had a funny look in his eyes. *Don't ever do that again or I'll open you up from your mouth to your arsehole.*

He jumped from the floor like he'd been awake

all morning and picked the boy up in the air in his thin arms and shook the child. *Don't ever do that again!* Then he put the boy down and punched him in the nose so there was blood all over the lino floor, and the blood went in with the beer and water and Bernard shook his head and said, *You clean that up we don't have time for your bullshit this morning.*

So the boy cleaned up the floor with some kitchen towel and it took a long time because the blood kept coming in gobs from his nose.

And then Bernard showered. And then he said the boy should shower and the boy showered and then got dressed in khaki pants because he liked them best and the blue checked shirt because his father had given him that for his last birthday so he liked that shirt best and the red shoes because they were the only shoes he had anyway.

The boy was hungry but they didn't eat. *I'm too rough for eating this morning rather make me some strong coffee, quickly hey.* So the boy put on the coffee maker and they both drank a cup but it tasted like cigarettes and Bernard spat his out on the floor and said for him to clean it up and the boy reached for the kitchen towel and as he was bending over the blood started to come again.

He ate an old banana that had been sitting in the kitchen for a week. He hadn't been living with his uncle, his mother's half-brother, for very long, a few months only, since the winter, and there was never enough for more than one person to eat.

They drove in Bernard's truck to a police station downtown and Bernard stopped at the entrance to the forecourt and said something to the guard, and the man opened the gate and let them pass and inside it smelled thick like toilets, and there was a black plastic mound. Bernard got out of the truck and looked at the mound and shook his head and lifted a corner of the black plastic, and then the boy could see what was underneath and didn't even look away because he had seen that sort of thing before but each time he forgot and looking didn't make much difference any more. Bernard and the man from the phone pulled the plastic all the way back and looked and laughed like they'd never seen anything so funny.

So Bernard drove them home and swapped the pickup for the big truck and then drove all the way back across town to the police station. He had to back the truck into the forecourt and it scraped against the top of the gateway. The boy thought maybe Bernard would just let him stay in the truck while he loaded but he said, *Come on man you gotta earn your keep* and he dragged the boy out of the front seat. The man from the phone with the funny voice said, *Isn't the boy too young for this?* and Bernard said, *You know what I was doing at his age?*, laughing and pulling at his nephew's shirt. They put on plastic jumpsuits and rubber gloves and masks and there were two policemen who were already wearing the same outfits and they started loading the bodies into

41

the back of the truck but the man from the phone didn't help because he was too important and he went into his office that had a window looking down on the forecourt and watched from there. Once he brought them tea for a break but the boy didn't want to put his hands near his face and Bernard said, *Suit yourself man, you take what you can get.*

The boy took the arms and his uncle took the feet and they would swing them and throw them into the truck and when it got overloaded at the back Bernard climbed in and moved the bodies around and then the boy had to prop the bodies left outside up against the truck and with one of the other policemen Bernard would drag them by their hands into the back. The boy didn't get the chance to see his mother and father dead. The police said there was nothing left of them.

Bernard and the two policemen were laughing because they were so close to being sick from the smell and then they were done and Bernard was still laughing when he closed the doors of the truck and bolted them and the policemen folded up the tarpaulin and began to hose down the forecourt, washing everything left into the drains. The smell didn't bother the boy so much. He had smelled it before and this was just another thing that smelled and looked like things he had tried to forget. Bernard went to the bathroom and was there for a long time and when he came back he looked greyer than he usually did and his teeth were yellower and he didn't even hit the boy, he just mumbled something and told him to get in the cab because it was time to go and they had a long trip ahead of them.

They drove out of the city across the flats and past the airport, turning east and going up and over the pass and then through the orchards where the lights on barns were orange against the dark and insects flamed in little explosions of fire when they hit the electric fencing. Bernard had forgotten to pack anything to eat and when the boy said he was hungry Bernard just said, *We'll stop in the morning, hey.*

But even Bernard, who only ate once a day, finally got hungry and about ten he pulled off the road and they went in to a petrol station for sandwiches. Bernard ate two and the boy ate one even though he was hungry enough for two. He'd learned not to ask for anything beyond what Bernard gave him. His mother had read him the book and he knew what happened to orphans if they asked for more.

SAM

Because of Clare's antipathy for the press and for interviews in particular, I come to these sessions knowing only the barest facts of her life. When approached, all of her family members refused to cooperate, as did her friends and former colleagues. A few people – academics with whom she's disagreed and other writers whose work she's savaged in reviews or essays – have clamoured to provide me with gossip: she blocked the appointment of an esteemed Renaissance scholar because the woman was both right-wing and a lesbian. Lesbianism and conservative politics were, Clare said, irreconcilable. She once berated a colleague in front of a lecture hall full of students for failing to recognize what to her seemed an obvious allusion to Petrarch in the text under discussion.

As always with successful or powerful women, there are rumours about her sex life. I dismissed most of these out of hand: she was promiscuous in her student days; she aborted several pregnancies; she frequented sex clubs in Paris during her wild years abroad; she spent a year as a kept woman in West Berlin; she had an affair with a

Soviet double-agent in London, betrayed him to the Soviets or the British or the Americans or to his wife or didn't betray him but was recruited by him and his wife to the KGB and served as an agent in the pay of Moscow from the late 1950s until 1989. There were many contradictory versions of that particular story. Even if such stories are true, they don't interest me, if only because they have so little relevance to her body of work. They tell me nothing about what I most want to know.

'You have one child.'

'Two,' she snaps.

'But your daughter, Laura –'

'If you are waiting for me to flesh out the scene, I will not. I cannot. As with my sister, the newspapers will give you the facts as they were reported.'

'Several years after she allegedly died, you published *Changed to Trees*, a historical novel about a vicar in Georgian England whose young daughter drowns during a family picnic.'

'Let me say one thing: I have never been provided with incontrovertible proof of my daughter's death.' Her voice is strangled. Not with sadness, I think, but with something closer to rage. I don't know where to look or what to say.

'So you believe she's still alive?'

'Believing her to be alive and feeling uncertain about whether or not she is dead are two distinct states of mind.'

'Would you care to elaborate?'

'No,' she almost shouts. I hear a door open

45

somewhere in the house: the assistant coming or going. I page through my notes to buy time and give Clare a chance to recover her composure.

'Going back to the book, then, *Changed to Trees*. It was seen by many international critics – particularly those in America and Britain, who were possibly unaware of the context of its writing – as an odd change of direction for you, towards a more personalized narrative, after a succession of acclaimed allegorical and resolutely secular novels.'

'You are saying it was seen as an artistic failure or a failure of imagination?'

'I think it was misread by some as indicative of a certain creative loss of direction.'

'It did not help that it was published so soon after the fall of the old government and the first democratic elections. My critics thought, *Aha! She has lost her natural enemy, she has nothing to criticize, so she turns to the past, and another country, and loses her way.* They all wanted me to attack or prophesy the failures of the new democracy, or else they wanted celebrations of it, something like hopeful propaganda, encomia to the Rainbow Nation. But I do not work programmatically. I write what I am compelled to write – and by compulsion I refer to interior compulsion of course,' she says, on a roll again, as if I had never made any reference to her daughter. I don't know how to get us back to that territory, or what map to follow if we get there. 'One of my many parts, call her the governor of my internal nation, says to the clerks in her government, *This is what you will write today*, and so it is. Most of writing is secretarial drudgery, hard work looking for the right word. You are correct, I don't think the international critics knew then about Laura's disappearance, which was not reported outside this country (it hardly made news here), and they thought I was changing tack or aiming for a broader audience. I should say as a side note that I have never been concerned with money. I would have become a lawyer like my father if I had been worried about that. Any of the critics who thought I was suffering financially need only have come to visit to know that was not the case.'

'You are divorced.'

'Yes.'

'Your husband was a lawyer. Like your father.'

'Yes. Are you interviewing him?'

'I was unable to contact him.'

'Which means he hasn't returned your calls. He won't. He is an even more intensely private person than I am.'

'And your son?'

'My son can speak for himself.'

'He has also declined to be interviewed.'

'Yes. He would. He leads an unexceptional, unimpeachable life.'

'And his politics?'

'He's what we might call fractionally left of centre.'

'And your daughter, Laura?'

'Yes, my daughter. A radical. A revolutionary.'

'What did she do?'

'I thought we covered her already. She was mostly a journalist, until she became wholly invested in the armed struggle. But I won't speak about that.'

I decide to leave Laura for the moment, hoping, I suppose, to keep Clare unsure where the questions might be going.

'You wrote your first published novel not long after the birth of your son.'

'Yes. It was bad.'

'You described it once as a "deconstruction of the feminist protest novel".'

'It succeeds on its own terms, but I have never given permission for it to be reprinted. It was very much a first novel, even though it was the third I'd then written. The real first two are languishing in my safe and no doubt one day they will go to Texas or be published after my death, undermining every assault I've made on the canon. But the first published book, *Landing*, was about the culture of my childhood. I was struggling to make sense of my own past, and the country to which I had decided very consciously to return.'

'You mentioned earlier that your books were never banned, and unlike some of your peers, who were forced into exile, you were left relatively unmolested by the old government.'

'Relatively unmolested. What a careful construction.'

'Would you say that's an accurate description?'

She pauses and looks past me, and then without saying anything stands and walks out of the room. I can't tell if this signals the end of the interview or if she's only going to get something, or perhaps going to the bathroom. I'm hungry and thirsty, and forgot to bring anything to eat or drink today. After ten minutes she comes back with a notepad and sits down without comment.

'Would you – ?' I begin. She raises a hand to silence me, glances down at the pad, and begins to speak.

'Compared to five or six others I can think of, who were proscribed, whose work was banned, who could not even smuggle their manuscripts out of the country without paying huge bribes they could ill afford, who were forced to flee and live abroad for many years, I was, as you put it, relatively unmolested. But for a writer trying to work in the conditions of repression and censorship that existed in this country under the old government, every moment, waking and sleeping, was a form of intellectual and artistic molestation. It is like the abused wife who chooses to remain with the battering husband, or believes that she cannot escape without risking her life or the lives of her children. She will cower and supplicate, plan every word and action, knowing – because she knows her batterer intimately – the effect of everything she does and says, so she can speak and do for calculated effect, or for no effect at all. She knows the reaction of her assailant better (and before) he does.'

She is paler, fiercer. Her words come in a staccato beat, half-read, half-improvised from the notes she holds before her. I look at her long ankles, gnarled sticks protruding from the cuffs of her linen slacks. She turns the page of the notebook and continues.

'This kind of knowledge requires missteps and bad bruising, even broken limbs. Some are not so quick to adapt, or refuse to do so, and when the battering becomes too severe' – she pauses for a moment, makes a change with her pen, then continues – 'when their lives (or in the case of these writers, the *life of their work*) is placed in mortal jeopardy, then they must flee, go to a shelter, hide themselves away, take on an assumed identity, travel under false papers. I adapted. I came to know my molester as intimately as I knew my husband – perhaps more so. I chose to adapt, to keep my children and myself alive. At least that was the rationalization on which I built my career very specifically as a writer in this country in that historic moment.'

'Just before the old government was overthrown, you published "Black Tongue", an essay about censorship.'

'I think I am too tired to continue today. You will come back tomorrow at the same time?' She looks up from the notebook, her face somewhere else.

'Yes, if you wish.'

'I do not wish. But I fear that now this has started, I cannot stop you.'

Marie appears from another room. She's been listening and leads me to the front door. She opens the gate at the end of the drive, waits until I've reversed the car into the street, and closes it again.

When I arrive back at Greg's, I find an email waiting for me:

Dear Dr Leroux,

Further to your previous message, I do entirely understand that my mother has, quite unwisely, given her consent for you to write her official biography. I do not know whether this was her idea or yours or her publisher's, but that is irrelevant anyway. Why you in particular have been contracted to carry out this ill-conceived project is my real concern. Perhaps I know more of your reputation for exaggeration and character assassination than my mother or her representatives do.

I can do nothing to stop you telling the story of her life so long as she cooperates, but I counsel you in the strongest possible terms to attempt no depiction of my father, my sister or myself. I speak in an official capacity for my father, Professor William

Wald, and can only assume to speak for what my sister Laura would wish. My mother is a duplicitous and self-serving woman who says whatever she thinks will make her appear in the best light. She is vain of person and vainer still of reputation. Her statements about her children – myself in particular – are not to be trusted. I hope I make myself clear.

I categorically deny you permission to publish this letter in any form or to forward it to any third party.

Yours sincerely,
Mark Wald

★

Next day. Every time that I've arrived at Clare's house, Marie has said nothing to me. Today, however, she makes a sound, a grunt of irritation, and leads me down the corridor past the reception room where the first interviews were conducted to a door at the back of the house. There isn't anything remarkable about the rooms we pass. They don't suggest the daily haunts of a writer. Everything is antiseptically clean. It looks too uncluttered to be the home of a mind as complicated as Clare's. I was expecting random collections of books and orna-ments, stacks of newspapers and ephemera, as in the over-stuffed apartments of bohemian academics I've known in New York. Instead, this house looks like it came to life out of a design magazine.

Marie knocks twice. She looks at her watch. Thirty seconds pass, and then she opens the door to a bright room. Two of the walls are glass. They meet in the corner opposite the door, giving views of the garden, and the high rocky slopes rising precipitously behind the house. The other walls are lined with bookshelves, the volumes all flush in a line. Marie gestures towards a couch where I sit as she leaves, closing the door behind her. I'm tempted to examine the bookshelves, but guess that this – being left alone in what is obviously Clare's study – is a test of my trustworthiness. A moment later one set of bookshelves swivels across the floor and Clare emerges from an adjoining room.

She looks more relaxed today, dressed in a long white smock and blue slacks, her hair loose around her face, feet bare. She sits behind her desk. Intimacy, but mediated. Without looking at me, she pages through her desk diary. After a moment she says, 'Yes? All right.' I turn on the voice recorder, uncap my pen, and open my notebook.

'Yesterday, I was beginning to ask you about "Black Tongue".'

'Yes.' She still looks down, turning the pages of her diary.

'You write movingly about the effects of censorship on writers. I wonder if you could speak at a more personal level, about the ways in which the possibility of censorship affected your own writing?'

Her lips part and she blows out a stream of air. Adjusting the diary so that it is square on the desk, she turns the pages, but I think I see her glancing peripherally at the garden, where a man is pruning an already compact-looking bush whose name I don't know, though I can recognize it as some kind of indigenous shrub. Such plants should make me feel at home, but their musky, wild animal smell always catches me by surprise, like a mugging.

'I would have thought that the essay could be read either personally or impersonally – relevant either to all writers who find themselves working under the threat of censorship, or just one particular writer,' she says, punctuating the sentence with a distracted cough that I'm beginning to recognize as one of her conversational tics – the cough, the snort, the involuntary throat-clearing.

'Are you inviting me to read it that way?' I hesitate in asking a question like this; I know she resists being asked to interpret her own words. A colleague of mine once wrote to ask Clare what she meant by a particular passage in one of the novels that referred obliquely to Sophocles. She responded politely but firmly, '*The sentence says . . .*' and quoted the line verbatim without further comment. The text spoke the meaning, and she could or would do nothing to explain it.

'It would be ridiculous not to read it that way, given what I have just said.'

'You argue that institutionalized censorship tends to empower individuals with "unsubtle minds" and that the ideal censor, if censorship *must* be practised, would be someone like yourself – reflective, academic, widely read, a rationalist, someone with an objective mind.' Her eyes flicker briefly up to mine, as if to say, *Don't even try, flattery is futile.* She puts away the diary and begins shuffling papers on her desk, moving them from one pile to another. It's a game to show me that I'm unimportant, that her mind needs more to occupy it than my facile questioning.

'I don't think those are quite my words, but yes, broadly, that was my argument,' she finally says, giving me another quick glance before looking down again, absorbed by a pile of recycled envelopes.

'The problem, you say, is that people like you would never choose to be a censor, because there could be no more painful work than being forced to read works – books, magazines, articles, poems – not of your own choice. And one would think, also, that it would be anathema to a writer – particularly one like yourself – to have to ferret out offensive works and bar their publication.'

'If one could ever agree on a universal standard of offence.' A little cough again, clearing the throat, and a surprising, girlish toss of the hair, another peek at the gardener and a tight pursing of the lips. She opens the window, calls out to the man in words I don't understand. They're full of politeness, and a smile that looks genuine spreads across her face as she bows her head. The gardener responds, smiles (not so genuinely, I think), bows his own head and leaves the shrub alone.

'It's the wrong season for that. If you prune it in spring it won't flower,' she mutters to herself, and returns to my question. 'It was Milton's argument – reading unchosen works. "He who is made to judge . . . upon the birth, or death of books . . . had need to be a man above the common measure, both studious, learned, and judicious." But for such a man – or woman, we should certainly wish to say – "there cannot be a more tedious and unpleasing Journey-work . . . than to be made the perpetual reader of unchosen books," or something like that. It has always seemed a logical and worthy argument, to me at least. I think I credited him.'

(Later, I check the transcript of the interview against Milton's text and am impressed by her memory for quotation.)

'And Milton argues that censors are typically "ignorant" and "imperious". Would you say that was true of those who worked as censors in this country under the old government?' It's an unsubtle question and I wish I hadn't asked it, or had found a different way to phrase it.

She's silent, stills her hands, draws her head up, looks at me for a second only and then out the window. Something's been mis-communicated. The gardener is back at the already compact bush, cutting again. Clare opens the window, calls out to him with a lengthy preamble, bows of the head, and what I take to be a questioning reply from him, an uncertainty about her earlier direction, or uncertainty about its wisdom. She replies, more forceful, hurried, and then the shears are on the grass and the gardener has trudged off across the lawn to an unseen part of the garden. I look at my notes and hear her head move, the window close; glancing up I find her eyes fixed on my face with a sadness that surprises me.

'There is no mystery, really, about who served on the Publications Control Board, as it was called. There were, as you no doubt know, even some cases of writers who worked as advisory readers – minor poets and novelists – as well as a number of academics, a fair number. Perhaps that – the academics, I mean – is not so surprising. But there are periods for which almost no reports survive, so we may never know entirely who served the Board, who was complicit. The writers who worked as censors were not, as one might rather perversely hope, compelled to do so, coerced into the activity and the role of censor, but because they believed in the rightness of what was being done, or else believed they might make the process a little less philistine, hoping to subvert the system from within. Their reports make for depressing reading. As a definition of the common (meaning the *usual*) type of censor – let us say, for the sake of argument, that it includes those people whose complicity may have remained secret – I would not disagree with Milton's statement.'

I'm transfixed by her speaking voice, by the shapes her mouth makes, the sharp planes of her face and the fine geometry around her eyes. At the conference in Amsterdam I almost didn't meet her, thinking it would be better for us not to do so. I told myself that I feared the person could never match the words on the page, that I was afraid she would disappoint, that I would never achieve the kind of intimacy I desired – or not intimacy but rapport, a friendliness possible only between equals. Aside from her brittleness, she is, I'm beginning to think, exactly the person her works suggest. There is no disappointment in that respect.

There was and is a greater fear. I packaged it up with old tape and tied it with fraying string. I did a bad job of it. I can feel it trying to escape.

The gardener comes back for the shears, leaving the already compact bush alone for now. I see Clare watching him, trying to pretend a hadeda ibis has caught her attention. It's clear this is a ruse, either for my benefit or the gardener's. She has no interest in the hadeda or any other bird, except a bird she might conjure in her imagination. The hadeda here and now is an excuse for her to look interested in one thing to deflect my attention from her interest in – or call it irritation with – the gardener.

It feels strange to think of Clare as 'Clare', to think of her not by her last name, Wald, which is the shorthand I've tended to use when talking about her with Sarah or with colleagues and students. Until these interviews began, in my mind she was her surname, a name acquired through a marriage that has now ended. *Wald* meaning 'forest', 'woods', 'wood' or simply 'timber'. The surname has made me think of her and her work in this way – a forest of timbers that might be put to some practical use. Out of the forest emerges the person I've created in my head: half-ogre, half-mother, denying and giving, bad breast and good breast, framed by wood or woods. I try to find my place again in the list of questions I've prepared, questions that now seem rude, reductive, too peremptory, too simplistic and ungenerous in what they appear to assume.

'In the years after the first democratic elections,' I begin, 'there was a programme of amnesty. Many applications were made, many people were granted amnesty for serious violent acts – ostensibly "legal" under the old government, because enacted by, and ordered by the government itself, but clearly violations of human rights, and quite obviously illegal by the standards of the country's new constitution – but I can find no evidence that anyone submitted a claim of amnesty for having worked as a censor or for the censors.'

'No?' Clare says, her face blank. 'I suppose they did not see their work as violent. Violence is the key, doing violence physically to someone. So much of the testimony, you know, it hinges on personal experiences of violence. Inability to publish a book, that's relatively minor compared to what has happened to so many.' Her eyes are tired, looking not at me, but again at the gardener, who has returned to the vicinity of the already compact bush to bully a neighbouring protea into a different shape. She makes no effort now to pretend anything else preoccupies her.

'Even though the act of banning a book, or banning its author, might have had serious – one might even argue *mortal* – implications for the livelihood and life of the author and that author's friends and family?' I ask.

'Yes. It is strange, as you say. I don't have an answer.'

'Perhaps no censors came forward because they trusted that their identities would remain secret.'

'More likely they thought that no one would care, given the violence of so many other atrocities,' she says, for the first time today looking directly at me for more than a brief moment. 'I don't know that anyone would have regarded the banning of a book as a gross violation of human rights. Which is not to say that one shouldn't think of censorship in that way, as that serious. But we are speaking of degrees of violation . . .'

'Were your own books ever threatened with censorship?'

'Threatened in what sense? If you are asking

whether the censors ever came to me and said, "We will ban this book unless you delete x, y, or z," then no. No one ever did any such thing. It didn't quite work in that way, although I know that the censors reviewed several of my books and in one case there was an import ban until they could read the text in question and conclude it offered nothing that might threaten to destabilize the country. I have seen the reports. They're quite amusing in their way – amusing and depressing and strangely, perversely, flattering. Woe to the writer who is flattered by the praise of a censor. But this is beside the point, really,' she says, pulling her body into focus again, 'because, as I say in "Black Tongue", any writer working under the threat of state censorship, no matter how general, how diffused, is effectively threatened at all times. It is back to the battered wife syndrome. Worse, even, because as a writer living under the old government, I – and doubtless many other writers in the same or similar positions – found that the censor infected my consciousness, like a worm. It lived in the brain, and ate around in the skull, living side by side with me, inside me, occupying the same mental space. I was always aware of the worm. It exerted a kind of psychic pressure that I experienced physiologically, right here in the sinuses, between and behind the eyes, and in the frontal lobe, pressing against the brow. It was toxic, excreting hallucinatory chemicals that twisted my thoughts. I became obsessed by its very presence:

the heart raced, the brain erupted, trying to purge itself of the worm; I have often thought it was like a brain storm – but not in the sense you Americans mean, not a storm of ideas, but a literal electrical storm, raging inside the skull, trying to strike down the worm with a fatal bolt. When I went outside, out in public, I was embarrassed, horrified and disgusted lest anyone should guess that the worm had infected me – as if such infection could be seen on the face and betray the fact that I had become host to the terrors of the censor. The terror suggests – or the afflicted writer fears it suggests – a kind of guilty conscience that betrays guilty acts, and this makes the infection all the worse. One begins to scrutinize every word written, every phrase, trying to detect meanings hidden even to the mind of the writer, and this is the source of real madness. A friend of mine, a fellow writer, has described his own mental relationship with the censor as that of a tree (he, the writer) being embraced by a strangle-vine. One thinks of the love-vine, *Cassytha filiformis*, leafless and tangled, overtaking an entire tree, smothering but not killing it. For me the love-vine is too external a metaphor. In my case, the censor was a bodily invader, always with me, entirely with*in* me, inter-nally bloodsucking. I knew what the censor would look for in my words, and the kind of mind that would undertake the looking; it would see suggestion where there might only be document, though my work could never be accused of being documentary, perhaps because I knew what attitude the censor would take to the documentary form, to journalistic writing. My own evasion of social documentary is itself a symptom of the illness that *is* the relationship with the censor. If one looks at the writers who were banned and the books found "undesirable", a great many fall into the social realist school, representing in fairly unmediated terms the state of this country in the period of its emergency. And while our censorship was often arbitrary and inconsistent and changed its targets over the decades, it was no less malign and wide-reaching for all that. I spent decades writing in such a way as to avoid having my books banned. I wrote books, effectively, which the censors could not understand, because they lacked the intelligence to read beyond the surface, and the surface itself was almost opaque to them, darkness etched in darkness. Is that the confession you were hoping to extract – that I consciously wrote evasively, to remain in print? I did. I don't consider it a crime. I consider it a means of survival, a coping mechanism, in the language of pop psychology, and one at which I seem to have excelled.'

'And if one reads the censor's reports on your books, they're all judged too "literary" to pose any risk of fomenting unrest among "average" readers.'

'By this they mean the majority. I have read the reports. Books and pamphlets in simple, polemical language, books that outlined in undisguised terms the realities of this country under the old

63

government – those were the books the censors were most inclined to ban, not mine. They could have condemned my books, found them "undesirable" in that peculiar erotics of the language of their censorship, on any number of grounds: indecency, obscenity, offensiveness to public morals, blasphemy, ridicule of any particular racial or religious group, being harmful to the relations between races or a threat to national security. Instead they found them "not undesirable", which is not to say that they were judged in any way "desirable", only that they were not offensive enough to be actively *undesired*. They were tested and found, simply, passive things, hanging in the liminal space between desire and repulsion, want and rejection. It is a curious way to think of literature, particularly for people – the censors I mean – who so naively fancied themselves sophisticated arbiters of the literary. But all of that does not mean I was immune to the effects of censorship.'

★

On Greg's suggestion I went to Robben Island on my own yesterday to see the former prison buildings. He thought it might help me 'reconnect' with the country. It was overcast and the views of the city were obscured by cloud and mist. I couldn't see anything beyond the boat, and visibility was even worse on the island. After disembarking we were loaded onto a tour bus and a young man, tall and thin with dreadlocks, began giving his prepared speech. He showed us the settlement, the Maximum Security Prison, the old leper colony, the house where Robert Sobukwe had been isolated, the quarry where prisoners did hard labour, and where we spent far too long because a visiting American senator was having a private tour and holding us up.

With only twenty minutes left of our allotted time on the island, we were allowed to walk around the cells with a former political prisoner as our guide. Greg told me this would be the most moving part of the visit, but our guide was reticent. When people asked him pointed but polite questions about the movement, he became defensive and parroted the party line. Whatever the leaders said was right must be so. I began to feel ill.

The most famous cell moved me only insofar as it represented the place where so much of one exceptional life had been spent, but it was difficult to feel the trace of any presence there. It is bleak and small and cold. It contains no life or spirit of its own.

I paused to photograph the office where the prison's censor read all the inmates' incoming and outgoing correspondence. I tried to imagine the experience of receiving a letter that might begin with the normal salutation, in the hand of the beloved, only to discover two lines later that the body of the letter has been deleted by the censor's hand, that the very words meant to give succour in a time of enforced isolation were judged too great a risk – or to know that anything one might write to those on the outside could itself be obliterated, that attempts to reassure, console, answer what could not be answered because of the censor's obfuscations, would be blacked out anyway.

We were hurried back to the boat. I hoped the fog and mist would clear, but everything was grey and all the passengers hung around inside sulking.

'It was disappointing,' I told Greg that evening. 'I wanted it to be moving.'

'You can't buy catharsis,' he said, feeding Dylan spoonfuls of yogurt. 'To think you can is perverse. The tour guide, the bus driver, the ex-prisoner, all of them, they spend every day there. They have an endless stream of people like you wanting to hear the stories, expecting to be moved, to be made to feel less or more responsible, depending on who you are and where you're from.' He catches a drip of yogurt before it rolls from Dylan's chin to his shirt. '*You* complain about not being moved. Imagine what that must do to them. Maybe it was an off day. Maybe they spent all their energy moving people yesterday and didn't have anything left to give but the automatic narrative. Maybe they spent all their energy on the lone American dignitary. Think what that means to the local people,' he said, shaking his head. Dylan squirmed in his chair and reached for his cup of juice. 'For them the island isn't just a tourist site but a place of pilgrimage, and their one visit, maybe the only one they'll ever make, was ruined by an American. Don't get me started. For foreigners it's just atrocity tourism. We can't rebuild a society on atrocity tourism. I don't know, maybe I shouldn't have told you to go. I feel guilty that you're not as connected to this country as I am, and jealous, too, that you've been free of it for so long.' Dylan drank his juice, ate another spoonful of yogurt, and his eyes began to droop. Greg lifted him out of the chair and handed him to Nonyameko, who took him off to bed. 'Don't get me wrong,' he said, 'I'm thrilled you've finally come home. It's just a shame you and Sarah are going to live in Jo'burg.'

We sat for a while in front of the fire, drinking a cheap bottle of pinotage that would cost four or five times as much in New York. Greg has been more or less single for as long as I've known him. There's never been anyone else permanent in his life until Dylan. I know the boy is biologically his, but I don't know the other details. The mother was either hired, or a friend I don't know.

I think of our first meeting, at a depressing drinks event for new graduate students at NYU. Greg stood out in a pink sweater with his tattooed hands and black hair that had been dyed a shade of blue so dark the colour appeared only when the light hit it, making him look like an eccentric superhero. Discovering we had something more specific in common than mere foreignness, we spent the night talking in the corner and soon became close friends. A year later, he returned to Cape Town while I stayed in New York, finished my doctorate, married Sarah, and taught part-time at three different colleges, running up and down Manhattan until I was senseless with fatigue. When I was commissioned to write Clare's biography I knew it was the opportunity I'd been looking for to do something different and, more importantly, an opportunity to try coming back home.

ABSOLUTION

They saw only one house, and it was so obviously perfect that Marie looked as though she had decided Clare would buy it even before they went inside. Clare was not as certain. The estate agent, a sunburned man with an overhanging stomach and a voice like curdled cream, met them at the entrance to the driveway, opened the gate with a remote control, and indicated they should follow him. The perimeter wall, half a metre thick, was topped with barbed wire wrought and painted to resemble ivy, with a staff of electrified wires above. It was self-effacing security for people embarrassed to think they needed it.

'You've got all the security features here,' the agent said, stepping from his car. 'Cameras watch the exterior of the house, the entire perimeter wall, the gate, all the time. These guys are the best, *primo*. If they could smell the intruders they would, believe you me.'

They stood in the front garden, in a paved courtyard overlooking the steep terraces of the lawn falling down towards the street and the electric gate, now shut again, enclosing the three of them and their two shining cars. A group of gardeners, arms lax with fatigue, unloaded from a truck across the road, spilling out and trudging to the properties they were paid to tend, each announcing himself at a residential intercom, then waiting until the doors or gates opened, allowing access. It was the kind of neighbourhood in which Clare swore she would never live: a warren of celebrities, foreign dignitaries, and arms dealers. Perhaps it was fitting that she and Marie, scarcely less foreign in their way, possibly more dignified, should retreat to the company of such rabble.

'So I should be paying for the privilege of being surveilled.'

'Huh? Ja, well, they've got dogs, too, fully armed response with semi-automatic weapons and there are panic buttons in every room of the house, even the bathrooms and cupboards, in case of real emergency, but they're disguised, so the attackers won't know, and they're not an eyesore, not red like some are.'

'Then how should we be able to find them if we panicked?'

'Ja, well, absolutely nothing to worry about. At least as long as we got rule of law. God knows how long that lasts, though, hey?'

The *real emergency*, he suggested, was that one might flee in stark terror to the interior of a cupboard and be trapped, quarry awaiting a hunter. But who would get past the wall in the first place? Inside, the house itself was, without question, splendid, and Clare could imagine being happy in it. With space enough for Marie to have a proper administrative area, Clare would be able to remove herself entirely from all external concerns, should she so wish. There was a vast garden, too, and no neighbours to the rear, save the slopes of the mountain and the occasional hikers who followed its trails – and they, it seemed certain, would never attempt to scale her deadly ivy. The trees were tall enough and the wall itself so high that there was no fear of being overlooked, even outside, swimming in the pool, except perhaps by the neighbour on one side. Still, she disliked the idea of paying for her own imprisonment, paying to be watched by a security firm likely as not to turn over its surveillance to a branch of the government, or perhaps even worse, to a corporation that would compile records detailing her daily habits, her food preferences, her alcohol intake, her sleeping and waking, and sell such data to other companies wanting to market their goods to her, goods made by the wives, daughters, and sisters of the petty intruders against whose incursions she would be employing the security firm to protect her. There could be no protection against the currents of history.

Marie was ecstatic. The windows were equipped with remote-controlled metal shutters manufactured by a company called Tribulation; these could be closed at night, entombing them in reinforced steel. There was a special ventilation system with a reserve generator. What would happen in the case of a fire or an electrical failure? Would they ever escape? The alarm could be set to exclude their bedrooms and bathrooms at night, while motion sensors in the rest of the house would respond to something as innocent as a cushion resettling itself on a couch or a spider crawling across the wall.

'Once the alarm is set,' the man said, 'nothing must fall down, nothing must drop, nothing must stir, or you'll have the guys down here in no time. Guaranteed response is five minutes max, but they're just around the corner anyway, so it would be more like two for you. Not much can happen in two minutes. You can go to sleep at night feeling nice and secure.'

Clare wondered if the estate agent, blond and fat as he was, knew what could really happen in two minutes. Anything was possible within two minutes, but perhaps with a panic button the two minutes could be rendered inconsequential, the response always already responding, the dogs always slavering for battery-acid blood and orange disinfectant skin. She guessed that the estate agent, let her call him Hannes, had a wife and daughter, and that he had recently had cause to fear for them both on some horrible occasion – and fear, too, what intruders with a will and no conscience, no system of moral principles, might commit.

When she heard it, the price was astounding, although she could easily afford it. Her knowledge had not kept pace with the property market and she was still thinking in rates of nearly five decades past, when she and her husband bought that vulnerable house on Canigou Avenue, her house with a gaping wound in the wall of its master bedroom. She wondered if the estate agent recognized her name. It seemed more likely that he did not read, and would not like what he read if he opened one of her books.

'You two ladies will be very safe here. And it's that kind of neighbourhood, if you know what I mean, where people don't mind what two ladies do.'

Marie looked at Clare. There was no reason they should correct his misunderstanding. Clare had never imagined herself as anything but feminine, even if feminine at one-and-a-half times life size. But her very size made men – and for all she knew, other women, too – speculate about the alignment of her affections.

'Yes. The rich don't care *what* two ladies get up to. I'm sorry you thought it remarkable,' Clare said, smiling down on him, and she could tell from his flinch that she had been ungenerous. He was only trying to be cosmopolitan, a man of the world.

Clare expected that her invasion and subsequent move would make news, appearing in the headlines and on the nightly broadcasts, off and on, for several weeks. There were only a small number of national celebrities and she liked to count herself amongst them. The media, she thought, would enjoy gloating over the apparent retreat of a champion of an open society into a fortress of personal security. Reporters would deliver dull updates from outside her new home. Editorials would wonder if she herself kept a gun, suggesting that one should know the business of one's own house; guns were anti-progressive. Marie might have killed one of the invaders, but there was no way to know. As far as Clare knew, no one had turned up at any hospitals complaining of gunshot wounds that matched the calibre of Marie's elegant little arm – then again, the police had not been in touch to tell her one way or the other.

In the event, Clare's move went unnoticed. But if the press ever did come to call, she knew what she would say:

'My fortress is the envy of the president; he says all old ladies should be so lucky. He speculates that I shall die here. Do you think that's a veiled threat or an acknowledgement? An admission of guilt? Never mind, the fortress will protect me. I do not keep a gun, though I know how to use one. That is the legacy of frontier life, knowing how to care for and fire a gun, knowing what a gun will do. Have you ever fired a gun? No? Ever held one? No. Oh, someone once had a gun in your house, but he was a guest, a policeman, and unloaded it, and placed it on top of the refrigerator, to put you all at ease while you ate your dinners, as if that would put you at ease. No, that is not the same thing as knowing how to handle a rifle, which I am entirely capable of doing. We had ours hidden in a safe in the floor. My father learned to shoot a gun as a boy. His father, my grandfather, was a farmer who thought it sensible that his sons should know how to protect themselves in the bush. He taught my father and his brother to shoot, and when they grew up into men, they taught my sister and me and my cousins to shoot, frail English girls shouldering guns nearly as long as our own bodies and taking aim at nothing to start with, the usual nothings (tins, bottles, trees), then being encouraged to take aim at more horrible targets. The first thing I killed with a gun was my cousin's horse, because she could not kill what she had loved. To the men it was just my cousin's horse, and it was injured – I cannot recall the nature of the injury – and nothing could be done for it, and this, my irresponsible grandfather and uncle and father thought, should be my initiation into killing. It took five shots; I had such bad aim at first. The first two struck nowhere near the head, and I nearly shot off my father's foot, and the poor horse had to be settled again, and then three more shots until it was dead. They should have let me kill a dog first, because a dog is only a dog, it degrades itself hourly, but a horse is something more than human. It was like killing a god rather than an animal, and I did it badly. What does that do to the mind of a child? Today they would put my father in prison on charges of child abuse or endangerment, but at the time he thought he was instructing me in the ways of our country. He was a man of the law, not of the land. How was he to know the harm he was doing? Of course he should have known.

'Did my sister kill anything? I cannot remember. She was not inclined to shoot. It is better not to imagine my sister armed. But after witnessing the appalling execution of my cousin's horse (where was my cousin in all of this? this, too, I have un-remembered) my sister put down guns forever and, one might say, bided her time, waiting for the gun to come back, to find her, to answer her rebuke.'

CLARE

There is the struggle between what I know – what was reported officially, what was reported to me in the last letter from you, the notebooks you kept before you disappeared completely, Laura – and what I imagine. I feel towards the place where the line between the reported and the imagined must lie. But how do I know when and where my own mind pushes that line in one direction or the other, questioning reported fact as possible imagination, crediting fantasy with the reliability of fact? Can you imagine the force of my desire to know the truth from you, who can no longer tell it or else refuses to do so?

No more demurrals, no more waiting or delay or hesitation over what it is possible to know. This must and can only be my own version of your last days, culled from what you chose to tell me, and from what I can piece together from the official record. There will necessarily be other versions, perhaps more complete, less subjective in their way – versions not so far removed from events as this fractured narrative of longing and lamentation that is all I can muster.

It was quiet at first, a radio to fill the gap in conversation, a woman wailing a country ballad. Bernard glanced at the route on his map, and Sam fell asleep against your arm, his breath coming heavy and warm. You squirmed under the heat of the child's body, hard and trusting, smelling sulphurous and unwashed, a small insect crawling in his hair.

You checked your watch. It was after three in the morning, and you knew how long it had been since you emerged from the trees, crossed the broken fence and skidded down onto the road. You could not sleep.

When you left the old house a month before, neither one of us can have imagined it would be the last time, the last meeting, the first and only final farewell. I nearly write *final failure*, because there were so many between us – farewells that were failures, shortcomings that were also, in some abstract way, incremental steps away from each other, so that we were always saying goodbye, and failing to do so in ways that did neither of us justice. I cannot count the number of times I failed, have failed, continue to fail you. Perhaps you alone can make that tally.

It was only in the previous few days, through the *strange felicities of chance*, as I once wrote, that you threw yourself into what you must have realized was the inevitability of exile. At our final meeting, when we sat in my garden, the shabby cottage garden of the decaying old house on Canigou Avenue (the garden I loved rather than the garden that now intimidates me with its meticulous beauty), my home-grown beets mixing with soured cream and paprika bleeding on a plate, I wore a smug grin at seeing you dishevelled again. You're allowed to hate me for that, for my smugness, for so much else. Know at least that I never hated you. You said, *This is just the first in a new cycle of meetings, and we'll go on meeting like this, for many years, until one of us dies.* It was not much of a beginning for a reunion. It was your decision to meet again. I suppose you were finally able to stomach me, even on my terrible terms, to bear my smugness, my judgement, and my failure to judge, too.

In that last letter to me you wrote, *For your sake, I hope you are okay.* Is it true? Would you really have been worried about my feelings, my well-being, in those terrible few days? Apart from yourself, did you not care for me least of all people?

No, that is unfair.

I know that you've never approved of my decisions, you wrote, *or the kind of life demanded by my activities. But I don't regret. What I've done is what I feel has to be done.*

I knew all that. You did not need to tell me.

As Bernard drove, humming along to the radio, you forgot for a moment what had brought you to this point, and, staring at yourself in the rear-view mirror, you wandered through imagined confrontations with him. You beat him to death when he tried to force himself against you, and then you fled with the child into the wilderness, living on scrapings from the bush, deserting sleep-walking civil society for the full consciousness of hermit life. You would raise this boy, Sam – *Samuel,* you would call him, renewing him – alone in a cave, teaching him the world, the names and uses of plants, how to steal eggs and trap birds, the best ways to disappear into the landscape. Or perhaps you would fail to overpower Bernard and he would imprison you in his own remote fastness, teaching you a different vocabulary of power, until you escaped, a serpent prophetess entering the man's mouth in his sleep, consuming him from the inside, heart first.

The sonic jolt was so strong that the truck swerved off the road to the unpaved shoulder. Bernard clutched the steering wheel, veering back onto the tarmac as a thundering wake thudded through the truck, rattling the windows. Tiger began to howl and Sam woke, grabbing at your waist. You felt the hairs on your body quiver and isolate. Sam's hands were hot on you and you tried to push him away but he held fast, dumb with fear.

Bernard was trying to catch his breath while a man whined through the radio's speakers: *pure love, it's pure love, it's our love, baby, my love.*

'Jeez. Must be the power station. Or the gas works. Look at the sky.'

Behind you the horizon was bright with an orange fire. It backlit isolated trees ascending the line of the mountains and the ragged heads of dense forest along the highway.

Tiger pushed his body against Sam, who cringed and whimpered himself, holding tighter to you. 'The whole coast will be dark. It won't be safe to stop until daylight.'

At the next crossroads the streetlights had gone out and an abandoned car was ablaze, tendrils of flame leaping into the air and igniting the trees. Ten minutes later a caravan of ambulances and fire trucks passed, sirens droning, strobe lights picking out the trees on either side of the road. Bernard slowed, pulling aside to let the convoy pass.

There had been similar blasts, other kinds of sabotage – you and Bernard both knew what this explosion meant, though your knowledge was more complete than his.

'Maybe just an accident,' you said.

'I wouldn't bet on it. We'll see in the papers tomorrow.'

'I wouldn't trust the papers.'

'You're not one of these sympathizers are you?'

'No. Not a sympathizer,' you said, knowing you should stay awake as he drove, listening to the radio, waiting for a news report that would not come, while further convoys of ambulances and fire engines passed, dispatched from the closest city and other neighbouring towns.

Bernard clucked. 'If it's *them*, well, you can bet they'll be hitting other places, too. Lucky I've got a full tank. We'll be okay until it's light. Can you stay awake to watch the road? Sometimes I don't see so well at night.'

'Then why drive at night?'

'Less traffic. But more risks of course. Hijackings. And what happens if I get a blow out? Then I'm really fucked. Hasn't ever happened, but I'd be in God's hands if it did, I'm telling you, you know what I'm saying? That's why I always bring Tiger.'

'And your boy?' Sam was falling asleep again, arms constricting your waist, his head wedged up under your breasts.

'*Ag*, he's used to it now I guess.'

'Not easy.'

'Naaaa. He likes it,' he said, like a man insisting a woman enjoys being knocked around. 'You have any kids?'

'No.'

'Husband?'

'I'm going to my mother's. She lives near Ladybrand. You can see the peaks of the Malotis from her back door.' I know you said this, a fact I can count on, me as the excuse, the point of destination. But I lived nowhere near Ladybrand. Is it ungenerous for me to think I was always a convenient excuse for you?

'I'll take you as far as Port Elizabeth, but you'll

have to find your own way from there.' Bernard began to hum along to another song, a woman lamenting the loss of three husbands. He knew it by heart, anticipated each note, could not resist mouthing the words, then singing himself. 'Your mother know you're coming?'

'I'll phone her when we stop.'

'That's if the phones are working.'

★

My biographer pretends to be American now, but there is something unfinished about him that I know like my own breath. Of course, I remembered Sam at once. Rather, in Amsterdam I half-recognized him, and in the weeks that followed learned to trust my memory of him. How could I forget? I do not acknowledge this to him when he sits so uncomfortably before me, squirming on the couch in my study, his palms sweating in this room that I always keep cool. It would be a lie to say I remain silent about our connection because I wish to torture him. I have no such wish. In truth, I am terrified of what may yet be revealed.

So call it, my dear daughter, my Laura, a kind of restitution – my letting Sam in, at long last, much later than I should. I have been tardy in so many things, terrified by so much else. Perhaps in letting him in, I will begin to understand why you did what you did.

But as the days pass and he asks ever more intrusive questions, I begin to see, just barely, the magnitude of what I have done by allowing Sam to come here, to sit in judgement before me, as my auditor, interlocutor, and elegist. I have summoned my own judge, perhaps even my own executioner – executioner of spirit and will and certainty if not in fact of life. I find it toxic to explain myself, but this is the bargain I have made – the mistake I've made at being intrigued by him, at recognizing someone I should have forced myself to forget, for my own sake, ignoring whatever his own needs might be, whatever my debt to him, real or imagined, might yet prove to be, and how it will be settled. What is it he needs? I sense it is not just one thing. I want to say *How dare you?* and know I cannot, because all this turning over of my old soil, hoping a poppy might emerge, was my idea. I wanted it, I agreed on him, which means he is, by my hand, not just conjured, but *authorized*. I will not be one of those who invite and then refuse to accept the consequences of that hospitality. He is my guest and I his hostage. I have invited him into my life because I was curious, because I thought, foolishly, that *on my terms* meant *in my control*. But he is always coming from more than one direction. He does not himself know what he thinks of me. I suppose there is a kind of power in that, but I am too exhausted for an exercise of power.

Was he always so tentative? How did he behave as a child? Is your account of him accurate, or itself a performance for my benefit? What would you make of him now, Laura? In your notebook, he is always cowering and flinching, clinging and trembling. I see some of that now, but also a more sinister quality. He is like a beast that feigns vulnerability to put its prey at ease.

★

A cloud of toxic smoke was moving along the coast, following the weather patterns. You could already see its black mass approaching behind you on the western horizon. Bernard stopped for fuel at a station that had its own generator; everywhere else along the coast was in blackout, as he had predicted. Sam was asleep in the cab, Tiger standing guard over him, panting his sticky breath. You knew that it would have been easiest just to leave them, but you pretended to phone me, you mimed a conversation, laughing in a way that you have never laughed with me. I told you that I couldn't wait to see you, in a way that I had never told you. You had a story ready, you were going to tell them that plans had changed, that I was about to leave for our beach house – a house that does not exist – and that I was getting a little forgetful these days, had been confused about plans. But when you returned to the truck Sam was awake and staring at you, his body crossed into a tight knot against the vinyl upholstery. He asked if you were coming with them and before you could remember your invented story you said yes, because he looked afraid.

You bought a newspaper, peaches, another packet of Safari Dates, and bottles of water, which you put into your red rucksack on top of your clothes, folded neatly over your notebooks, hidden at the bottom.

The interior of the cab was ripe with human sweat and dog breath, vinyl and petrol, the rotten egg of the child's skin. As Bernard drove, Sam sat looking blankly ahead at the road. Every few minutes the child turned his head to stare at you. His mouth pouted, grime at the corners, sometimes opening to show his small teeth. There were globs of sediment in his tear ducts. No one had taught him to care for himself, even to scratch the sleep from his eyes. You smiled at him as if to say, 'Yes? Ask me anything you like, tell me something, what is wrong, why are you afraid?', but Sam only stared at you, his mouth hard and impassive, eyes yawning vacant in his skull. It was not a normal child's expression.

Near dawn, Sam's nose began to bleed and you helped him with a tissue, pressing until the blood stopped. You wiped his face, and he turned away from you to bury it in the seat. You were accustomed to the smell of blood, but it was overpowering in the heat of the enclosed cab, the hot-iron stench. You opened your window, but Bernard told you to close it. 'Gravel sometimes flies in. Rather I'll put on the fan. We'll stop soon. Always getting bloody noses. You'd think he was a girl. What a girl, Sam, what a little girl you are, hey?'

After another hour of driving Bernard stopped at a picnic ground. He parked the truck in the shade of a grove of eucalyptus trees clustered next to the road, their sharp-edged leaves rattling. It could have been anywhere along any road in the Cape. There was nothing to mark it as unique – the same stand of trees, the same concrete bench and picnic tables, at this one, perhaps, also a standpipe for water. There were no toilets, not even a barbecue pit or emergency phone.

'I'm going to sleep,' Bernard said. 'You can stay and wait, or you can leave. Suit yourself. Don't mind your company, but don't want to keep you if your mother's expecting you.'

'What about the boy?'

'Sam's fine.'

You walked around the picnic ground, looking for somewhere to sit out the day, while Bernard stretched along the length of the seat. Tiger was between his legs, the dog's tail slapping the man's gut. Sam slipped out of the cab after you and sat at the base of a tree, fiddling the earth with a stick, boring into the dust between his feet, red canvas shoes, withdrawing the stick, boring again, deeper, withdrawing, a chimpanzee using a stick to harvest ants from a hole. His dark hair was red with a layer of dust and his skin was peeling from sunburn.

You knew it would have been wiser to keep

moving, but the child kept staring at you, opening his mouth as if to speak, then turning again to the stick and the earth, grinding and digging into the soil, up and down, one hole after another.

Cars were passing. If you wanted to play your part properly you would have continued your journey. Instead, you ate a peach and read the newspaper, which told you nothing you did not already know, nothing the authorities did not want everyone to know. Terrorists would be blamed. At that moment the police were raiding several properties and two remote farms suspected of operating as training camps. Did you imagine the knock on my own door that morning, the men, the memories that knock conjured of an earlier knock, many years ago, on the morning after a similarly horrific night? You dismissed the consequences for the rest of your family – you had to in order to survive. I understand that, at least.

And me? What of me? What should I have said when the men asked, when they shouted? What did I know? I tell myself that I knew nothing that could have changed anything at that point. Earlier, though – if they had come the day before, or the day before that, demanding I confess what I knew of my daughter's plans and her associates, I can no longer say what I might have given away. And why, I ask myself now, every day that passes, did I not take the chance myself? To save you, to save others, I might have betrayed you. Would a defeat on that day have changed the course of anything, the balance of lives lost against lives saved?

There was no news for you, who knew all that mattered on that day. You clawed in the sand trying to make up your mind – cruel, an ostrich in the wilderness.

1989

The boy understood that his Uncle Bernard had been a soldier once and still called himself a warrior. This was a reason for doing and not doing all kinds of things. A warrior did not listen to music except when going into battle and a warrior trained his body to live on less, to eat only once a day, twice at most. A warrior knew the psychology of his enemy. A warrior had to rely on nature for survival and so a warrior had to be – what was it he said? – intimately acquainted with the bitch.

This meant that when they went on these drives there was no music.

Are we going into battle? Bernard barked, when the boy asked if he could turn on the radio.

No, the boy said, even though he didn't know if this was the answer Bernard wanted to hear.

Then no music, hey? No battle, no music. You got to keep your mind focussed. Music and food, these things distract a person, man.

Was my father a warrior?

Bernard laughed and rolled down the window and spat into the wind.

The boy remembered car trips with his parents to see his Aunt Ellen in Beaufort West, and once to visit friends in Kenton-on-Sea. The radio was always on, all the time, even if his parents complained that the music was terrible. It was something to drown out the sound of the road and the hot wind that came in through the windows if it was a dry month, or the rain on the roof that hammered them deaf if it was wet. Music made time pass, sped up the hours that seemed so much longer driving fast in a car. The boy would fall asleep to music, especially if it was the old-fashioned music his parents liked, and wake after dark when they arrived on the street where his aunt lived, and felt himself being carried inside by his mother or father and tucked between sheets stretched tight over the cushions of the sofa in his aunt's lounge, a sofa that smelled like one of his parents' parties if it were held in a sweet shop or bakery.

On the road that night with Bernard, the boy thought about how he hadn't seen his aunt in at least a year. He wondered if he would see her again. Somewhere he was sure he had her phone number and address. If only she knew how things were, he couldn't imagine that she'd let him stay with Bernard. He'd asked Bernard if they couldn't get a cat or a dog, to have some company on the long trips. *I'm not running a blerry zoo*, Bernard had said, *I don't like animals.*

The boy tried to stay awake, to watch Bernard out of his right eye, the road with his left, but the images kept coming together so that the man's face turned black and the road turned white. As he fell asleep, the boy imagined that he had the strength to tie Bernard to the front of the truck, so that his head was like a plough or the guard on the front of a train, and he dreamed of driving the truck fast and forward, so that Bernard's face became black with the road and the road became white with his face.

SAM

Saturday night. At great expense, Greg has Nonyameko come in for the evening so the two of us can go out to dinner. We drive around into the City Bowl, park up on Kloof Street and have a drink with one of the artists represented by Greg's gallery. The night is warm, so we decide to walk down the hill to Saigon for sushi. As we pass Hoërskool Jan van Riebeeck a young woman comes out of the darkness.

'Excuse me gentlemen, I don't mean to be rude,' she says. Moved by some kind of metropolitan instinct, I turn away. I don't hear the next words. Out of the corner of my eye I look at her face and clothes, wondering where the clipboard is. She's either doing a survey for the city, I think, or she's selling magazine subscriptions, or canvassing for a charity.

Then the story comes out and I can't help listening. She does odd jobs for people but was unable to find work today. She doesn't think that ninety rand to pay for a night in the shelter is going to fall out of the sky. She has a daughter. They lost their house. She begins to tremble. I keep my body turned away. New York has hardened me against this kind of plea. But Greg listens, asks me if I have any money, any coins, he doesn't have any change. I take out my wallet, remove the largest silver coins I have in the change compartment, and ignore the hundreds of rand in notes. The woman has an educated accent; she isn't drunk and doesn't appear to be high. As I've been trying to decide whether to give her fifteen rand or twenty, she's covered her face and started to cry. Maybe, I think, she's a drama student. I knew drama students in New York who were sent out to beg on the streets as a test of their skill. Grades for the exercise were awarded on a scale pegged to how much each student earned in handouts. The thinnest ones always got A's.

'Here,' I say, and empty the coins into her hand. She mumbles, 'I'm so ashamed, I am so ashamed.' I know that the money's too little. I tell her not to be ashamed and hold her gaze and say it again. She has a crescent of dark freckles around her eyes and brow. Her clothes are good but dirty.

'There's nothing shameful about asking,' I say, and we leave her. Fifteen or twenty rand is nothing to me – less than five dollars, less than four.

As we walk down the hill Greg says, 'I couldn't pass her knowing that we were going to spend several hundred rand on raw fish and beer. I think she was telling the truth. It could have been drugs or something else, but I think she was telling the truth.'

'It doesn't actually matter,' I say.

★

At the end of our interview yesterday I asked Clare what my purpose was, why she herself didn't write about her past.

'You mean why I didn't choose to write a memoir?'

'Yes. Or autobiography.'

She had me at the door and was trying to transfer me over to Marie, so that I could be ushered out of the house. 'I can't see my life as a totality, or as a continuous narrative. I wouldn't know how to write my own life in that way.'

'But what about fragments?'

'Yes, fragments, I suppose I could write fragments – I have written about moments. Transitional periods. Narratives of personal trauma, specific traumas. I can write about periods of my life but not my whole life. I wouldn't know what to put in and what to leave out. Or, I guess what I mean is, I would want to leave out so much there would be very little left. That's why I need you.'

★

I wasn't looking for it. The image comes when I don't want it, in the middle of the night, bloated with fish and beer.

I'm standing at the screen door, not alone. Someone else puts his palm against the wooden frame. He tightens the palm into a fist and knocks three times. It's a polite knock, not an insistent one. We hear steps inside and then the interior door opens, and we see her face behind the screen. She asks who we are and what we want. *What is your business?* she asks, and I can hear that she's trying to be polite but is alarmed by the sight of us. We're strangers and we must be strange in appearance, too, ragged and bony. I can almost smell myself then. One of the others says who we are and holds up a bag. She takes us through the house, down the dim central corridor and out to the garden. She gives us tea and biscuits. She sees that we're still hungry and goes back inside to make sandwiches.

Or do I imagine that hospitality? Did she keep us on the front porch, a screen separating her from us, a discreet hand tripping the lock on the door, which would not have been difficult to break down, not for the three of us, travelling for days with so little, so hungry and thirsty we could have broken through deadbolts. Or is that a false memory, too?

It's her face behind the screen that comes to me. It's the only thing I can see with any clarity. The rest I don't know.

★

It's possible that the conversation late on Friday has changed things between us. This Monday morning I sense that Clare and I have reached a new level of understanding, or at least that she's beginning to trust me. She speaks more freely, so I return to questions about censorship, since those have produced her most fluent responses so far.

'You've described the mental effect of living under the threat of censorship, but how did it specifically impinge on your writing?'

'Quite simply, it acted as a constant distraction. Under such conditions, one cannot even begin to put pen to paper in the morning without weighing the implications of every letter, because the censoring mind, parsing and legalistic, looks for meaning even in spelling and punctuation. And that is when one knows that the censor has won, because, ultimately, what the censor most desires is not total control of information, but for all writers to self-censor.'

'Did you?'

She draws herself up but her shepherd's crook spine keeps her always somewhat stooped, vulture-like. How tall she must have been before her body began to turn on her. I remember that height from the past, and how it intimidated.

'Yes and no. I never wanted to write the kinds of books they were inclined to censor. You know that. Protest is not difficult, neither is journalism; even good journalism today requires nothing more than a notebook, a recorder – look at *you* – and the ability to ask dogged questions of someone who does not want to answer, or else merely to observe the world and describe it with insight or a particular point of view. People will always write protest novels and reportage and pornography. One might argue that the tyranny of the censor fuelled my writing as much as defined its parameters. The body of my work is at least in part a product of the place the censor held in my own imagination.'

'Was the censor embodied in your imagination?'

'Why?' She looks startled; the question seems to catch her by surprise.

'I wondered if you envisioned the censor as a person, rather than an abstraction, or a worm, as you said last week.'

'Yes, I did,' she says – no hesitation now.

'Would you care to say what he, or she, looked like?'

'Why?'

'Curiosity.'

'The censor looked like me. She was an internal doppelgänger, hovering just behind me with a blue pencil, poised to attack. I often thought that if I was very still, writing at my desk, and turned around suddenly, I might see her there, just behind me. You will think me insane,' she says, sounding amused by her own confession. 'It is a good question, you know. No one has ever asked me that. I called her Clara – the censoring half of my mind. Not half – maybe quarter or eighth, the little bit I allowed her to occupy, the bit she claimed.'

'Clara?'

'It sounded smug to me. A smug little housewife censor who thinks she knows what literature is. The fear I've always had –' She stops and raises her hands. 'Turn off your recorder.' I switch it off and put down my pencil. 'The fear . . . I'm just a smug little housewife who thinks she knows what literature is. Unlike you, I have no doctorate. I belong to a generation of academics who could build a career on a first degree alone, and a generation of writers who did not go to school to learn how to tell stories. Often I wonder how much of Clara I have let take over. More than an eighth? More than half?' She holds my gaze, shaking her head. 'I don't know, you know, that's the thing.'

The gardener, who seems to be here every day, draws her attention away from me. 'What does one do with a man like that? I certainly don't know what to do. I don't want to be thought rude, even by him. Especially by him, I mean – by someone like him. I don't want to be like my mother was. I don't *want* to be the imperious white madam who can't help being an autocrat with the servants. Even that, you know – I'm aware what I give away in calling them *servants* instead of *staff*. Don't think I don't know. But what is one to do? This is life on the feudal estate. I want to tell him to go away and not come back. *Fire him* as Americans say – such a violent way of ending a professional relationship, burning the terminated, or firing upon them, executing them. But I don't know how to fire him. My mother never taught me how to

99

terminate a relationship – any kind of relationship. What is one to do? If I fired him, how many lives would I imperil?'

I shake my head and hunch my shoulders. 'I don't have any experience of staff. I wouldn't have any idea how to terminate a relationship. I've never been in a position of authority over another person.'

'I'm not sure I believe that,' she says, glancing back at me. 'All right, let's get back to it. You may turn on your recorder thingy again, darling.' Do I imagine the *darling*? No, I hear it distinctly. It's the word I've been waiting for that I didn't know I needed to hear. My chest is a hot flood. *Darling, darling.* I shuffle papers to kill time and fiddle with the recorder. *Darling.* I try to find my composure.

I invent a question.

'Do you think other writers in this country imagined themselves as their own censors?'

'How should I know? Ask them,' she says coolly, and it's as if the conversation of a few seconds ago never happened. It was off the record. The record is something separate. It's a different register and another kind of contract. There is no room on the record for *darling*.

The sun flashes into the room, reflecting off the windows of a neighbouring house. She draws the blinds and returns to her desk, again to shuffle papers, as though it's a code we've agreed: to shuffle papers is to buy time. It isn't about pretending to be otherwise occupied, or at least this is how I begin to interpret it. Without looking up at me she speaks.

'Don't you want to ask me about my childhood?' Three fingers pull the hair away from her face on one side.

I want to hear her call me *darling* again, that's what I want. I want her to hug me at the end of each meeting, pat my head, tell me I'm doing a good job. She teases me with a photo of her as a girl, on a horse, somewhere on a farm in the Karoo.

'I thought there were no clues to your fiction in your own life,' I say, trying to tease back.

'That is true, but you are writing a biography, are you not? Should we not be talking about my life instead of my work? Or what kind of biography is this?'

'As you've said, much of your life is a matter of public record.'

'If not my own life, then the lives of those around me.'

We spend a further two hours talking about the themes of her works, historicizing the texts, exploring obvious resonances with her own life that even she is willing to acknowledge, while asserting *the process of mystification and mythification* she undertook to make *the personal more complex and more significant than mere autobiography.* Her words, not mine.

At one o'clock Marie taps once on the door,

doesn't wait for Clare's reply, and wheels in a cart bearing two covered trays. Placing each tray on the low coffee table in the middle of the room, she removes the covers: sandwiches, a selection of salads. She bows (is that my imagination?) and wheels the cart from the room, closing the door behind her.

We eat in a concentrated silence, punctuated by the sounds of our chewing and breathing, our movements across upholstery, readjusting our weight to find more comfortable positions. A hadeda screams in the garden. One gardener shouts to another. A plane passes overhead. A house further down the street cries out in alarm. We say nothing over the food, and nothing about it.

In all the hours I've been in the house I've never heard a telephone ring. Maybe there's a phone in the other wing, with a quiet ringer that only Marie hears and answers. There's no phone in the office. Clare has no contact with the rest of the world except through the windows, which she opens throughout the day to direct the gardeners in an unbroken stream of language that I know will only ever be sound to me. It's a language I won't learn because I don't have the time or the will.

She chews, her movements slow and methodical, as though every bite demands full attention. Her large, straight teeth work through the bread and fillings, the salad leaf and tomatoes, all simply but carefully prepared. She likes good things, good food, good clothes, good furniture, and a good house.

The success of her books has afforded a comfort-able lifestyle – an extravagant lifestyle compared to what most have in this country, or in any country for that matter. When we've finished the sand-wiches, she presses a button on the wall by her desk. A minute later Marie returns with coffee and a plate of Tennis Biscuits and Romany Creams. She takes the empty plates, and again leaves us in privacy.

'I thought I was supposed to bring my own food.'

'I don't like strange smells. Everything becomes more intense when one lives alone. I don't like going out. I hate travelling. Going to London was almost more than I could manage. I slept for a month afterward.' She affects a smile. 'I wasn't always this way. I haven't left this house in over three weeks, nearly a month. Twenty-four days: a single day containing many.'

ABSOLUTION

After the initial police investigation into the house invasion, as Clare insisted on calling it, she had no further contact with the authorities. No suspects were presented for her to identify, no one apprehended, and no one, so far as she could remember, had ever asked her for a description of the invaders. The police had failed to recover her father's wig in its black tin box. And then, a few months after moving from the old house on Canigou Avenue to her new fortress in Bishopscourt, there was a buzz at the outer gate and Marie admitted a black car with government registration plates. The driver, a man with pinched features and a thin neck, opened the door for a petite woman whose hair was swept up behind her head.

The woman did not wait to be offered a seat, but slid down onto the couch opposite Clare's desk, and opened a binder containing a thick wad of documents.

'You were previously resident on Canigou Avenue,' the woman said.

'Yes, that's correct.'

'You suffered a house invasion, I believe.'

'Come to your point.'

'You employ a personal assistant, Ms Marie de Wet.'

'Correct.'

'*She* repelled the intruders,' the woman said, and sniffed.

'That is also correct.'

'With a *gun*.'

'Licensed. With a licensed gun. She did all that was necessary – a competency test, background checks, registration. I was unaware of it all. I did not know she had one,' Clare protested. 'I have since made her get rid of it. I believe she turned it over to the police, to have it destroyed. There are no guns in this house. I have very strong feelings about guns.'

'Indeed.' The woman curled her lip, as if to say, *We all have strong feelings about guns.*

'Have you caught any of the intruders?' Clare asked.

The woman, who Clare thought of as Ms White, looked startled, as if it were a strange question, and jerked her head in silent answer, *no*.

'Why would you wish for so long to live in such an insecure house?' Ms White asked.

'I don't think I understand your question.'

'Why did you choose to live so long on Canigou Avenue when your house was clearly no longer safe? You did not even have a proper gate or razor wire or an electric fence, as you do now. Any so-and-so could have got in. Why did you stay there so long when it was clear the neighbourhood was no longer safe for a woman such as yourself?'

No longer safe because the neighbourhood was too mixed, not white enough any more, too near the crime of the Cape Flats, even if only psychologically so? Clare knew that her intruders had nothing to do with those places, nothing to do with poverty or material deprivation.

'It was my house. It was where I raised my children, and where I spent the whole of my former married life,' Clare said. 'Is this relevant to the case? Could I see your identification?'

The woman produced a badge, but Clare had no means of judging its authenticity.

'You must have known it wasn't safe to be there, without even an alarm, without the proper measures taken. You are a celebrity of sorts, madam, aren't you? You are wealthy. People know you have money, even in this country.'

'Even in this country, Ms White, where the government does not necessarily like what I have to say.'

'I did not say *that*. I meant only that not quite so many people know in *this* country who *you* are, but that enough do that you must look after yourself.'

'It is *my* country. You need not refer to it as "this country", as if to suggest I am a visitor,' Clare said, hoping she sounded authoritative.

'Are you not a kind of visitor?' the woman asked.

'I was born here, as were my parents and grand-parents. And while they may not have done so, I have made a point, a very conscious point, of washing myself in every culture of this country, of making myself a part of it entirely.'

'And yet you remain unchanged by the experience, madam. You are still quite foreign. Like those settler ancestors of yours. They were visitors – or maybe not visitors, something not so nice as just *visitors*. I can think of another word. Yes, I think with ancestors like that you are still quite foreign.'

'I am changed in ways you cannot see, Ms White, that are beneath the skin. We could, for instance, speak in your mother tongue if you wished, instead of mine, and then you would have an even greater advantage over me, but I would still be able to hold my own. I am not a stranger anywhere that I go. I can speak with everyone. How can you call me foreign? I have always been a citizen of this country. I have never been anything but a citizen of this country, no matter the history of my ancestors or the history of the country itself. This is *my* country. I have a birth certificate. I have a passport. I do not appreciate your tone.'

'And now you live in this grand mansion, with your high walls. It is almost like a palace. Perhaps you think you are some kind of queen.'

'I think no such thing. I am very humble.' Perhaps not humble enough. Clare had caught the scent of the hunt, knew that she was not going to

107

be accorded the rights and privileges of an innocent victim; she was a victim, perhaps, but not
innocent.

'You still employ the same personal assistant,
Ms Marie de Wet,' the woman continued.

'You know I do. She showed you into my house.
Forgive me, Ms White, but could you explain the
purpose of your questions?'

'All part of the investigations, to be sure we have
missed nothing that might help the case – nothing
that might help, as you would say, with appre-
hending your intruders.'

'They are not *my* intruders.'

'*The* intruders, then, if you prefer.' Ms White
managed to look down her nose at Clare, even
though, seated as she was, Clare remained taller
than the other woman. 'You use a private security
firm?'

'It is private to my knowledge. Perhaps the state
has some interest in it?'

'I do not know. Perhaps *you* know something we
do not,' the woman said, and sniffed again.

'No,' said Clare. 'Do you need a tissue?'

'It occurs to me, Mrs Wald, that surely your
private security firm employs men with guns. Would
they not respond with guns if you summoned
them?'

'I have not yet needed to summon them. We
might try now, if you like,' Clare said, daring a curl
of the lip. A silence rolled around between them
on the floor and Clare wondered how responsive

her security men would be. 'I hope you get them, the intruders.'

'Show them to me, madam, and I will. Just show them to me,' said Ms White, as if Clare herself were one of the intruders.

'Your officers never even asked me for a statement.'

'But that I think is a lie.' Ms White riffled through the papers in her binder and retrieved a single page. *'Four men, aged twenty-five to forty. Average height, muscular build. Race uncertain.'*

'I did not say anything of the kind. I have no idea what their age might have been. I could not even say with certainty that they were definitely men.' Clare wondered if, in the aftermath of the invasion, she had given a statement she could not now remember.

'You signed the document,' said Ms White, holding it up for inspection.

Clare was certain it was not her signature – too jagged, too unkempt. 'I did not,' she said, but then had a moment of doubt. If the panic had been as acute as she remembered, then it was entirely possible that a shaking hand would have distorted her signature. The name on the document was, she could see, the issue of a hand wandering free of the brain's control.

'Are you accusing my officers of something?'

'No, I cannot do that. I am – uncertain. All that I am doing is accusing someone of making a mistake. I do not *remember* giving a description. I do not remember putting my signature to that document. But no, thinking about it again, I am certain that I never gave an official statement. I was never taken to a police station – that is beyond doubt. I have never been called to testify or witness. That scrawl, the signature, it could be anything. I do not think it is mine. I say that emphatically.' In fact, Clare doubted herself even more, and, after all, the woman was only trying to do her job.

Ms White clicked her tongue, shook her head, looked concerned, sniffed again. 'It seems there is some very grave misunderstanding, then. Because here, quite clearly, someone purporting to be you – *I* can read your name – has levelled the blame at four men, aged twenty-five to forty, of average height and muscular build, and indeterminate race. Indeterminate race. Is that a euphemism, madam?'

'As I did not make the statement, how can I know whether it was meant as a euphemism or a statement of fact? I think you should leave, Ms White.'

'You should be careful, madam, because someone I think is pretending to be *you*. Or else you are forgetting who *you* are, and where *you* have been. Why do you think that would be? Why should someone give us evidence on your behalf that was not you, and pretend to be you? It seems a very strange situation. I think you are forgetting some-thing. I think you are not feeling well. There are places for the sick to get well, if you are sick. It could be arranged.'

'I am not sick. I am in perfect health. Consult my doctors.' Clare saw what was being threatened: the forcible hospitalization, sedation, electroconvulsive therapy, interminable confinement – an assault on the mind. She knew she would have to tread carefully, but was struggling to find the reserve to control herself.

'We will have to get to the bottom of it, madam. But I assure you, we are very good at what we do, and we *will* get to the bottom of it, one way or another, no matter how long it takes.' Ms White smiled almost benevolently and stood, signalling the end of the interview. She did not say goodbye or offer her hand, snapping the binder shut before dropping it into her briefcase. 'I can find my own way out.'

'I will show you,' said Clare. 'Allow me that courtesy at least.'

CLARE

Is it unfair for me to think your notebooks, your final letter, a load I must bear? It pains me to read them, to compare them with the official accounts, the TRC transcripts, the news clippings, the competing histories and revisions of the past that I have accumulated in an ever-expanding file of materials, compiled so long after the events they seek to describe. I begin to accept that distance can only breed distortion. I read a line in your handwriting, compare it with the other things I know, the memories of you, the birthday and Mother's Day cards you gave me over the years even when I know it pained you to offer me any sign of love. I cannot go on. Reading a single page is alpine ascent. A day's worth of writing – one of your days, your account of a single day – is ocean crossing. *I held Sam's hand and he looked so trusting*, I read, and put down the notebook before I make the ink of your words run lividly across the page. Why do I not have more in your hand, Laura? Your wild child's handwriting turned tight and regimented in adolescence, just like your politics, for a while so unlike ours, so foreign to anything your father or I would have countenanced as correct or proper or simply good. The flag you insisted on flying from your bedroom window. The salutes. The singing of the anthem. Your peculiar militarism. It was torture for us – torture and embarrassment. And the tiny marching rows of letters, so finely written your teachers complained that your essays were almost illegible and required the use of magnifying glasses. And then, along with your politics, the sudden shift in your hand halfway through your first year at university, the strange hybrid of cursive and print, your own invention, beautiful but unruly, adhering only to the barest outline of rule. Radical and unruly where once you had been so conservative. You were old enough to know what you thought, to realize when you'd been wrong in the past, to know your ignorance and realize the terror in that unknowing.

Even now, when so much has changed and nothing has changed, there are difficulties. There is something in your case, and others like yours, which pricks consciences and embarrasses your former colleagues. No one will tell me what or why. I admit I have made only limited enquiries, asked discreet questions of a few people at official events, where they cannot speak without fear of being overheard, where I must look like a pathetic and desperate old woman hungry for justification and reassurance and some explanation for why your name is not on the roll of heroes. I can only guess. Perhaps it is the cold-bloodedness of what you did, the extraordinary determination in the way you carried out your mission. You were nothing if not a zealot. You had innocent victims, if any one of us can be called *innocent* or *victim*.

Who do we believe? There are lacunae in the archive I have assembled, the filing cabinet that contains what remains of you, gaps yawning between your account to me in the letter delivered on your behalf, your account to yourself in the ten notebooks you bequeathed to me, and the accounts of the former government, the news reports, the testimony of your former colleagues, and that of your own victims. There are periods for which no one can account, missing ligatures of motivation and event and development between more or less established fact, without which the bones of the story would make no sense, fall to the ground, have no possibility of mobility or unity of structure, no life. I need to will those ligaments into being, put flesh upon the facts, decide whether it is a serpentine monster or a ten-armed goddess.

I remind myself that there is the other source, as yet untapped; given the chance, Sam might tell a quite different story.

★

You watched him suck at a bottle of brown-looking water, his hair flashing, dirty, dark and unlovable. You could hear his tongue cleave to the roof of his mouth. 'Do you have any bread?' he asked.

You did not reply, trying to resist being drawn into responsibility. He said it again. 'In your bag? Do you have another peach maybe? Or an apple?'

'No. I have dates.'

'Can I have some?' he asked, foot twisting against the ground.

'Don't you have any food?'

'Not like yours,' whining, beseeching, toe digging a cavity, 'not anything like that.'

'Then no. You can't have any of my fruit. I have a long journey ahead of me. My food has to last.'

You had come to desolation, a monochrome world, the bright colours of childhood disappeared, scarlet dresses lost and burned, or given to the maid to give to her own children, who might now have given them to their own children.

(Did you ever have scarlet dresses? Did I ever put you in a dress? I go to the albums to search for a picture, my little red-cap daughter, and can find you only in green or yellow, no red, no dress, a skirt at most, a stern blouse, khaki and white, brown and black, a brief surge of blue and orange. You must have had a red dress at some point; every girl in my family has always had at least one red dress. Did I fail you in this, too?)

You marched away from Sam, down into a ravine, where you hid yourself in the brush, lowered your shorts, and pushed until your bowels and bladder were empty. There were rolls of paper in your rucksack, sanitary napkins, too, which you had packed knowing that days might pass like this, that you would travel to your fate at the speed of contemplation; you did not want to be stuck without the few props that still separated you from the animals, who stared dumbly through the bush at your performance, furry faces sniffing your waste and unease, watching with bemusement as you buried your soil in the hard-packed earth.

By noon the winds began to rise and the cloud of black smoke appeared high above you, shearing the sky in half.

'It will be fine,' you said to Sam, who looked up, eyes wary, 'as long as the winds keep blowing. We worry when the winds drop, or if it starts to rain. You must not be afraid.'

'What is it?' he asked, staring at the growing weight of the sky, and back at you, and to the truck.

'Many things.'

Tiger jumped out of the cab, showing a stained tooth. He growled and nudged at Sam's leg. The boy stepped back and turned the tap on the stand-pipe for the dog to drink. Where it fell, the water cut a muddy red pool, and Tiger drank from this, too.

'Do you go to school?' you asked.

'It's the school holidays.'

'Of course.' It was January. He twisted his mouth and stood, hands on his tiny hips, staring at you.

'Why were you waiting by the road?' he asked, in such a tone of accusation it startled you into thinking he might be dangerous.

'Why shouldn't I?'

'Because people like us don't wait by roads,' he said, 'not in the middle of the night. That's what Bernard said.'

'Maybe I had no choice. Maybe the lift I expected didn't turn up and I had no choice but to hitch-hike. Did you ever think of that?'

Sam appeared to accept this and turned off the tap, which dripped with maddening persistence. He put his fingers into the hole, letting the drips run over them, turning the soil on his hands into bright red scars.

'Do you do this every day?' you asked.

'Do what?'

'Sit at picnic sites while Bernard sleeps.'

'For a while now. Not so long. Maybe for not so long now.' And then he nodded his head, as if that were the real answer.

'If he's not your father, then where are your parents?'

'Dead.' The boy looked at you, his face sour, puzzling, head still nodding, edging into a compulsive rhythm. He had little control over his body, it did things he did not expect it to, misbehaved even when he thought it was being still. 'Bernard took me when they died.'

'Was he a friend of your parents?'

'An uncle maybe. An uncle or cousin. *I'm your uncle or cousin maybe.* That's what he said.'

'Does he have a house?'

'Yes. We stayed there once. I slept on a couch. There was only one bedroom in the house, and that was his bedroom. So I slept on a couch. And then he said he had to go on a job. So we left his house the next day. After I slept on the couch. And then we started driving,' he said, a rehearsed speech, words he struggled to remember. Perhaps he knew there was something wrong with the order or the content. He shook his head.

'How long ago was that?'

'A while.' Sam stared at you, nothing but blank confusion in his face. He was lost, almost witless. He would illuminate nothing. His presence must have more material relevance. 'I want to go home. Do you know how to get there?' he asked.

'I don't know where your home is.'

'No?' he said, sounding surprised. 'I thought maybe you did.'

Making no noise at all, three women appeared out of the bush coming from the direction of the ravine. They each carried two plastic petrol jugs, variously coloured red, green, and blue. The women nodded at you and Sam, and went to collect water at the standpipe. You and the women exchanged words that Sam did not understand. Tiger growled at the boy's side as the women finished filling the jugs. There were a few more words between you and the women, and courteous nods, a language and a form you learned as a child on visits to the farm, before the women slipped away from the site and back down into the ravine. The black clouds had covered the sun, and though your watch said it was only 12.15 it was as dark as dusk. Many hours of day remained before the abrupt sunset, the quick dark-ening that spreads from the north-eastern sky, drawing a lid over the land.

'Should we pray?' Sam asked.

'Why?'

'For God to make the clouds go away.'

'It won't make any difference,' trying not to sound impatient.

'What do you mean?'

'What I say.'

'I think I'm going to pray.' The boy knelt in the dirt next to the dog, clasping his hands together, and looked up at the clouds, then dipped his head, closed his eyes, and mumbled for a long time. His face was fixed, intense in its devotion, head nodding in time to his prayer.

'It won't do any good,' you snapped. 'Either the winds will carry the clouds away from us, or the rains will come. There is nothing we can do. Praying will change nothing. All we can do is take cover if it starts to rain, so you might as well stop praying. That's just nonsense. Stop it now.'

But Sam continued his mumbling, and it worked at you until you walked over to him and shook him with such violence that he fell over in the dirt. As you did this, Tiger's teeth pierced your leg, enamel cracking against bone. With your free leg, you kicked the dog in the head until his jaws released. And then you kicked again, breaking the dog's back, and with a hissing whimper Tiger sprawled on the ground, immobile but still alive. You dragged him

119

by the legs under a bush, where you finished him with a rock to the skull.

The boy stood up, tears popping in dusty boils on his cheeks. It would have been logical to leave the boy and man. To walk away would have been the best choice, following the women into the bush, taking back roads, escaping the country at some remote point. By killing the dog you had done something that would have consequences, as if starting a chain reaction.

'We could go. Before he wakes up,' Sam said, looking towards the truck and then to the bush. At first you thought he didn't understand about Tiger, but then you saw it clearly. He was electing you as rescuer. But you could not take this child and walk into the bush. You could not raise him in a cave, a hermit. You had only enough for one, and Bernard would follow you, or send people to follow you, and that would be the end of everything – not just your life but also the lives of many others. Before killing you they would burn the names from your mouth, pull syllables from your fingernails, soak vowels and consonants from your nostrils, remind you of their authority with steel and wire, electricity and fire.

'Does he have a gun?' you asked.

'No,' head shaking almost out of control.

'Not in the glove compartment, or under the seat?'

'No.'

You looked around the picnic site for a stone large

enough to do the job but not so heavy as to be unwieldy. The one for Tiger was too big to carry to the truck. As you tried the weight of several others the winds dropped and the air pressure began to change. A front was advancing – dry air coming along the coast to meet the warm, wet air blowing from the other direction and converging over your heads. No other cars had passed for half an hour at least. You chose your stone and crept up on the cab. Bernard was snoring, but as you opened the door, he looked into your face, upside down, half in shadow; the stone sat heavy in your hands.

'Christ, woman! You gave me a fright, hey. Where's Tiger?'

'Chasing birds in the ravine.'

'I'll find him. I just need to answer a call of nature.'

You dropped the stone on the ground behind you as Bernard hopped from the cab, walked across the picnic site and down into the ravine, leaving the key in the ignition. You beckoned to Sam, who ran over and climbed through the passenger door. 'Lock your door.' Sam obeyed, staring at you, his face dumb and unreadable. You could not just drive away, so you started the engine, and revved it. Bernard ran towards the truck, his fly still open.

You gunned the engine again, threw the truck into gear, and accelerated as Bernard ran alongside, then, running faster, put himself between the truck and the road. 'Close your eyes, Sam.'

The boy put his hands over his eyes as you reversed, braked, revved the engine and sped forward, knocking Bernard flat. The collision threw you and Sam forward and then back against the seat.

You reversed again, revealing the fat man's twitching body, pink shirt stained dark, his mouth working, a gash of blood spurting from between his teeth. You shifted back into first gear, turning the wheel so the full weight of the truck ground into him.

'Keep your eyes closed,' you said, and drove back and forth over him until he was still. Each time, the truck bounced less violently, flattening Bernard as if something large and manmade had dropped on top of him, from out of the sky, from the dark clouds overhead.

To think I once said you lacked the mother's instinct.

At least, that is your version of what happened, the reason you give me in your final notebook for the change in your plans, and the responsibility you took for the child. Somehow, it is not a version I can believe. I try for another, one that fits with what I know you were capable of doing.

Bernard went on snoring, never regaining consciousness as you brought the stone down on his brow, over and over, until your arms and face were covered in a thick splatter.

So one could get blood from a stone.

You had done worse things in your life.

Taking the keys from the ignition, you shut

the door, walked around the cab and opened the passenger door. You grabbed his feet and pulled him out of the cab, knocking his head against the four metal steps. It left a red trail, speckled with stars of pale tissue. Sam was hyperventilating, his eyes large and dark, and without warning he convulsed, vomiting onto the ground, his body wracked with heaving until only foam dripped from his mouth.

You dragged Bernard's body into the ravine, hiding it in the same thicket of thorns where Tiger lay dead. Scavengers would clean up most of the mess before nightfall. You washed yourself at the standpipe, cleaning your arms and face, scrubbing the bite on your right leg, making yourself feel nothing. It was a talent you had developed.

Sam stared at you, his face and shirt splattered with vomit.

'Can you wash yourself?' you asked, putting your hands on his shoulders.

'Yes.' He splashed his face and hands, wiping his shirt with wet palms, getting himself wetter than he intended.

'Do you have any other clothes?'

'I have a bag. In the truck.'

'Go and change.'

'It's sticky,' Sam said, peeling his hand from the brown vinyl upholstery of the cab seat, a film of blood covering his palm.

'Wipe it on the floor.'

As you pulled the truck onto the highway, the rain started. You switched the cab's ventilation to recycle, to keep from breathing the worst of the fumes rising off the water that coated the windscreen, resisting the wipers that fought to clear a view. It would be impossible to drive at night if such rain continued. Sam pushed and pulled his bloody fingers apart, spat on them, rubbed his hands like someone trying to start a fire with friction, and bent double to wipe them on the cab's rough carpet, finger-painting in the pile. When he had exhausted this game, he sat up again, examined his hands, and tried to clean the arcs of dried blood from under his fingernails.

'I'm hungry,' he whined.

'Get in my rucksack. Have some fruit.'

Sam reached for the dates and ate four, watching your reaction to be sure he did not take more than his share. He flicked on the radio and looked at the map. 'Where are we going?'

'Back the way we came. Into the storm.'

He had only one picture of his parents together, with him in his mother's arms, and it was taken when he was only a few months old, and through everything that happened he kept it in his bag in a plastic sleeve between the pages of a book so that it wouldn't get bent or torn or broken. In the photo his mother's wearing jeans and a yellow T-shirt with a man's green head printed on it and his father's wearing shorts and nothing else, because it was January. Anyone could see from the picture why they would have fallen in love with each other. They're both tanned, nice bodies, nice faces. What is a nice face? Everything in the right place and the right size and smooth skin, but his father had a scar on his cheek, a scar that he loved. His father was strong and supple and the boy would kiss his father's scar whenever he was there to put him to bed, which wasn't very often because of the work that took him away from the house most hours of every day. He remembered the taste of that scar on the tip of his tongue. His parents were not bad people he was sure but maybe they were not very smart people even though they read books and knew all about the world.

When Bernard stopped the boy woke up.

I'm going to sleep over there. You stay in the cab. Lock the doors and don't let anyone in but me you understand?

What if – ?

But Bernard was already walking away from the truck to the only shaded spot. He had a towel and spread it on a patch of ground near a half-dead tree and then put a magazine over his face. It was hot in the cab and the boy was sweating so he rolled down the windows. They were half a kilometre from the road and there weren't any houses around, just fields in all directions. Bernard had left the keys in the ignition. The boy knew how to drive because his father had put him on his lap but Bernard didn't know that.

The boy waited until he could hear Bernard snoring and then opened the door of the truck and without getting out tried to pee onto the ground outside but little came out. There was nothing to drink in the cab and nothing to eat. There was an ablution block because it was a campground but the boy would have to walk past Bernard to get there. He wondered how long he could last without anything to drink. Was it two days? He didn't have a watch and the truck didn't have a clock, so the only way he could guess how long he'd been sitting there was by watching the sun, but even that didn't help. He'd never paid much attention to the position of the sun so that days might have gone by like that, and he wouldn't have known except for the coming of night. But he didn't last until night.

It looked like it might be midday and he edged the door open again, took the keys, locked the cab and walked towards the ablution block. His stomach was making empty noises and Bernard was snoring and there were pied crows fighting over a trash bin that hadn't been emptied in a long time, and over all that was the sound of wind blowing the dirt around and there was a red-brown layer of it on Bernard's body and collected on the bodybuilding magazine covering his face. A picture of a man who was naked except for a little green bikini flexed his muscles on the cover. Bernard's snores vibrated against the pages and the man's green bikini and his flexing muscles moved like a cartoon.

The boy went into the ablution block and tried the taps at the sink but no water came out so he went into the showers and when he pushed the chrome taps they didn't give. No one had camped here for years because it wasn't on the way to anywhere nice and the place itself wasn't nice so what was the point? The only water was in the toilets but he wasn't going to drink that. Half-dead flies were bouncing off the floor and the ceiling. One of them landed on his arm and he caught it with a slap, squirting blood against his skin.

He remembered that they'd passed a petrol

station before they stopped and there would be water there and food, but then he remembered he didn't have any money. What had happened to his parents' money? Bernard would have it because he was the boy's uncle and guardian, because the boy was *his parents' sole heir*, because he was too young to be trusted and then he began to wonder what Bernard might have done with the money, which was *his* money, not Bernard's to spend on beer or the new truck he bought after the boy came to live with him. Was the truck his inheritance? Bernard had never said anything about the money but the boy knew there would've been some, even a little, from the sale of the house, and money from his parents' insurance – he knew there was insurance, he had heard his parents talk about it. All that money had gone somewhere.

He started walking away from the campground to the open fields and took off his shoes. In the distance a group of men were walking in the other direction like they were half-drunk or exhausted or just couldn't care where they might be going. He wanted to run and join them, but knew he could not. There was nothing those men might do to help him.

His father had always been busy with the work he was doing, which was important work that was going to save everyone, and because it was important the boy had forgiven him for being away so much. His father most often wore shorts, even on a rainy winter day, and he said a house constrained him, so first thing after kissing the boy's mother he would pick up his son and carry him outside, lying down on his back and placing the boy on his chest facing him, either lying stomach against stomach, or with the boy's short legs straddling his ribs, under the fig tree in the small back garden. *What has my boy done today?* At first the boy could only laugh, but as he grew older, he would say, *I ate breakfast* or *I read a book* or *I played with Sandra*, the girl who lived next door and was the same age as him. When he got older still he would tell his father about the books he'd read and about his friends at school and his teachers, and his father would say, *You're getting too big to lie on top of me, you're going to suffocate me*, and the boy would press all his weight into his father and the man would gasp and they would both laugh. After ten minutes of this comfort, which was the best medicine for loneliness and a perfect balm for cuts and small traumas, he would lift the boy from his chest, place him on the ground, and walk him back inside the house.

Sitting at the edge of the field the boy watched until the sun started to go down and the clouds over the mountains were turning red. He felt dizzy and his eyes were scratchy in their sockets and his tongue was furred and heavy. He helped himself up and went back into the campground where Bernard was still asleep and he thought of kicking him. He'd stopped snoring but the boy could see he was still breathing and he was sorry for this because all he wanted was for Bernard to go away. How nice it would be if he died in his sleep. The boy sat down next to him for a while, watching him breathing and wondering how long they would stay like this the two of them. This was not the life his parents had promised him. This was the life that insurance was supposed to protect him against.

When it was dark the boy got back in the truck and turned over the engine. Bernard moved in his sleep. The boy put the truck into gear and accelerated. He was afraid that starting the truck would wake Bernard but then the wheels were on top of him before the boy knew it and before Bernard knew it. The branches of the half-dead tree were scraping across the windshield and the truck collided with the ablution block and it trembled and rocked away from the truck towards the field and almost collapsed. The truck was the boy's inheritance. He was only taking what was his. He didn't think what he was doing.

He reversed, rolling back over Bernard and then up toward the road and there was less crunching than you might have thought. It was a big truck and Bernard was only a small man, hardly bigger than the boy but so much stronger. The boy was moving the truck forward and then back. For a moment he thought he might have only pushed Bernard into the earth and he switched on the headlights and Bernard looked like he still could have been sleeping except for the rose at his lips and the strange way his arms and legs went like a spider.

The boy turned off the truck and left the keys in the ignition and the headlights on and walked through the yellow light to look at Bernard and said, *Bernard? Bernard? Are you okay?* But Bernard didn't say anything. The rose turned into red bath bubbles at his mouth and his eyes were open but couldn't see when the boy put his hand in front of them. If they were open then maybe he did wake up. The bodybuilding magazine was torn on the ground next to him. The boy leaned over and felt for a pulse like his mother had once shown him, and felt for Bernard's breath and listened for a heartbeat, but he knew that Bernard would make no more noise and the boy was happy and then he was surprised at being happy and cried and shouted and stamped the ground. He couldn't think of anyone left in the world that cared about him.

He sat down next to the man and put Bernard's left arm in his lap and held it for a long time, pressing his fingers against the dead wrist and looking at the hairs that went gold in the headlights. Bernard wore a signet ring on his pinkie. The boy stroked the man's arm. He could see the wallet in Bernard's jeans and took it out and counted the money and then took the ring off the finger and the gold watch and removed the new leather boots that were too big for the boy though he knew he would grow into them soon. The jeans and shirt were ruined so he left those and put the magazine back over Bernard's face. He folded Bernard's arms in a cross over his chest and straightened his legs. There was no one to see him do it except for a crow in the tree and even she was asleep.

The driver's seat in the truck was wet and the boy saw that his pants were also wet and he stood outside drying off for a while and looking at the wind pick at the magazine and the hair that was sticking out underneath. He put Bernard's watch on his own forearm and the ring on his right ring finger and the wallet in his front pocket.

Bernard had no family apart from the boy so no one was going to miss him, only maybe his friends and the people he worked for. But here was a problem. The boy could drive but he had no licence and if someone saw him driving the truck they would call the police and if the police caught him they would stop him and look at Bernard's licence and know that the boy was not the man and the truck was not legally the boy's even though Bernard was his mother's half-brother. It was too dangerous to walk back to the petrol station alone after dark so the boy decided to sit out the night in the cab of the truck and figure out what to do in the morning, knowing already he was going to have to give up his inheritance if he was going to live.

He turned off the headlights and locked the doors and watched the clouds begin to cover the moon. He'd still had nothing to drink since the night before and his tongue and teeth were moving against him. Every few minutes he switched on the truck lights to be sure that Bernard was dead.

SAM

Another weekend. Greg is free from work, so we decide to drive out of town for a picnic. He knows a place, one of the old wineries between Stellenbosch and Franschhoek, where there are tables with views of the mountains.

'And they have chickens,' he says. 'Dylan loves to see the chickens, don't you my boy?'

The drive from the city to the winelands, forty-five minutes, takes us past the townships and the airport. Going back and forth between Greg's house and Clare's, it's easy to forget where I am. It might be San Francisco, with a few more beggars on the streets, a few more people trying to sell fruit or trinkets or newspapers or offering to wash your car windows. At one intersection near Bishopscourt, at the turn-off to Kirstenbosch, half a dozen men sell identical mixed-media depictions of township life: canvas paintings with miniature tin shacks affixed to the surface to create a rough bas-relief. I've never seen anyone buy one.

FROM SHACKLAND TO DIGNITY say the billboards along the length of the N2, the road out of town to the airport and the national route, east along the coast. I half-remember driving this road with Bernard; I'd just as soon forget it completely.

A few years ago the shacks – made of cardboard, tin, plastic tarps, bottles, containers, tyres, mud, whatever could be found – had spilled out and were encroaching on the highway itself, Greg tells me. There was a clearance in the last year or two, so that foreign tourists wouldn't be so disturbed.

At the winery we park alongside one of the original seventeenth-century buildings, newly whitewashed, and find a table in the shade near a pond to spread out our picnic. Dylan makes chicken noises and Greg says in a gentle voice, 'Those are ducks, baby. What noise do ducks make?' Quacks instead of cheeps. We open a bottle of wine, give Dylan a cup of juice, and eat salads and sandwiches while he plays. He isn't hungry. He's been eating since breakfast.

I look up at the outcropping of rock on the mountain. The sun is so close it feels like a weight bearing down against me. The air smells like my childhood, like my parents, the home I grew up in – aloes and wood smoke, fynbos and pungent pollens that are as much like animal as plant, pollens and dust that leave marks on the pages of books and settle into the surfaces of objects with such permanence that the smell never goes away. I remember my parents obsessively dusting their books, wrapping the covers in plastic to protect them, watching the gradual decay they could only forestall temporarily. Books meant everything to them, books in false wrappers, ranks of dangerous books hidden behind safer ones, volumes secreted under a loose board in the floor of my own bedroom. What happened to all those books? What happened to everything we possessed? I don't have any of those things, nothing from my childhood. I have one picture of myself from infancy to early adolescence. The first continuous surviving record of my appearance begins with my arrival at my Aunt Ellen's house, after my parents were gone, after Bernard was gone, too.

After lunch we find the chickens in the herb garden that supplies the winery's expensive restaurant and Dylan cheeps with delight. He's a sweet child; taking both our hands, jumping up and down excitedly, *cheep cheep cheep*, he looks at us both for approval.

'He likes you,' Greg says.

'He's lucky.' I wonder if Greg knows just how lucky his son is.

On the drive back, we stop for ice cream in Stellenbosch and sit on the grass in a public park to eat. A group of students is playing football, and further away vendors are selling trinkets to tourists.

Two boys, younger than ten, eye us from a distance, and begin calling out to us. Greg calls back to them.

'What do they want?' I ask.

'They're saying, *Mister, mister, please we want some of what you have.*'

'What are you saying?'

'I'm telling them I'm sorry but they can't have any. Maybe next time. That's probably a mistake – the next time. They'll want to know when next time is.'

'I could give them mine.'

He shakes his head. 'Then they'd want mine as well, and then Dylan's, and then they'd want some money, and with the money they'd go buy sweets, or if we were really unlucky they'd go buy glue or something worse and hold other unsuspecting people at knifepoint while they're high, or overdose and end up dead in the street or trafficked. It doesn't stop. I can't believe I said that.'

'Are they with the vendors?'

'No, they're local. The vendors aren't even from here. They're probably all West African, or from Zim. The stuff they're selling isn't local either. Most of it comes out of containers from China.'

The boys keep calling, and Greg replies in a polite but firm voice. He might be talking to Dylan, whose face is now covered in melting chocolate ice cream, except I hear an edge of command in his voice that I don't hear when he talks to Dylan or Nonyameko, or his gardener or domestic. Or if it's not command, then it's panic. When the boys begin to approach, more brazen, we decide it's time to leave.

'Can you blame them?' he says in the car. 'If I were them and they were us, I'd do the same. Sometimes I don't know what to do, what's right

137

or wrong. It would be so much easier somewhere else.'

'There are difficulties of one kind or another no matter where you are,' I say. He looks at me for a moment as though he doesn't think this is necessarily true.

★

Dylan sits in his high chair, drawing ducks and chickens, while we make dinner in Greg's kitchen. I prepare a salad, he puts a roast chicken in the oven to reheat, we open a bottle of wine and are about to sit down to dinner when the dogs go crazy outside, growling and barking.

'It's the same guy who was here the other day,' he says, getting up.

'What guy?'

'He comes around offering to fix things or sharpen knives.' Greg pads to the door and calls off the dogs, who keep barking, five voices, a man and four dogs. There are two gates between us and the man outside – the gate between the garden and the driveway, and the gate at the end of the drive – and then there's the house itself, with its alarm, panic buttons, back-up generator, deadbolts, burglar bars, reinforced bulletproof glass. We could seal ourselves in and let the dogs go after him. Only when the man finally leaves does Greg come back and sit down. 'There's no such thing as tinkers any more. That's an extinct species. He's checking to see if anyone's here,' he says, picking up a drumstick. 'At least that's what I think. He might be harmless, but there've been break-ins. Do you think I'm paranoid? My assistant woke up with four men pointing rifles at her one night. But she doesn't have any dogs. One of the men was unbuckling and getting her undressed when the police came through the door. She has a panic button wired onto the bed frame. That's the only thing that saved her.'

ABSOLUTION

The move was an excuse, not for Clare but for Jacobus, the man who had helped her with the garden in the Canigou Avenue house since she and her husband bought it just after their marriage. Like Clare, Jacobus believed a garden ought to be functional, that it should produce crops its owners could enjoy, that it should not only be beautiful to look at but also a means of sustenance in an uncertain world. Together, Clare and Jacobus had plotted the beds on the patchy rug of lawn behind the house, a lawn that the previous owners had tended with maniac care for weeds but with no interest in anything else. With Jacobus and one of his cousins, a man whose name she could no longer remember, Clare had marked off the beds with string and croquet wickets, cut away the turf, and begun the laborious process of digging up and enriching the hard soil. Together they had chosen the seeds, planned crop rotations, conceded to Clare's husband William more than each other that there should be a perennial border across the back wall and that the beds themselves should be hedged, if hedged was the word for the profusion of growth they created, with bromeliads and clivia interspersed with agapanthus. An old poinsettia tree near the house came out and they planted a stinkwood in one corner of the garden and a yellowwood in the other. Clare missed that simple working garden now, organized on ancient principles, its lines clean and linear and its borders distinct.

The move was an excuse for ending the relationship. Like her, Jacobus was old. The new house was that much further away from his own home. It was going to be too far, too difficult to get there, and when he saw the new garden, four times the size of the other, he shook his head and apologized, it was too big a job for him, and anyway, the new garden was already what it was, an undulating showroom of mature specimens, a trophy gallery designed by the previous owners, with water features and delicate stone paths, a strange patch of woodland, and such a lawn, he confessed, as he had never hoped to find under his administration. He could not see where he would fit in the new scheme, he said. He was unsure of the steeply sloping grass terraces and beds, he preferred to tend flat ground where one knew one's footing, and besides, with the mountain so close now, and the garden bound to be in shade for half the day, the growing conditions would be different from anything he understood. He didn't trust himself to look after the place. Clare paid him a severance, bought him new tools for his own garden in

Mitchell's Plain, which she had never seen, and told him he must come to visit again once she was settled, knowing that he almost certainly would not.

The new man came recommended from her neighbour, Mr Thacker, a retired judge from London.

'With a garden like this, you need someone coming most days of the week, just to be certain nothing gets out of hand,' Thacker advised. 'Adam has been doing my garden for the last four years, but mine is the only one he does, and it doesn't take all day. He's a good, honest chap. I'll ask him. He could do yours in the morning and mine in the afternoon, when I'm playing tennis. I play tennis every weekday, you know, at the Constantia Club. The extra work would do Adam good, I'm sure, and not just the money, you know, but get him out of bed earlier and keep him off the gin, if gin is what he drinks. Honest enough, you know. Of course if you want to order plants from the garden centre I'd do it myself if I were you, or have your secretary do it. They're inclined to skim off the top. But you must know that, being a local.'

'I've never known anyone to skim off the top,' Clare said, in a flash of white rage.

'You didn't know it, you didn't know it is all,' the judge said, shaking his head, wagging a finger. He promised to speak to Adam.

When she finally met him, a week later, Clare knew at once that Adam was no Jacobus.

'What is your other name, Adam?' she asked, showing him around the garden, which he seemed already to know.

'Adam is my name,' he said, his voice so quiet Clare had to strain to hear.

She tried again, in what she assumed was his mother tongue. 'Adam is my name,' he answered again, in English.

'But your other name, your real name, what is your given name? What do you want me to call you?'

'Adam is my own name,' he said again, his voice firmer this time.

Clare remembered the family photos Jacobus had always produced – his neat wife, smiling children, Christmas gatherings and birthdays. Those had been taken in his own garden, so Clare had seen it in a way, knew it was a more modest version of the garden at her old house, but she had not been to see it in person, to meet the wife and children. An invitation had never been extended and she had not wanted to presume, she told herself. She had never said, *I should like someday to see your garden, Jacobus.*

It turned out that Adam's brother, who had also been a gardener, and was now dead (*He got very sick, he died,* Adam said) had been the gardener for the previous owners of Clare's new house, an elderly couple who had emigrated to live near their children in Vancouver. 'I know this garden well,' Adam reassured her. 'I know what to do for it.

You will see. I helped my brother when he was planting it for Mr and Mrs Mercer.'

'There are some things I'd like to change, though,' Clare explained. 'I want a vegetable patch here,' pointing to a place in the middle of the back lawn that seemed to get the most hours of sun, 'and a herb garden next to the patio.'

Adam put his hands on his hips and surveyed the garden, whistling through his teeth. He looked towards the sun and up at the mountain and knelt down to touch the ground in one of the perennial beds. 'This soil, it is not so good for those things,' he said, shaking his head and crumbling a handful of earth.

'But we can bring in new soil. We could hire a couple of other people to help, to prepare the new beds. I'm too old now to do it with you. I would have once. But I wouldn't expect you to do it alone,' she said, suspecting he saw more work than he wanted.

He shook his head again, rubbing the soil between his fingers, testing it on his tongue. 'These things will not live well here,' he said. 'We should leave this garden as my brother made it. We should keep it like this. For now.' He smiled up at her, a row of straight, bright teeth, and brushed his fingertips against his loose jeans. Without entirely knowing why, Clare hired him on the spot, thinking she would convince him of the possibility of herbs and vegetables in time.

Every weekday morning after that, Adam arrived

at eight and Clare would watch as he weeded the beds, pruned, mowed the lawn – she had to invest in a lawnmower large enough to manage what she began to call her 'Country Club' – watered, fertilized, and managed the place with a ferocious energy. After a month Adam came to her looking apologetic. 'It is too much just for mornings. You see, it is already overgrown.'

'Could you go to full-time?' She had heard of friends poaching other people's staff, but was surprised to find herself doing it with such ease.

'The judge has been very good to me,' he said, jerking his head towards Mr Thacker's property.

'I could pay you more than what you receive now from him and me combined.'

'No, no, it is not that.' Adam looked away from Clare and she realized he was not trying to drive a deal; he was only being honest. 'Maybe if we could have one other person, not every day, only two or three days a week. Ten days a month. And I could train him as my brother trained me and if there is more to do sometimes he could come in the afternoons when I am at the judge.'

'Do you recommend someone?' Clare asked, suspecting this might be the real ploy, to hire a relative or a friend. But Adam shook his head.

'Most of the gardeners here, the ones I know, they are not so good. They do not work so hard like I do. Maybe the judge knows someone,' he said and shrugged. 'But it would be good, because I don't want this nice garden of yours that my brother made to turn into a forest. It would be good to have one other person sometimes.'

Without wishing to, Clare went next door to Mr Thacker's house the following week, to thank him for recommending Adam and to ask if he could make enquiries. She herself knew no one else in the neighbourhood, and had no friends with gardeners, or at least not any gardeners they could spare.

'It's no problem at all, Mrs Wald. I'm a member of the Horticultural Society. I'll ask around,' Thacker said, looking pleased to be asked. 'Failing that, you could always enquire at the Botanical Gardens, see if they have any staff looking for extra work.' He was walking her around his garden, which might have been an extension of her own, but almost half the size, packed with indigenous shrubs and trees, punctuated by colourful exotics that flourished in the microclimate. What looked extravagant and only remotely menacing on Clare's own property was unseemly in Thacker's tighter plot – too mannered, too ostentatious for such a small space, everything out of scale. The garden was as overstuffed and florid as the man himself.

Thacker's connections in the horticultural society turned up a young trainee gardener who was looking for extra income and was happy to work under Adam's direction. 'A team,' Clare thought, 'I have a team of gardeners where once I needed only one. How many more will I need? Who else? A pool boy. The pool water is turning green.

Window washers, too. The windows are becoming glazed with dust.'

Months passed and the forms of the garden remained unchanged. The seasons moved through their cycles, rain beating through winter until spring came again. Clare became anxious for a vegetable patch, for the enjoyment of picking her own tomatoes, growing her own basil, cooking food she knew had been grown without pesticides, things one could not get so easily in the stores, even in the warehouse-like chain of produce markets. When she broached it with Adam, he again shook his head, said it was not such a good idea. She had never encountered this kind of resistance – not in Jacobus, not in Marie, not in any of the various women who had at times come to clean her house – and she had no idea how to deal with it except to accept it mutely and then plan behind Adam's back. The young apprentice, Ashwin, who was now working every weekday morning and two afternoons a week (it transpired that the previous owners had employed one full-time and two part-time gardeners year round just to keep the place in order), was alone one afternoon when Clare approached him with her plan. She explained where the beds should go, how big she wanted them, and asked him to come over the weekend at double pay to create them.

'With Adam?' he asked.

'No, on your own. Tell me what equipment you

need to get it done and I'll hire it. Rototiller, plough, whatever. I want a vegetable patch and a herb garden. I don't think it is so much to ask, but this garden means something to Adam, you understand. It has a certain importance to him. But in the end, it is *my* garden now. I must be allowed to grow what I like. Will the beds work here? Do you think there's enough sun?'

Ashwin looked around, made some calculations, and agreed to the plan.

That weekend he cleared the lawn, enriched the soil, and planted what Clare requested. On Sunday evening, with the new beds laid out in aggressive rectangularity against the otherwise fluid forms of the garden, Clare looked at the clean black furrows and mounds, the promise of cabbages and tomatoes, beans and squash, melons and lettuces, protected and nurtured under shimmering white lengths of floating cover, and felt at last that she might grow to love this new house, with the mountain glowering over her, a trailing cloth of mist cascading down its iron-grey flanks.

When Adam arrived on Monday morning, she watched his reaction from her study. She could not have wished for a better effect. He started physically, paced around the new beds shaking his head, and went to the back door of the house. A few minutes later Marie came to the study, explaining that Adam wished to speak to Clare in person.

'It is not a good thing. These plants will not grow.' He looked grief-stricken and Clare felt sorry for him, if not for what she had done. 'You cannot grow these things here. They will not grow. And it does not look good.'

'We're going to try it this year,' Clare said, trying to make herself sound resolved at the same time that Adam's vehemence opened up a fissure of doubt in her mind. 'If they don't grow, we'll turn them into flowerbeds next year, or back into lawn. But for now, we do it my way.'

'It is a bad thing.'

'It is not a bad thing. It is merely different. You will see. And if you are right, then I shall see. But you must let me grow what I want, Adam, otherwise we will only come to grief, and in the end I should have to ask you to leave. It would not be pleasant. Everyone would be unhappy. This way, I shall be happy and you will have to wait to see how unhappy these new beds will make *you*, and how much upset they will cause in my garden. But give them a chance. See if they will flourish.'

CLARE

The TRC transcripts are all accessible now. I have printed out only some of them, and these run to hundreds – no, thousands – of pages, several toner cartridges. I read through the ones I think relate to you in some way, Laura, to your case, your activities. I reread the official submissions from the ANC and other bodies; I look for your name, but it occurs only rarely, often misspelled – *Lara*, *Lora*, *Laure*, even *Laurie*, only sometimes *Laura*. *Welt*, *Wal*, *Wêreld*, *World*, and finally, in the last one I read, *Wald*, and sometimes, even in that one, *Waldt* and *Weldt*. Often your name is not there at all, and I have no choice but to infer your involvement in the events described: the opening of a letter bomb at a government office, the aftermath of an attack on a refinery.

Your actions are indecipherable to me. Could you have done that? Can I understand why you did it? I look again for correspondences in your notebooks, in the archive of you I have assembled, but I find myself overwhelmed. I cross-check and collate and decide I must try to build a portrait of your movements for the relevant period, a portrait and a map. You were here *then*, there *later*, back home a few days *after*. In the end, it is mostly guesswork. I can guess where you might have been, what you were doing, what you were thinking, what compelled you. I keep hoping your former colleagues will come to see me, give me whatever information they might possess, if there is anything yet that has not been revealed to me. I would be polite, I would accept it with gratitude, I would not ask too many difficult questions, nor sit in summary judgement, either of you or of them, for your failures of communication, for their failure to speak of you and for you, to me and to others. I would be hospitable. I have studied hospitality. *Thank you* for telling me where my daughter was on *that day*, I would say, for at least now I can imagine with certainty what *that day*, whatever day it might be amongst all others, was like for you. It is not a story they are eager to tell, even in private, you understand. You horrify them. A woman is not supposed to _____. Fill in the blank. You did everything a woman is not expected to do, is not supposed to do. You horrify because in action you appeared more man than woman, and more woman than man in every other respect. Neither one thing nor the other.

I sit in this new garden, which is now no longer new to me, but one you never knew, belonging to a house you would have scorned as a betrayal of familial principles. *You have sold out*, you would tell me, always courageous, but I no longer need you here to tell me what I already know about my choices. You are entirely within me now, voice echoing always, a million different voices, all you, borrowed from moments when I heard you as you wanted to be heard, moments you did not realize anyone was listening, perhaps in particular me. These are no substitute, they are all that I have, those million necromanced fragments of you, summoned around the pit of fire yawning between my ribs. Would that I had a sorrowful song to sing, *un sí pietoso stile*, to win you back, as Orpheus did Eurydice. I offer you the cup to drink, a song of prayer, wish for you to cohere again, *Etemmu*, the wandering soul. I pour milk and nectar on the fire, wine and water, sprinkle white corn meal around, grind it against my flesh, cut my throat to summon you, sacrifice myself to body you forth, but you will not rise. If you will not rise, you are not dead. I have seen no remains. It must be thus.

I have tried to learn this garden like a book, interpret it by reading its lines, studying to understand its form, its four discrete zones, its moments of horticultural mirror-gazing, the nature of its construction, its constructedness, its absence of irony and humour, or is that absence my misreading? There is a long lap pool that stretches away from the house, acting also as a reflecting pool for the garden itself and the mountain above it. I push through the water each morning, my long old body, otter in a tank, the underwater lights blinding me at first in the darkness of dawn. What does this pool say to the garden, what is its dialogue? I ask it and myself. What do the woodland, the perennial borders, the indigenous specimens, the exotic interlopers, and my own aggressive vegetable plot, carved rectilinearly into the fluid forms, irrupting into formal life, say to each other when I pause to listen? I lurk at the end of the pool, fingers curling over the smooth concrete edge, peering up, nostrils just above the surface, dead hair fanning out from a dying head, floating on the surface, as I gaze on the wonderland around me, a landscape of fantasy. I have thought of tearing out the lawn and replacing it with a carpet of succulents, impossible to navigate, organic, left to themselves, a fortress of life, ramparts pregnable only by flat stones spaced close enough to leap between them. It is tempting.

*

Sam tucked his knees under his chin, and turned from you to stare at the highway. The weather report said the rain was localized along the coast and it would be dry in the mountains. You would follow a road that, while longer and slower than the coastal highway, would take you up into the interior, away from wherever Bernard had been going. A backtrack and then a sharp turn north, over passes, heading towards your destination, which was at least twelve hours' drive – but surely more in those days, in that truck, say sixteen hours to Ladybrand if you were lucky, and what then? There would be roadblocks long before you got anywhere near there. You thought it strange there had been none already, but put your faith in providence, knowing its unreliability.

You knew a town where you might stop for the night without attracting attention. In the dark, it would be easy to masquerade as Sam's mother, even if your hair was fair and his dark. Lightning filled the sky behind you as the truck laboured up into the pass that would take you over the mountains and out of the storm. Oudtshoorn, the first town after the Outeniquas, was at least an hour away, waiting flat and feathery against the red soils of the valley.

Near the top of the pass you left the rain behind and were high enough to look back on the dark mass of cloud. Where the rain fell the earth looked black.

'I want to go home,' Sam whined.

'Where is home?'

'Woodstock.' Frame and plaster houses, their paint flaking, with curtains made from old sheets in floral patterns, all faded from the low-swung sun. Inside, there would be the ubiquitous collapsing picture rails, holding cheap frames with family photos or pastel illustrations of gods and saints, mimeographed prayers, disembodied heads torn from dolls or icons, suspended in effigy over oily beds pushed against stained and cracking walls whose paper or paint had begun to disintegrate from the floor up, new continents forming in exposed plaster, glaciers pushing up from the warped floorboards. It was a place of houses inhabited but already half-abandoned by people only partially there.

'But do you have a home any more?' you asked, unable to say, *I've killed the man who gave you a home, any home you have has been lost.* 'Do you have any grandparents?'

'I have an aunt.'

'Where does she live?'

'Somewhere. Away.'

'Away where?'

'In the Karoo.'

You were trying to concentrate on the hairpin turns that forced the truck into a jack-knife waltz with the precipice. At each corner you blew the truck's horn, terrified you might surprise a vehicle coming from the opposite direction. 'Do you know the name of the place?'

Sam clutched at the door handle, bracing himself against the erratic movement of the truck. Beaufort West, he said, across the Little Karoo and beyond the Swartberge, black mountains that reveal their reddish-brownness only once you are on top of them. It was on your route, the one you were inventing as you went. There was luck in this, or perhaps no more than coincidence.

You decided to push on, grinding down into the valley and racing past Oudtshoorn, then rising

155

again into the fertile ribbon of land south of the black mountains. You stopped for petrol near Kango, breathed the cool dry air and bought sandwiches and biltong from the shop. The two of you paused to eat, feeling for a moment like an ordinary mother and son on a holiday excursion to drive the seven passes on that dirt road made by convicts. And then it was time to go. Night was brisk and total, and you took the truck up the unpaved road of the pass, the lights picking out the precipice edge. Going slowly, you prayed to your body to make deliberate movements, be alert, know the curve of the road by instinct, sense how it would bend, know where it would end, because the slightest wrong movement, a flick of the wheel too far to the left, even a whisper too much acceleration, and it would be tickets for both of you. You could not look at Sam in those minutes. Time wound into a single moment of tension that unspun itself into all the years of your life. Your muscles ached, your head throbbed; Sam's breathing drummed in your ears and the higher the truck climbed the more aware you became of the burden you had taken upon yourself by your own actions. He had become yours, you his.

(But how can we say that? You say in your last notebook, *He is mine for now, I his, it has been silently agreed.* We have not asked him. How can we presume to know his thoughts, to assume his consent?)

At the top, where the mountains levelled off, you

relaxed for a moment, exhaled the breaths you had been holding, knew you would have to stop, realizing it would be suicide to navigate the hairpin turns winding across and out of those mountains at night. A stand of pines in the landscape of low shrubs and grasses reared up, darker against the sky, concealing a campsite with rudimentary facilities. You half-remembered it from our family holiday, when the four of us drove the passes in a state of anxious wonder.

A campfire was visible amongst the trees and you decided to take the risk. Keeping to yourselves, you would sleep in the truck. There were chemical toilets at the edge of the site, a hundred metres from the campfire, against which you could see a figure hunching. Waiting by the outhouse, you scanned the darkness for noises and movement, listening to Sam urinating and vomiting and the boom of an eagle owl, *hoot HOOT, hoot HOOT, hoot HOOT.* You called to Sam through the unit's blue plastic wall.

'Are you okay?'

'Yes,' his voice was wet and choked.

'Do you need help?' you asked, turning your back on the campfire.

'No.'

It had the suddenness of an attack, the man appearing out of the night, silent, standing beside you, his head shaved, glistening, eyes pale and metallic in the dark. 'Howzit?' he said, casually offering his hand.

'Hello.'

'Are you okay?' the man asked.

'We're fine. The boy's sick.'

'Shame. I have some medicine if you need it.'

'That's very kind.'

'I'll go get it. Wait here.'

You did not know whether to trust him, and were deciding to leave when a second man appeared, as tawny and fair as the other was hard and dark. A jackal and a lion. The first man returned with a bottle of tablets. 'Do you have water? Good. He should take only one now, and then another in the morning if he's not better. I'll give you four,' he said, handing over half what he had. 'You can get others tomorrow if you need. You're driving through the pass tonight?'

'I have to get to Prince Albert,' you lied.

'This road isn't safe after dark. Quite apart from the road itself, and the size of your truck, there have been hijackings. You're welcome to stay here with my friend and me. I'm Timothy. He's called Lionel. You and your boy can have our tent. We'll sleep outside. It won't rain up here tonight. You don't need to be afraid of us' – an easy assurance, one you would have been foolish to accept at face value, but Timothy's voice and his accent (if not his eyes) reassured you, as did the tablets with a brand name you recognized, triggering an unbidden memory of an advertisement, an animated graphic of a simplified digestive system, angry red, turning reassuringly blue.

'Thank you. You're very kind.' You caught yourself again, doing what you did not intend. Had you lost the capacity to say no, or did you sense some kind of salvation in those men who presented themselves like angels, and believe in their beneficence?

TRUTH AND RECONCILIATION COMMISSION
4 JUNE 1996, CAPE TOWN

VICTIM: Louis Louw
VIOLATION: Injured in ANC Bomb Attack
TESTIMONY FROM: LOUIS LOUW

CHAIRPERSON: Thank you for your patience Mr Louw. I believe the microphone is working now. Please would you just lean forward and be good enough to speak into it clearly.

MR LOUW: What do you want me to [*indistinct*] or what?

CHAIRPERSON: That's fine, Mr Louw, the microphone is working now and I [*pause . . . indistinct*] begin again. No, there is still a problem. The translators are having difficulty. A moment while they make an adjustment. There it is? Okay? Is everything in order now? Good. We may continue. My apologies, Mr Louw. You may take your time, there is no hurry. Now, are you comfortable as you are?

MR LOUW: As comfortable as I will be.

CHAIRPERSON: Very well. You will tell us please if you need anything, or if you want to take a break. We all appreciate how difficult this can be. Have you been following the other hearings, and the testimony of those who appeared earlier today?

MR LOUW: Yes.

CHAIRPERSON: So you know the kinds of questions we might ask and the kinds of things we will want to hear from you, or that you might tell us about yourself, to give us a, a better sense of this, of the terrible impact of this event on your person and on your life and on the lives of your loved ones, your family, I mean, and those close to you.

MR LOUW: Yes.

CHAIRPERSON: Could you tell us something about yourself, about who you were, and where you had come from, so to speak, at the time of the bombing?

MR LOUW: You see, I was just an ordinary man. I had grown up here, gone to the schools here, member of this very church. I was baptized in this church, and so were my brothers and sisters. My people have always been here, you see, for hundreds of years.

CHAIRPERSON: Please, can we have quiet in the room. Please. Mr Louw must be allowed to speak. If there are any further interruptions I will have to clear the room. Please continue, Mr Louw.

MR LOUW: I was just a clerk at the time of the attack. I pushed paper back and forth, you see. I was just only a clerk at the time. I had never raised a hand in anger at anyone in my life.

CHAIRPERSON: Did you not fulfil the national service requirement?

MR LOUW: Yes, but that was orders. I'm talking about in everyday life you must understand. This attack happened in everyday life, me just minding my own business, and in everyday life we always got along with everyone, our family. We were always good to the people. I married just before I got the job as clerk and at the time of the attack we had a boy aged three and a baby girl, just turned one. We had a little house over on Weymouth Road and everything was good. My parents were proud of me because I had a good government job. I had been not such a good student at school and I think they were worried that I might not do so well in my life, that perhaps maybe I was on the wrong path when I was a youth but I decided to turn my life around after my national service and I was committed. I was a very hard worker at the time then. So you see what it was I lost in the terrible thing that they did to me and others. I had my family, my livelihood, a good job. So what I want to know is, what is this committee going to do to make up for what I lost? What are you going to give me? Because I did nothing to deserve this.

CHAIRPERSON: Can you tell us, Mr Louw, about the day of the attack and what exactly happened on that day?

MR LOUW: Ja, it was a long time ago now, almost a decade, and because of the medicine I take the doctors say I have places that I black out, my memory has holes in it and so I cannot say that it is that I remember everything clearly you understand from that day itself. If you don't believe me you can ask my doctor here what the names of the medicines are and he will tell you they keep me from making bad memories of that day. It's very special medicine this stuff. You can ask if you don't believe.

CHAIRPERSON: That won't be necessary, Mr Louw. We believe what you're saying.

MR LOUW: It is all a little too confusing in my memory for me to know that I remember it as it happened so you will forgive me if there are gaps in my story but I am trying my best to help and to cooperate with this here today because I hope that maybe the government is going to be able to do something to give me back what I lost on that day.

CHAIRPERSON: We understand, Mr Louw. You have been diagnosed with PTSD, treatment for which is ongoing.

MR LOUW: I'm getting treatment, yes, but I don't think I'll ever be cured you see, and as I say the medicine they give me might be affecting my memory and other things also.

CHAIRPERSON: That is all understood. Perhaps you could begin with what you remember from that day.

MR LOUW: I remember getting up and already my wife had breakfast ready. And I remember standing at the sink in our kitchen and my two children there at breakfast looking happy and that was a wonderful thing that day, a wonderful feeling that started that day, and I thought things are good, the family will go on, continue. You may think that is funny some of you, but it was important to me that I maintain the family line if you like, and it was good to look at my two healthy children who looked like me and my parents and my wife and her family there that morning. That is a good memory and the doctors say I should try to focus on that, so I remember the orange housedress my wife was wearing and that I had eggs and bacon for breakfast because it was the end of the week and it was a treat. But it is also a sad memory too because it was the last time we were like that, the four of us. After breakfast I had a shower and put

164

on my uniform that my wife had ironed and I drove to work. It was a slow morning and a very hot morning, I think, it must have been at least thirty-five degrees that day. If you don't believe me you can check with the weather records and they will show you that it was hot and you know what it is like when the weather is that hot, you have difficulty thinking quickly, clearly, that's the way it was that day. Your brain does not work so well on hot days. I think perhaps there were forms to fill out or a memo to write at the office, an end-of-the-week report or an internal memo of some kind but that's something I don't remember clearly any more you see, what exactly I had to do on that day. You understand you are asking me to remember what the doctors have tried to help me to forget and I am trying [*indistinct*] I am trying very hard to help you with this because I want people to know what happened to people like me.

CHAIRPERSON: Would you like to take a break to compose yourself, Mr Louw?

MR LOUW: No, I'm fine. Rather let's just get it done. So after the morning I had my lunch, and it was just after lunch that it happened. You understand, it was because it was a government office, that was the reason we were targeted. They did not care, those people, who they went after, what lives they might be destroying in the process. It happened so quickly I don't think any of us understood what it was. The post had arrived and I had the box on

165

my lap and didn't think twice about it because it looked like all the file boxes I would receive every Friday through the internal mail. I just assumed it was the ordinary batch of files for me to process and the next thing I knew I was on my back on the floor and there was water falling down into my face and there were fires burning all around me and people screaming and crying, and there [*indistinct*] explosions, because none of us knew that they had [END OF TAPE 4, SIDE B.] and if not then I say we should have been told. I couldn't move and had to wait to be rescued and I just lay there wondering if anyone was going to come for me and then finally one of the cleaners, I can't remember her name, God save her, she saw me and she lifted up what was left of me and she carried me outside into the street and the ambulance took me away. I slept a long time after that and when I woke up finally it was only then that I realized I had lost everything, my legs almost to the hip, my right arm to the shoulder, and my left arm to the elbow, sight in one eye, my right eye, and the doctors said I was lucky it wasn't worse.

CHAIRPERSON: And how did your family react?

MR LOUW: To them I was a hero just because I survived but I said no, you must rather not call me a hero because I was the one who set off the first bomb that day. I was the one that opened that box. I should have been more careful with the package. Maybe I don't know there was some clue on the box if I'd looked carefully that would have told me it was rigged. They trained us for that kind of thing but you get careless, you get a little lazy I guess maybe. My wife was good at first, she looked after me, and there was the pension, but then she couldn't take it any longer. I could not blame her, if I'm being honest, because you know I simply was not a man any more and imagine what I looked like then, you see what I'm like now when the wounds have long healed. I could do nothing for her. And with the two kids it was too much for her to do on her own, so she went away and took the kids to live with her parents up north and I sold the house and moved back in with my own parents because I could not look after myself at the time then. I am getting better now and the government has looked after me somewhat, even the new one. I have to give them credit for that at least. My wife is remarried now and I don't get to see my children so often because I can't afford to visit and she can't afford to send them to see me. It's not the way it should be you see, and I blame that on the attack that day, not on her, I know it's not her fault. What else can I do? I ask you, members of the committee, what else am I supposed to do? What are you going to do to help me?

CHAIRPERSON: Would you like to say anything, Mr Louw, to those who have accepted responsibility for the attack?

MR LOUW: What can I say? I guess it was war. But they were fighting us, and we were just defending ourselves. That's all. And me I was just a clerk.

CHAIRPERSON: Quiet please. That really is the last warning. If there is another outburst I will have to clear the room.

SAM

Despite her initial insistence that she wouldn't do so, Clare begins to let me see business correspondence with her agents and publishers. When I arrive now for further interviews, there is a file waiting for me on the coffee table in her study. We talk in the morning, eat lunch together, and then I'm allowed to examine the papers in another room, make notes, photograph them if I want, and ask her questions, although there's still an edge of ice beneath the surface. She is reserved and distant and acts scornful about the project. Biography is the work of the second rate, she says. Biography is cannibalism and vampirism. I have not heard her say *darling* again, and suspect I won't. It was an uncharacteristic moment of weakness.

A week later. Instead of correspondence, today she begins to show me manuscripts and typescripts with her own marginalia, allowing me again to take these to another room where I can work on them uninterrupted. I make notes, comparing variations between the printed editions of *Landing* and its early drafts, composed by hand in school exercise books. There is enough work here to keep me busy for months. What is essential is getting copies while I can, which means photographing every page Clare puts before me. I buy additional memory cards for the camera, a better tripod, and a small light. She looks on with amusement as I set up my studio and she even apologizes that she doesn't have a photocopier or a scanner; it's out of the question that I should be allowed to remove any papers from the house. 'Too many hazards,' she says, 'you understand. I have lost precious things in the past. I cannot bear loss. But record all you want, all that might be relevant.' I know that at any moment she may change her mind. It's within her power to end the project and buy me out of my contract. Technically, my notes and transcripts don't even belong to me, but to Clare and her publisher. I think twice about the camera and buy a portable scanner, duplicating my earlier photographs, and e-mail everything I copy to Greg, who agrees to keep the files safe. Everything must be compiled, copied, archived, backed up. In all likelihood, this is a chance no one else will have. Who can say what's going to happen to the papers once she dies? Her son has already proven himself uncooperative, so I can only imagine the restrictions he'll place on access to Clare's papers after her death. The key is to get the book written and published before then.

She tells me that she hasn't given anyone else this kind of access before. No one has seen the author in her workshop, 'through the fluidities of her texts', she says. I know that in many ways I'm just being used, even as I'm using her, never mind her performance of scorn for the project. There's her reputation to consider – the biography can only enhance it, as well as my career. This could make me a full professor by the time I'm forty. There's the money as well. She and I, we're feeding off each other. It's a relationship of mutual interest.

Beyond the money and my career, there's the other thing as well. The subject I haven't had the courage to raise. I allow my mind to indulge in fantasy, to imagine that I spent my adolescence living with Clare and her husband in Cape Town, the city that had always been home.

Most days we have lunch together in her study and I ask questions about the manuscripts, or about her life, trying to clarify key events and establish a detailed chronology. She has also given me access to her personal library, which numbers in the thousands of volumes on shelves throughout the house and has its own catalogue, maintained by Marie, who, I discover, is a trained archivist. When I happen across an unusual or unexpected title – Liddell Hart's *A Greater Than Napoleon: Scipio Africanus* (1926), for instance – I ask Clare if she's read it. Often, she can summarize it with a cryptic phrase ('the deadly indirect approach' in that case). Other times she admits the book was a gift or an impulse purchase and she's never opened it. 'Who has time to read everything?' she says.

There are few photos around the house – only two of her children, one of each, though the photo of Laura is taken from childhood, and her son Mark is pictured more recently. Smug and prosperous, he is also dishevelled, and nothing at all like Laura except in his fair hair and complexion. It's the first time I've seen a picture of Laura. I wouldn't have recognized her, prim in pigtails and a school uniform, but of course it can't be anyone else.

Leading from the room where I'm allowed to work into the main body of the house is a corridor painted the colour of unbleached bones, decorated only with a long textile hung across the span of one wall. Like the paintwork throughout the house the colours of the textile are muted: granite, flax, a wave of ochre. In the large L-shaped lounge that faces the garden there is a small art collection, mostly third-rate Dutch masters, but also paintings by Cecil Skotnes and Irma Stern, and an etching by Diane Victor that depicts the Voortrekker Monument as if in catastrophic ruins. There's a black tin box with Clare's father's name stencilled on it sitting in a locked glass cabinet surrounded by what I take to be the family silver.

Food deliveries are made every few days. The mail arrives each morning. Sometimes a courier delivers boxes of books. The phone never rings. I've offered to take Clare on a drive for a change of scenery but she says she has already seen enough to last a lifetime. The outside world has become too much for her. The garden, the house, her own work will occupy her mind for the rest of her life. She's retiring from the world, she says, in full retreat. And in any case, if she really wants to go out, Marie will drive her.

'It's like a story she published early in her career,' I tell Greg, 'like a self-fulfilling prophecy.'

'Read it to me,' he says, making dinner while Dylan sits in his highchair playing with a toy that helps him learn the alphabet. He sings along with it.

'I don't have it here, but I can tell you about it. It's called "The Prisoner". In it a blind academic who made his reputation attacking a growing tide of philistinism in public life falls out of favour when a reactionary government comes to power – a particularly philistine government. The academic is dismissed from his position at a university, stripped of his pension, evicted from his home, and because he's homeless and jobless (and vagrancy and unemployment are outlawed under the laws of the new government) the authorities detain him. Now, because the prisons are filling up and because the new government doesn't value knowledge or art, they convert all museums and libraries into prisons, and inmates are expected to use the contents of those places, those palaces of culture, as fuel – to burn books and artworks to keep themselves warm. So along with several hundred others, the blind academic is locked inside the Central Reading Room of the National

173

Library. Every day, guards bring the prisoners two meals so they won't starve, and that slight edge of hunger keeps their minds even more alert. They have access to the toilets, because the government prizes hygiene above almost anything else. The detained academics make beds from old encyclopaedias and sleep under the library tables, and when winter comes and the heating is inadequate they burn newspapers and periodicals for as long as they can, then start to burn all the commercial fiction, and finally have to hold votes to decide which worthy books should be burned – in other words, to decide which works are less worthy than others. Of the classics, Dickens and Shakespeare are the first to go by unanimous agreement, not because they all hate Dickens and Shakespeare, far from it, but because they're certain that the library holds nothing unique from those writers and they won't be destroying anything irreplaceable. Dickens and Shakespeare, the logic goes, are everywhere since their works have been reproduced in their millions.

'The blind academic can't read during this incarceration because there aren't any books in Braille in the library, so the other prisoners read to him in turns, and he finds that he's happier than he's ever been before in his life. He no longer has to worry about publishing, or about the purchase and preparation of food, or reading through his fingertips. He is happy to wait for food to be brought to him, books to be read to him, a bed of leather and felt stripped from the library tables to be made for him. The other prisoners petition the guards for paper and ink, using the pornographic eighteenth-century titles they've discovered in the rare books collection as items of barter, and begin taking dictation for the blind academic, as well as writing themselves.

'When the reactionary philistine government eventually falls, as the story suggests is inevitable from the beginning, the political prisoners being detained in the libraries and museums are liberated. The blind academic, however, begs to be allowed to remain in his place of imprisonment. His former fellow prisoners enter pleas on his behalf, and the new government agrees that a small cell will be constructed for him, in the corner of the reading room, where he has spent so many happy years against his will. His friends look after him, bringing him two meals each day (to maintain that mind-sharpening edge of hunger), reading to him in turns and taking dictation. At night, the guards lock him in, and he sleeps soundly, listening to the silence of the books that surround him, expecting nothing of him, except that he listen when they speak.'

Greg smiles as Dylan sings 'l, m, n, o, p'. 'That's very good my boy,' he says, and shakes his head at me, his attention always divided. 'You know what I think, Sam. It's not healthy to be so obsessed.'

'Is it obsession?'

'You know everything about Wald that it's possible to know. You know her works backwards.'

'But that's what my job is. I agreed to write this book. I was the natural choice, even if I'm the only one who knows that's the case.'

'And you don't see any ethical problem in that?'

'I'm not letting it – I'm trying not to let it affect me. I'm trying to be unbiased. I know how to be objective.'

'I wouldn't be able to do it if I were you. If it had happened to me. If she had done to me what she did to you, given the circumstances, given what should have been obvious about the state you were in – I mean, I can only imagine the state you must have been in.'

I don't know how to answer. On the one hand, Greg is right – there is something unethical about my role in the project. But I don't know what other choice I have.

ABSOLUTION

Clare switched on the monitor to find the same government car that had come before waiting on the street outside her front gate. Ms White's monochrome face stared, unblinking, into the lens. It was eight in the evening and Clare could no longer remember how many weeks or months it had been since the woman's last visit; perhaps three weeks, perhaps six months or a year or more. Clare pressed the intercom to speak.

'You are here at an inconvenient time. I am about to go to bed,' she said, and switched on the security floodlights at the front gate. Ms White raised her hand to shield her eyes against the glare and pressed the button at her end.

'We have a group of suspects in your case, madam. Now would be convenient for you to come see them.' It was the first time Clare had used the intercom; she was surprised how clear it was, how Ms White sounded as though she were in the room next to her, disembodied.

'Now would not be convenient.'

'Now is convenient for me and for the suspects,' said Ms White.

The roads were quiet so it was a twenty-minute drive from Clare's house to the brick government building in the city centre, near the old castle and the harbour. Ms White did not speak during the journey. They entered the building through the narrow arched gate on Parade Street and parked in the forecourt, which was full of cars, although it was nearly nine by the time they arrived. The driver opened the door and Ms White led them into the building and up two flights of stairs to an ordinary-looking office corridor. Men and women walked briskly and silently between offices, carrying files, staring at the floor. Had the government become so industrious? Ms White led Clare to the end of the corridor and into a viewing gallery, where a panel of one-way glass separated her from a line-up cell.

A dozen men of varying ages, heights, weights, and races were paraded into the cell. Ms White asked each one in turn to step forward.

'This one?' she asked Clare.

'I have told you,' Clare said, impatience fraying her voice, 'the intruders all wore hoods and head masks – ski masks, balaclavas without eye slits – a mesh where the eye slits would have been. Gloves, too, long-sleeved shirts, polo-neck jerseys. I could not see their skin. I do not know what they were. I do not even know with certainty that they were men.'

'This one?' Ms White asked, sounding unperturbed.

'I have told you already,' Clare whined, ever more exasperated. 'Why do you refuse to listen?'

Ms White remained unruffled, patient as a good parent with a recalcitrant child. 'This one?'

'This is an absurd exercise. I cannot see the point,' Clare cried out, hitting her fist against the chair and breaking her own skin. 'You have brought people here who bear no resemblance to each other. It is not what I call a normal kind of line-up. And anyway, it is pointless to show me anyone. I saw nothing of them that would help. They all wore black, and it was night, so not even a description of their clothing could possibly help. The only thing I know is what they smelled like.'

'What they smelled like, madam?' Ms White turned from the detainees to Clare and switched off the light, leaving the prisoners in darkness. 'You never spoke of *smell*. Do you think you know what they smelled like? That might be helpful.'

'They smelled of disinfectant,' said Clare. 'Orange-scented disinfectant. Industrial cleaners.'

'The intruders were industrial cleaners?'

'No. For pity's sake. They smelled of industrial cleaning solutions. Solvents. I don't know. I would know the scent if I smelled it again. It was distinctive, distinctively unpleasant.'

'But this is a major development, madam,' said Ms White. 'Why did you never tell us you could smell the intruders? Please come this way.'

Ms White led Clare out of the room, back into the corridor, around a corner and a further corner, and into a laboratory next door to the viewing gallery. A group of men in white coats, men as heterogeneous and generic as those presented in the line-up, so similar that they might have been the same people in different costumes, looked up, faces passive, as if old women were routinely delivered to their lab at bedtime. Ms White indicated Clare should sit on a stool near the door and, after a few minutes, a young man came over and presented her with a number of vials to smell.

'This?'

'No.'

'This?'

'No.'

'This?'

'Closer, yes.'

'This?'

'Yes, that's it. But . . .'

'Ah. Let me see,' he said, thumbing through his rack of vials. 'This one?'

'Yes. Definitely. This is it.'

'Lady Grove.'

'Lady Grove?'

'Lady Grove. *The housewife's friend.* Have you not seen the ads?' the man asked. He hummed a calypso jingle and shuffled a dance, hips swivelling, arms becoming branches. '*Lady Grove,*' he sang, shaking his head, as if even the blind and deaf would know it.

'I don't watch television,' Clare lied.

'Not an industrial cleaner after all,' said Ms

White, clicking her tongue. 'A *domestic* cleaner. But madam would not know that. Madam does not know about domestic cleaners. She still has a maid, whom she no doubt calls a maid.'

'She only comes a few times a week,' Clare protested. 'Marie and I do most of the cleaning, it's just the heavy things, the windows . . .'

But Ms White had already taken Clare by the arm, leading her back into the corridor, around a corner, a further corner, and into an empty waiting room. 'I will be back just now, madam. Madam will please wait.'

'I should like to go home. I have cooperated with you, Ms White. I think that I have been exceptionally cooperative given the circumstances, not to mention the time of the evening. May I remind you that I am not the criminal?' Clare found herself wiping away tears. The wound on her hand left a streak of blood across her face.

'Not the criminal? No. Of course not, madam. What a suggestion. What a silly thing to say. You had the *misfortune* to be a victim. And that is a very grave matter, although some might say that victimhood is a kind of delinquency. Some would say you should have been more careful, as you are being now, in your nice, safe house. No one should wish to be a victim. Please wait here. I will be back *just now*.'

It was decades since Clare had been left alone in a waiting room. The last time she had been waiting in a hospital for her parents to come, to see their eldest daughter and son-in-law, or what remained of them. It was to be expected, Clare supposed, that the police had come for her first in that case, so long ago. They had been polite enough initially, a man taking her elbow, much as Ms White did, leading her to an armchair in her own living room, in that house on Canigou Avenue, and sitting her down, kneeling himself, explaining in his crude English that her sister had been murdered, and that a positive identification by one of her family members was necessary as her husband's family were away on the other side of the country and would not arrive until the next day. Official confirmation was needed. They had been murdered in their guest house.

Leaving her husband and son at home, Clare had gone with the police in a government car to the hospital. She had expected to be shocked, the sheet removed to reveal a quarter of a face, just enough remaining to be unmistakably her sister: the beauty mark below her lips, pursed even in death, as though her own assassination had triggered nothing but disapproval. The policemen with her had held their breath, as if they expected Clare to throw her body against her sister's, slake her grief with blood, but she had only nodded curtly, saying in her cool voice, *Yes, that is my sister, now let me see my brother-in-law.*

After she had identified both bodies, the policemen took Clare to a waiting room with rows of orange plastic seats all facing towards the door, where she sat alone, monitoring her heart rate. The policemen had offered to leave a nurse with her, but she shook her head, keeping two fingers on her neck and her eyes on the red second hand of the clock on the wall, timing eighty beats per minute, ninety, slow breaths, seventy-five again, down to seventy. How long had she waited alone, facing the clock on the wall and the door beneath it? Only seconds were recognizable, each second counting beats and after perhaps fifteen thousand of those seconds her parents had appeared in the door like two grey monuments. Her father, she remembered, wore an opposition pin.

'Are you trying to test them?' she had hissed.

'What?'

'The pin.'

'Pin? Oh. No, sweetie. It was on the coat. It was the first coat I grabbed. I didn't think.'

'Let me take it, Dad.'

'No one will care. I'm an old man. I don't mean anything now.'

After being interrogated all night by the police, Clare and her parents had left the hospital the following morning. The murder of press photographers caught the pin on her father's lapel. When the photos were published in all the papers, the whole country believed that even in the hour of his daughter's death Christopher Boyce had staged an act of defiance.

The funeral, another kind of waiting, had been unpleasant on several counts. Clare later heard that before their arrival a crowd had been gassed into submission, clubbed, and taken away in hand-cuffs, two later dying in custody. Worse still, she and her parents had to stand in the company of the Pretorius family, who had already refused them access to her sister's papers and belongings. They sang hymns that were foreign to the Boyce family, whose own suggestions for the service were ignored, judged too secular, inadequately Christian. 'We're not having a circus here,' her brother-in-law's father informed them. While the minister lectured the mourners about the sins of man, Clare had fixed her eyes on a wild fig tree and the mountain in the distance, dust rising from its slopes in spiralling devils around the great pale domes of granite; mute tortoises rearing up from the earth. They had waited then, she and her parents, for the two caskets to be lowered into the ground, dropped on canvas streamers by the muscled hands of her brother-in-law's family, men red from the sun, sweating under heavy pads of fat. After the others had left, Clare and her parents threw handfuls of dirt on the coffins before two men began to shovel. Later, she wondered why she had not grabbed a shovel herself, and added more than handfuls of dirt instead of just watching the young men, their shirts soaked with sweat, dust running down their faces. She wanted to be sure her sister was in the ground, was not going anywhere.

Sitting again in a waiting room of orange chairs facing a door and a clock, her hands were damp and cold, an old woman with few allies in her own country, a foreigner even in the land of her birth. Crime had set itself upon her, victimhood had been thrust upon her, and as a victim she was somehow also a suspect.

It was hours before Ms White returned, by which time Clare had fallen asleep in the chair. The other woman cleared her throat and Clare righted herself, found her mouth had been open, a line of drool on her shirt. She squinted up at Ms White, at the clock behind her.

'I apologize, madam. I got delayed. I did not expect you still to be here,' Ms White said. 'Why have you not gone home already?'

'Where did you think I would go in the middle of the night without a lift from you?'

'I'm sure you could have found your way home. You are good at finding your way, aren't you? Anyway, you were free to go all this time. Really, I can't understand why you came with me in the first place if you weren't prepared to cooperate,' Ms White huffed.

Clare looked at the woman's eyes. There was no glitter of irony or sarcasm, only blankness. Who is this stupid woman who abducts me at bedtime and leaves me alone in a waiting room for hours? Surely this is not how the police now operate, surely not.

'Why didn't you say so before you left me here?' Clare tried to control her voice but a screech of rage slipped out.

'There is no reason to be angry, madam. I will have you driven home by one of my officers just now.' She turned her back on Clare and, as she walked away, paused, head half-turned. 'We also discovered something about Lady Grove, the domestic cleaner you say you smelled on your invaders. It is sold in nearly three thousand separate retail outlets across the country. Not unique at all. Any of us could smell of Lady Grove.'

'I see.'

'Yes. So you would call us all suspects, I guess, madam.'

'I can call no one a suspect, for I have no other evidence to provide. There was blood on the floor, was there not? You could conduct DNA tests. There was a car registration number.'

'There was no match for the number. It does not exist, that registration. Perhaps your assistant made a mistake,' Ms White said, and sniffed.

'It is nearly three in the morning. Why are we having this conversation in the middle of the night?'

'Because you did not order a taxi when you might have, madam.'

'Stop calling me madam. Call me by my name if you must call me anything. I am in no mood for this. Test the blood that was on my floor. Find DNA matches. Or don't. But leave me alone now. I don't want to see you again, Ms White, or hear from you, unless you have firm evidence linking a suspect to the blood that was shed all over the floor of my old house. Is that clear?'

'Perfectly, madam. You are interested only in blood.'

★

Days or weeks passed in which Clare stopped thinking about the house invasion and carried on settling into her new home, learning its peculiar rhythms and idiosyncrasies, the way a closet door would catch or the shower in the master bathroom would drip if the washing machine was on. She had to admit that all the elaborate security features made her feel more protected, while they also made her think constantly about her security in a way that she had never done in the old house on Canigou Avenue. If security came at the cost of paranoia, she supposed it was something that had to be borne.

Then, on yet another evening, when Marie was working late, finishing a batch of correspondence while Clare watched the news, the intercom buzzed.

'We have good news, madam,' Ms White said through the intercom. 'We have caught the miscreants.'

'Why must you always come unannounced, and always at such inconvenient hours?' Clare shouted into the microphone, cross with her voice for once again betraying her irritation.

'The law does not rest. And now we know who is responsible, madam.'

187

Marie showed Ms White into the living room. Clare did not offer her a seat.

'Three men and a woman. One of them is known to you,' Ms White said, consulting a file.

'What do you mean?'

'Jacobus Pieterse, the man who was your gardener at the house on Canigou Avenue, he is the killer.'

'But there was no killing, and –'

'Yet his DNA matched the blood found in your house. We had almost forgotten that bit of evidence. Why did you not tell us you had a criminal in your employ?'

Clare was astonished by the suggestion. Jacobus was the gentlest, least violent man she had ever known. He had refused to use poisons of any kind in the garden for fear of killing the birds. 'Jacobus is no criminal. He is certainly no killer. I refuse to believe he had anything to do with it. It's nothing to do with him. You have the wrong person. He's been in and out of that house a million times. There are perfectly innocent reasons why his DNA should be present. I remember a time he cut his hand in the garden on a pair of secateurs and I brought him inside to bandage it. No doubt he bled on the carpet.'

'But he has a gang this one. Him and his wife,' said Ms White, tapping a binder with the long nail that extended from her index finger like a pointer – a pointer or weapon, Clare thought.

'Gang? The man is nearly my age.'

'Yes, but he and his wife are major players as

we say. You would have saved us so much time had you told us in the first place he had been your handyman, instead of waiting for us to question your former neighbours.' Ms White sniffed, wagging her finger at Clare.

'My gardener. Not my handyman. I never needed a handyman, only a gardener. This is quite impossible. Jacobus and his wife are devout Christians. They would never be involved in any kind of criminal activity. What claim do you make against him?'

'He invaded your house, madam.'

'But you said he was already a criminal.'

'Yes, he invaded your house with his gang. That makes him a criminal, but he was already a criminal. You can tell the type. Or,' and Ms White laughed at herself, '*I* can tell the type, but clearly you cannot, otherwise you would not have hired the man in the first place.'

'Jacobus was in my employ for more years than I can remember. He would have had nothing to do with this matter. He had opportunity for years, decades, to break into the house, and I never once had a problem. Nothing ever went missing, nothing was stolen, no blood shed in defence or malice.'

'Biding his time, madam, waiting for the right moment to strike, a viper,' Ms White said, sniffing again. 'He waited until after your husband left you, didn't he? You are lucky you came away with your life.'

'And what about my stolen property? Do you

189

mean to say that Jacobus is in possession of my father's wig?'

'Oh no, madam. He has disposed of the property already. A very clever thief. No doubt he sold it for a high price on the black market.'

Clare felt the room spin and slant. The woman made her feel nauseated and unsure of everything she knew to be true. 'This is madness. The wig is all but worthless to anyone but me. You are very mistaken. This is all a mistake. I want it to stop.'

'But you have put it in motion, madam. It is a serious crime. We go until it is finished,' said Ms White, opening and closing the binder with a final tap of her fingernail.

CLARE

I have been experiencing recurring dreams of such vividness I would be certain they were reality if not for the fact of your presence in them, Laura, and even that makes me wonder if you have not reappeared, or I have slipped unwittingly into a space where the impossible is routine. Each time, Marie wakes me out of a deep sleep in which I have been dreaming another dream – these other, prior dreams are the only things that change, and they are almost always banal: cows in a field, me on the farm as a child, or in a boat off Port Alfred, memories conjured up out of darkness. In the recurring part of the dream it is always half-past six when Marie wakes me, and she says, *You have to get ready, you have to be at the studio.* I am making an audio recording of my new book, doing my own reading. This is what makes the dreams so real, because this week, in my waking life, I am in the process of recording the new book, *Absolution*, a volume of fictionalized memoirs (although it is nothing like the memoir the publishers truly wanted, hence the official biography). In the dream, I thank Marie, go to have a shower, dry off, all very deliberately. I choose black slacks and a black shirt, tie my hair back with a black satin bow and rub moisturizer into my face – always the same actions in every dream, in the same order. Marie has made me a light breakfast – no lemon, no dairy, nothing to constrain or confuse the vocal cords. Hot tea, a soft roll with honey. In the car, Marie tells me this is the last day of recording, and after that we can get back to the usual routine, the humdrum that keeps us happy. I remind her of my biographer's presence, remind her he may continue to visit daily for months to come, except when I tell him, as in this week (and as in the real week happening now), that other things keep me busy and we will recommence after a break of ten days. (I know it is cruel the way I play with him, both in dreams and in reality. He knows nothing about the actual contents of this forthcoming book. It is embargoed.)

We arrive at the drab glass and metal building that houses the studio. A girl who always mispronounces my name greets us warmly at reception and escorts us upstairs. In the dream I sit down at a desk in the studio, and the production team smiles at me through the glass window of the control booth. They are waving . . . waving *fondly* I think, fondly because there *you* are, Laura, one of them. Not just one of them, but the boss, the head of the team, the one *calling the shots*. You lean towards your microphone and tell me just to let them know when I'm ready and they'll begin recording. You show no sign of recognizing me as anyone other than the writer in your studio, the semi-celebrity who can walk down nearly any street in this country without being recognized, who is only noticed on the campuses of a few universities, and even there by a mere handful of students and professors. Abroad is a different matter. In the dream you appear unaware of – or wish to conceal – our kinship, and I sit there bewildered. Why should you be so pleasant but so distant? Is it a matter of not knowing? Are you not the daughter you appear to be, but her doppelgänger? Or are you ashamed of me, wishing for your colleagues not to know that you are the child of the monster who sits before them to read into a microphone, all the voices of her mind merging into a single furious shriek, for there is so much anger in the pages of this book (both the real and the dreamed, though they are different texts, telling different stories, equal in their rage) that in the dream (as well as in the real recording sessions this week) I have memories of previous sessions (dream memories of the real recording sessions, I presume) in which I have come to the point of shouting, screaming, breaking down in tears. My urbane New York editor will be unhappy with this. In his fey voice he asked for tension and suspense in my oral delivery, but controlled, modulated, made safe for the ears and feelings of my auditory readers. In the dream I look down at the transcript of the book, open the cover, and find nothing but blank pages. *Go ahead,* you say to me, coaxing, smiling, *Go ahead, whenever you're ready, just speak clearly into the microphone.* But there are no words on the page, I protest, holding up the transcript. There is nothing here to read, and I cannot remember it, I don't remember the words, it doesn't work like that, a memoir, even a fictionalized one, is a work of memory on the page; the individual words might lodge in my brain, but I cannot summon the text complete in my head. The text I have written does not reside within. You smile at me, looking patient, rather indulgent, and nod your head. *Take your time,* you say, *there's no rush, we have the studio for the whole day, and you should just let us know when you're ready to begin.* I page through the script, thinking perhaps I missed the text, that it will be there if I look again, but it remains obstinately blank. I cannot read from a blank book, I say. I cannot pretend there are words here when there aren't, you must bring me the text that I used yesterday and the day before. I don't have time for games, for these kinds of April Fool's jokes. I am an old woman with feelings, and this is a serious business, the reading of one's life. Suddenly you look cross, push back your chair, and stomp into the studio. You stand over me, pointing your finger, your face twitching as it used to when you were consumed with your own anger, but magnified a hundredfold, blocking out the rest of the room. Leaning over, you hiss at me, *You will read now, old woman, and you will read until you are done.* (Not *until you have finished*, but *until you are done*, dead, kaput.) *We don't have all day*, you whisper between clenched teeth. *This is a very expensive studio to hire and you're wasting our time and money.* On your body I catch the scent of wildness, of rage. I begin to tremble, and it is invariably at this point that I wake up, covered in sweat.

Waking from this dream and its multiple iterations over the course of the week, I have turned each time to your notebooks or journals, I know not what to call them any more, because they are as much plans and appointments and random thoughts, all apparently giving nothing away that would be of use to anyone but me, the person in the position of the grieving parent, as they are a record of your life before you disappeared. (Am I not the grieving parent? I grieve and I was your parent, but I cannot fit my own position and my feelings with the image I have when the phrase *grieving parent* is pronounced: the sobbing woman with white hair, in a babushka, holding a broken body in her arms. I have not sobbed, there has never been a body to hold, the babushka my mind has borrowed from photos of disaster zones, wars, and battlegrounds. I could never be that woman I see, searching for her unburied dead.)

Every Saturday, I speak to your father on the phone. We ask each other, *Have you heard from her?* We've been asking this for two decades. I tell him about the dreams I have been having of you, their vividness, my belief that they signal your continuation, and your rage – rage directed at me specifically. It is something we both feel. We are both responsible. Your father is convinced he failed to support you adequately in your beliefs – beliefs that, at the very least, we both shared, even if we drew the line at some of your activities. You talk to us, relentless, haranguing, banging around in our brains, beseeching. We cannot put you to rest.

★

You and Sam sat apart on one side of the fire, with the lion and jackal, Lionel and Timothy, on the other. There should have been obvious questions from each party for the other – questions you would have asked them, questions they must have had for you. Why were two young students – for that is what they said they were, at least that is how you describe them in your notebooks – camping alone in the mountains? Why was a lone woman with a small child driving a truck through a hazardous, untarred mountain pass after dark? The two parties looked at each other across the campfire. Did you trust them intuitively, as the boy trusted you? Your notebook is silent about this. You had locked the cab of the truck, the keys were safe in your pocket, so there was no worry about the men stealing the vehicle, though perhaps you allowed yourself to imagine the worst in order to be prepared, to see yourself being forced to the ground, the keys stripped from your body, the way you would fight, how you would claw at their faces, call on Sam to attack them, to bite at their legs as the dog had bitten at yours. But these men had innocent, children's faces. You brought out your Safari Dates, and the men offered to share their dinner. Sam nibbled a hot piece of bread and drank water, but had no appetite for anything more substantial. He laid his head against your side and you put an arm around him.

'Lionel and I were wondering if we could ask you for a ride, if you've got room in the truck?' Timothy said. 'I know it's presumptuous, and we're strangers, and two men, and you're a woman, but, at the risk of being inappropriate, I can assure you that you'd have nothing to fear from us. Nothing to fear, I mean, in the way that women so often have cause to fear men.'

'Are you priests?'

'No, not priests,' Timothy laughed. 'Though even if we were, would that really reassure you?' This made him laugh even harder.

'No,' you agreed, trying to make yourself look relaxed and unafraid. 'Where are you going?'

'The Nuweveld. Outside Beaufort West.'

'I'm going that way. Sam's aunt lives in Beaufort West.'

'Your sister?'

'No.' Through the fire and smoke you thought you saw Timothy raise a sceptical eyebrow. 'What's in the Nuweveld?'

'We're going to a clinic. It's nearer Beaufort West than anywhere else. There's nowhere particularly near to our clinic.' Timothy held his hands over the blaze and Lionel muttered to him in a voice so low you could not make out his words. 'You haven't told us your name,' he said.

'Lamia.'

Lionel coughed and laughed. 'Ah-ha, the night-monster.' A cagy smile slashed through his face as he ran his hands down his hair, pulling it away from his body.

'A sea monster, too. A shark. An owl. And a beetle,' you said. *With brazen brows and lips that smile.* 'My mother's sense of humour.'

This was your invention, sowing confusion, as if to say you were and were not Lamia. You laughed to show you took it lightly. You were not your name, or not entirely your name, and the name was more than it suggested.

The two men looked at each other as if uncertain of you; Sam, filling the silence, moaned in his sleep, his arm twitching violently against your leg. You stroked his head, smiling to reassure the two men. They helped you put Sam to bed in their tent, tucking him into a sleeping bag, head on a pillow. How long, you wondered, since the child had slept as a child should, head cushioned, covered in blankets? How many nights had he slept in a moving truck, upright, or slumped against the door, the dog standing sentry over him?

You and the men returned to the fire and sat

198

together drinking Old Brown Sherry out of tin cups. With antiseptic and cotton wool Timothy treated the wound on your leg, which had swollen up red and black. 'A stray,' you explained, 'at a picnic stop. It was trying to get our food. I didn't see it.'

'You'll have to see a doctor about it. It might have been rabid.'

'I've known rabid dogs. This one was not. It was just mean.' You asked them about themselves. They explained that it was the long vacation, the time when they could be away from university, doing good works, gaining experience, whatever boys who leave the city do when they're away. And then Lionel turned the conversation.

'Terrible things going on.'

'Yes, terrible things,' you agreed.

'A dangerous time.'

'A very dangerous time,' you said. They did not know how dangerous.

'Particularly for people like us. Young people.'

'Yes, particularly.'

'A very bad time.'

'Indeed. The worst.'

To get this far, they had hitchhiked from Cape Town to George where they collected medical donations, and then from George to Oudtshoorn, before going on foot from Oudtshoorn into the pass. They had their tent, their sleeping bags, medical supplies for an emergency and enough food for a week of travel, which was the longest

199

they reckoned it might take them to reach the clinic on foot if they couldn't pick up another ride.

'The clinic is funded by Lionel's parents and their rich friends,' said Timothy, smiling.

'Which makes it sound like he's from the gutter.' Lionel elbowed his friend. 'His mother is the head doctor at the clinic. What do you do?'

'I used to be a reporter,' you said, half-truthful. 'I worked for the *Cape Record*.'

'That must have been interesting.'

'Yes, interesting.' Too careful to say more, you watched the men hold their breath, as if doubting whether you were all on the same side. Were the sides so clear? you wondered.

'And now you drive a truck?' Lionel asked.

'Now I drive a truck.' You did not speak like a truck driver and Timothy again looked sceptical.

'And your boy?'

'As you say, it's the long vacation. He comes with me when he's not in school.'

It was late and you all began to yawn and stretch as the silences lasted longer. After half an hour you left the two men, saying goodnight as family would, with a familiar kiss on the cheek. In the tent, you folded your body into a corner, lying on the ground next to Sam, but unable to sleep yourself, a curse that returned always at the worst times, when sleep was what you needed most. As a child, you remember, you would pray to be able to remove your eyes, to dream as others dream, as if the eyes alone were responsible for waking or sleeping.

You watched Sam breathing, his thin lips parted, crooked teeth catching the light from the fire that filtered through the green material of the tent. The light carried the thick odour of wood smoke and returned you to earlier fires on the beaches of childhood holidays, to the farm for funerals and weddings, numberless ceremonies of the everyday and the extraordinary, fires built of acrid-smelling brush and lemon wood, fires built of pines that popped and fizzed with sap, fires built with coals and lighter fluid over which slabs of beef and fish were grilled, dripping juices that spat and sizzled. Below the crackling and hissing of the campfire that night, you could hear the men whispering.

Before dawn you rose and crept to the truck, slipping past them, arms pillowing their heads in sleep. Using one of Bernard's shirts stashed in a bag under the seat and water carried in a plastic bottle from the showers at the edge of the camp-site, you scrubbed the worst of the blood from inside the truck's cab, until what remained was only a brown stain that bled into the lighter brown vinyl upholstery. If they asked, you would tell them that Sam got nosebleeds, since children often do, and then you remembered that Sam *had* actually had a nosebleed. The deception would itself be a kind of truth.

You washed in the shower, bracing under the cold water, and changed into shorts and your last clean shirt. Outside, it was light enough to see yourself in one of the truck's mirrors. There were purplish bags under your eyes and you had recently chipped one of your front teeth. It was not a face you liked, too much of me in the jaw and complexion, too slack in the cheeks.

Stealing back to the camp, you found Sam sitting outside the tent, staring up into the trees. Since arriving at the campsite the night before, he had become affectless, less human, less present. 'Did you sleep well?'

'Can we phone my aunt? I want to go home now,' a long high whine like a dog.

'There's no phone here. Come. Let me help you.' You put Sam's clothes, dirty with blood and vomit, into the campsite dumpster, and then dressed him in the last clean shirt and shorts in his small bag. At least you could count on delivering him to his aunt and being rid of the responsibility.

When the men woke, they brewed camp coffee and you drank in silence while Sam sipped from a tin of condensed milk. The usual formalities of travel, discussing a route, speculating about time and distance, detours, the boastful talk of men, these were all superfluous. There was only one logical way from there to Beaufort West, one road through the mountains.

After you finished your coffee, you helped the men collapse and pack the tent and bedrolls, everything compact and well maintained. You thought of your apartment and its scarce effects, now abandoned, already ransacked. You knew your files were being read, a search undertaken, looking for stray telephone numbers, addresses, names, illicit books in brown paper wrappers, the few items you had dared accord sentimental value being knocked over, broken. Even these things, apart from the books, would not have been obviously valuable to anyone but you, and perhaps me. A blue glass carafe you used as a vase. A woven raffia textile with a geometric pattern. Two plants. A photograph of your father as a boy. An assortment of small shells collected on various beaches. The apartment came furnished, the chairs and tables were not yours. Even as a child you distrusted ownership. It was inevitable that the authorities would summon me to collect what remained of your possessions after they completed their task. It was inevitable, too, that they would find nothing to help them in their investigations. Banned books, yes, but no phone numbers, no names, no addresses, no dates paired with locations. The landlady clucked over the unscrubbed oven, the dusty skirting boards, the cobwebs on the chandelier, the missing marquetry plaque in three kinds of wood in the design of a fish, the plastic bowl of potpourri, the rubber plant in a glazed pink pot – those things on the inventory you had hated and wilfully discarded. I forfeited the deposit, too busy and careless of money to clean the apartment myself. We lived ten minutes from each other and for so many years I never knew your address. I would have come every day if I'd known. Perhaps that is why you never told me.

'Are you ready to go? Lamia?' You did not respond. *Sie war in sich.* You were deep inside yourself. 'Lamia? We're ready, if you and Sam are ready.'

'Yes. We should be going.'

The sun was already high as you pulled away from the campsite and into the full glare of the treeless mountains, volcanic red rocks flowing in undulating vertical waves. The remainder of the pass road was less harrowing than what you had negotiated the night before – fewer hairpin turns, less dramatic precipices. Now it was only a matter of not riding the clutch or the brakes. You feared how much a night's sleep might have cost you.

Sam turned his attention to the two men, fixing them with the same uncompromising stare that had so moved and unsettled you. It was a relief not to be the focus of his attention. Sam did not just look, he studied, as if adults were an invasive species, alien to his experience of the world, creatures from fantasy. The men tried to bring him out of himself. Timothy had a length of rope and showed him how to tie different knots.

'You can't untie this one, can you?' he said, smiling and gently elbowing the boy.

'If I had a knife I could cut it,' Sam said, grim and determined.

'Ah, but there is a way, man. You don't need a knife to cut this knot.'

'A knife would be easier.'

'But that isn't the point, Sam. Try with your hands.'

You could not explain to them why Sam was so removed, so joyless. You scarcely understood it yourself, but wanted to shake him again, to say, *Be happy! I have freed you! You are free! I killed to free you!*

Prince Albert spilled out from the mountains, a white and green pool bright against the hard brown interior. You stopped on the edge of town to refuel the truck and buy more food and water. Timothy and Lionel bought sandwiches for themselves, and paid for half the fuel. Sam brightened after eating a peach, smearing juice and flesh over his face and shirt. The men doted on him, wiping his face as if he belonged to them. He withstood their attention like a dog that has learned not to snap when fussed for fear of being beaten.

Driving through the grubby northern outskirts of town, inhabited by filthy children and curs that stopped traffic on the road to fight over a piece of carrion, you passed a police car. Your chest tightened and as you slowed down the cruiser pulled into the road behind the truck. It followed you for half a second before turning around, lights flashing and siren shrieking, to race after a car travelling in the opposite direction.

'This is the real Wild West out here,' you said. The Wild West: cowboys and Indians, farmers and natives, lawmen and outlaws. Lawmen gone wrong in our case, at the time, and outlaws on the side of justice. To be outside the law, to place oneself beyond the rules because the rules are wrong, that's what you had done. Apart from our books, hidden in their camouflaged cavities, and our circle of associates, my associates in particular, hidden in their own ways, your father and I were always so law-abiding. Where did you learn to be more than just a paper rebel? Not from me. I was no model for action. Even my work, my papery protest, it could hardly be called daring.

The rest of that day you passed few cars. A truck had overturned, scattering lengths of metal along the roadside. The driver stood next to the wreck, looking bewildered. He waved to you but you shook your head – an apology and a dismissal. Along the highway people trudged with loads on their backs, bundles of firewood balanced on their heads, children tied in sheaths of cotton cloth against erect adult bodies. A group of boys had found a trolley from a supermarket and were taking turns pushing each other in it, pretending they were motorized. They waved when you passed, throwing dust in their faces. Agave and yucca broke the monotony of the flatland, sending up flowering spikes and curving their forms into succulent arcs. On the horizon a bustard broke into a run.

Sam fell asleep and Timothy read a book. Lionel sometimes read over Timothy's shoulder, and when he grew bored he stared at the road being endlessly consumed by the maw of the truck, or watched you driving, your face hard and scarred as the road itself.

I look at the last photographs I have of you, the last trace, together with your notebooks and the final letter. You are somewhere on a hill, perhaps in the Nuweveld, with long white acacia thorns behind you, and the skimmed-off surface of the Karoo in the distance, hazily exposed, Sam standing beside you. This photograph of you and the boy demonstrates your possession and affection for him – your hands are on his shoulders, he squints, you look at him with a caring smile. In another you look into the camera, hold him out in front of you, his hair brushed away from his face, your hair blowing away from yours, so there can be no mistaking the two identities. These were meant for me. They were evidence, the case you were presenting. Not of maternity, but of responsibility. *This child has been mine to look after*, your face says. *And now he is yours*.

Mine.

How I have failed you.

TRUTH AND RECONCILIATION COMMISSION
19 JUNE 1996, GEORGE

VICTIM: Jimmy Sukwini
VIOLATION: Killed in ANC Bomb Attack
TESTIMONY FROM: ETHEL SUKWINI (WIFE)

On continuation.

CHAIRPERSON: And on the night of the explosion?

MRS SUKWINI: I did not hear about it until sometime the next day. My husband worked the night shift and when someone phoned to say that the refinery had blown up I knew in my heart that he was dead. In my heart I knew already something was wrong before my friend phoned to say what the news was about the explosion.

CHAIRPERSON: Can you tell us, Mrs Sukwini, how your life changed after your husband's death?

MRS SUKWINI: Mr Chairman, this is the worst thing that can happen. I don't think I have to [*indistinct*] very hard for us after he died and we went to live with my parents. I was missing him all the time and my girls were missing their father. I still miss him. He was a good man. I understand why the comrades did what they did but I think maybe it should not have been like this. I don't know. I was not a part of these things. I am only a teacher.

CHAIRPERSON: Thank you, Mrs Sukwini. Is there anything else you would like to say?

MRS SUKWINI: Only that I am still waiting for someone to come to me, to say to me that they are sorry, that they wish for me and for my daughters that my husband did not die. I am still waiting. Please, will you tell them to come find me?

1989

The blast and the flash woke the boy and when he looked back to the north he could see the mountains on fire and a moment later her face was at the window of the truck and she was pointing a gun at him. Then she recognized him and put down the gun and said *Open the door.* They had known each other for a long time. Except for his dead parents he didn't know anyone better in the whole world than Laura.

What are you doing here? she asked, looking at the boy's face in the dark. *Where's Bernard?*

He turned on the headlights and pointed.

Laura turned off the lights and perched on the steps leading up to the cab with the door open. *Is he dead?*

The boy nodded. *He was sleeping. The truck went into gear.*

We can't leave him there.

Laura climbed down and together they went around to the back of the truck and they had to lift their shirts to cover their noses. The clouds were clearing and there was enough light from the moon for her to see the bodies inside and the boy didn't have to tell her who they were because Laura knew the kind of work Bernard did. *So let's put him back here*, she said, and together they lifted him up and carried him to the back of the truck and pushed him inside, and Bernard rolled against another body with its left arm missing and its hair burned off and the lips were curling away from the teeth. They closed the doors, locked the back, and rubbed their palms against the ground.

The boy tried to work out how long it had been since they'd seen each other. It was definitely before his parents died, so maybe no more than seven months, but Laura had been away and she looked different, her hair was short against her head and her face was like a carving and her eyes were darker. She hadn't come to the funeral. At the service he'd sat alone with Mrs Gush, the woman who took care of him in the days after the accident. He had waited for Laura to arrive. He'd asked Mrs Gush, *Did you tell her?* and the woman said they had tried to contact Laura and left word, *but did not reach her directly*. There were people from the university who were his father's fellow students and professors who came past and shook his hand. And then there was his father's mentor Professor William Wald with his dark hair and grey beard, and he came very gently over to the boy and took his hand and whispered what good people his parents were and what an extraordinary woman his mother was, and how sorry and sad he was that they were gone. The boy knew that

Professor Wald was also Laura's father, and this made the boy trust him. The man had put his hands on the boy's head and said if the boy needed anything at all he just had to ask, and if there was no one else to look after him then something could be done about that. Professor Wald gave Mrs Gush a funny look and she gave the Professor a funny look, and then Professor Wald went away with his tall wife and the boy never saw the Professor again because Bernard took over but now Bernard was dead.

There were no grandparents since all the boy's grandparents were dead. His father had no siblings and his mother's sister Ellen said she couldn't come *Because it's too far away and I can't afford to come, sweetie, so you'll have to forgive me and I'll see you soon, okay?* After the funeral Mrs Gush told him that although Ellen had been asked to look after him, she had refused – it would be too great a burden. Bernard was the only other choice.

The memorial was at the university because the officials thought that was what he'd want although the boy knew that his parents would have preferred everyone to gather on the beach at Camps Bay to sing, and then lift them up to the air and let them float away, but in a way it didn't matter because their bodies had already gone into the air. *No remains recovered*, the report said on its funny paper. He could tell that the flowers were leftovers from some other function like a banquet. They looked too happy with their big scarlet pink faces, and instead of live music there was a tape recording of some low and crying organ and the sound wobbled and it was the kind of song his parents would have called *music to dig death by*. And throughout the music and the man at the podium talking and talking and talking and raising up his eyes to the ceiling the boy kept turning around to look for Laura who was the only person in the world at that moment he wanted to see. But she never came and he only saw her again that night at the truck when she pointed the gun at his face.

SAM

Clare sends me away for a week, claiming other responsibilities. Some days while Greg goes to work I stay at his house, lying by the pool and listening to the recordings of my interviews. Other days I go to his gallery on Loop Street, where I sit in one of the vacant offices and work on the materials I've gathered, or I explore the city over long lunch breaks while Greg deals with his artists. One day I go to buy a car, agreeing with Sarah over the phone that it makes no sense to carry on renting until she arrives in December. A car is a car, she says, one is as good as another, and she trusts my judgement.

On Wednesday I walk all the way up Long Street until it runs into Kloof. I drop off some dry cleaning and go to a movie in the middle of the afternoon. As I'm coming out of the cinema and waiting to cross the street, a young man approaches me. He's polite, well dressed, but his clothes are dirty and he smells.

'Excuse me sir, I'm sorry to bother you. My name is Derek,' he says. Derek isn't like the woman we saw the other evening. There's no trace of privilege in his accent, and little education.

'I'm sorry I don't have any change,' I say.

'Thank you, sir.' As he begins to walk away I call out to stop him.

'Listen, I'm not going to give you any money, but I'll buy you some food. What do you want?'

'Some bread and some sugar and some coffee,' he says. 'That's what we need most in the shelter. Bread and some sugar and some coffee.' He says this like he's said it before. His body falls down around itself. His eyes are clear. He hasn't been drinking. He looks listless with hunger.

I tell him to wait and I go into the KwikSpar up the street. I choose a loaf of vitamin-enriched brown bread, half a kilo of sugar, and then look for the coffee. There's no coffee for under 50 rand, so I decide to skip it. The bread and sugar come to 18 rand, a little over two dollars at the current exchange rate. Less than I'd pay for a cappuccino. I know that I have to stop comparing, that soon dollars will mean nothing to me, that I will measure my life once again in the currency of my childhood.

Derek has come to wait outside the shop. I give him the loaf of bread and sugar. He looks disappointed with the bread, as though I've chosen the wrong kind. I tell him I didn't have enough money for the coffee, which is true in a way, since I wouldn't have had enough cash to pay for it.

'Thank you sir,' he says, and walks away.

On Thursday, as I'm going to fetch my dry

cleaning, I see Derek again: even from the short distance across the street, he looks almost prosperous, or, if not prosperous, then not on the skids. And then he pushes up his sleeves, puts down the plastic bags he's carrying, and begins to search through a trashcan.

★

Greg called out to me a moment ago to say he was setting the alarm, which means the kitchen, dining room, and lounge are all out of bounds until morning. I have nearly a wing of the ground floor to myself, including my bedroom, its adjoining bathroom, and Greg's study – a room that would have been intended for a live-in maid when the house was built. There aren't any outer doors in this section of the house and motion-sensing beams operate all along the perimeter fence, at the doors, and at each exterior corner of the building. Greg and Dylan sleep marooned on the upper floor, and the stairwell off the kitchen, which ends at the back door, is also alarmed. The dogs stay upstairs with them.

It's easy to become paranoid about noises. The house settling or weight on a floorboard? Wind in the chimney or a window opening? I know that no one could enter the house now without triggering the alarm, unless they were more than petty burglars. They'd need whatever technology is necessary to disarm the system without any of us being aware of it. Greg isn't anyone of real importance, and I'm definitely not, so I know that we have nothing to fear except petty burglars, and even then the fear is more about confrontation than loss of property. Confrontation, pain, and death.

I'm nearly asleep when the electronic howl pulls me up, eyes throbbing in time to the siren. I haven't felt like this since I was a child. My heart's in my tongue, every part of me vibrates with fear. The alarm echoes down the corridor and I slip out of bed to the door, crack it open, but can see only darkness. I sprint back across the room to the windows and edge the shutters open. The garden is dim under its night lights and my breath comes out quick and shallow. The dogs are silent. And then the alarm stops all at once, pulled into a vacuum of silence, and Greg calls from the end of the corridor. He can't see anything outside. It must have been an animal, or a power surge. The dogs aren't concerned. The alarm company phones to be sure that everything's okay, and Greg gives them the password that indicates it is, that we aren't being held at gunpoint – there's a different password for that – and we all go back to bed.

I begin to drift into sleep again when the dogs go crazy and seconds later the alarm splits my ears open. I run into the hall without thinking and see a face at the kitchen window, a palm flattened against a pane of glass. Greg comes down the stairs with Dylan in his arms. He sees the man at the window, gives Dylan to me, and orders me upstairs

217

into the bathroom. It locks from the inside and doesn't have any windows. The handle of the back door rattles and Greg pounds the panic button in the kitchen. *Our number is up*, I think, *our number is up*. I run up the stairs with Dylan, who's crying now, and lock us in the bathroom. Downstairs Greg shouts into the phone, 'There's a man on the property, he's trying all the doors and windows.' I hear glass shatter below, then silence and more glass shattering somewhere else. I think of the sliding doors in the lounge, which don't have burglar bars. I hold Dylan's head tight against my chest, rocking him back and forth. It's quiet for a long time and then the sirens come and feet stomp around downstairs and upstairs. Greg is at the door. It's okay, he says, and he gives me the pass-word that tells me it really is okay, that he's not being held at gunpoint. 'Chocolate sundae,' he says, 'we're all clear.'

The intruder is on the ground in the garden, spread-eagled, with the security company guards holding him down at gunpoint. He looks tiny, half as big as Greg. It's the man who was here before, claiming to be a tinker. He doesn't resist or protest.

Saturday morning. After sweeping up broken glass everywhere, we eat fruit salad and French toast on the patio with the dogs circling and whining for scraps. They go wild when a hadeda lands on the lawn and the bird shuffles back into the air. A glazier is coming to replace the windows and

218

the security company will be here later to check the whole system. Greg has decided to install a gate outside the sliding glass doors. 'It's going to ruin the room,' he says, 'but what can you do? It's either enjoy the view and pretend this is paradise or sleep soundly at night. I've been thinking of moving to one of the gated communities, up in Constantia or Tokai. Not for my sake, but for Dylan's.' Greg says what I thought last night. 'I was sure our number was up. It's only a matter of time.'

For a while, before he had Dylan, Greg was living in a rambling old house in edgy Observatory. One day while he was at work an intruder beat his five dogs to death. 'You can almost get over that. At least I wasn't there,' he says. 'But when you face the man who wants to take everything from you because he doesn't have anything himself, and sees us whiteys living like pharaohs, I don't know how to get over that. He didn't even have a gun. Just a knife. The police said he was high, probably on *tik*. I locked myself in the study. I cried in there, thinking I might die without saying goodbye to Dylan, or thinking that the man might get to you and Dylan first, and I'd have to live with that. I was too terrified to confront him. What does that say about me? I think maybe it says we shouldn't live here any more. We don't belong here now. But I can't imagine living anywhere else. I could never live in New York again. I don't know how you did it for so long.'

As happy as I am to be home, I can't help wondering what kind of place I've come back to, and what sort of country and life I've convinced Sarah to move to. I've tried to forget the reasons I left, all the history of my own life that I left behind, but it keeps coming back, like a chronic illness.

★

Nearly four months have passed since the first interview. My work on Clare's papers is as complete as it can be for now, and anyway, she tells me there's nothing more she's willing to share. The personal correspondence that I'd hoped to see hasn't and won't appear. I leave next week for Johannesburg.

'We could have a final series of conversations, if you like,' she tells me today. 'Not that I mean to suggest finality. You may contact me in future, if the need arises, but since you are here, why don't we cover anything you may have been holding back. I am not easily offended. I've begun to think you rather hide your lamp under a bushel. You are cleverer than you like people to think. There is something both endearing and unnerving in that. Why don't you kick off that bushel these last few days? Ask me the unaskable. Give truth the reins.'

I have to stifle a laugh. It seems such an unlikely, even absurd thing to say after everything she's said in the past, what with all the hostility at the beginning, when even the most basic question seemed exactly that: *unaskable*. I think – how can I help but think? – that she's already guessed the questions I have to ask, what this whole project is really all about, assuming she has any idea who I am. It's like being allowed to ask your mother anything about herself, and finding that a million questions suddenly spring to mind, each one even less possible to formulate than the last, even when you've been given permission.

The weather has grown warmer and we take the opportunity to sit in the garden. I return to some earlier points, clarifying questions of authorial intention, which she bridles against – 'You are poisoning me,' she complains – and larger thematic links, details about her family, her childhood, her relationship with her sister, which she is more willing to discuss than at our first meeting. She seems to brighten, in fact, when I mention her dead sibling.

After three days of this kind of discussion she again loses patience.

'You are still hiding under that bushel. I have dared you to join me, but you go on screening yourself. Come out into the daylight. I am inviting you. Stop prevaricating. *Neither was any thing kept secret, but that it should come abroad,*' she says, and I know I should be able to recognize that – a quote from which of her books? 'Listen Sam,' she says, now more like a mother than ever, 'you won't know whether I'll refuse until you ask, and you know me well enough by now to know that I *will* refuse if

221

I don't wish to answer. I won't bear you a grudge for any question you choose to ask. This is what you are here for after all, darling.'

I don't imagine the *darling*. It makes me shiver. Marie suddenly interrupts with a plate of biscuits and a pot of tea. She says nothing and leaves as quickly as she came.

I try to pull my thoughts back into focus, but the flutter of courage I felt at *darling* has gone. Of course I have two questions in mind: the askable question and what remains the unaskable one. So I go with the former, and know I'll regret it.

'There *is* something else.' The trick is to set up the question in such a way that I don't deceive, and don't present myself as being ignorant of the answer, which I already know, so that when the question comes she won't feel betrayed. I don't want to corner her; I just need to see how she answers. 'In the first few meetings – I can't remember which now – we spoke about the process of writing under the threat of censorship.'

Her face draws to a point. She has something else entirely on her mind. I'm disappointing her again.

'Yes. I remember that conversation.'

'You mentioned a few cases of writers who had worked for the Publications Control Board as advisory readers.'

'Yes. Some were true believers. Others naively thought they were defending literature from within a hostile system.'

'Did you know any of them personally?'

'I knew them as colleagues of a sort, yes, as fellow writers do. But they were not close friends. Why don't you come to your point?'

'When it became known that I was going to write your biography, lots of people sent me letters offering anecdotes about you. Most of them I ignored, because most were, frankly, libellous, never backed up with any evidence. Someone, however, and I don't know who, because he or she acted anonymously, sent me a photocopy of a document,' I say, handing her a folder. 'I've been to the State Archives to look for the original, but files from the period have been lost. I was hoping you might be able to tell me if this is genuine or not.'

'I think I know what I am going to find inside.' She opens the green flaps and removes a slim stack of photocopied pages, stapled together, bearing her initial and surname at the top of the first page. There's nothing to prove she actually wrote it; some enemy might have wanted to put her name to the advisory report that argues in the most legalistic style on what grounds a novel, summarized and analyzed in the pages therein, might be banned under the country's old publication control laws. She skims the pages and sets the report to one side.

'It's genuine,' she says, the corners of her mouth turning up. 'That's my handwriting, my signature, my words throughout. You want me to offer some kind of defence for my actions, but I won't. I will say only that I did it as a challenge to the system, believing I might be able to subvert it from within, or prove that there was nothing high-minded about its aims. Then one day, they simply stopped using me, and no more books were sent in my direction; notably, it happened after I wrote this very report – coincidence or not, I don't know, nor do I care. If you were to read all the reports I wrote, of which there were perhaps twenty over a period of two years in the early 1970s, this one, the one you have, is the only one that advocated banning, and I argued for banning on strictly legal grounds, as you can see. Whoever kept the report knew what they were about, or at least they thought they did. I assumed I had the only surviving copy. The author was totally unknown, and the book, *Cape Town Nights*, was quite obviously written with the express purpose of challenging the publication control laws; it was obscene, blasphemous, and openly ridiculed the government and the police, all of which were forbidden. The small press that risked publishing it made a habit of these sorts of crude attempts at challenging the system. It had a certain futile nobility. In every other case, the books upon which I reported were ultimately made available to the public without change or emendation, as far as I know.'

'And the author of the book you reported against?'

She smiles and shakes her head. 'You already

know her.' Having been unable to trace the author of the banned novel, which was embargoed and nearly all the copies apparently destroyed, never to be republished, never published abroad, I'd assumed the man, for the author was a man, Charles Holz, was dead.

'You banned your own book?'

'I thought perhaps you would be sympathetic, since you are, like I was, an intellectual – or a kind of intellectual – trying to survive in a time of madness.' She smiles for a moment only and then purses her lips together, sticking them out, as if to kiss. 'What will you do now? Will you tell the world that the woman who argues so fiercely against censorship collaborated with the censors, became one of them, and worked against herself? Do, if you wish. I won't stop you. I cannot. It will change no one's mind. If you present it fairly, as I know you will, being yourself of a highly legalistic frame of mind, then those who hate me will go on hating me, and those who do not hate me will merely think this new information adds to my complexity. It is a shame that this is all you could come up with, this impotent little squib. I thought you had caught the real scent. I was sure you knew,' she says.

'Knew what?' I ask, feeling my heart race, wondering if she is referring to our own buried connection – if it's possible she remembers me from decades ago – or something else altogether, a secret about herself I can't begin to imagine.

She shakes her head. 'You asked the wrong questions. How do you think you can write my life? You have nothing but a skeleton of facts, which you will flesh out with your own conjectures. I have shown you nothing. Because you now think that you know why, at one period in my life, I might have violated my own elaborate ethics, you will paint a pad of muscle and skin, and say, "That is who she is, there, as I've drawn her." '

She takes the photocopied report and places it back in the green folder. 'You are caught under that green bushel, lighting up what? Nothing. A dark empty space. My greatest secrets are left unillumined. You cannot see me from underneath that bushel. I was ready to show you demons. But that is work you have left for me to do, if I should choose to do it.'

This is how she appears to me, and these are her words, as I recorded and transcribed them, but when I reread them I find I've lost who she is: that system of continuous small explosions, contained in a tall pouch of skin.

ABSOLUTION

Since it was going to be cool over the weekend, Marie suggested they go for a drive.

'To the beach?' Clare asked, and then thought better of it. 'No, not to the beach. There will be a wind.'

'To Stellenbosch, then?' Marie said.

'Yes, all right.'

'And perhaps you would like to stop at the cemetery, to see your sister's grave. We haven't been there in such a long time.'

'Yes, very well. Perhaps it's time I paid another visit to check she hasn't unearthed herself.'

Clare's parents were not so easily visited; they had both been cremated, their ashes scattered in a high wind at the tip of the world, falling in eddies around her head and into the air above the waves where two oceans meet.

Marie drove them from the house and along the N2, turning off at Baden Powell Drive, going through Stellenbosch, and then up into the vineyard-covered slopes and around into Paarl.

The cemetery felt unnaturally white, headstones of white marble surrounded by whitewashed walls, the graves tended by fat white men with burned skin, replacing the faded white lilies on Nora and Stephan's graves with fresh ones every day, at private expense. The wild fig was still there, outside the walls, covered in vines, and the language monument was now visible beyond the tree. Nora's grave was in a place of honour next to her husband's, adjacent to an eternal flame, which, it was rumoured, had lately been allowed to go out at night. But on that day it was burning, blue-gold under the leaden clouds, stark against the white crosses that faded into invisibility against the white wall that surrounded the acre of dead, the burial farm.

It was a space of such whiteness that Clare, in black for fashion rather than respect, looked like an intruder. And then she noticed that there was another intruder as well, black and small and round, nestled against the base of the monument that marked Nora's grave. Clare knew what it was before she had seen it clearly; she knew at the first dull metal glint of black, half-revealed, itself half-concealing the eternal flame. It was her father's black tin box. She felt cold in the heat, and put her hand on Marie's white-sleeved arm. When they reached the grave, Clare leaned over and took up the box in her hands.

It was impossible; it was too horrible to find it there. It was somehow exactly what she had been expecting. She opened the lid. The wig was there, and she imagined for a fractional moment that her father's head was there as well, tipped up, staring at her, though this was impossible, for his head was in ash, scattered to the sky. Clare thought she heard herself scream. She knew that they knew. She knew who they were – Stephan's family, his brothers, his cousins, nephews and nieces for all she knew. It was clear what the wig meant, clear to her that her own complicity was known, that someone wished to remind her that she was not above the law, and not above the claims of history.

Surprising herself, Clare found a small white stone and placed it on her sister's monument. It was not the tradition of her own family's religion, but somehow it made sense, the stone as a private acknowledgement of a feeling she was unable to describe. It would have been too much to say that she grieved for her sister, and certainly she had no fond feeling for her brother-in-law, but there was a turbulence in her heart that, for a moment, the movement of the stone from the ground to the monument put to rest. When Clare was finished, she asked Marie to drive her home.

'Would you not like to go for lunch somewhere?' Marie asked, sounding hopeful.

'Not now, no, I'm sorry. We can stop for a sandwich if you're hungry, but I've quite lost my appetite.'

Later that day Clare realized that she should phone Ms White. It was near the end of the month. When had the invasion occurred? The beginning of December a year ago, or the end of November a year before that? The dates were fuzzy in her head. It seemed as though it had still been spring, only just warm enough to have had the windows open at night. Ms White was perfunctory on the phone.

'Well, that is good. You have found the wig. I guess the case is closed.'

'What of Jacobus and his so-called gang?'

'You pressed no charges against them, so we have let them go.'

'Is it as simple as that?' Clare asked, incredulous.

'As simple as you make it, madam.'

'And what of the invaders? Are there no clues?'

'Invaders?'

'The people who broke into my old house, of course.'

'But we had him, Jacobus and his gang, and you said it could not be them, madam. I do not understand. Is it now your wish that we should charge them with robbery?' Ms White sounded truly perplexed, as though she could not begin to understand the nature or logic of Clare's intentions.

'It was not Jacobus, but I need to know who it was. I only wish to know, exactly, who did it – the invasion, the theft. I can tell you only that it was someone from the past. Someone from my brother-in-law's family. His associates, his brothers, or even his sisters. They wish to punish me.'

'If this is a family matter, madam, then why did you ever bring the authorities into it? If you knew who it was, why have you wasted our time?'

'It is not that simple.'

'Perhaps you should take over the investigation. You are so good at finding. You found your father's special wig. That is good. Perhaps you will find the intruders. And then you will phone me if you wish. And we will come fetch them for you.' Like a ball, or a stick, Clare wanted to say. Intruders that were only playthings, a wig, a tin box, two women of a certain age. 'Or you will settle the matter as it should be settled, madam, as a family.'

But they are not my family, Clare wanted to say. *They are nothing to do with me. They know what I have done. They are sending me signs. They are terrorizing me.*

CLARE

There is something I have never told you, Laura, a thing about me that makes us more alike than you might imagine. While I have many regrets – in particular about the kind of mother I was to you, and the kind of mother I never managed to be – I have no greater regret than this: that I failed to tell you the darkest truth about me when you were present to hear it, that I failed to show you, when you needed it, how alike we were. This is my true confession. To confess is all that I can do for you.

It is a story about sisters: my sister Nora, and me.

Perhaps I never told you, but even as small children, Nora teased me mercilessly. I was *Giraffe Girl, Goosey, Noose-neck. I'm going to hang you high, Noose-neck,* Nora would scream, threatening me with a length of rope. And then when I cried she would clasp me to her and say she didn't mean it, *No offence, Clare,* it was all just joking, that's what sisters did. I stopped loving her when I was eight, after she cut off all my hair while I was sleeping and burned it in the garden. I stopped thinking of her as my *dear sister* before I ever came of age, even before I was a teenager, long before Nora left home.

At sixteen, Nora was always threatening. She threatened our parents that she would marry that great bullock Boer, Stephan Pretorius, with or without their permission. She once threatened me with a hot griddle from the stove, chasing me through the house and screaming *I'll kill you! I'll kill you!* after I used her lipstick. She threatened the cats with drowning and switches. She threatened our parents that she would never see them again if they refused to attend her wedding. She threatened to elope, never to let them meet their grandchildren (a blessing, perhaps, that there were none). She threatened too much. Why, I wondered, was she so unlike me? How do two people become opposites in every way while being raised by the same parents in the same house with the same values and rules? I hardly have an answer today. They were stricter with her, but not in a way that should have produced a tyrant. My father used to say the ghost of his grandmother, whom he remembered with terror, must be haunting Nora, for how else could one explain her wickedness? There were times when I wondered if you had inherited that haunting, Laura, if the echo of Nora's name in your own betokened some generational curse.

Even as a child, I understood why she would marry Stephan. It was not about love. He was older than her, a man already – a man to replace our father, who was a better man by half. (I know you will protest – that I, too, married a man to replace my father, a man of the law like him, to take his place. Unlike Nora, I was conscious of my folly, and your father was – is – no monster.) Nora's husband, so unlike our father, had a strong, stout body, florid with health and indulgence. What could our parents say but *Yes, we give our blessing*? And even though his was, if you like, a parallel branch of the same Christian tribe (if we can still speak of tribes these days), the Pretorius family seemed as foreign to my parents as we must have seemed to them. On my sister's wedding night I heard my father weeping in his study in a way that he wept only when he remembered the dead.

One of our father's clients loaned us a limousine for the day, and we paid the gardener extra to drive us to the church, then to the banquet, and then home afterwards. On the way to the church, the gardener was so excited by the car that he tested the windscreen wipers but could not discover how to turn them off, so we arrived in the blazing sun at the church in our borrowed limousine with the wipers screaming over the dry glass, and even when the car was turned off, the wipers kept screeching back and forth until the car's battery died. After the ceremony, we had to walk through town to the wedding banquet because there was no room in the limousines that my brother-in-law's family – dozens of them – had hired to carry themselves. Or perhaps they simply did not wish to risk such intimacy with us. My sister had become one of them, embraced their church, turned her back on our quiet Methodism. Stephan had caused scandal by choosing an outsider, but he stood his ground. He said he loved her. And who could not? She looked like Marilyn Monroe in those days, blonde and flawless as a goddess.

We arrived at the banquet sweating and covered with dust while my sister and her new family were dry and cool, already eating their chilled soup. There had been a 'mistake' with the seating arrangements, so that my parents and I were not at the long head table with the wedding party and my brother-in-law's parents and six brothers and sisters, but at a separate table just to the side, with my aunt and uncle and cousins, a knot of slender, pale bodies, suffocating under all that beef. We were not in any of the wedding photos, except those taken by my uncle, with my sister and her husband out of focus in the background, chewing their *braaivleis*.

In the months after the wedding, when they moved to his grandparents' farm, into the long white house outside Stellenbosch, Nora learned the ways of her new tribe, the formalities of the language with all its cloying diminutives, *the little pot*, *the little sister*, *the little mistress*. In private, our mother asked my sister if her new husband's family was treating her well. My sister did not answer at first, then said, too brightly, *Yes, Mother, they treat me well.*

When we were visiting her I upset an antique plate hand-painted with delicate blue flowers, breaking it on the dung floor that was polished with ox-blood and studded with peach pits, perhaps imagining how my sister's mother-in-law would react.

Years passed. By the time I returned from Europe my brother-in-law was something important in the National Party. My own politics had been, as is so often said these days, 'radicalized' – chiefly by my time in England, and the people I met there, the books I was suddenly allowed to read without fear of discovery or sanction. On returning home, I met your father. We found each other through like-minded friends who arranged for us to meet, and, liking each other well enough, we decided to get married. I had your brother Mark, and as your father became more cautious, more concerned not to jeopardize his newly won place in the university, I became more radical, writing and publishing and attending meetings the wife of a professor should not have attended. It was enough to get me noticed by people on both sides, and at a meeting one night I let slip that my sister and her husband were going to be in Cape Town for a few nights. One of my associates asked, as casually as you please, if they would be staying with me. Don't be ridiculous, I said. My sister's husband would never accept my hospitality. They're staying at some fancy guest house. Did I know the name? The name of the guest house? Of course I did – and let it trip from the end of my tongue.

I did not know it was supposed to be a secret, or that their arrangements were for my ears only, that my sister, in trusting me, was trying to extend a hand of friendship, even of reconciliation.

You are right to protest.

Without doubt I knew. I knew the delicacy of the information I held. I chose to forget. I have spent the rest of my life speculating why.

I imagine the moment of horror, the two of them caught by the intruder in the room of the guest house. Nora and Stephan were in bed together, sheets slick with hair oil, sticky with him, socks on the floor, cold and sharp, sour in the hot room. Woken by the sudden opening of the bedroom door, pushing her body upright in bed, damp with perspiration, seeing the figure outlined in the intruding light from the corridor, she must have wondered, *Where are the guards?* It must have seemed impossible that they should find themselves bargaining for their lives. Logically, Nora would have expected her husband to intervene to save her, but she must have known there had never been much evidence to suggest he would do anything to endanger himself, to put anyone's interests above the instincts of his own self-preservation.

I have read the testimony. My sister's assassin reported that she threatened to scream, to call the guards, to wake the entire guest house. Why, I wonder, at that most crucial hour, did she threaten but fail to act? She looked to her silent husband clutching the bedclothes in terror, and the smell of shit filled the room. (The police, the coroner, they confirmed this.) The intruder went first for my sister while her husband pleaded for his own life, on his knees in the bed. And then it happened. He moved, but not towards the assassin; he scrambled from his bed to the open window, trying to escape, and in the instant in which his legs planted themselves on the floor and his bare white back turned against his wife, the gun moved from her eye and fired into her husband with a soft *pffft*. She did not scream, or move, but looked at the assassin, who was, the man said, surprised by her silence.

When I saw their bodies the following morning I thought, *I have done this. I have made this happen.* I delivered the assassin to my sister's door. I was not shocked by their deaths or the violence done to their bodies. I knew what bullets fired at close range could do to living tissue; I had done it myself, to my cousin's horse. The only thing that shocked me was my own capacity to give away the very information that led to my sister's death and to feel, in the aftermath, no remorse. They were, I told myself at the time, on the wrong side of history. About that, at least, I was right. About my own role, I can no longer be sure.

You see, Laura, how I played my own part – not as brave as you, but as wilful and headstrong, anxious to make a difference, or at least to appear useful to people more involved than I. Was I callous? Were we both?

In your last letter to me you write:

You know that I don't ask for absolution, since that's something you don't believe in and therefore can't give, or won't give. I only offer this document as my version of the truth, a truth among many. Bernard's truth would be different, but he can't speak. Sam's truth would be different still, and he may yet speak. If you refuse to absolve me, will you also refuse to judge me, or does judgement belong to a different order of ethics?

Come back. Come back that I may say it all to your face, that I may rethink my ethics, beg for absolution from you, prostrate myself in the name of reconciliation and love. You are all that I love now. I want only you.

★

As the earth spun you out of the eye of the sun, Lionel directed you to a point he recognized in a folded shadow of the Nuweveld Mountains. The clinic was a long low building in a tiny settlement of whitewashed plaster houses surrounded by a grove of acacia. Lights were on inside and a radio played. Timothy knocked at the largest of the houses, and his mother opened the door. She was a much older woman than you were expecting, short, in a neat smock dress. She kissed her son on both cheeks, then turned to Lionel with the same greeting.

'Mother,' he said, 'this is Lamia and Sam. They gave us a ride.'

'And they've come all this way with you? Shame! Are you sick, my dear?'

Inside, the house was bright and incongruously modern. Timothy's mother, Gloria, poured you tea and said that you could sleep in the clinic. 'There are no patients now, and plenty of beds. You're welcome here for as long as you need.'

'Perhaps a night. Just to rest. I can pay,' you offered.

'That isn't necessary. You've given the boys a ride. That's payment enough. Won't you have another slice of malva pudding? It's always nicer the next day, I find.'

'We won't stay long. I'm taking Sam to Beaufort West tomorrow. To his aunt.'

'Of course,' Gloria said, as if Beaufort West were a town peopled solely by aunts awaiting the delivery of prodigal nephews.

Like Gloria's house, the clinic's rustic façade masked an up-to-the-minute interior equipped with consulting and waiting rooms, an operating theatre, and a dormitory with sixteen single beds. Gloria and Timothy helped you make up two of the beds, showed you the toilets and showers, the kitchen with facilities to make tea and coffee, and

invited you to return to Gloria's house for breakfast in the morning. Left alone, you put Sam to
bed and looked at him square in the eyes.

'Perhaps we should have a talk,' you said. 'Do
you know where your aunt lives in Beaufort West?'

'If I saw it. I don't know the name of the street,
but I've been there before. I know the way.'

'And you're sure she's still living there?'

'I think so.'

'When I take you to your aunt, I'm going to
leave you with her. And after that I'm going away.
I'm leaving the country.' Sam screwed up his face
and kicked his feet against the bed. 'People will
ask you questions about what happened to Bernard.
You must tell them what I did to him, the way I
killed him. Only give me perhaps three days after
I leave you, before you say anything.' Sam looked
up at you again. 'Do you understand?'

The next morning, you left your notebooks and
the last letter, every document important to you,
in Timothy and Lionel's care, telling the young
men, these strangers you trusted, to deliver the
papers to me in person when they could.

★

Between the clinic and Beaufort West there was
only a dirt track that twisted through hills the
colour of dead skin. It stopped a kilometre from
town, north of the national route, so no one who
did not know what to look for would ever find

it. It appears on no map and does not exist today.

From the clinic approach, the white spire of the church appeared first, rising in defiance above the dusty trees. You arrived in town on a street of depressed storefronts and a petrol station where you parked alongside other rigs, glinting bright and aggressive in the summer heat. At a phone booth across the street you paged through the slim Beaufort West directory, looking for the name Sam gave you. When you found it, you phoned the number and after a single ring a woman answered.

'Yeeees. Who's this?' The woman sounded suspicious.

'Do you have a nephew named Sam or Samuel?'

'Yes. What is this about exactly? Who is this?' It was not a voice that seemed to care about a nephew.

'Sam is with me. I wondered if I could bring him to you. His guardian is dead. Bernard – he's dead. We're here in town.'

'No kidding,' the woman said, with a flatness that surprised you.

'May I bring him to you?' You looked down at Sam, who had wedged himself into the phone booth next to you. He was playing with the cord, twisting it into an unnatural shape, and staring across the street at a fruit and vegetable vendor.

'Who are you? Who is this?' the woman snapped.

'We'll be there now.'

Sam's aunt lived in a single-storey house with a broad covered veranda. She was standing on the steps as the two of you approached eating peaches, juice dripping down your arms. You hoped the woman would run out to embrace Sam, but instead she just stood waiting under the canopy, slouching in a pair of blue jeans and a dirty white shirt, arms crossed over her breasts. She had Sam's sharp features, the same peaked nose and narrow eyes, but with a shock of ginger hair.

'Sam? Is this your aunt? Is this the house?'

Sam looked at you and looked at the house and looked at the woman.

'Don't you know your auntie, Sam?' the woman asked.

'Yes.'

'Don't you want to come see your auntie?'

You watched Sam climb up the three shallow steps and stand in front of his aunt, one hand holding the peach to his mouth as he sucked the flesh from an exposed hemisphere of pit, the other dangling at his side. The woman put a hand on his head, smoothing his unruly hair. 'Are you his guardian now?' she asked, squinting. 'Are you some kind of friend of my sister?'

'No. I happened to find him. He said his parents were dead. He said you were his only relative.'

'I guess that's right. How do you know that bastard Bernard is dead anyway?'

'I saw his body. I saw him – I mean I saw him dead. I was hitchhiking and came upon the truck and Bernard's body. Sam was hiding in the bush. They were hijacked.' You knew the hijacking story was plausible, hijackings being not so uncommon. And in a way, it had been a hijacking.

'So much the better. I mean Bernard dead. Not the hijacking. Would you like a cup of tea or something?' the aunt asked.

'I should be getting on,' you said, anxious to get moving. 'You'll look after Sam?'

'You mean you're leaving him with me?'

'He's your nephew isn't he?'

You stared at each other. The aunt's lips spread and flattened against her teeth.

'I guess I have to take him, then.' Sam had finished the peach and turned back to you, rolling the stone around in his mouth, eyes confused. You thought again of taking him into the wilderness, renewing him, as you thought of it, calling him *Samuel*. But you knew this was impossible. 'You've dropped a real burden on me, *Miss* – what's your name?'

'It doesn't matter.'

Sam's aunt rolled her eyes and snorted. 'I don't mind saying I think there's something funny about all this. Just turning up with nothing. I don't mind saying I think it's *strange*,' she said, grabbing Sam, pulling him towards her and clasping him against her faded jeans. He shuffled his red shoes, trying to squirm out of the woman's grasp, but she held him closer, her arms tightening around his chest. 'That's right. I think this woman is strange.' She coughed, a deep productive cough that pushed her off balance, freeing the child.

You studied Sam with the same intense focus he had once turned on you. After all the unwanted embraces, the grabbing and clinging, you found yourself desperate to be held by him, to hold him, to feel that heat again around your waist. You reached out three dry fingers to touch his cheek. He did not flinch. You wanted him to throw out his arms and cling to you, cry out not to be abandoned, force you into doing what you could not.

But he had nothing to say.

Of course I remembered him at once. Not just here. I knew him immediately in Amsterdam. And finding him suddenly before me, it was like being faced with my own assassin. I wondered if he had come to exact his pound of flesh. But he has only ever been charming. *What does he want?* I ask. *Why can he not say what he has come to say?*

1989

It wasn't chance that Laura and the boy knew each other already, before she found him there in the dark, in the truck, with Bernard lying dead on the ground. The only chance was them being in the same place at the same time. When his parents blew themselves up with three other people outside a police station the only person in the world the boy had wanted to see was Laura because she was as close to a mother as any he had left in the world. He put his hand out to her and she took it and drew his head against her arm and for a moment he couldn't remember whether she'd only appeared after Bernard was dead or if she'd been there earlier. They sat in silence for a while looking out on the darkness. The boy wanted to ask Laura if she could be his mother, now that his own mother was dead, but he didn't. He knew it was impossible.

There was a roadblock on the way, but she showed her ID book, as well as the boy's, and explained she was going to meet his uncle, the owner of the truck. The boy wondered what would happen to them if the police opened the hold and discovered what was inside. But they were lucky. The police sent them on their way and told them to be careful.

Laura drove almost until dawn to a farm outside Beaufort West where she found her associates waiting for her and there the boy met Timothy and Lionel for the first time. Laura told the boy he must trust the men but that she had to leave – there was something she had to do. It was possible she might see him again and she promised to look for him and said he should look for her and if they were both looking they would find each other someday. She told him to go to her mother, to look for her if he ever needed anything. *My mother is a good person*, she promised. *My mother won't fail you.*

The boy watched her leave in a car with a man, but he didn't know who the man was and never saw his face. He only knew that Laura and the man had something important they had to do and that it was too dangerous for him to go with them. He never saw Laura again. If she was going to come back she would have done it by now.

She left behind the truck that was the boy's inheritance and in the coming days he watched Timothy and Lionel and other men dig graves for all the bodies, Bernard included.

Timothy stripped the truck of its identifying marks, put on new number plates, and one of the other men left with it. The boy never saw the truck again but he didn't care any more.

At first, when he asked them what was going to happen, Timothy and Lionel would laugh and say, *You're going to be our mascot*. But as the weeks passed they didn't know what to say and the boy reminded them that he had an aunt in Beaufort West and for days everyone talked about whether or not they should take the boy to his aunt or if that was too risky, and wouldn't it be better just to let him stay with them because he had been born into the movement and shouldn't he grow up in it since he was already almost a man who could be taught to shoot? Lionel said it would be wrong, that it wasn't fair to the boy, and they should take him to his aunt.

But the boy barely knew his aunt and the others didn't know if she could be trusted. And then he said to them, *What about Laura's parents? Laura said I could go to her mother. And her father – her father told me that if I ever needed anything . . .*

And that was how they came to be on the woman's front porch, staring through the screen door, and how the woman shook her head and took her daughter's papers and said they should go.

The boy and the men stood there, the door slammed in their faces, and though they were in the shade it was a hot February day with no wind and the boy came out in a sweat all over his body and the men turned to him and told him not to worry. He stood on the porch looking up at the mountain so that he didn't have to look at the men or at the windows of the house. He did

248

not want to be seen or to see anyone else as he listened to the rush-hour traffic on Camp Ground Road, thinking of how it became other roads, Liesbeek Parkway, Malta Road, Albert Road, roads that curved around to the north, following the contour of the mountain, circling back to his own neighbourhood, to the house that had once, until recently, been his.

They walked back to the car and sat for a while in the shade while the men argued the boy's fate in front of him. *I think we should ask the boy,* Lionel finally insisted, and when the boy was asked he said he did not want to stay with them. He wanted to go to his aunt in Beaufort West, where Laura was taking him in the first place, or not in the first place, but as a last resort, after rescuing him from the situation he had gotten himself into. Sitting in the car, he was sure it was his fault that these men had to decide what to do with him, his fault that Laura had been forced to look after him, his fault that his parents disappeared in the first place. It was his fault and his failure.

He promised he wouldn't say anything about them to his aunt or to anyone else.

Not until all of this is over, not until, you know, all of this is history, my friend, Timothy said.

They would leave him on his aunt's doorstep. If anything went wrong, if his aunt refused to take him, if he felt he couldn't live with her after all, they gave him a number to phone, and someone would come get him.

CLARE

You drove for the rest of the day and into the night until, an hour's walk from the border, you abandoned the truck and began following your compass to a place where you hoped you would be able to slip out of the country unnoticed.

The mountains were dry and the scrubby trees old and thickening. As you walked a mist settled in the depressions, wafting through the low branches. A light wind was coming from the south-west, but the sky above was clear and would be bright for another few hours. If you kept your pace, you would reach the border well before dawn.

As you walked, your thoughts began to fill with the deaths of others, and your own inevitable death, and the absence of Sam – an absence you felt in the weight of the bag on your back, the mesh of red vinyl bearing into you, opening and inhabiting you. The thought of deaths you had caused – the deaths for which you alone were ultimately responsible – filled the whole of you, was played into fullness by a song beating through your memory. You were deep inside yourself, absorbed, death

250

filling you past the point of contentment, *erfüllte sie wie Fülle,* sweetened by the thought of your own death, the death that must come, that might arrive within the hour or the next day.

Your sandals hit the first bale of razor wire before you saw it, but you stepped back in time to keep from lacerating your hands. You took the rucksack from your shoulders and put it on the ground, listening for any noise. Digging to the bottom of the red vinyl cavity, you found wire cutters and a pair of thick leather gloves, then returned the pack to your shoulders and began cutting through the bale until you could pull the two ends apart and pass through. You had trained for this, cutting through heavy wires, and the muscles of your hands were strong and responsive. You knew there might be multiple lengths of baling, each separated by a treeless stretch of land. On the other side you paused, turning your ears to the wind and then sheltering them, listening in the vacuum. There was no sound apart from the wind. Moving forward, you tried to walk a straight line from the first bale but had no idea how far apart the lines might be. Your heart began to race as the sounds of your footsteps and pulse thundered in your head. The mist was too thick to see beyond the end of your arms and your lungs were filling with the damp air. After five minutes your feet met another bale. You cut through this as well, opened a passage, and began walking again. Five minutes later, another bale, and then another after that.

You worried that you might have turned, that you were walking parallel with the border rather than across it – that there might be perpendicular sections of baling designed for the very purpose of confounding anyone trying to cross. You remembered your compass. Its glowing green dial confirmed you were still moving towards freedom. After another two lines of baling you began to lose hope, and fell to your knees, exhausted, heart echoing, your breath irregular, labouring under the damp rucksack. Only the ground immediately around you was visible. Your watch said it was two, but it felt much later. There were places, some said, where watches did not work.

When you tried to stand, you found you could not, and had to crawl. At least at dawn, you thought, I will see where I am. You crawled for an hour, always south-south-east, but came to no further bales. Your mouth was dry, joints aching. Finally you managed to stand and, as you did, lights exploded from the right. A man shouted. A dog barked.

And then the man and the dog were upon you.

You could not recall how many days it had been; perhaps five, perhaps as many as fifteen hundred. You had been deprived of any means of recording the passage of time, and living permanently inside, in a windowless cell, with transitions down windowless corridors, to other windowless rooms, windowless showers, windowless examination chambers, all lit by the same orange lights, you could not say how many days it had been since you had last seen the sky and the sun. And the sun! The shock of its brilliance initially left you blind. They had placed you supine, your face burned in hard sunlight, so that instead of examining the world, to be sure it was still as you remembered it, you had to close your eyes against the glare; although compared to the time you had spent inside, those moments of closing your eyes against the sun and seeing the orange brilliance through your greyed lids was no more than a pause. It was a relief, after the stagnant air of the prison, to breathe ocean winds, to feel the sun heating the length of your body, so that even the constraints that held you in place were almost forgivable, and the fact that your spine and legs were supported by nothing more than a slender metal pole, no thicker than your own wrist, almost forgettable for the first minutes. You could taste salt in the air, and shout if you wanted to, but you had long since lost the courage to shout, and dared only to whisper to yourself, barely moving your lips, the salt on them sharp white flowers. They had closed the cage and trudged off, up the dunes, and you were left listening to the waves breaking down the beach, and when the wind shifted, the voices of others like you, whispering to themselves, whimpering, crying silently, and then a throttled scream.

'It is a simple system, ladies and gentlemen, not

unlike a fishing rod, but with an almost opposite purpose, as you can see here. The cages, made of ultra light titanium, are tethered to these gear mechanisms, which can drag them on their cables up beyond the reach of high tide, or allow them slack enough to be pulled out by the retreating waves as much as half a kilometre into deep water, depending on what's required. On this stretch of beach, very secluded – an hour's drive to the perimeter fence, as you well know, and another hour still to the nearest artery – there are twenty-five cages, usually operating at full capacity.'

'What are the dimensions?'

'Each cage is a metre square and three metres tall, and inside, along the vertical axis, is a pole, with an adjustable crossbar that can be raised or lowered according to the height of the detainee's shoulders; it's essential that there always be a good fit, so the detainee is held securely in position, even when submerged. Shackles at the feet, the neck, and the wrists hold each detainee in place, and these are also adjustable, so there's no chance that someone could slip out when wet, and swim to the top of the cage.'

'Even then, they wouldn't be able to escape, would they?'

'No, but they might be able to catch a breath.'

The memories were very clear, the early ones; it was your grasp of the recent past that was inse-cure. You knew the first time you had walked on a beach, when you were two, with your father and me and your brother, and could feel your red swimming suit with its yellow fish design tight against your skin. You could remember the first steps you had taken, wholly unafraid, for you knew all about the ocean, knew it was for swimming, knew also that it was colder than it looked. You had marched into the surf and began paddling with confidence, your father and I swimming on either side. There was the thrill of the buoyancy, which made swimming easier than in the dam on the farm, but also the force of the waves, which made you work harder. After ten minutes in the water you were ready to rest on the beach, to let your chest rise and swell in time with the surf, hair salty, stringy round your face as you watched the waves approach and recede. Collapsing on your back, you stared at the white-blue sky until your father opened an umbrella to shade us.

'If you watch the one closest to us, you can see that we've given the tether substantial slack, and the water is already around her ankles. Not long now and the waves will take the cage out into the surf, and that's what we call the "testing threshold". If they withstand that without screaming, then we know there's no breaking them, and we might as well just let them go all the way. It's a clean system, too, because once we've let them out to five hundred metres, there's an automatic release function, which opens the cage to predators, to sharks and the like, and we just leave them out there until we see a little activity in the water, and then we know we can bring the cage back in, more or less empty.'

'So there's no burial necessary.'

'Anything left over is incinerated. Sometimes the predators take everything. What we call a "clean sweep". No work for us to do but put the next one in.'

'But there are some, presumably, who do break?'

'Like that fellow over there, the one who screamed a few minutes ago. You see, my men have gone out into the water, they're getting what they need to get from him, and if he doesn't give them everything they want, then back he goes. Sometimes it takes a dozen trips out before they realize we're serious; they scream every time, but don't tell us everything we want to hear, and back they go. Ones like that always break down eventually, though. It's the most efficient system we've found, and it serves an ecological function, too. Fish stocks in the area have increased ten-fold over the last three years.'

'This is the court of last resort, so to speak, for the hardest cases.'

'These are the ones who've been through everything else and still not cracked. I can't explain what it is about the ocean, some kind of natural rhythm that just scares the hell out of them. We figured out how to do it best, too. You leave them out for a day, in a secure position, and let them roast. Then the next morning, after they've been shivering all night from the burns, we drag the cages down to the water line and let the tide start to work its magic. It's a beautiful thing to watch. There's something redemptive about it.'

Your fingers and toes were throbbing and burning as the salt worked on the exposed tissue where the nails had been torn away, and the sores that covered your back were alive with sand kicked up by the breeze and the persistent sting of fleas. You were aware that you were beginning to burn when you chafed your bare thighs together or shifted your wrists in their shackles. The inside of your mouth was cottony and you closed your eyes to preserve the little moisture that remained. Sleep was impossible because of the strength required to hold yourself in place; if you relaxed, the shackles at your wrists and ankles would cut into your flesh, and it would be a short time before they began to cut into bone. *I have resisted this long, I can go longer. It is not like illness or fever, not even like shame. Nakedness no longer matters. They can do what they want to me, they can watch me pissing and shitting myself, if I had anything left inside me to piss or shit. No food in my stomach to vomit, not even bile. This is not the worst they have done. This is almost a reprieve.*

Suspension over sand might not have the hot flush of shame, or the chills of sickness, but was nonetheless both hot and cold. Shame had been rife indoors. You did not want to remember what they had done to shame you; it was impossible to return to that and still remain yourself.

You could hear the voices of the guards and the officials who accompanied them, but couldn't catch individual words; they were spending more time watching than you would have expected, as if they were attending a test match, with lunch and tea breaks. Turning your head to one side or another, you could see cages just like yours, stretching out on either side, nine to the left, fifteen to the right, the furthest at the limits of your vision; some were in line with your cage, others were closer to the water. In the cage to your left was a young woman. Like you she was steeling her body, holding it in place so that the shackles would not cut into her extremities. You thought you recognized her from inside, but without any hair, and several metres distant, it was difficult to be sure. You clicked at her, as you had taught yourselves to do, but she did not respond; perhaps she had gone elsewhere, travelling. The guards were too far away to take any notice of what you were doing. Turning your head to the right, you found the cage on that side was closer, and you recognized a friend from inside. Together you had learned the ancient alphabet, taught by one of the first prisoners, the knowledge passed down over the years. To the guards, it was only noise, mumbo jumbo.

'Hello, friend. They're not watching us.'

'Did they bring you this morning?'

'I don't know. You should hold yourself up. Your wrists.'

'It's all over tomorrow, either way.'

You tried to remember how long you had been friends. You had met at least five years before being captured. Your bodies had not changed markedly; you were thinner now, your faces drawn, but you were still recognizable as yourselves.

'I won't scream. Will you?'

'No.'

There was no point in screaming. You thought you knew what it would be like to drown, you had almost done it at the age of three in the deep end of a pool. At first you had panicked, forced to swim out from the ladder into the depths, and then, finding yourself dropping to the bottom of the pool, you had relaxed, come to the end of your air, and suddenly found yourself on the concrete poolside, the mouth of the swimming instructor clamped on your own, the wrinkles in her face dripping with water, and a crescent of other children standing near you, looking curiously as the great fat woman breathed the world back into you. *It was not so bad almost drowning; I would have preferred it to resuscitation. Why did I panic? I knew how to swim; I swam before I walked. I was talking to someone, a boy with brown hair, and I was trying to tread water, and then I was under the surface, falling past those other small bodies, and the round abdomen of the swimming instructor.*

The light was beginning to shift, and a hot breeze blew down from the interior, throwing sand against your burned body, and you began to feel chilled, wracked by the nausea of sunburn that comes

259

when the light fails. The woman on your left and the friend on your right were also beginning to shiver and shake.

Is this where you end? Is this how you end?

It is my nightmare. I dream it every night, every hour, have dreamed it for two decades now.

It is all I can see.

PART II

SAM

Before I leave for Johannesburg tomorrow, Greg suggests a visit to my old neighbourhood. We stop first at the weekend market in the Old Biscuit Mill, jammed with hipster locals shopping for overpriced baked goods, handicrafts, African masks spray-painted matte white to make them look more chic. Alongside all that there are still the run-down shops on Albert Road, the car guards with manic arm motions insisting that it's fine to park on a solid line because everyone does it and the traffic police don't give a damn and anyway it's a Saturday so what could happen?

At the market we sit on hay bales and eat while Dylan plays with some other children. Greg seems to know everyone and after two hours of eating and playing and squeezing through the crowds to buy vegetarian wraps and pastries and iced coffees I tell him I'm going to look for my old house and will meet them later.

I dodge through the cars on Albert Road and with the map in my head walk back towards the

City Bowl; after a few blocks I turn up Dublin Street, cross Victoria, and turn off onto Kitchener.

Devil's Peak looms above, though it doesn't seem as massive as I remember it. And while the street hasn't changed much in two decades, it feels narrower, cramped and enclosed. Some of the houses are more dilapidated than they once were, others look like they've been recently refurbished, repainted and encased in burglar bars that enclose the front verandas. Kwaito pulses from one of the shabbier houses. Further up the hill, from a house with a new extension built above the original one-storey structure, there's the sound of a string quartet coming from a stereo, the windows all thrown open and the curtains limp with heat fluttering out through the bars.

I thought I would recognize the house without having to look for the number, but before I know it I'm at the intersection with Salisbury and have to retrace my steps to the house with the new extension, and then I see that they've knocked together our old house with the one next door. Both used to be white but the new structure is painted dark grey with black trim and has a glass and steel cube jutting out of the top in place of the original pitched roofs. There's a new gate and the whole front porch has been caged in burglar bars cast in geometrical patterns. Through the open windows I can see the interior: the walls have been painted the colour of blood, the ceiling clad with bamboo, Congolese masks hang on the walls – 'hectic, bad magic', Greg would say. A woman in one of the front rooms watches me through the window.

Three boys on bicycles ride past, shouting to one another. A cat runs across their path and they whoop until it disappears under a parked car. Above us a helicopter thwacks the air and in the distance, towards the mountain, car and taxi horns wail along Eastern Boulevard. I remember this as a quiet neighbourhood but maybe it never was.

The woman comes out on the porch and looks at me and then glances up and down the street as if she's expecting someone.

'Can I help you?' she shouts. Her accent isn't local – possibly German or Dutch.

'I used to live here – at least, in that half,' I say, pointing at the southernmost part of the house.

'Oh? Long time ago? We've been five years here. We put the two together. One was just too small. They were both real dumps. This street used to be hell. Now it's improving. Maybe we think of selling. I'll make you a good price. You want to buy it again? You lived here a long time ago I think?'

'Yes, a long time ago.' I see my parents in the front room as it used to be with its beige walls, my father hunched over his books at one end of the dining table, my mother banging on an old portable typewriter at the other, while I drew with crayons and pencils on lengths of white butcher paper unrolled across the bare floorboards.

'Oh, I guess so then.' The woman again looks

up and down the street. 'I'd invite you inside but I'm just now in the middle of making lunch and my husband isn't here and I don't usually invite in strange men if you see what I mean.'

'It's okay. I didn't expect to come inside.'

I try to imagine what version of my life would have allowed me to stay in Cape Town with my parents, to grow up in that house, to watch them grow old in it, perhaps finally to sell it and move somewhere quieter, a bungalow in Hermanus with views of the ocean, for the three of us to come back together and marvel at how the neighbourhood had and hadn't changed.

I feel it could have been that way if only I'd known what they were doing. But surely I must have known something about what they did when my father was not studying the law and my mother was not taking care of me or banging on the typewriter. Maybe the typewriter was part of it, though. They went out in the evenings and left me with Mrs Gush, the old woman who had no teeth and hissed songs into my ear and made cold 'soup' from ice cream and milk with tinned guavas sliced into it. Sometimes my father went away by himself for days or weeks at a time. Other times, friends of my parents – including Laura – would come over and talk through the night. I listened at my bedroom door and tried to understand what they were saying. Some of them weren't from here; they had strange accents or spoke broken English. My parents knew people from all over. That, I now understand, was also a part of it – the company they kept, the danger of their circle, both the formal and informal ties.

I must have been aware that something about our family was different. They would have let something significant slip. If I remember the type-writer, then I must have known that it was important in some way. Like Laura, my mother was a journalist. That was how they knew each other – that way, and perhaps other ways as well. Like my father, my mother had also studied the law; they had both been William Wald's students, but while my father finished his master's degree my mother helped support us by working as a journalist. Sometimes she took me with her in the car after school and I sat reading a book while she interviewed people. But when I searched through the archives of the *Cape Record*, the paper both she and Laura worked for, I could find no articles with my mother's by-line. Laura is there, but my mother is not. Perhaps she worked in some other capacity, as an editor or an assistant, or perhaps I've always been mistaken and she only let people believe she was a journalist because she was doing something else entirely.

I see my parents as I last remember them, on the porch of the house in Woodstock, the way it was when we lived here. They both lean over to kiss me as they leave me in the care of Mrs Gush. My father is in khaki trousers and a blue checked shirt. My mother has her hair tied back in a bandana and wears a red tank top and a wrap-around calico skirt. After they left, Mrs Gush sat in the lounge while I read a book in my bedroom. An hour after my parents were supposed to have been home, Mrs Gush came to ask me what I thought might have delayed them. I said I didn't know – they were going to see some friends. An hour after that the police were at the door. Mrs Gush took me outside and held me by the shoulders as the police searched the house. I couldn't understand why they were searching, and at the same time I knew exactly why. After half an hour they came out with books and files and my mother's typewriter. 'Someone will be in touch about the boy,' one of them said. 'Can you look after him tonight?' Mrs Gush protested and then they said that if she couldn't do it I would have to spend the night at the police station. When I realized they were taking my mother's typewriter I screamed and tried to pull it out of the arms of the officer who was carrying it. 'Won't you control this boy? Otherwise he's going to be in trouble just like his parents,' the policeman said. Mrs Gush pulled me away and took me back inside the house. Drawers had been emptied onto the floor and the furniture turned over, the bottoms of the couch and armchairs slashed open. My bedroom, always neat and tidy, had been twisted into a splatter of toys and books and clothes. I began to cry. Mrs Gush said there was no use crying and helped me put the house back together.

If I had known what my parents were planning, I have to believe I would have pleaded with them not to do it, not to do anything that would have put them in danger or risked taking them away from me. It isn't enough to say they were doing it for a 'good cause', or that they had 'noble aims'. The equation doesn't balance, the losses are too great.

★

I leave Cape Town this morning before the sun is up. Greg and Dylan stand at the gate with the dogs to wave me off. I'll drive to Colesberg today and on to Johannesburg tomorrow, in time to get the keys for the house we're taking over from Sarah's colleague before he leaves for his next posting. Sarah arrives Tuesday from New York.

On the drive I keep myself awake listening to the recordings of my interviews with Clare. It's also a way of distracting myself from the landscape, which, after leaving the Hex River Valley, settles into the monotony of the Karoo that I could never bring myself to love when I lived here. After Laingsburg there are long stretches of road maintenance and I sit in endless queues of traffic held up by female traffic wardens in orange uniforms; they perch in mobile white units, waiting to let the traffic proceed, while the pied crows hover and dive for scraps. When we move, we go at a crawl over rough surfaces, half-finished, corrugated and unstable with loose bits of asphalt that glint like coal dust against the paler layers of grit and gravel. This may be the main route through the country but it's still a two-lane road.

I listen to the recording of one of our later conversations, when I asked Clare if her parents – her father in particular, who was active in opposition politics from the early 1950s until his death in the mid-1980s – influenced her own political views.

'If you mean to ask whether they indoctrinated me, then be direct,' she says, and gives her dismissive cough, which explodes through the car's speakers. 'Don't prevaricate.'

'So did they, indoctrinate you?' I hate the way my voice sounds so tentative, obsequious and wheedling.

'Not quite in the way that you mean. Listen, my parents represented the first generations of their respective families to rise above the soil, to turn themselves into fully educated professionals, so they had a particular sensibility about the world. That is to say, they held a constellation of values that were both reverent of tradition – they were not exactly secular, while my grandparents and great-grandparents were, I think, seriously devout – but they were also naturally suspicious of totalizing and totalitarian ideologies, as well as authoritarian ones. By the end of their lives, my grandparents on both sides were, perhaps, in the process of being transformed into humanists by circumstance and experience and observation. They were latent progressives forced to look outward and forward, to imagine where possibility might lie for their children, my parents, beyond their rural and quite insular experience – men and women who were in the process of *passing from orthodoxy*, as much as Methodists might ever be called orthodox, or were compelled by history to make that passage, to alter their view of the world because of what they witnessed happening around them, though the Methodists had what we might call a fair if imperfect record in this country. My parents, on the other hand, seemed to have entered the world as fully formed humanists who were religiously observant in a rather casual and fluid way – my mother more than my father, though.' At that moment, as I recall, Clare was distracted by one of her gardeners, who started up a lawn mower that registers as indistinct static in the background of the recording. 'That man does make a terrible noise, doesn't he? I'll ask him to stop.' She shouts out the window in Xhosa and closes it abruptly, but the gardener continued, I remember, and the sound of the mower is still audible, making some of her words difficult to pick up. 'What I'm saying is, our parents might have trained my sister and me in the ways of their faith, had us christened and confirmed, but I was never instructed that I had to marry one kind of man or another, although if I had come home with an Afrikaner or a Jew or a Muslim, or especially a man who was not white, I have no doubt that would have given them pause – pause or worse than pause. I think of their shock when Nora announced her engagement to Stephan, and my mother was not entirely happy when she discovered that my own intended was from a Catholic family, no matter that he himself was an atheist. Even humanists have blind spots.'

'But did they indoctrinate you, politically speaking?'

I remember Clare looking surprised at my implicit suggestion that she hadn't answered the question. There is a long pause in the conversation as the noise of the mower continues. I can hear the blade catch on a tree root or a stone. I hear myself shift on the couch, move a folder against the recorder, and click my pencil to advance the lead.

'I was about to say that obviously they had, given the relative unity of my and their political beliefs. But there is nothing obvious about that relationship. My sister was as un-indoctrinated by my parents as it was possible to be. She chose the opposite way. So it was not inevitable, it was not a natural relationship. It is a question I cannot entirely answer. I do not know, in the end, how much influence parents can have over the beliefs of their children, or how they choose to act on those beliefs. One can but sow the seed and provide the proper environment, and hope that the flower promised by the illustration on the packet is the one that will grow, trust that the hybrid will not revert to the characteristics of some earlier generation, or be so transformed by unpredictable and wholly external factors – a drought, a storm, environmental pollution – that the seed mutates and something unrecognizable grows.'

'And that is what you're suggesting happened with your sister?'

'A mutant, yes. Nora's soil, the water she drank, the air she inhaled, it was all polluted. And while she and I grew up with the same conditions, more or less, I had higher tolerance, natural immunities against the environment that tried so hard to twist our growth to its own malign purpose. But not Nora. She was always susceptible. She was weak.'

'And your daughter? Would you say that you indoctrinated her?' I hear the tension in my voice, the way it suddenly sounds choked, afraid of the very words it says.

'Sometimes a plant is more vigorous than its parent. But Laura – I do not wish to speak about her, as you well know.'

I stop in Beaufort West for lunch, buy a sandwich, and sit in the car down the street from Ellen's old house. The town looks unchanged since I was last here, except for the new speed cameras and the sign warning that it's a WATER SCARCE AREA; the dam is dangerously low and they have to truck in water from elsewhere. After years in the States I'm struck by how American the town seems – the American fast-food franchises, the strip motels, the scrap-metal yard and trailers. Only the occasional sign in Afrikaans or Xhosa reminds me where I am, and the residential architecture, the township, and the people themselves. Demographically, it's like taking a small town in the Deep South and plopping it in the middle of a Nevada wasteland.

Ellen's old house looks as unchanged as the town, and I realize I'm parked in the same place that Lionel and Timothy must have stopped twenty years ago.

'Is that the house?' Lionel asked. Of the two, he was always the more concerned about me.

'Yes, it's that one,' I said, looking out the rear window. I had been there enough times to show them the way from the outskirts of town. Though I didn't know the exact address, from the prison roundabout I could find the house without difficulty. At the time there was bougainvillea with orange flowers growing all along the roof and spilling down to enclose the front porch with heavy drapes of leaves and flowers. The porch is now bare – less cover for anyone to hide.

Lionel had handed me the bag that contained everything I owned.

'You'll call us if you need anything, if it doesn't work out,' he said. I nodded and said goodbye. I hadn't known them long enough to feel anything at the parting, except a kind of hope that I wouldn't need to call on them, that everything with my aunt would be perfect.

They sat in the car watching as I walked up the street and knocked on Ellen's door. Before I went inside, I turned back to look. Lionel waved, Timothy turned over the engine and they drove off. I've never seen them again.

*

I rely on the satnav to direct me through the swirl of Gauteng roads, the N1 to the N12 and into central Johannesburg on the M1, then off and up leafy Jan Smuts Avenue, past the zoo, left at the Goodman Gallery and onto Chester Road, then right at 1st Avenue and a hundred metres further up on the left side. Despite the rush-hour traffic I'm in front of the house in dizzying time and find that when I finally let go of the steering wheel my hands are shaking and I'm out of breath.

From the street the house is invisible: the property appears to be nothing but a white wall concealing a forest of trees with a gate on the left side protecting a long brick-paved driveway. Halfway up the street there's a small wooden shed, just large enough for one person, where a private security guard sits on a black plastic conference chair twenty-four hours a day, monitoring the whole block, from Chester up to 7th Avenue.

I buzz the intercom at the entrance and Jason, Sarah's colleague, lets me in; the last three Africa correspondents for the paper have occupied this ersatz Cape Dutch house. 'It's what Americans prefer,' Jason says, handing over a ring with no less than thirty keys on it and showing me around. 'Big, old, high ceilings, high walls, heavy security, nice area. You'll be fine here.' There's a garden cottage at the back, once intended for a live-in maid, which Sarah will use as an office, and a shiny black SUV that comes with the job. Jason gives me the names and cell numbers for the domestic worker and the gardener, the utility and telecoms account numbers and passwords, the password and emergency number for the security company, a list of decent restaurants in the area, and a whole booklet of information pertaining to security – where it's safe to go, where it isn't. Nowhere, according to the pamphlet, is especially safe to walk alone, even in the daytime. Drive if at all possible, and tell someone where you're going, when you expect to arrive, and when you'll be back. This seems excessive to me, but then I've never lived in Johannesburg and can only go by the stories I've heard. Jason points out the panic buttons – at least one in every room, sometimes two or three – and gives me two mobile panic buttons on lariats that Sarah and I can wear around our necks.

'You should wear these at all times,' he says, 'because you just never know when the woman who comes to the gate selling mealies might actually be a man in a fat suit with a gun. You don't want to end up murdered in your bed. Change the passwords regularly. Rose has worked for me four of the last five years and I'd trust her with my life. Andile, the gardener, you have to watch like a hawk, but as long as he comes on a day that Rose is here she'll do that for you and you won't have to worry. But you're a local, I hardly need to tell you all this.'

I offer to drive Jason to the airport, but he's already arranged a car service, and half an hour after arriving I'm left alone in this luxury bunker. Growing up I could never have imagined that I'd live like this, with staff (even if part-time), two cars, a swimming pool, and security as extensive and high-tech as anything Greg has in Cape Town.

I order a pizza – 'Never let a delivery man in, always take the food through the slot in the gate,' Jason warned me – and then phone Sarah before she leaves for the airport. We've adjusted to these separations, though in the past it's always been her work that has taken her away from home instead of mine, and that's only going to continue once she arrives. After the holidays she'll be off to Angola for two weeks to cover the oil industry; Nigeria after that, Sierra Leone, and no telling where else. She's braver than I am, so I know I don't need to worry about how she'll adjust to living here. Given the work, she's unlikely to be in Johannesburg more than half the year.

With the TV news in the background, I get online to look at the profiles of my new colleagues at the university. Like the jobs I've had before, this is only a fixed-term position. Sarah's is the job that

matters, at least for now, and the one that deter-
mines where we live and for how long.

On a whim, I search the university site for anyone
named Timothy or Lionel. Not knowing their
surnames, I've been looking for likely Lionels and
Timothys over the years, but there are countless
people with the same first names in the archive of
TRC testimony – the first place I thought to search
– and none of them seems to match the little I
know about either of the men or their activities.

There's a hit in the Anthropology Department
for a Professor Lionel Jameson. I click on the link
for his staff profile. When his picture comes up, I
know at once it's the right man.

Sarah's flight is delayed so I wait at the Woolworths
in the concourse of shops between the International
and Domestic Terminals. I order a bran muffin
and coffee and sit at the long white communal
table, my back to the entrance.

After a few sips of the coffee, a hand reaches
into my space, dropping a tattered rectangle of
brown cardboard next to the saucer. I look up to
see a giant scarecrow of a man who doesn't make
eye contact with me, but just stands there. In a
scrawl of Afrikaans on one side and broken English
on the other, the slip explains that he is deaf and
needs money. I'm short on cash, so I give him a
five-rand coin, dropping it into his hand, which
stretches out the moment I reach for my wallet.
A look of disappointment flashes across his face

when he registers what the coin is, like he can't believe I'd be giving him so little. He doesn't thank me, still won't even look at my face – does nothing to acknowledge the coin apart from appearing crestfallen. Without bothering anyone else, he walks out of the store, and as he goes I see that his jeans are completely sodden and stained. He's doubly incontinent, and only then do I smell it, as he's walking away, unharassed by the security guard. The jeans are frayed to above the ankles and his shoes are both missing the heel and quarter, the entire back part of the shoe, so they're more like clogs, flapping and thwacking the floor with each step. I watch him leave and go back to eating my twenty-rand bran muffin, which tastes like the best muffin I've ever had and has been served with a ramekin of grated cheddar cheese and an individual pot of jam. I wonder in a surge of irritation why the guard, a plump uniformed woman who seems aware of nothing in particular except the romance novel she's reading, failed to stop the man from coming in to bother paying customers. I'm outraged, and just as suddenly I can't believe that I'm outraged, and then I become outraged at my own outrage. I worry that Sarah will regret moving here the minute she's off the plane and we're surrounded by men offering to help us, to show us the way, to carry our bags: a minefield of opportunists, the genuinely desperate and the criminal.

Sarah finally arrives and when I see her come

through the doors from customs I feel a flood of relief to be with her again. I hate these separations because they always remind me of other separations. Men offering taxis and directions begin to swarm. I pull us out of the melee to a quieter corner. She kisses me and I try to feel calm, but I can't help looking past her to be sure no one swipes the luggage.

She laughs at my vigilance. 'Please, Sam, this place makes JFK look like a third-world country. Where's the car? How are you? You're so tanned.' She studies me and at the same time takes in everything around her. I want to tell her to be careful, to remember where she is, that you can't let down your guard for a moment. I have to remind myself she's been here before, she knows how things work and knows better than I do how to look after herself.

In the car I ask her if she remembers what she said when we first got together.

'That you need to relax?' she laughs, her head swivelling around and staring past me to look at the skyline of the city centre.

'You told me you admired my courage to come halfway across the world to a place where I didn't know anyone. And you said you weren't sure you could do the same.'

Sarah braces against the car door as I merge through the fluid lanes of rush-hour traffic. 'I don't remember saying that, honey, but that was more than a decade ago. My father was a good model.

He threw himself into so many different places. I knew when this job opened up that I had to apply. You've lived in my country. Now it's time for me to live in yours for a while.'

At the house we rearrange the furniture that Jason and other correspondents have left behind. We'll need to buy chairs, a new couch, but will wait until the container arrives with our things. For now we can live with what's here. Though she's exhausted, Sarah feels compelled to check in with her editor in New York. There's no gradual settling in with a job like this – she'll be working on a story from first thing tomorrow, getting herself set up, 'learning the lay of the land,' she says, with the kind of enthusiasm that made me fall for her in the first place. There's a study in the main house where I can work when I'm at home. The garden cottage has always functioned as the resident correspondent's office space, and we've agreed it should continue that way – a clear separation between work and home, even if they're only a few metres apart. In any case, I'll have an office at the university. Before going to bed, I send Clare a message, my first communication to her since our last meeting.

★

Dear Clare,
I write with greatest appreciation and gratitude for your patience over the last four months. I hope,

as you say, that we'll meet again. It seems likely that I'll return to Cape Town at some point in the next year.

I have started to transcribe the interviews and will undoubtedly have further questions as I begin to map the shape of the book. In some cases I may send you the transcript if the recording is poor. In fact, I include a transcript here, from early on in the process, where the sound suddenly goes and your voice with it. I think there was a house alarm going off in the background. I've done my best but there are some unintelligible passages and I would be grateful if you felt able to reconstruct what they might have been (or to construct them anew or revise them or insist on their irrelevance).

I hope I do not overstep the mark in saying that the last four months have been transformative for me in so many ways. It is my fondest hope that we'll meet again someday soon and continue our conversations. I also hope that you may be able to forgive me for my less honourable questions and revelations at our last meeting.

With all best wishes for a happy holiday season and prosperous New Year,

Sam Leroux

*

I hold it together until we're in bed, and then, finding the reassurance of Sarah next to me, the experiences of the last four months all burst from my face, running out of me, my heart seizing up, limbs twitching. I lose control, I rock, shake against her as she holds me, wait for her to put me back together again.

ABSOLUTION

Now that the terribly hot days had all but passed and the mist fell down more abundantly from the mountain, spreading its cloth of ephemeral whiteness through Clare's garden, she gave Marie, who so rarely had a holiday, the week off for Easter.

'I do not know how I shall cope on my own,' Clare said, performing an exasperation she did not entirely feel. 'I have almost forgotten how to cook.'

'Shame, Clare. You'd think you were helpless. Listen, I've left meals in the freezer and all you have to do is take one out in the morning, let it defrost throughout the day, and just put it in the oven in the evening. I've written up some instructions for each one,' Marie said, tying a scarf round her neck and handing Clare a printed sheet with cooking and household directions for each day of her absence. Marie was going to see a niece in Rustenburg and had plans to indulge in a little gambling, church going, and game viewing in the Pilanesberg Reserve. 'I'm going to see a black rhino this time, finally. I've never seen a black rhino. And a *wildehond*. I can't tell you how I long to see one of those. The countryside in that part of the world is unequalled in my mind. It is where I shall retire –' she said, laughing, and then caught herself, a hand to the mouth in tentative regret. She was already past retirement age and for her to suggest the end of her working career was somehow also to imply the end of Clare's life. For all that Clare knew they lacked common ground on the most basic and fundamental beliefs, Marie was a more efficient archivist and manager and all around help-mate than Clare had any hope of finding elsewhere. Mutual disagreement was part of their contract, and while she had no wish to hear Marie's old-fashioned opinions on the majority government or blacks in general or the rights of sexual minorities, Clare could not live without her; it was impossible to conceive of going forward without Marie.

With no one else to flick switches or close cupboards, open doors or answer the telephone on the rare occasions it rang, the few sounds that did occur of their own accord were magnified, rever-berating as if in an echo chamber and imposing themselves upon Clare's ears as a tangible rush of pressure. The crunch of the freezer contracting brought Clare to her feet, certain that someone must be in the kitchen, that perhaps Marie had changed her mind and would not abandon her after all, or that an intruder had somehow managed to stride across the dry grass, disable the alarm, force the locks, and was brazenly liberating Clare's posses-sions in the next room. This was how it would happen, alone, the predators of the world sensing Clare's vulnerability, the oldest member of the pack abandoned by the others and left for dead, for nature to work its efficient illusionism in which those who disappear are not merely offstage, slipped through a trapdoor, but are gone entirely, bodily.

After a day of starting even at the wind at the door, Clare spent twenty minutes closing all the curtains and blinds against the fast-falling night. Then, in a moment of irrational panic, she engaged the armoured external shutters that motored into place, sliding with the penitentiary ping of metal meeting metal. The special ventilation system came on automatically, blowing air of such bracing freshness, the moist feral smell of the mountain rushing in, that Clare felt almost liberated in her cell. She would put the alarm on later. She had never used the shutters before, insisting to Marie they would not succumb to the siege mentality. Unlike her neighbours' houses, there was no threatening plaque with the face of an Alsatian on her perimeter wall, only the wall itself and its subtle fortifications, its shocking iron ivies and invisible motion-detector beams. The electrified wires bore no warning of GEVAAR or INGOZI, those conscientious betrayals alerting the criminal to present danger. Those who would dare to intrude, Clare had decided, could risk pain or worse.

The defrosted meal for the first day of Marie's absence was a tuna quiche typical of her culinary skills, which had been honed in the middle part of the last century when tinned vegetables and commercially preserved meats had their vogue. Since moving to the house Clare had taken to eating in front of the television, fatigued by the formality of laying a table every night, the two of them sitting and trying to make polite conversation about days that were so alike as to be indistinguishable one from the other. Now they had adopted a new pattern. Putting out a small dish of pretzels or potato chips for Clare, shredded kudu biltong for herself, and two glasses of wine poured from a box, Marie would ask at six each evening whether Clare wanted *table or trays*. Although making a performance of considering her mood, Clare would nonetheless now always settle on *trays*. Then they would sit in the lounge, eating from the freestanding wooden trays and watching Marie's favourite soap operas. Outraged at the latest high jinks and proof of social chaos the soap stories seemed to offer, Marie would comment on the lives of the characters as if they were real people. 'It's this teenage pregnancy story again,' she would say, shaking her head and clicking her tongue against her palate. 'Remember earlier this year Teresa was pregnant from Frikkie.' Or 'It's this whole discrimination story again, as if we haven't had enough of that already.' *Story* for *problem* or *palaver* – it was a way that Clare's sister and the Pretorius in-laws once had of speaking. After a couple hours of such entertainment Clare would excuse herself, going to bed with a book, which she would read on and off throughout the night between short periods of sleep.

Without Marie, Clare went through the evening routine on her own as well as she could, although she became distracted by the news and overcooked the quiche, having to peel a layer of burned custard from the top. She forced herself to make a salad, eating without much appetite in front of the television. It was half in her mind to watch something other than the two soap operas that she and Marie usually followed, but the theme tune of the first came on and she was surprised to find that she wanted to know what was happening with Teresa and Frikkie and Zinzi and Thapelo. At some point she fell asleep with the tray rolled to one side and woke after nine with an American action movie banging across the screen. The dishes would have to wait until morning. She piled them in the sink, knowing that Marie would be disgusted.

'Dirty dishes attract vermin,' Marie would have said. 'And I don't just mean mice and roaches, but *snakes*, I'm telling you. I heard that Mrs Van der Westhuizen had snakes last month because she'd been leaving the dishes out for her girl to do the next morning.'

Mice and roaches, snakes and other creatures, they were welcome tonight if they wished, provided they could penetrate the shutters that transformed the carapace of the house into a patchwork of steel and stone.

Clare was too tired to read, but kept the book she was trying to finish next to her on the bed. At some point in the night she would be wide awake and need to make the hours pass. Initially she had blamed the house for her insomnia, convinced there was something wrong with its chemistry. She'd had it tested by half a dozen environmental experts and no problems were detected. Then she had been certain it was the orientation of the structure, or some shortcoming in the way she and Marie had arranged the furniture. Though not believing in such things, she had consulted a woman from Mowbray who claimed to be a feng shui master. She made small adjustments to the placement of chairs and sofas, turned Clare's bed to face the window, hung two mirrors, and pronounced the space well balanced for a house of its kind. This still did not solve the problem. Then Clare had paid a German interior designer from Constantia to repaint all the rooms in soothing neutral colours with non-toxic paint, but this made no difference either.

'Maybe it's a problem with you and not with the house,' Marie had said. 'I have no trouble sleeping myself, unless I forget to drink enough water during the day and then I get the most *terrible* cramps in the middle of the night.'

Clare snorted and rolled her eyes.

'I'm only suggesting that maybe you should see someone about it. They say that insomnia may be, what did they say – ?'

'You've been playing doctor online again. Practising medicine without a licence.'

'– *indicative*. They say that insomnia may be *indicative* of a more serious problem.' There again was the click of the tongue, one hand on the waist, one pointing in accusation. 'You should get it checked out, I'm telling you.'

More to satisfy Marie than out of any hope of a cure, Clare had subjected herself to blood work, heart monitors, and brain scans. All established there was nothing physically wrong with her – she was remarkably healthy for a woman of her age. Her doctor suggested psychoanalysis, but this was something she could not face. She spoke with her cousin Dorothy, who had suffered insomnia in the past, and she suggested Clare consult a traditional healer, a sangoma.

'They know what they're doing. It's not just witch doctor's bones and that kind of nonsense. They use herbs. It might help,' she had said. 'It couldn't hurt, I don't think, if you get a reputable one.'

'Where is one meant to find what you call a "reputable" traditional healer?'

'Look in the phonebook – or ask your gardener. They always know.'

Clare worried that Adam might misconstrue such a request and could not bring herself to do it. More to the point, the *kwaksalwers* of 'western' medicine were one thing, diviners and interpreters of the spirit world, mediums for the souls of ancestors, quite another.

Certain the problem would eventually go away, she stopped fighting the insomnia and made an accommodation with it, coming to know it as a shadow self that, like an infant, commanded attention and amusement and sustenance. It would not be cajoled into silence until some number of pages had been read, notes taken, thoughts rearranged into a tentative grid of stillness and order, each tucked tidily in its compartment, maintaining the peace for an hour or two until the insomnia grew bored or restless and demanded the game start all over again, thoughts spinning themselves in circles of frenetic repetition. It was a way of being, if an unsatisfactory one.

When her husband had first left her and she was forced to sleep alone after all those years spent with a warm body beside her, Clare had been astonished at how cold the bed was with only her bones to fill it. He left in winter and for the first few nights she had continued to sleep on her customary side, nearest the door, stuffing pillows along what had been William's side to block the draught created by her own body. After a week of being crowded by these soft objects that remained lifeless and motionless, never adjusting themselves to her nocturnal movements, she realized the most sensible thing was to sleep in the middle of the mattress, flexing her body to its limits. This helped with the warmth, but ultimately she blamed that earlier bout of insomnia on William's absence. They were still cordial with each other, although he had left her for another woman, someone only a year younger than she. It seemed to suggest that her husband's straying attention had nothing to do with Clare's face or ageing body, but instead that he had grown tired of her personality. A month after his departure, she had phoned him to complain.

'I cannot sleep without you,' she snapped.

'Take a lover,' he said, in a way that sounded half-mocking. 'Or get a blow-up doll.'

'Don't be ridiculous, William. I can't get used to the extra space. You've left a gap.'

'Then downsize. Buy yourself a luxurious single bed, a canopy. Make yourself over into a dowager princess.' He could be like this, teasing in a way he claimed was affectionate.

There was a silence between them on the line. On his end, only the other side of the city, around the mountain on the Atlantic coast, she could hear seagulls braying.

'Did I do something wrong?' she asked. 'Was there something else I should have done?'

He sighed and she could hear him adjusting the receiver against his face, the microphone amplifying the sound of the plastic surface making contact with his stubble.

'No, my dear, there's nothing else you could have done or should have done. Don't torment yourself by thinking that you failed to do anything. You can blame me with good reason and tell everyone that's the case. The acrimony can come raining down on my head. I've been selfish and I'm not proud of it, but there it is. The truth is, I'm happy now. I imagine I would have been happy in a different way if I'd gone on living with you, if I'd never met – sorry, I know you don't want to hear about her.'

'What is her name?'

There was another pause and a hesitation and then he said, as if the name itself were a sigh or exhalation of breath, 'Aisyah.'

In a flash Clare had understood. William's leaving really did have nothing to do with her. There had been many mistresses in the past, she knew, including a number of his students. She had suspected on one or two occasions that the relationships had resulted in serious complications and entanglements and unforeseen responsibilities. But with this new woman it was all about the possibility of a wholly different kind of life, a new way of living in a country alive to new promise.

That she might not wake in profound darkness, alone in her new house that would always feel too large, too self-directing and sentient, able to reorganize its own architecture into something completely unexpected – a museum or morgue, for instance – the moment its inhabitants lapsed in their vigilance, Clare left the light on in the passage and put herself to bed.

After an hour of turning first left and then right she had nearly fallen asleep when there was a sudden interruption in the light, as if from a momentary power outage – or worse, from the movement of

293

someone passing between her and the door. She lay as still as she could, listening for a noise, remembering she had forgotten to engage the alarm. There was no sound apart from the hum of the ventilation system and the soughing flow of air, but Clare was certain she had registered a change in the light through her closed eyelids. She supposed it might have been a power outage – *load shedding* was the supplier's euphemism, as if provision of a basic service were a burden to be borne – but it had not felt like that, and the transition from the public utilities to her own generator should have been seamless. No, there were people in her house, friends or family of her dead brother-in-law, one of his six brothers and sisters or countless cousins, men and women as old as Clare herself, come to remind her once again of the knowledge they possessed about her. The removal and return of the wig was not enough; now they were intent on tormenting her in new and more terrible ways. As with the invasion at the old house on Canigou Avenue, her heart took over, beating in terror and outrage that anyone should dare to enter.

The light was interrupted again, and then remained so, half of what it should have been. Someone was standing in the doorway to Clare's room. If this is going to be the end of me, let it come, she thought, and opened her eyes.

CLARE

I cannot bear it any more, my vision, conjured out of horrible imagination, of you trussed like a lean pig, waiting for your fate in that titanium cage, clicking for your sanity. I try again what I have tried before. I offer you the cup, a song of my own invention, and wish for you to cohere again, my wandering daughter. In the garden I make a fire of dried leaves from the neighbour's eucalyptus tree and a pile of twigs cut last winter from the branches of the stinkwood. It crackles and smokes and turns itself over into a gentle blaze. I pour honey and milk on the flames, a glass of wine, and water that has run down from the mountain. In the absence of barley, I sprinkle white cornmeal over the fire, grinding the grain between my palms. I do it correctly this time. I pray to you Laura, plead with you to come forth, promise to sacrifice a black sheep in your honour. I prick my finger to summon you, extract a drop of my blood to body you forth. I did not do it properly before: the bloodshed was only in my mind. I drone and squeak. I dance with steps of my own devising, an unbalanced dervish, hair in the wind, a blue crane, a crone. I keen as I should have keened before. The ibises watch me and cry out in chorus.

I wait until the fire burns itself out, knock the coals apart, heap them with ash, see the windows of my neighbour's house go black as, bored by my theatrics, he finally puts himself to bed. I told Marie I did not wish to be disturbed, but no doubt my neighbour has been watching as neighbour-men do, passing judgement in his way. He will tell the other neighbours, the grandees of the Constantia Club, that Clare Wald practises witchcraft. They will read the new book to see if there are any hints to the nature of my devilry. I predict a spike in local sales. I no longer care if I am seen and thought mad – or worse, sane and an agent of evil.

In the darkness with the moon spitting off the mountain, I sit before my pile of ash, running my fingers through the grey feather-petals. Silence, and breeze that stirs the cinders, but you have not come. Myth is only myth. Perhaps you are too long dead. Perhaps the recipe or incantation had a flaw.

I go inside, locking the doors behind me, engaging the alarm that makes Marie and me feel secure until morning. With the disappointment at your failure to appear, there is also comfort. If you do not rise, there is still a chance you are not dead. But if not dead, then where are you, Laura? Where have you taken yourself? It does not seem possible that you would wander the world without contacting one of us – and if not your father or me, then at least your brother. You cannot still be in captivity; that is only a discomforting fantasy. No, you can only be dead, and I am no believer in the supernatural. It was foolish to pretend I was.

I shower and roll myself into bed, crack my back straight, turn on my side, and bury my head half in the pillow. In sleep I drift through dreams of you, always dreams of you abandoning me, and if not abandoning, then caged, your body exposed, waiting to be consumed by sharks, the bones picked by palm-nut vultures when the tide goes out, bones sinking into the estuary silt, waiting for the next age to discover you, this country's own bog woman, victim of the gladiatorial ring with victims of your own.

My scream pulls me out of sleep and I sit erect in bed, blankets swirling around me, because I felt your breath and the coldness of your hand, and now, out of sleep, you come screaming back at me on black rag wings burned with blood, chanting a haunting cry into my eyes. You worm yourself between my toes and infect my bowels, a tapeworm foetus angry for rebirth.

I wake up screaming, and Marie comes to my door. She is the keeper of my secrets. I could never let her go. 'Nothing is wrong,' I say, 'only a bad dream.'

But it was no dream, and you have not come alone.

As quickly as you arrive you disappear into the shadows, leaving only Nora, who flies on currents of white noise, the sound of wind coming down the mountain or the air of this house being stirred by its hidden rotors.

She arrives with the murmur of two cushions compressing, air being forced out by her weight, the ripping sound of two pieces of fabric rubbing warp against weft. She sits on the chair nearest my bedroom door. I know immediately it is Nora, and her presence is so real that my brain, lesioned by trauma, tells my hand to reach for the panic button until I hear Nora's voice in my head, warning me that she will be long gone by the time the security guards have arrived and I will be made to look like a mad old woman, asked if I have been sleeping well, if I have spoken to my doctor about the things I think I've seen, if I am taking all my medication. I take no medication.

'Then perhaps you should,' she says.

Nora's voice, the sing-song amusement of young womanhood, consumes me in an acid bath. I know it as well as the voice of my parents and your own lost voice, Laura. I can summon you all to ring in my mind, you and your brother, your father, my dead and my living. I can speak all of you aloud in my own feminine way. And now I learn I can summon you all too well. I want to send you back. I have made a mistake! This is all the proof I need. I accept you are dead, now leave the living in peace.

My sister, the Nora I have unwittingly conjured, has a sense of humour that she lacked in life. She sits with me for hours through this night, passing comment on my works, all the books she never had the chance to read, speculating on their meaning. She has turned herself into an eternal reader, benefitting from the underworld's great lending library. Rightly, she finds herself in each of my books, appearing in one form or another, sometimes young, more often old, male and female, human or lesser animal. Once I cast her as a hurricane, a storm of such unpredictable ferocity that it defeated the meteorologists and destroyed an unprepared swath of American shoreline. Another time she was a drought of long duration, teasing the suffering heroine with storm clouds that never broke into rain. She is an admirably flexible talent, bending to suit my purpose.

She wears the yellow taffeta cocktail dress in which I last saw her, its skirt arranged coquettishly around her knees, spine erect, lips pursed into her customary pout. Her skin remains firm where mine is now loose, her eyes bright and clear where mine have lately begun to dim, to cloud, wandering independent of my will. The only change I see in her now is the presence of a round, dark cavity. It is a perfect circle on the left side of her face: a hole into which one might insert a finger. Around it a reddish-black fire rages in quiet stillness across the surface of her pale skin. It is the hole for which I must bear responsibility, the fatal orifice and eternal flame burning from beneath a marble slab. In the last moment of her life it opened to consume three-quarters of her face.

'I have only been speaking about myself. But how are *you*, dear sister?' she finally says after hours of explicating my texts. 'By the by that last book was a *triumph* if I may say so, but what a lot of obscenities. Mother and Father were not at all sure what to make of the language.' After another quarter hour of such annoying small talk – not quite my idea of a proper haunting – she falls silent and approaches me, her movements halting as if her bones were centuries older than my own, and leans over, placing her hand against my heart. I feel pressure as through the cold numbness of anaesthesia, and then that pressure penetrates my skin and wraps itself around the beating organ, slowing the heart to a less panicked time. I wish I could say that her trick does not frighten me, but in fact it does. My hands tremble; I mewl like a kitten and ask her to stop.

I try to consider the situation with my usual logic. It occurs to me that I might actually be asleep, and that I am experiencing a new kind of dream giving vent to the guilt I have carried for so long. The problem with this logic is that my customary stress dreams are always of an entirely different order and have no physical effects.

Some weeks ago I dreamed that I was visiting a busy European city, half Paris, half London, walking from one side of the metropolis to the other, at once escaping some ill-defined threat and running towards an appointment whose exact nature I could not discern, but which I knew I could not afford to miss. At the intersection of two wide boulevards I was compelled by a local guide, a short woman with a brown pageboy and wire-rimmed spectacles who spoke with a stammer, to take a detour into a subterranean museum, the entrance to which was red and mouth-like, the walls scarlet and stairs black – altogether a quite unimaginative rendering of hell – from whence clouds of steam billowed. I was wearing a wool coat that I had recently bought in my waking life, and which I decided to leave at the entrance, knowing it would be too hot to wear inside. I assumed I would only be a few moments and that no harm could come to it. Once I had made my way down into the museum (which had exhibits that made little sense – dioramas of civic worthies who had been recast by history as traitors and rogues, a tableau of slum clearances, a collection of the skulls of murder victims housed in reliquary boxes), the air cooled by several degrees and I began to shiver. At the same time that I felt need of my coat once again, I realized that in order to continue my journey I would have to progress to the very end of the museum, on the other side of the river that bisected the city. Only forward movement was allowed. It was impossible to turn around and retrieve my coat, and in realizing this I felt the tour guide had tricked me into abandoning the very thing I would need most on my visit. It was forbidden to go back to the entrance and every time I attempted to do so I found that the museum itself had closed off its passages behind me, walls and gates and barriers rolling themselves into place. The coat was lost – I had no idea on which street the entrance to the museum had been, meaning that I would, in all likelihood, never retrieve it. This sudden loss filled me with a dread disproportionate to the real value of the thing – coats and clothes are not, moreover, items that much trouble me in waking life. A garment has utility and may be replaced when worn out or, indeed, lost. I have never endowed my own clothing with sentimental attachment.

Last night I dreamed that I had agreed to reprise a role I'd played as a girl in a school production of a holiday-themed play, filling in for an ill performer as the adolescent love interest of the main character. But as the night of the performance approached, I realized I had failed to study the script and knew none of the character's lines. Nor could I remember the blocking, which, it occurred to me, would have changed anyway since it was a new interpretation of the story. More significantly, at the last minute I agreed to take the unsympathetic lead role, which I had never studied. The character had the most lines and was on stage for nearly every minute of the play. As I was panicking about learning the script, which I could not even locate, an old lover phoned to ask if he should come to the performance and I insisted, yes, he *must* come, and he *must* bring his mother (a common woman with a weakness for

Victorian sentimentality, she had been a pub landlady in London's East End) because she would
love it – a haunting production, it was done with
the utmost professionalism, with extraordinary
sets and wonderful performers, a genuine evoca-
tion of nineteenth-century Christmas festivity.
When I hung up I felt sick, knowing there was
nothing remotely professional about my failure to
prepare my lines.

I know what such dreams mean. The loss of the
coat, being tricked into abandoning something I
will need in the future that protects and comforts,
I can only assume is about the fear of disposses-
sion, of becoming dispossessed. I would not believe
in such things if the dream and its variations were
not so persistent in my unconscious life. The
dream of ill-preparedness is more obvious, and
comes most often when I am worried about an
impending public appearance. I know why this
dream has returned. I have agreed to something
I should never have, the appearances at the
Winelands Literary Festival in five months' time
that will put me before my public, such as it is,
and the series of lectures in Johannesburg that are
the price Mark has extracted from me for hijacking
his identity in the new book. It is a kind of expo-
sure I can barely stomach.

But Nora's presence, and your own brief coming,
Laura, does not have the quality of a dream. If it is
not an actual haunting, then it is some kind of
hallucination or delusion, a projection of my own

disturbed mind. And if that is what it is, like the insomnia I have been suffering off and on for the last several years (perhaps it is even an effect of the insomnia, the hallucination brought on by sleep deprivation), then I can see no point in resisting it.

'You wish to do what? To make me realize my faults and my failings, I suppose,' I say to Nora now. 'To remind me of everything I did to wrong you.'

'Yes, there is that,' Nora says, a smirk pushing out through her pout, a smirk and a pout we share. 'And after all, *you* have summoned *us*. What's more, you're not sufficiently *penitent*, Clare. You are a *terrible* sinner, and yet you don't go to church, you ignore tradition, you do nothing to demonstrate that you regret or repent.'

'Each person has her own form of repentance. I repent in my own way, in private,' I insist. 'I repent in ways that even you, the dead, may not see.'

'And if I am, as you appear to think at this very moment, nothing but some hallucination of your own mind, then wouldn't that suggest your attempts at repentance have failed?' Nora shakes her head and those eyes that so often flashed in fury, eyes that screamed and raged as loudly as her voice when she bellowed wrath at me as a child, eyes that judged and condemned, autocratic as any dictator, grow gentle before me.

We sit in silence for a further hour in the middle of the night, two sisters, so alike, separated by time. 'Is this the price I must pay,' I finally bring myself to ask, 'this waking of the living?'

'Price? You speak of a single price? There is not one price. There are many prices for what you have done, all the acts you have committed. Prices, debts, and balances against you, Clare. You have but begun to repay them.'

★

Now that I have summoned you and Nora, brought you forth, how do I make you go, Laura? If I wore black, if I fasted and lit candles and recited incantations, retreated to hermitage caves in the wilderness, perhaps you would allow me to live out the rest of my days and nights unmolested.

After her wedding, her embrace of her husband's church, Nora chastised me for failing to be observant. 'Faith is what you need,' she said. 'You need faith to put you on a better course. You are an evil woman, Clare, and someday that evil will catch you up.'

'As a child I played at faith,' I remember saying, furious that she should presume to lecture me about something so personal, 'in the way that one will play at dressing up as princesses. I always knew it was imaginary. To you, I know, faith has always had a corporeal reality. I cannot explain how we came to see things so differently.'

Nora clucked at me, looking more superior than she usually did. We were in the old house on Canigou Avenue and Mark was crawling around on the floor while Nora photographed him. 'Someday

God will find you,' she cooed, and snapped a photo. 'He will choose you and take you. You are mistaken if you think you have free will. Faith is not a matter of individual choice.'

'It is *my* choice!' I shouted, feeling the rage pulse in my eyes. 'It is my choice not to believe in comforting fantasies. Comforting fantasies are undoing this world. By the laws of comforting fantasies one group feels it right and proper to subjugate all others.'

'And what about my nephew? Are you going to let my boy grow up outside of the church, without God?'

'He is not *your* boy!' Mark looked up at me, startled, and began to cry. 'He is my child and William's child and we will raise him to be an ethical man, a good man, not a man who feels himself above any other person because of the colour of his skin or the god he bows down before.'

'Children can't find their own way,' Nora said, taking a picture of Mark wailing in my arms, my face wild with fury. 'They must have guidance. They must have adults to guide them properly.' Another photo: a flash and more screaming.

'It's time for you to go,' I said, opening the door.

Nora came again last night, looking much as she did on that day I remember. She speaks as she always now speaks, with a salutation followed by hours of annoying pronouncements about my work. And then, rising from where she was sitting, she placed her ghostly hands over my face and I could feel my eyelids through her fingertips. As her hands fell away and I opened my eyes once again, I found myself in an unfamiliar room, still sitting at the end of a bed, but not my own, not in this house. I looked down at my legs and saw Nora's in their place, sheathed in a nightgown. A man was lying beside me and I knew from the smell of his aftershave and the camphor cream rubbed into the soles of his feet that it must be my brother-in-law, Stephan. The door to this new room rattled with a sudden force and my hand rose to my mouth, though I had not thought to move it. My feet twitched but I had not compelled them to do so. Stephan murmured in panic and I turned to look at him. The body I inhabited was acting of its own volition; I was merely a visitor within it.

The door rattled again and I found myself running towards it, Nora's body bracing against the wood, looking back at Stephan cowering on the bed. Nora hissed at him to call for help, but as his hand went for the phone her body was thrown back by the door crashing open. We landed on the floor against the bed's footboard, a report of pain echoing along Nora's shoulders – a pain I could feel, but only at one remove, more pressure than pain.

A man came through the door and closed it behind him, although the latch no longer engaged and it swung back open, letting in light from the corridor – just like the light from my own corridor coming into my own bedroom. The man did not bother to wear a mask. If a person could be said to look rational, this man did. But his was not the face of the man I had come to know in the weeks after Nora's death, the man who was charged and found guilty and never denied the charges.

I wonder, Laura, what you looked like when you killed, if your face was composed, if you were fully conscious of your actions, as this man appeared to be, or if you were overcome with rage and the blaze of the moment. I picture your mouth drawn in a line, see the lips pushed together: a rational mouth, a mouth in harmony with what the rest of the body is doing. And then I cannot help seeing a different you, a woman enflamed, screaming vengeance, unfurling a tongue of fire.

There was nothing wild-eyed or impulsive about my sister's assassin. He knew his task and undertook it without breaking a sweat or allowing his hands to shake. The smell of shit filled the room as the man rested the silencer of his gun against Nora's face. I felt something release in my sister's body and a hot wetness spread across the legs. In an instant Stephan had moved towards the window and, as if strings connected the two, the man moved in the same direction, firing his gun three times.

I did not want to turn around to look but Nora's body did. I knew already what Stephan Pretorius looked like in death. The stench of shit and urine that seared my nostrils billowed out from Nora's lap, mingling with the smells of gunpowder and the gun's oils, the odours of a crude beast created by the highest of animals – a beast with no place in nature.

The man with the gun then turned to Nora. As he took aim, I felt the bowels of the body I occupied loosen again, the liquid warmth continue to flow down onto the floor, and though I wanted to plead, to beg this man to pardon my sister, I could not make Nora's mouth move, could force no sound to come out.

As I watched the man's finger curl round the trigger, I woke alone in my own bedroom with the memory burning across my eyes of Nora's destroyed face – a screaming pope disintegrating into darkness.

Such experiences can be explained in only two ways according to the logic by which I live, a logic which does not allow for the supernatural, though it was by the trappings of supernatural practice, my sham nekyia round the fire, that I seem to have occasioned these recent phenomena. The cause is either psychological, meaning that my own sense of guilt and complicity in evil acts has grown to the point that even my conscious mind is affected as if in a dream state. Or the cause is physical, and perhaps, in that case, the crueller of the two: the loss of my mind by the process of a self-annihilating dementia, though I am not aware of any other psychological abnormalities, memory problems or confusions, and the doctors have all pronounced me sound.

I can understand the allure of the supernatural. To explain your and Nora's visits as a haunting, as the intrusion of a world beyond the physical one before me, would be the more comforting explanation. And in the absence of any other, it may be the one I am forced to believe.

★

Now that Sam has left me in peace for the foreseeable future, I set aside the last of your notebooks, Laura, my guide to the final weeks before your disappearance, the days you spent in the company of Sam. I turn instead to one chosen at random from the middle of the pile, wondering how it is possible that for twenty years I have left these ten volumes largely unread. It is not entirely true. At moments of greatest weakness and need and grief, I have picked one up, read a single page until I could not see clearly enough to read any further, and put them away again in the safe for months or years. Any hope I had that the books might provide clues to your whereabouts was overcome by my own selfish grief.

The notebook I take up now dates from the year you began working for the *Cape Record*. You had moved into the furnished flat above a shop on Lower Main Road in Observatory. On a typical morning you got up early to sit outside on the covered balcony, watching the traffic, people and cars, waving to the neighbours, calling out to them, a young white woman in a grey neighbourhood. ('Don't you want to live somewhere safer?' you reported me demanding. Your retort: 'I don't want to live in deepest darkest suburbia like you.')

Your father was giving you money to help make ends meet, though this was something I did not know at the time. I would have protested, said that you should first try to make a go of your life without our help, forgetting the way my own parents subsidized my itinerant years abroad, so much less focussed, so much more extravagant than you ever were, less noble in my aims. *You* wanted to tell the truth, *I* to fabulate and fabricate. In such a time and place, who better to support than you? You and your brother both inherited your father's love of the truth. I cannot help seeing that as an indictment of my own professional lying.

After your morning coffee you showered, dressed in simple and unfeminine clothes, and went downstairs hoping your battered yellow Valiant would still be where you parked it the night before. (It was stolen once; your father helped you buy another, paid a former student to let you park it in his driveway a few streets away – another secret I did not know.) Each working day you drove fifteen minutes along Victoria Road and into the City Centre, parked, and went to your office.

At first, your editors only allowed you, young and recently finished with your degree at Rhodes as you were, to write obituaries. In the notebook you recorded brief sketches of your subjects:

> A retired shopkeeper with three absent children, all emigrated to England. He had nothing but a crippled dachshund to keep him company. The dog will have to be destroyed because no one will take it in. I make the man over into a local prophet, exaggerating his importance and the effect of his death on the neighbourhood. Out of curiosity, I go to the funeral. Two of his children (snobs, but they grieve loudly; the son looks terrified by everyone he meets) come from London, and some old ladies from the street where the man lived. That's it. Less than ten people at the funeral. Next time I should rather say the man was the second coming, not just a prophet, and then watch the crowds turn out.

Every morning you pored over the death notices. Some days you would arrive to find the night editor had flagged two or three that merited an obituary; on other days you chose for yourself, people of obvious local or national importance, but also others, like the former shopkeeper, men and women never thought important except by the few who knew and loved them.

In between the obituaries, your editor allowed you small general reporting assignments: human-interest stories, court reporting for minor local cases. The truth was, you enjoyed the obituary assignments and made the most of them. Families responded to you. You listened patiently and spoke politely, no matter the person you were addressing. You checked and tripled-checked the facts of the lives you wrote, and then made embellishments so the nobodies sounded even more important than they were (an inheritance from me, I like to think, despite your passion for truth). Families wrote expressing thanks for the quality of your notices and the managing editor joked that you should be employed to write nothing but obituaries, a scribe and chronicler of the dead.

A month into the job you met a woman who had gone back to work as a freelancer for the *Record* after having a child, who was now in school. She was older than you by nearly a decade, but on that first meeting the two of you discovered a connection.

'I'm Ilse,' she said, her dark eyes looking out from an even darker fringe of hair. 'Have they let you out of the obits prison yet? Tell them you want the crime beat. That's where the real news is.'

You told her your name and she crossed her arms over her chest and looked at you.

'You're Bill Wald's daughter, aren't you?' The tone was more accusation than enquiry. She was tiny, a head shorter than you, but you felt intimidated by her, as though she were an older member of your own family.

You had never heard your father called 'Bill', but yes, you said, you were his daughter.

'He was one of my professors, and a very good friend. I haven't seen him in ages.'

You thought you recognized her from one of the garden parties your father always insisted on hosting for his Honours students. But that would have been years earlier. Before you knew what you were saying, it came out: 'Yes, Ilse. I remember how fond of you Dad was.'

Is it possible that you knew, even then, that your father and Ilse had been lovers? I knew it, had known it for years with something like certainty, but you were only a child when she was his student, when the brief affair kept him away from home more than usual, then ended with no explanation and weeks of sulking from him. The next I heard, Ilse – I only ever knew her first name – had married another of your father's students, and was pregnant.

You were so observant, it is not impossible that you knew – not just about your father and Ilse, but about what all of us were doing in ways we thought would be illegible to a child.

You prefaced your account of this meeting with a line I do not know how to interpret: *Succeeded in meeting Ilse.* I feel a chill at the base of my spine when I reread it, as though, from the start, you had contrived everything that followed, setting the players in motion by placing yourself in their midst.

★

Dear Sam,

God what a ninny I sound! Much as you might have enjoyed the process, your careful transcription is a sad and salutary reminder to me not to agree to face-to-face interviews in the future. The things one says off the top of one's head! Yes, for the sake of your book, I shall attempt to reconstruct the garbled passages and, with your permission, revise what I say elsewhere, maintaining the conceit of the conversational so far as I am able. What know I of politics? I fear I shall have to do some research and recast my feeble political opinions in a more sophisticated light if this is destined to find a place in your work of record. Now that I think of it, you must let me see the other transcripts – all of them, in their entirety, whether garbled or not – that I may work to make myself better understood.

I am also sending something to you, although I have little idea of how long it may take to reach Jo'burg. (By the way, why swap New York for Egoli? I should have thought the former could not be beat, but perhaps you are a masochist, coming back to Africa.) The woman at my local post office shrugged and said something about unpredictability and instability and the like. I asked her if she thought the country any less stable now than it had been at any time before and, wise woman, she said she feared it might be. You see what a pessimist I've become, but perhaps now that you've been here for an extended period you will understand why I have actually given up despairing of this country's postal system and instead console myself with hoping that what I send will reach its intended recipient before I die so that I might, at the very least, have some acknowledgement. No doubt that is why we now communicate in this improbably sterile way, which is to me, in my old-fashioned training of penmanship (*there* is a term, if ever there were one, that demands deconstruction*), a markedly inelegant, impermanent, and cumbersome one.

This 'thing' I send – a proof of my new book, *Absolution* – will not, I hope, upset you. In any event, it will be available in bookshops in May. It does not, I feel strongly, risk usurping the position of your own work, but will provide a kind of augmentative prelude *avant la lettre*. Moreover, in sending it to you now, you will have time to

---

* I consult my dictionary. *Penman* may refer to a clerk (which suits this writer's sense of her own vocation), a recorder of scripture (scrivener of the divine, if you like), a calligrapher, an author, but also, from the 19th century, a forger (a counterfeiter, a criminal) remembering that *forger* did not always bear the negative sense it now does. Ecclesiastes 11.5: *God, that is forgere of alle thingus*. I like this idea, God as creator whose creations are all perhaps no more than counterfeits of lost originals which probably no longer exist, if ever they did.

consider and incorporate it into your surreal portrait of this old woman. As for the why and the wherefore (*why* I did not tell you, *wherefore* it came, etc. – since every why hath a wherefore, and one must take nothing for granted), let me say only that I tell no one of or about my work apart from my woman of business and my editor in London, and between the two of them they put the pieces in motion and effect the kind of result people expect every two or three years, and only once *everything* is in place do the publicity people take the reins and by then there is no stopping the machine. Chug, chug it goes, whirr and buzz and out plops the tome.

This is all to say that I hope you find something of interest when the parcel finally arrives and that you will not judge me too harshly for the secrecy and deception that has become my default mode of engagement with all but those I have known for years.

Yours,
Clare

1989–98

Life with his aunt Ellen was the beginning of something like a normal life, a life of memory, a life the boy – that is, Sam, in other words me, or some version of me – would remember fully and not just in fragments of odour and light and noise.

That is not to say it was a particularly happy life, or even an unhappy one. Ellen adopted him, took away the name of his father's family, Lawrence, and gave him her own name, Leroux, without asking whether he wanted it or not. Like the loss of his house, its contents, and the money from his parents' estate, it was another kind of disinheritance. He had always been Sam Lawrence and now, with the filing of papers and a series of signatures, he was not.

Once, when Ellen went out to the shops and left Sam alone, he phoned the number that Timothy and Lionel had given him. There was no answer. A few days later, he phoned it again. The number had been disconnected.

At first Ellen wanted to know what had happened, asked him dozens of times to tell her exactly how he had come to be at her door. *There was a hijacking. And the hijacker killed Bernard while I hid. And then I hitchhiked. And the last people who gave me a lift were in a hurry, so they left me at the end of the street before they went on their way.* It was the story he'd rehearsed with Timothy and Lionel, and after hearing it enough times Ellen finally stopped asking, though Sam knew from the way she squinted and turned to look at him out of the corner of her eye that she didn't really believe him.

Well never mind then, she said. *You're safe here now and we can forget about the past.*

If she called the police to report the hijacking and Bernard's death, Sam never knew. He remembered there was evidence, in the form of Bernard's watch and signet ring, that there might be another story, another explanation for how he'd come to her. A hijacker would have stolen a ring and a watch. Sam kept them rolled up in a sock hidden at the back of the bottom drawer in the dresser of the room that became his. Every night he checked to see if the sock was still there, rolled just in the way he remembered rolling it.

I'm sorry I didn't send for you in the first place, Ellen said several weeks into his life with her, but she didn't sound sorry, not at all. He had hoped she would be like his mother, or even like Laura, that she would allow him to hug her, that she would treat him something like her own child. But she did not hold him, nor did she indulge him when he slipped into long silences, staring out the window, sitting in the garden, lying on the couch and looking at the ceiling. *Stop mooning now*, she would say, sounding like the teacher she was. Sam remembered his mother complaining about her family, about Bernard and Ellen. *We have to pull ourselves together and move forward*, Ellen said. *You're not a little boy any more. You're practically a man, even if you don't look it. Find something to do with yourself. Read a book.*

The few books Sam had managed to keep with him were, he knew, nothing more than children's stories. He understood that he was no longer a child, or not in the same way he had once been. If he was practically a man, then he decided it was time to read adult books. At the end of the central hallway off of which all the rooms of the house opened, there was a bookcase with four shelves. He started with the bottom shelf and its half-dozen volumes of *Reader's Digest Condensed Books*, speeding through them in a week, and feeling afterwards as though he'd eaten too much cake. Next there were bibles in English and Afrikaans, hymnbooks in both languages, too, but these he ignored. Mysteries followed – Agatha Christie, Ngaio Marsh – less like cake than the condensed books, but still not very nourishing.

When Ellen enrolled him at the local school, he had less time for his own reading, but began to jump around the bookshelf, teaching himself what he could without realizing it was an education. He read Schreiner and Millin, FitzPatrick and Bosman,

Paton and Van der Post. These were all stories he could read and have no trouble understanding: the story was exactly what it claimed to be. He exhausted the contents of the bookcase, and then, as the autumn began to close in and the days shortened, he discovered another collection of books in the lounge, hidden behind stacks of *National Geographic* magazines. Why, he wondered, were these books hidden? They were not hidden as carefully as his parents had hidden books, with some of their covers removed and brown paper pasted on in their place, secreted in plastic packets under the floorboards. Ellen's hidden books were still intact, with their covers and all their pages, but they were tucked out of the way, where visitors could never chance to see them. Sam began with a book called *Dusklands*, which at first appeared to be one kind of story – a story unlike any he'd read before – and then turned into another kind of book altogether halfway through. He wasn't sure what it all meant, but as he read it in his room at night, with a torch under the covers of his bed, he felt a kind of thrill that no other book had given him before. There were others by the same author that confused and excited him even more than the first. From there he moved to another writer whose stories he found still more confusing: *The Late Bourgeois World* he had to read with the dictionary open next to him, but he became convinced that such books were teaching him, both about the country and himself.

The last of the books hidden behind the stack of *National Geographic* magazines were by Clare Wald. When he'd first discovered the cache, he hadn't noticed her name, and now, picking up the first of Wald's books, *Landing*, he wondered if she could possibly be Laura's mother. He opened the book to the back flap and looked at the photo of the author holding a baby cheetah, its tongue sticking out. He had only seen Mrs Wald twice in his life, but he knew it was Laura's mother, the woman who had stood in the background at his parents' funeral, and who later slammed the door in his face. He tucked the book under his shirt and read it through the course of a single night. And though it made even less sense to him than all the other books he'd read, slipping into Laura's mother's words was like discovering that the house he had lived in with his parents had other rooms – and not just rooms but whole floors and staircases and wings of space that were at once in keeping with the architecture of the small house he knew, but at the same time made it something else altogether, so that he understood the original space in a new way. He read the other books by her – *Cacophony*, *Dissidence*, *In A Dry Month* – and began to understand that Wald's stories were not only spaces to inhabit as real as the house he lived in with his aunt, the house he might have hoped to live in with Clare herself, but they were also keys that opened the library of his memory.

Sometimes, at night, he would hear Ellen on the

phone. *It changes everything,* she would sigh. *All my own plans are finished. But what can I do? There's no one else to take him now that Bernard's dead. If I could, you know, I'd leave in a heartbeat. Maybe he'll be hit by a truck. No, of course I don't mean that.*

There was something about his family, Sam began to think, that was careless of life. His mother had it, Bernard certainly had it, his aunt had it too. And Sam himself had it. He knew he did.

You need a better school, Ellen said when the winter holidays arrived. *It's time to set our sights higher.*

With Ellen's tutoring, he won a bursary to a school in Port Elizabeth and moved there the following year.

Life at school was normal boarding-school life. Holidays were normal holidays, mostly at Ellen's, sometimes with trips to the coast. He read other books from other countries, but kept coming back to his own, and especially to Clare Wald's.

Ellen suggested he try to forget the years before he came to live with her. *It's better that way,* she said. *You can remember your parents but try not to think of those times. Your parents didn't know what they were doing, in so very many ways. The poor fools. Better to forget everything they ever did.* Sam didn't know how to separate events from the people involved in them, and once Clare's books had given him the key to his own past, he did not want to close that door again.

He moved to Grahamstown for university, voted for the first time in 1994, finished first in his class, read for an MA and finished first in that class, too. All the while, he read and reread Wald's books. Every time a new one was published, he bought it the first day it appeared in the bookshop. If he could not actually live with Clare, he could live in the house of her words.

★

When Sam first arrived he went straight from the airport to the high-rise that had been converted by the university into a student dorm. It was around the corner from Bellevue Hospital so he heard sirens at all hours and couldn't sleep without earplugs. He had thought of Cape Town as a city, but he knew after only an hour in Manhattan that this was something else entirely. Trees were stunted and corralled into holes surrounded by concrete. He strained to see a large expanse of sky. Everywhere he looked the space was crowded with buildings that dwarfed and enclosed him. It had not occurred to him that he might miss the great openness of the Karoo, an openness that had often felt claustrophobic and oppressive in its own way.

Once his phone was working he called Ellen to tell her he was there safely. She believed that phone calls were not for chatting but for the brief communication of essential information. They promised to write to each other and hung up after two minutes. Sam would have liked to talk for longer, only he didn't know how to keep her on the line.

At the end of his first week in the city there was a party for new graduate students in the Arts and Humanities at one of the brownstones owned by the university. As Sam arrived a jazz trio was playing and a caterer pushed a glass of white wine into his hand. He saw a group of people he recognized from one of his seminars, but when he joined them he had difficulty keeping up with the references to plays and concerts they had attended just in the first week. Plays and concerts would require money Sam didn't think he could afford to spend, even with the scholarship that had allowed him to come. He had vowed to himself to save as much as he could, in anticipation of returning home.

Without being missed, Sam retreated to a corner table where finger food was arranged on platters. As he was making up his mind to leave a voice next to him said, *God this is depressing. I'm Greg. What are you? You're familiar.*

Sam looked up at the man, surprised to hear a Cape Town accent.

I decided you were the only person I could bear to talk to, other than the Israeli over there, Greg said, nodding at a woman with a shaved head who was talking to the Dean of Arts. *These Americans undo me.*

How did you know I wasn't American?

Your clothes, Greg said. *The way you stand. Your hair. Your shoes. Your hair especially.*

Sam put his fingers to his hair and brushed it away from his brow.

No, like this, Greg said, mussing his own hair to demonstrate. The backs of Greg's hands were patterned with tattoos of astrological symbols. *Say something else and I'll tell you where you're from and where you went to school.*

What makes you think you can read me so well?

Because there aren't that many white South Africans and we're mostly all related. We're probably distant cousins. I'd say you spent time in Cape Town but went to school somewhere in the Eastern Cape. Grahamstown?

Port Elizabeth, Sam said. It was unnerving to be so transparent.

Greg had come to New York to do a master's in art history. *When I go back I'm going to open an art gallery and sell to all the rich Europeans who come looking for authentic Africa*, he said, making horns with his fingers and pulling a horror face. *My parents say I should try to stay here.* He raised an index finger and wagged it at Sam: *'It's just a matter of time,' my father says, 'before they have us all strung up from the trees my boy.' So you see I have no choice. I have to go back to prove him wrong.*

★

Sarah was presiding at the first club meeting Sam attended. At the end he approached her to sign up and pay dues for the year. These amounted to fifteen dollars, and even that felt like a stretch, but the club was the kind of thing he thought he should be doing to meet people. When he saw her smile with her eyes as well as her mouth he thought this was also a reason for joining. Her teeth were straight and she had thick, light brown hair and there was something wholesome and unmistakably American about her looks – as if she had woken up that morning on a farm and drunk a glass of milk fresh from a cow milked by her father, and eaten pancakes made from scratch by her mother. Her clothes were spotless and unrumpled. Later, when he learned she knew nothing about farms and that her father would have no idea what to do with a cow, Sam wondered what her childhood had really been like but didn't know how to ask. Asking about Sarah's childhood would only invite questions about his own.

When the members of the club weren't meeting to listen to local poets or reading their own work, they were usually at bars on Bleecker Street or gathering at someone's apartment. It was one of those nights – at the home of an exiled Somali poet who lived far into Alphabet City and walked with her keys poking out from between the fingers of her left hand, pepper spray at the ready in her right – that Sam first had time alone with Sarah. He knew that she was regarded as a rising star in the journalism department, that she was approaching the end of her masters programme, that she had already published articles in leading news magazines, and that she lived nowhere near the university. No one in the club knew where she lived because she had never invited anyone to her apartment. The two of them talked about Sarah's thesis on American media coverage of the Iran-Contra scandal. As she spoke, moistening her lips by rolling them into each other and taking long slow sips from a red plastic cup, now and then popping a chip into her mouth, Sam began to feel that he needed her. He realized that she reminded him, strangely, of Laura.

My father spent time in Africa, she said, *in the Foreign Service. He was in the Congo and Rhodesia in the Sixties, in South Africa, too – in the Seventies and Eighties. I think he spent quite a while in South Africa.*

But you never went with him?

He always said the postings were too dangerous, so Mom and I always stayed in Virginia. I don't know – maybe we could have gone with him, but I think he was too worried about our safety. He liked South Africa. He said it was a beautiful country. I can't imagine what it must have been like growing up in such a dangerous place.

Even though terrible things had happened, Sam had never considered that the country as a whole was a dangerous place, any more than America was. He tried to make out the expression on Sarah's face. She looked curious and preoccupied, but it could have been the light refracting through the glass lampshade, which patterned her face in a labyrinth of strong shadows.

328

As they spoke, Sam thought more and more of Laura, seeing in Sarah the same energetic curiosity, but also a physical likeness, in her muscular limbs and sharp features, a bundle of angles and olive-blonde complexion, and eyes that were always active, when not scrutinizing Sam then taking in their surroundings, logging everything and everyone around them. If she was interested, Sam intuited, if she smelled a story, then this was a woman who wouldn't stop until she understood everything about a person, until she discovered the truth.

SAM

We wake to the sound of birds, a jungle cacophony like nothing I've ever experienced, not in Cape Town or Beaufort West or Grahamstown. Along with the hadedas, which are familiar to me, there are grey loeries that look as prehistoric as the ibis and make a blood-chilling cry like a baby being strangled.

Sarah runs across the patio to the garden cottage first thing this morning, starting research on a story about American oil companies in Angola. The pool is tempting but I know I have to get to work. We say goodbye for the day, I implore Sarah to be careful and not let anyone in, and she reminds me to remain calm. As I pull out of the drive and watch the gate close behind me, a woman approaches on foot, hand-woven baskets stacked on her head and grass whisks tied to her body, looking as though she's just arrived from some rural area.

As hectic and congested as Cape Town traffic can be, it has a kind of fluid logic that makes sense to me. I know its neighbourhoods and landmarks, its energy and codes. But Johannesburg has its own aggressive rules and an unrelenting pace that leaves me in a cold sweat, even with the satnav voice issuing constant directions to change lanes, to turn in so many metres, to watch out for speed cameras. By the time I arrive at the university I feel like I need to be sedated.

The faculty has arranged a parking space for me in the garage beneath Senate House, which on the outside looks like a late-Soviet grand hotel. Inside it's an Escher nightmare of lifts and staircases and galleried walkways that never meet up in the way I expect they should. After losing myself twice I finally arrive at English Studies where the administrator tells me I need to go to another office to fill out paperwork, and then another office after that to get my staff ID card. An hour and a half later I return with the ID and requisite paperwork and no memory of how I got where I went. The department administrator shows me to my office, teaches me the code for the keypad, and explains that I must always remember to deactivate the silent office alarm when I arrive or the security services will be dispatched to investigate.

Left alone in the office, which is bare except for a desk, a chair, an empty bookcase, a filing cabinet, and a computer, I download all the recordings of my interviews with Clare and the scans of her manuscripts. My teaching duties won't begin until February, and they've given me a light load for my first semester, but I intend to work on the book here at the office, even though the house, which offers the distractions of the pool and the television, is much more comfortable, particularly on a hot day like this. I spend the rest of the morning transcribing one of the interviews, and reply to Clare's message, which arrived in the middle of the night.

★

Dear Clare,

I hope this finds you well. A French friend once told me that one should always begin a letter with a statement about, or wishes for, the recipient, rather than beginning with something self-reflexive. I'm afraid I've never quite mastered that. *I* do hope that you are well as you read this. How artificial it would seem to begin a letter with some-thing like 'Dear Clare, You will no doubt now be enjoying these long December days and preparing for the festive season.' Perhaps it is something only the French can do – or do well – or perhaps it is the kind of form only truly possible in French. So instead I begin with myself, because it's the only way I know how.

Please don't be offended when I say that I was shocked to hear that the new book might in some way be a memoir – that's certainly what your last message seems to imply. Of course I look forward to it, and can only say how intrigued I am. I've managed to bully an editor into letting me review it. Do you read reviews?

Knowing *Absolution* is now on its way, I feel more than ever that other areas need to be explored for the biography, and doing so in person would be the best possible way. I have teaching duties here from February, but would like to see you in the next six months if at all possible.

I also feel that I need to apologize again. In the process of transcribing our interviews, I realize now how stupid my questions were, and how juvenile. I don't know how you found the patience for them. I can sometimes hear the irritation in your voice on the recordings, but only in your voice. Thank you for that – for the restraint you showed, and the patience of your words.

Yours,

Sam

*

Before going to find lunch downstairs, I look up Lionel Jameson's office location in the main building. If it's him, as I know it must be, I'm not sure what I'm going to say when we meet. Perhaps it would be better to phone or e-mail first, but when I'm outside, eating my sandwich on the front steps of the Central Block, I decide there can't be any harm in going to see where his office is, even if I don't intend to knock, even if I lose all courage and never end up meeting him.

His door of heavy brown wood, covered in posters about direct action and anti-globalization rallies, is midway down a long corridor with high ceilings. It's enough for now to know where it is. I can make contact in time, once I've mustered the courage. Though I tell myself that I want to ask him about Laura, my hesitation, I realize, is as much to do with what he may remember about me as a child.

I turn to walk away when the door opens. He stands looking at me, unmistakably Lionel, though his hair is thinner and wilder than it was two decades ago. It's a relief to see him and I feel an unexpected flush of happiness. For the first time, I understand that we're not that far apart in age – he must be only six years or so older than me, but at the time he seemed remotely adult.

'Are you waiting for someone?' he asks.

'Lionel Jameson.'

'That's the name on the door.' He's gruffer than I remember him, louder too, his voice booming down the corridor and bouncing off the high ceiling.

'I'm Sam.'

He studies my face and shakes his head. 'Sorry, are you one of the candidates for the lectureship? The interviews are down the hall.'

'I'm Sam Leroux. I used to be Sam Lawrence. That was the name you would have known at the time. Laura Wald brought me to you.' I watch his face change, the furrows in his brow flatten, his pupils dilate.

'Come inside,' he says, swinging open the office door. 'I'm afraid I'm in a hurry.'

Lionel's office is full of book boxes that have never been unpacked from some prior move. It has the feeling of antiquity, of a storehouse forgotten by everyone except its lone attendant. I'm making him more than he is. He's just a prematurely ageing academic, a typical professor, blind to chaos or too overworked to bring order to his own mess. The shelves are stacked with papers and files and it looks like nothing has been dusted in months.

'I'm so relieved you're okay,' he says, studying my face. 'Not a boy any more! You are all right, aren't you?'

'So you do remember me.'

'You sound almost as American as I do now. Tell me you weren't in Chicago too?'

'New York.'

He shakes his head, crossing his arms over his chest and laughing. The drawers of the filing cabinet in the corner of the room are open, disgorging bundles of paper-clipped documents and hanging folders. 'There are so many questions,' he says, pulling his red hair away from his head. 'But you are *all right* after all? I worried so much when we left you.' His face twitches as he fidgets with a paperclip holding together a sheaf of papers. I reassure him, tell him I'm fine. This was never the reaction I expected. 'You must have questions for me, too. Whatever I can tell you –'

He pauses, shakes his head again, as if thinking better of something he was about to say.

I tell him that I'm writing Clare's biography, that I've almost finished the research, but still have a few leads I'd like to pursue. Even though Clare has been unwilling to talk to me about Laura, I don't feel I can let the story go. It deserves at least a small place in the book.

'I was hoping you might be able to tell me something about Laura.'

When Lionel hears it again the name seems to hit him like a bullet: his chest deflates and all the animation in his face dies; his body becomes rigid as he turns away from me to shuffle the countless piles of paper on his desk. My entrance into this space is somehow a transgression that I didn't intend. I want to go, and I can see that Lionel needs for me to go.

'Yes, of course you would. I'm afraid I have these interviews just now, so you'll really have to excuse me. Perhaps we can take this up again at another point. I'm sorry I can't talk now.'

I invite him to dinner but he's going away for the holidays and says I should phone him in the New Year. I know he's trying to give me the brush-off. I resolve not to give up, no matter how long it may take.

Tonight Sarah and I go to a busy restaurant at the mall in Rosebank and get a table outside where we can watch the foot traffic. We place our order, but then decide we want cocktails instead of wine so I go inside to the bar. There are half a dozen wait staff running around – too many of them for the small space at the cash register behind the bar, and too few of them for all the patrons in the restaurant at this hour. I change the order and decide to wait while the bartender makes the drinks. There's a young woman behind the cash register who looks shyly at me, and then smiles. Without thinking, I smile back and as soon as she sees me smile she returns the smile, looking ecstatic, but then she winces and swoons, like she could die from embarrassment, spinning around and sinking below the bar. Her co-workers look at her and pull her up and look at me and ask the woman what's going on. She shakes her head and disappears into the kitchen.

I take the drinks back out to Sarah.

'Cheers,' she says, clinking her glass against mine. 'What just happened there? All you did was smile and the girl acted like you'd presented her with a diamond ring or something.'

'I don't know. Most whites look through blacks. Security guards. Servers. Clerks. You get what you give. I smiled back, and maybe it was the first time a young white guy ever did that to her.'

Our dinners come and we order another round of cocktails. The night is warm with no breeze and there are buskers further down the street, a group singing an old Dolly Rathebe hit. As we wait for a dessert menu an elderly white woman weaves along the pavement towards us.

'*Ek soek 'n honderd rand,*' she says, putting out her hand.

I tell her I'm sorry, that I don't have a hundred rand to give her, even though this isn't true. I can see Sarah start to go for her wallet until I give her a look that makes her stop. The woman curses us and moves on to another table where the diners, too embarrassed not to give her something, offer a handful of change. She picks out the large denomination coins and leaves the rest. A few cents – forget it, she doesn't want it.

'Who can blame her?' I say, accepting a dessert menu from our server. 'Five rand buys next to nothing. Greg says he should get a special tax break for being white. This is Greg, who must be the most radical-thinking person I know in the country. He calculated he gives away ten thousand rand a year to people asking for money. And that's not even factoring in all the help he gives to his domestic worker and gardener and nanny, or the official charity work that his gallery sponsors. "Life on the plantation," he says. "This is the price." 'I gesture at the well-dressed diners around us, the extravagant portions of food, the booze sold at a premium but still running like water.

'It's not so different in New York these days, or London,' Sarah says. 'It's not a matter of one place or another. These are not just problems of place.'

ABSOLUTION

The man reached out his hands, removing a pair of thin leather gloves. Squinting into the light from the corridor, Clare recognized him all at once. It was no one she might have expected.

'Heavens!' she cried out, her heart leaping about against her ribs. 'What on earth do you think you're doing here?'

'You knew I was coming,' her son said, taking off his jacket. 'You told me to let myself in.'

'I did nothing of the kind, Mark! I'm minded to phone the police.'

'Don't be ridiculous, Mother. I've come for the week, as you must remember. What are you doing in bed so early? It's not even ten.'

'You call that early? I have no memory of inviting you to visit.' Clare watched as Mark slumped on the taffeta-upholstered chair nearest her bedroom door. Propping herself up against the headboard, she turned on the bedside light. Her son looked tired, his skin bluish, claws of wrinkles deepening at his temples. How irritating it was to be interrupted in this way. She knew she would never get back to sleep, and feared that the entire week, which should have been one of intense, undisrupted work, would be lost to the demands and petulant whims of her son.

'I didn't realize I needed an invitation to come home,' he said, loosening his green silk tie and unbuttoning the neck of his shirt to expose a ruff of chest hair that repulsed Clare. The law, which had kept his father and maternal grandfather lean men, had given Mark Wald a paunch he could ill afford.

'This is my home, not yours. The old house on Canigou Avenue, the house you and your sister grew up in and stormed through and abused in your way, that house might yet have been your home, but this house is mine alone and no one else's until I die. I sold your home at a considerable profit and for the sake of my own security. Any home you might now have must by necessity be of your own purchase and deed and responsibility. How did you come by a key to my house?'

'You made me a copy the last time I was here.' He sounded as tired and short-tempered as his mother. 'In case of emergencies. You *wanted* me to be able to get in. At least that's what you said then.'

'How short-sighted of me. And why do you trouble me and not your father and stepmother?' It was a way the two of them had, this needling banter, half-play and half-contretemps, the two of them thrusting at the same time they wished only to tease.

'Dad's doing renovations. It wasn't convenient for me to stay. I can see what you're thinking but really there isn't anything else to say about that. You can't expect me to gossip. Can I make you a cup of tea or something?'

'I should not presume to know what you *can* or *cannot* do.'

'*May* I make you a cup of tea?'

'Allow me the courtesy of offering refreshment in my own house. You realize that because of your intrusion I won't be able to sleep all night. You've disturbed my rest, which is hard won at the best of times,' she said, swinging her legs out of bed. 'I suppose since you offer me tea that you want food or drink yourself.'

'If it isn't too much trouble.'

'It is a terrible imposition, but let us see what we can find. Marie left behind a banquet in the freezer. You can eat, and I shall watch.'

Clare found bread and cheese, chutney and mayonnaise, and made her son a sandwich in a way that she had not done for many years. When he and his family came to visit they usually stayed with Clare's ex-husband, because Mark's wife Coleen complained that staying with Clare made her nervous, and Clare, who saw little of interest in Coleen (a believer in what the woman described as 'traditional feminine roles'), made no objection to the arrangement. The twin grandchildren were too small to be reasoned or conversed with and were themselves chiefly interested in swimming

341

pools, ice creams, and long visits to the aquarium. It was only when Mark came alone to Cape Town on business that he sometimes stayed in his mother's house.

'Why are the shutters closed?' he asked, pouring a glass of wine from the box in the refrigerator.

'Aren't you going to ask if you may have any wine?'

'Don't change the subject, Mother. The shutters. Has something happened?'

'You do ask irritating questions. Don't you want to offer your mother a glass of her own wine?'

'Would you like a glass of your own wine, Mother?'

'No, thank you, it will only keep me awake, but do help yourself,' she said, and winked at him.

'The shutters, Mother,' Mark insisted, trying not to smile and swallowing half his glass of Stein. 'Why do you drink this appalling stuff?'

'Marie likes it. The shutters are closed because, if you must know, I was feeling vulnerable. Is that what you want to hear? Without Marie here, for the first time since we moved to this country-club fortress, I felt an old woman alone in the world with nothing but fragile glass between me and those –' for a moment she nearly stopped herself, and then without completely fathoming the implications of what she was about to say, continued '– between me and those who would wish to visit their recriminations upon me.'

'I don't know what you mean.'

'Nor do I, perhaps. In any case, raking over the past is something best left for daylight,' she said, rising from the table. 'If you wish to stay up, stay up. Watch the television if you can find anything decent at this hour, listen to music, whatever you do to make your own nights pass.'

'Thanks, but I'm exhausted.' Mark rubbed his face, which had once been so taut and pale, and was now thickening into a pasty blob. 'I've been going since five this morning. There was a hearing at ten and I got the last flight out this evening, which was delayed by an hour. I could sleep for twenty-four hours if I didn't have commitments tomorrow.'

'Client meetings?'

'Meetings, yes. I'll need to be up early, but I was thinking that maybe we could have dinner together. Would you like to go out somewhere? I could make a reservation. We could even go up to that restaurant in Franschhoek.'

'I don't relish the idea of a night out, or being on the roads after dark.' In fact, Clare had to admit, she no longer wished to be outside her own locked and gated property after sunset. On the rare recent occasions that she had received evening invitations she turned them down, excusing herself with the lie that neither she nor her assistant could see well enough to drive at night. 'And in any case, Marie left plenty of food and her cooking is good enough for me. My taste buds are not what they were, so your fine dining would be wasted. You know where the guest bedroom is. No one has stayed here since you last came to visit, so any dirt on the sheets is your own. If it is too disgusting there is clean bedding in the linen closet. I trust you have not been so spoiled by servants that you have forgotten how to make a bed.'

She stood in the doorway for a moment and wondered if she was meant to hug or kiss her son. They had never been demonstrative and after a score of agonizing seconds they both nodded and Mark turned out the light.

Clare was up before dawn the next morning. Too tired to swim she instead went to work before emerging from the study adjoining her bedroom. That was perhaps the greatest advantage of this new house – being able to move from bed to desk before the spell of night had completely lapsed, and without having to encounter anyone but her own reflection, which was disturbance enough on some mornings. Marie knew not to knock before eleven if the door remained closed. Mark was not so well trained.

'Are you up, Mother?' he called from the other side of her study door.

'A closed door means one wishes not to be bothered,' Clare shouted, opening the door and taking in the vision of Mark, already showered, his remaining hair combed back and gelled into place, his gut filling out his shirt.

'My first meeting's been cancelled.'

'And you expect me to entertain you.'

'I thought it would give us an opportunity to talk. Were you working?'

'Unlike you I am always working, even when it appears I am bent to nothing in particular. But now that you've interrupted me I might as well stop the actual mechanical work. The interruption comes at a very high price, you understand. I won't get back what I've lost.' She pressed her lips into what she hoped was an ironic smile. 'Perhaps you could make us some coffee, and find where Marie keeps the rusks, and we can reconvene in the garden in half an hour. Adam was going to mow today but I will ask him to wait until tomorrow.'

She was not accustomed to so much intrusion, especially now that she had, at long last, begun to feel at home in this new house. Quite apart from the adjoining study and bedroom, it afforded her a much larger measure of privacy and separation from the wider world. Mendicants could no longer come directly to her door. Only the truly brazen or desperate rang the intercom at the gate to the drive. Marie, feeling even this was inadequate, had proposed a secondary gate such as she had seen at some homes in Johannesburg, thereby creating a kind of security decontamination zone. The idea was that if one needed a delivery of groceries, for instance, the deliveryman would be allowed through the first gate, could deposit the groceries in the secure zone, Marie could sign for the delivery while remaining separated from the deliveryman by the secondary gate, and only after he had left and the first gate closed would she open it to retrieve the delivery. Clare had dismissed the proposal as ludicrously paranoid. Cape Town was not yet Johannesburg, where entire neighbourhoods had become privatized security zones and armed guards patrolled grocery-store parking lots from bulletproof watchtowers. Besides, the truly determined would still find ways around any number of secondary or tertiary defences; they would cut through wires and tunnel under walls. Nowhere was truly secure.

Mark produced the coffee tray and Clare could not help taking note of the mugs – mugs rather than cups and saucers – and the plastic container of milk. Marie would have laid a placemat or cloth on the tray, used the china, poured the milk into a pitcher, and put the rusks with slices of cake on a plate. Such things made life in this country more bearable at the same time that they pointed up the irony of living as one did in the place where one happened to have been born.

'It seems terribly unjust, this life,' Clare said, accepting a mug. 'That we should be able to live like this. It would not surprise me if, one day very soon, it should all be taken away from us. Nor would I think it an entirely unjustified deprivation.'

'The government should make you head of land reform, Mother. You sound like some kind of radical.'

'Have you ever thought I was anything else?'

'I once thought you were a liberal,' Mark said, stirring milk and sugar into his coffee, tapping his spoon on the mug in a way that made Clare flinch. He had learned the tapping habit from his father. 'A good old-fashioned white liberal.'

'That's a very offensive thing to say. Whatever could have made you think I was a liberal?'

'It was before I understood what it meant. I was only a child. And then, when I realized you weren't a liberal, nothing so tame or easy to label as that, I thought you might be a pragmatist.'

'An even worse offence. What else would you call me? An opportunist? A reactionary? An appeaser?'

Mark laughed and shook his head. 'Now I see that you're not only a radical but also a strict non-conformist, if such a definition is possible.'

'Let's say that it is and leave it at that. This need not be a pinning down of my politics, which become ever more mercurial. I see ineptitude and shoddiness and for a brief moment think of how efficient things once were. People in this country don't complain enough when goods or services – services in particular – are substandard. I am of the generation, as are you (more's the pity), who will be able to say that they lived through two corrupt nationalist governments. The question is whether we will survive the second, some members of which see us as its unfinished business, its potential fifth columnists, and its dormant antagonists. One settler, one bullet. They are the ones who see all whites as parasites, and *they* are the analogues to those of the old regime who saw all blacks as terrorists or idlers. It may only be a matter of time before the likes of me, and you in particular given the nature of your work, are described as enemies of the state. We are the new sleeper cells, the plotters in the dark. To dissent now is to commit treason, in a way that could not even have been imagined by the old apartheid government.'

'And now you do sound like a racist and a reactionary.'

'And truly I think myself neither. I know that *I* am the one – one of the ones, one of the few remaining – who is keeping faith with the struggle. Not the men and women who now use their struggle credentials as smokescreens, who pull strings and make magic happen and watch as their speeding tickets and even worse disappear like pixie dust. Your sister would have had something to say. She would have been scathing. She would have spoken as I speak, but even more boldly. We may yet find ourselves relying on her, claiming her legacy as our own political bona fides. I wish Laura had seen fit to trust us more, and that we had given her greater reason to trust.'

Mark wheezed and shifted in the white wrought-iron chair, looking uncomfortable, as if mention of his sister were too painful to bear. It was possible, Clare realized, that there were things about Laura he knew and had never shared.

'You make Laura sound like some kind of hero – or heroine. I'm not at all sure that was the case,' Mark said. 'She was a terror as a child. And not much better as she grew up.'

'The media has debased and perverted the idea of heroism. Successful sportsmen and women are now almost habitually accorded the status of hero. Laura does not fit that kind of category. What she did, what I assume she did, was both too great and selfless as well as too dishonourable and horrific to be called heroic. The term lacks the necessary ambiguity to describe your sister's activities – what I know she did, and what I can guess she may have done. She was something more than human, but less than a goddess. Unlike heroes of antiquity, I don't believe that Laura was a favourite of the gods, or even of one particular god – certainly not the God of Christianity, who was, besides everything else, a god in whom she did not hold much faith. Do you think that's a fair assessment?'

'Before she was ten years old she was already terrifying me. I suppose she was a kind of heroine to me, as a child, if not the typical kind. I can't speak for what she did or might have done as an adult. To be honest, I've tried to remain ignorant of the details, to protect my sense of her.'

'And what sense is that?'

'As a person of total independence. Like you.'

Clare looked for a smile but Mark was as solemn as if preparing for the judicial chamber; if there were humour or empathy there, another part of him sat holding down the cage that contained them. She wished he were not so inhuman.

'No one can flatter as a child can flatter. Total independence, for me at least, is long in the past – if I ever had it to begin with. It was to your father that I first ceded control for the routine manoeuvres required to get myself through life on an ordinary day. Your father hired and fired the staff, managed the household accounts, arranged a cook to be sure we did not starve and a nanny to look after you and your sister when I refused to do so because I was too busy with my work. Your father played all the domestic roles that society, culture, religion, and the state had for centuries ascribed to the wife. That was not, however, the reason for the end of our marriage. About that I want there to be no misunderstanding. There were a great many other women, and I would not be surprised if he had other children besides you and Laura. Don't look so shocked. What I hope for him now is that he is happy with his new Mrs Wald.'

'Aisyah.'

'I am told that is her name.'

'I'd be lying if I said I had a totally easy relationship with her. She acts as though she expects white people to treat her like a maid, and then she goes and acts like one anyway: lots of milk and *four* sugars in her coffee. She doesn't like me at all, I think, and can't stand Coleen or the kids. She dotes on Dad day and night – half-maid, half-concubine. It's quite disgusting.'

'Now you sound like the reactionary. If your colleagues could hear you . . .'

'You've already tricked me into saying too much already. I don't like it when you put me in the middle. Dad does it too.'

'I'm surprised he would ask about me.'

'He wants to know that you're okay, that's all. After the robbery he was very concerned, but didn't know what to do to help.'

'He always used to know exactly what to do. He eventually reached a level of awareness with me whereby he could anticipate what needed to be done before I had even thought to frame the request. He was truly intuitive in that way – Marie has the same talent. With others – the men I knew before marrying your father, men dependent on me and astonishing in their ultimate indifference – independence was my passport and papers of freedom. If I could do for myself, then I knew I was free to escape situations that became untenable. If I had enough money in order to eat and to find somewhere warm and dry to spend each night, whether or not that involved sleep, it was enough at the time. These kinds of attitudes are possible when one is young and unattached, unencumbered by issue or the responsibility of relationships made legal, the slow accumulation of things that accrue meaning, endowed with sentiment knowable only to their owner, things that define what one may do, where one may go, what one may risk. I have never been a great one for objects or trifles. As the collection has grown, it's been the library that matters, and the few belongings from my parents and grandparents that I have chosen to keep.'

Clare noticed Mark checking his watch beneath the table, as if he thought she couldn't see. At the same moment Adam came round the house from the garage carrying a strimmer. Clare felt the mountain pressing against her back, the sun burning layers from her face.

'One tells him not to mow and he finds some other way to make a noise. I suppose one shouldn't fault the industrious,' Clare said, turning back to her son, who was still wheezing but was too proud to excuse himself. 'We've run out of time. You have your appointments.'

★

'You are back sooner than you indicated you would be,' Clare said as Mark let himself in the front door that evening. For a moment earlier in the day she had toyed with the idea of changing the alarm code and the locks, and then realized how unreasonable that would seem to anyone but her. It was one thing to love one's children, quite another to cede them unconditional access to one's life, as she unthinkingly had done. In truth, she had no memory of giving Mark a key to her house – neither a key nor the code to the alarm. If only she could undo that breach without offending him. She knew, however, that he was quick to take offence, to see a slight where none was intended. How he screamed as a child, shouting threats to sue his friends, his teachers, even his parents and grandparents and siblings – how like his Aunt Nora he had been, it occurred to Clare for the first time. 'I wasn't expecting you for another hour at least,' she said, leaning over to be kissed. He did this with dutiful quickness, as though he found the contact almost repellent. 'Dinner is not, therefore, anything like ready. I suppose you must be hungry. I suppose you expect to be fed all week. Are you staying all week? *Are* you hungry?'

'I am, Mother, but why don't you let me do it? I'm quite a capable cook,' he said, and kissed her other cheek.

'There's no cooking to be done apart from turning on the oven and putting the defrosted meal into it. You might make a salad. Or do you eat salads?' She glanced at his waist, worrying about his heart as she had since he was a child. He no longer spoke to her about his health, though she knew there had been surgeries in recent years. 'What were you doing today?'

'As you know, I was meeting with some clients.' Following her through to the kitchen, he stood watching as Clare took a head of iceberg lettuce and an avocado and two tomatoes from the refrigerator. 'That avo isn't ripe, Mother. You should put it out with some bananas in a paper bag.'

Clare looked at his plump hands and the jaw that had lately begun to lose definition, and put the avocado back in the refrigerator.

Out of respect for Mark's unwavering belief in confidentiality, she had learned not to ask him prying questions about his work. Most of the cases he undertook involved defending individuals' rights to privacy as enshrined in the country's new constitution. Sometimes the cases had surprised her, such as one in which the claimant argued that the right to privacy protected his work as a prostitute. Mark had lost the case, but argued passionately on behalf of the young man, who contracted HIV during his brief incarceration and for want of adequate medical treatment died of an AIDS-related illness not long after his release.

Clare had attended the hearing at the Constitutional Court – her first visit there, still in the court's early days – and found that she was both moved and bewildered by the physical space and the institution it housed. The building itself, she thought, failed as a piece of architecture, although it had been celebrated in many quarters. It achieved a sense of openness and transparency and consciousness of the country's history at the cost of monumental gravitas, which it wholly lacked. While it was obvious that the planners and designers wished the central piazza to be a place of casual civic life, of picnics and impromptu social events and community celebrations, it felt instead like what it was, a converted jail yard with the enclosed ruins of two staircases from the demolished block where prisoners once awaited trial. She could not help but compare it with the grandeur and monument of Herbert Baker's Union Buildings in Pretoria, where the black middle classes now played on weekends, teenagers practising dance moves, adults posing for wedding photos, spreading out in a space of green lawns and sculpted trees and classical vistas. It was possible to be both monumental and welcoming, to command respect without intimidating or alienating the citizenry. The Constitutional Court had failed fundamentally in this respect. Noble ideas had usurped practicality as well as beauty.

Inside the chamber, the pervasive sense Clare had was of symbolic chaos, of the hotchpotch. Brown tiles stretched across some sections of the floor, a white carpet with an incongruous grey and purple organic design covered the lowest portion. The walls were either rough red brick salvaged from the demolished awaiting-trial block or white plaster, with grey concrete pillars. Counsel sat at brown wooden desks that looked like castoffs from a lending library, while the justices themselves were seated, higher than the level of the lawyers but below that of the public gallery, behind a bench faced with black and white cowhide – a nice African touch, Clare thought, and the only moment of originality and artistic integrity in the whole mess. It was both contemporary and traditional and yet had too much glass and steel and too many competing angles and pointless balconies and cacophonous surfaces ever to cohere into a whole. What Clare had liked, what impressed her as well as troubled her in its audacity, was that the public, the spectators, were physically above the justices. There was something too populist about this arrangement for her to be completely comfortable with it, but the idea that the judges should be servants to the people was, in theory, good. That the lawyers themselves, the counsellors appearing before the court, occupied the lowest physical position in the space was an even nicer ironic touch. Through the long horizontal window slanting behind the justices, the street life of the city – foot traffic and cars – remained just visible. Sirens were audible. Everything was permeable and transparent. This highest authority on the law of the land was not a star chamber, not a place of secrecy or privilege, but open to all. What concerned Clare more than anything, however, was that in its effort to be accessible and transparent, the Constitutional Court, the highest court in this fragile new country, could too easily be ignored – or worse, attacked.

Unlike some of his peers, men of the old dispensation who still argued with the illogic of apartheid, the logic of illogical privilege, Mark seemed to have an instinctive understanding of the tone of the court, the casual formality of its discourse, the critical interrogation and titanic frustrations and teasing good humour of its justices. He commanded the space and performed convincingly even if the justices did not find in favour of his clients. It was a noble thing to champion, the right to privacy, but Clare wondered if her lawyer son did not perhaps take it too far, if the supple intellect that could always see a more pliant interpretation of the law did not also risk perverting it. There were limits to privacy, and always had been and always must be. A state of unlimited privacy would inevitably be a state of chaos – a state that could not for long remain a state.

This, however, like his health and a great many other things between them, was something that Clare and Mark did not discuss. When she asked about his work, he turned either silent or defensive. She hoped that he could talk about the law with his father, who had been his model in so many things. For the sake of both men, she hoped that they enjoyed that kind of intimacy, though as the years passed she believed this was not so, that Mark's best and closest interlocutor was his own mind. And in this, perhaps, he was more like his mother.

CLARE

As the day progresses and I try to ignore Nosipho's enthusiastic vacuuming, Adam's mowing and hedge-trimming, and Marie's clip-clopping back and forth from her study to mine, I become incapacitated by a migraine. It starts at the base of the skull, and then grinds across the right side of my head like tectonic plates sliding against each other in a crescent arcing from my forehead to occipital bone. Then comes the nausea and visual distortions, the twin kidney shapes I always see, forms that pixelate the world within their borders. The first time it happened I thought I was going blind. I have learned that the only way to make it stop is to close my eyes and hope it may pass in an hour or two. So I put myself back to bed, but the headache is relentless, and the pain spreads, running along my clavicle and radiating demonic wings across the planes of my shoulder blades. After an hour of turning first left and then right, lying on my stomach and then back, pillows over and under my head, I finally fall asleep to one of the most troubling of my recurring dreams, one which takes various forms but always involves a similar scenario.

At some point in the recent past, so the narrative usually goes, I have made a commitment to look after the dogs belonging to a young couple that lived down the road from my childhood home. In most versions of this dream, on the afternoon the owners are due back from their holiday, I remember at the last minute that for several days I have failed to attend to the animals, leaving them without food and without access to the garden. Visions of frantic dogs, paws smeared with their own shit, the house rendered uninhabitable from the mess, overcome me. Knowing that, at worst, one or both of the animals might be dead, I race to the house, arriving just as the couple does; there is no hope of rectifying the situation before they can discover it. In the variation of the dream I have today, however, I remember the neglected dogs only after the couple's return, making my irresponsibility all the worse. I become aware that the couple has not phoned me to retrieve their spare keys, but, being overcome with shame, I cannot bring myself to contact them. The threat of some kind of legal sanction against me lurks at the edge of the dream's contents: I will be marked in the courts, and thus in the public record, as an abuser and neglecter of animals, someone so irresponsible I cannot even be trusted to look after myself and should therefore be locked away where I can do no harm to anyone.

Each time I have dreamed this particular dream it involves the same couple. They either have two dogs, or one dog, or a cat and a dog. I always fail to do what I have promised, resulting not only in acute embarrassment, but also potentially in the deaths of those entirely innocent other lives, the companion animals who relied upon me for their most basic needs. What always troubles me more than anything on waking is that I can think of no reason for feeling I ever disappointed this particular couple. They had no pets, but as an adolescent during the school holidays I was sometimes paid to look after their young daughter. I know that I always took good care of the girl, reading stories until it was her bedtime, tucking her in, consoling her when she cried for her mother (always her mother and never her father), waiting up for the parents to return from their dinner party, then being walked home by Rodney, the husband, who looked like a more dissolute Cary Grant. He would always press the money into my hands as we reached my gate, his palms sweaty and the notes limp with perspiration. At the time, I would not have minded if Rodney had drawn me aside, against a tree, and kissed me. Although nothing of the sort ever happened, this feeling runs like under-stitching through the fabric of the dreams, invisible but holding firm the lining that keeps everything else tidy, the seams obscured, the construction masked under a shimmer of subconscious satin. Looking back on my desire for Rodney I suspect that if he had actually kissed me, pushing my body up against the bark of a stinkwood, insinuating his tongue into my mouth, I would have been horrified.

I know, too late, that this series of dreams has nothing to do with Rodney, or his wife, or their daughter, whom I looked after so well, and about whom I have no reason to suffer a guilty conscience. These dreams have everything to do with you, Laura, the wild beast daughter I neglected, failed to feed and water, failed to hold myself account to in the way that you needed. I should not have waited for you to ask for help. I should have known what you needed, anticipated your requirements, and foreseen what you would feel compelled to do. I should have known you could not be domesticated or broken. If I had tried to stop you, would you have let me?

'No,' you say, coming into my bed tonight, unfurling yourself around me, enclosing my limbs in yours. 'You could not have stopped me.'

'But if I had been different, if I had known another way to be, if I could have given with both hands instead of always, *always* holding something back, then surely you might have let me help you!'

'There is no undoing the past, old woman. You must accept what you are.'

'What am I?' I implore, as you rise and retreat. 'Tell me what I am!'

'A monster,' you say, your voice unravelling sadness. 'A monster like me.'

★

Since I don't know what else to do, I return to what I was reading the other day. I realize, for the first time, that all ten of your notebooks are nothing more than school exercise books – the very same kind that I used to compose the first half-dozen of my novels, convinced that if the authorities ever raided the old house on Canigou Avenue the police would assume they were nothing but the work of children and posed no threat. I intentionally made my handwriting juvenile, even sloppy in places. But your handwriting, Laura, is always precise and, though unusual, unmistakably adult. One would look at your script and say it was the hand of a writer, unlike mine.

After first meeting Ilse at the newspaper you saw her again a few days later and, trying to sound as though you'd been struck by some spontaneous inspiration, invited her to join you for lunch. She suggested a small hostel on Church Street.

If you knew about her relationship with your father, you gave nothing away, attempting instead to play the ingénue seeking advice and friendship from a woman more experienced of the world – a role I never fulfilled for you; if you ever asked for

362

my advice, I cannot remember it. You turned to the men of the family, to your brother and father, and even to your uncles, but the women you ignored – not just me, but your aunts and cousins in equal measure – as though you suspected that only men had access to the truth, that women were, in this society, no more than ornaments, impedimenta on the path you wanted to travel.

Throughout lunch, Ilse raged about the repressive new laws imposed on the country and spoke hopefully about the return of opposition figures from abroad, come home to liberate with jewels of fire. Afraid someone might be listening, you looked around the café, monitoring reactions, comings and goings, whilst Ilse spoke, her small body generating so much anger it was like suffering an assault just sitting across from her.

'It's a reasonably safe place,' she said, noticing your unease, 'and the owner is a fellow traveller of sorts.'

'You should be careful in any case.'

'Careful people don't make things happen. Until people like us – like our parents and cousins – begin to feel directly threatened, then nothing will change.' She groaned and put her head in her hands, always dramatic. It was the kind of explosive passion that your father found irresistible, a quality I could never offer. 'I must apologize,' she said, looking up at you through her dark fringe of hair, 'it's unfair of me to assume that you would necessarily agree with my opinions. But I know where Bill's sympathies lie, so I imagined that you –'

'No,' you assured her, taking her hand across the table, shaking it as if in compact, 'you're exactly right. I agree with you completely.'

She smiled, folding your hand between both of hers. 'I knew it. I'm so pleased. You must meet Peter. We've been looking for someone like you.'

You were flattered by this opening, but felt you could not trust her. Perhaps you were right: she had been your father's lover, had forced herself into his arms when you were still a child, knowing that he had a family. She had been to the house, met the wife and children, and still she seduced him, aware of the harm it might do.

'I would like that very much,' you said, almost flirting with her. You decided that day to accept whatever invitation was extended, to infiltrate yourself into her life, finding a way to return the sting of her transgression.

★

I have told Adam to come later today so that I may enjoy my swim in private, watching the early morning light penetrate the dark teardrop blossoms of the agapanthus on one side of the white gravel path that bisects the most formal beds, and on the other side catching the dew that rests on the fireball lilies. I realize with horror that the previous owners arranged this planting to suggest the old South African flag, stripes of blue, white, and orange. I make a mental note to have Adam pull out the lilies; I have never liked those poisonous hot colours anyway.

When Adam arrives I go inside and spend the morning reviewing a transcript from one of my interviews with Sam, who now writes to me as if I were something like a lover, or if not a lover, then the mother he wishes he'd had. It pricks my conscience but I cannot yet bring myself to give him more than I have already.

After lunch, I return to your words, Laura, feeling with each page that, rather than bringing you closer to me, far from leading me to the truth of your destiny, your notebooks only push you further from my sense of who you were. With each line I know you less and less, to the point that I begin to think you are not even yourself, not in this notebook, not in the way you are in the final volume, the one where, even when you confound my expectations, I can see the humanity of your choices, or if not that then your rationalization of those choices, the ways you saw that they might yet be humane. But in *this* book, in these pages, you are nothing but cold intention, a young woman of focussed determination, doing only what you wish to do, what you have decided or been directed to do. What I cannot discern is the precise nature of that desire.

On their suggestion you arranged to meet Ilse and Peter at a tavern in Observatory – it meant that after coming home from the office on Friday you could park and walk less than a minute up the street to find them, already at a table in a private corner, out of the flow of traffic, a place where the three of you might talk and not have to worry about being overheard.

Given Ilse's exuberance and reckless pronouncements at lunch, it was a surprise to find Peter so controlled, conservative in his dress and demeanour – the kind of thirty-something graduate student who would have spent his entire school career at Bishops or SACS and gone directly to the University of Cape Town, before, say, winning a Rhodes Scholarship to read Politics at Oxford; in other words, he appeared on the surface to be a carbon copy of your brother or one of your brother's friends. He was nothing at all like what he appeared. He'd never lived outside the country, and years after finishing his undergraduate degree and surviving national service he was only now about to begin work on a masters degree under the supervision of your father. You wondered to yourself what and how much Peter knew about Ilse and 'Bill', as she insisted on calling him. (He was never 'Bill' to me, not once in our life together, and the revelation of it in your notebook wounds me more than I could have expected. Foolishly, I assumed the old weapons had lost their power to maim.) I stagger across the line when I come to it: *I know about Ilse and Dad. Does Mom?* How could you not bring yourself to confide in me what you knew?

Despite yourself you liked both of them, finding they were easy company in the way that your other colleagues – mostly men, mostly older, hardened and hard-drinking, some risking their lives to cover stories the government did not want told – might never be, at least not with you, a young woman who had no right to look as striking as you did and yet remain so unreachable.

At first, politics was not on the agenda that evening and the three of you swapped life histories. Ilse had survived a cloistered girlhood in Graaff-Reinet with a doctor father who shot himself in the head one Sunday after church.

'And your mother?' you asked, curious to know as much as you could about them both – especially the woman who had so attracted your father.

'Not so long after my father died she drank herself into a fatal car crash – drove off a cliff in the Valley of Desolation.' You could see the high mound of rock and soil, the pinnacle outcroppings and the sheer drops to the unyielding floor of the Karoo.

After her mother's accident Ilse moved to Cape Town where she and Peter met as students. They married just after graduation, to the disapproval of Peter's banker father and housewife mother, who had both died in the past year – he of cancer, she of a heart attack.

'So you're orphans now,' you said, 'adult orphans.' They looked at you as though the idea had never struck them before and was something that changed how they thought of themselves, both as individuals and as two people together in the world. And you, though younger than them by more than a decade, childless as you were and always would be, an orb to the grave, presented yourself as the mother they both sought.

It was clear, however, that this was a topic that disturbed Ilse. She did not want to talk about parents and children, least of all about loss.

'Don't you hate the *Record*?' she demanded, as Peter went to get another round of beers. 'They won't print a story about a stray cat if they think it might get them into trouble. And when they *do* cover the townships, which is almost never, they act as though they're reporting from the darkest heart of the Congo.'

'Then why do you work for them?'

'The alternative papers don't pay as well. I have a child, Peter's at university again, what can you do? We have to make compromises. It won't always be this way. Things will change. We're going to make them change, aren't we?' She stared at you intently, unblinking, her gaze half-obscured by the lengths of dark hair that fell around her face.

As the evening wore on and Ilse continued to rage there in the corner, Peter consoling her now and then, cooling her fire, you felt a tickle of resentment in your chest, a complex stirring. Who was this woman to be so sanctimonious, to say and do what she wanted without having to face the consequences?

★

I put you aside, Laura, for as long as you will remain silent, and reply to Sam, teasing him, coaxing him onwards, hoping to show him the way, to force him into making the first move, which I am too great a coward to make.

Dear Sam,

Thank you for your message. Have no worry, I am not offended at your shock, although I suspect your French friend would also have counselled you not to direct the recipient of your correspondence to react in a particular way to your words. One reacts to what words say, and sometimes – too often – intent can be opaque. A case in point: the words I have written sound pricklier than I mean them to. If you were here, you would see the smile on my face and know that I am amused, but my brain lacks the energy to put that amusement into my words, if you see what I mean. So we read, interpreting the intention of the other according to what the text says (the text that the other has written). In the end there can only be *that*, the words on the page, or in this case on the screen. So let me reassure you that I am never offended by anyone being shocked at what I may have done or what I may have said, least of all by what I may have written. It has often been my intention – my dearest hope – to shock in one way or another. (There's a revelation for your book.) I fear that I have very rarely managed it, so your shock is a kind of gift to an old woman, and it will keep me warm at night, although I have no need of warmth at present as the heat here is truly terrible – 33 degrees Celsius today and a southeaster to make it that much more unpleasant. They say sharks have been spotted in False Bay, sharks the size of helicopters or dinosaurs, sharks the size of minibuses, sharks as big as nuclear submarines. One does not know what to believe. Marie will not go within twenty metres of the ocean so convinced is she that sharks are destined to start coming out of the water and taking their prey from land. For myself, I have not been swimming in any other water but my own pool for a long time, and have no intention of changing that habit. There it is again – intention, that old bugbear.

You will not apologize again, please, for your questions to me. (It is different, I would say, to command an action in one's correspondence than to demand a certain kind of response to one's words; and here, you should know, I smile again, tongue in cheek.) I know I am a difficult prospect for an interviewer. Reputation has made me so. It is my suspicion that your time in America has made you more direct, though you retain some of your South Africanness; if anything, it was that directness that surprised me on occasion. With the British and even with local scholars, there is more circumlocution – questions in the form of paragraphs or mini-essays, questions that quite intimidate the questioned. I always think if the interviewer has so much to say to the interviewed, then what use am I? Know that I appreciated your (general) restraint on that point. I don't know if it was conscious, nor does it really matter.

Reviews, yes, I read them. I shall look forward to yours and trust you will be honest about the places where I have failed. Be sure, I know there are failures in the book, things I wished to say but could not, for the sake of others, things I said badly, less directly, than I should have liked. It is all about protection – protection of myself, protection of my family. (I can be direct here, in private. *My* instead of *one*.) That is why the book, as you will discover, is so distanced and distancing. What safer way to write about the self than from a distorting distance?

An eager young man at the University of Stellenbosch who writes rather a lot of nice, perfectly well-intentioned (there it is again) but quite mad twaddle about my books has asked me to give a reading at the Winelands Literary Festival; you'll no doubt know who I mean. I have momentarily dropped his name into my mental waste bin and cannot be bothered to retrieve it. Anyway – I accepted before I could think better of it. I wonder, perhaps, if you might consider coming?

Yours,

Clare

PS I suppose you 'do' holidays. I do not. But I shall wish you 'happy holidays' nonetheless. I used to escape from holiday gatherings on long walks, when one could still walk 'relatively unmolested' (I remember that phrase of yours) in this city, up on the mountain above the Rhodes Memorial where the trees and the university architecture almost fool one into thinking it the Palatine Hill. Such walks are no longer possible, not for me or for most in fact. Even groups of hikers with whole packs of dogs are no longer safe. If you came to Stellenbosch in May, perhaps we could find a way and a time to walk. I should like that.

1998–99

Life since the death of his parents had felt like a series of corners: a corner of his aunt's small house; a corner of a room or a series of rooms at school and then at university; a corner of an airplane cabin; a corner of his dorm room in New York, half-inhabited by other creatures and layers of dirt that reappeared a day after washing them away. Sarah offered more than a corner. She was space and light and airiness and a confidence of movement and grace that was so natural and unconscious he could only marvel at her.

He didn't know what it might mean, to begin a relationship with an American, to throw in his lot with a different country. He accepted that he was getting ahead of himself; he also knew that he had almost no one else in the world – just an aunt in a dorp in the middle of nowhere, someone who hadn't wanted him in the first place. He had no connections to speak of, no money, no privileges other than those he might earn.

Tell me something about your exotic childhood, Sarah said, tracing an ellipse on Sam's cheek over a scar whose origin he could not remember because it had been made when he was still an infant. A part of him had a memory of his mother telling him a cat got into his crib, while another echo told him he had fallen against a barbed-wire fence. Another still said he had been pulled up into someone's arms and his face slashed with a broken bottle when his parents had taken him somewhere they shouldn't have. Whatever the case the scar was there and was not going away. It had been a part of him for as long as he could remember looking like the person he recognized as himself. To imagine his face without the scar on his left cheek was to imagine someone else's face, another person and a different identity, a self he might once have been but could now never be. It made him remember the scar on his father's face, a face so unlike his own that at times it seemed as though scars were the only things that connected the two of them.

She traced the ellipse over and over with her fingertip until he told her to stop and wrapped his hand around hers and examined the swimming surface of her eyes. *Exotic* was a strange way to describe it since his childhood had never seemed anything other than routine to him, apart from the death of his parents and the circumstances that had delivered him into the care of his aunt. But there was nothing exotic even about those events in the way that most people mean 'exotic'. To Sarah he supposed he *must* appear exotic and, strictly speaking, that was the correct way to describe him. Compared to her, he *was* from outside, from a country as foreign as it was possible to be, even though he felt strangely at home in America, which was both as much and as least like home as anywhere might be. Before coming to New York he had always assumed that Britain was his country's model and frame of reference, but the longer he spent in the city he realized how wrong he must have been. America felt like his country in different terms, its inverse and possibility, its cultural twin and opposite.

When Sarah spoke of his *exotic* childhood he feared that she meant not just foreign but also strange and barbarous, spiced and scented, a childhood glamorous in its outlandish landscape, creatures, and customs, tribal and tropical, though *tropical* was far from accurate.

He told her his parents were dead and that after their deaths his aunt had taken him in and that although he would now see her once a year when he returned home for the holidays he was otherwise alone in the world. He said nothing at first about Bernard. He said nothing of the way his parents had died. He realized later that he'd spoken of their deaths in a way that didn't invite questions.

Or perhaps Sarah asked him how they died, and he said only, *They died. They're dead.*

And after they died, she said, as if understanding that he wasn't ready to speak about them, *what can you tell me about those years?*

As he began to recount his life after going to live with his aunt, he realized that the memories were all folded into the books he had been reading, the books he had inhabited in order to make sense of his life, in order to unlock the earlier memories – Clare's books. His memories were as much his own as they were scenes from the books he had been reading at the time the events occurred. In each case, the story he told Sarah began as his own and then, without intending it, changed into something he hadn't experienced that was derived from one of Clare's novels.

There were stories from school. Stories of pretending to be sick to escape revelation that he had bribed a group of boys to vote for him in a school election by promising to give each of them a chocolate bar every week for the rest of the year – and then of being discovered by a black member of the cleaning staff, and insisting in front of the headmaster that the black man was lying. Stories of listening to records in the bedrooms of dayboys whose parents drove him back and forth from school to play at suburban homes with high walls and swimming pools, gardeners and maids – and of discovering an elderly relative of one of the maids hidden in a garden shed, covered in perfectly round suppurating wounds that he knew had been made with a lit cigarette. Stories of finding a scorpion in his shoe – and watching as the scorpion turned to

376

stare at him, lowering its *metasoma*, its tail, and its *aculeus*, its sting (words that could only, he knew, have come from a book), and retreating from conflict. Stories of sneaking out of the residence and back into the school and playing piano in an empty room at night.

What did you play? Sarah asked, examining his fingers.

Schumann, he said, knowing that mostly he had played Chopin's Études. One of Clare's characters, Sam remembered, was a pianist and Schumann scholar.

He told her stories of an Afrikaans teacher who fell in love with him and gave him a book of C. Louis Leipoldt's poems.

Did you report the man?

He left the school the next year. I never saw him again. No one ever told us where he went. In fact the teacher had stayed at the school, and nothing more was ever said about the gift.

Stories of holidays with Ellen spent at Bushmans River and the blue-green waves of the Indian Ocean crashing like terror – the mist coming off the foam that rushed around tortured outcroppings of rock, directing the waves into mesmerizing eddies and swirls, and him running in fear to the grassy crest of the dunes to get away from the shore, inhaling and exhaling rapidly, his chest rising and falling under a thin cotton T-shirt. He had never been afraid of the ocean.

What colour T-shirt?

Green with gold sleeves, he said, thinking it might have been blue and orange.

When they had been together just over a year he finally told Sarah something about Bernard, although he spent days building up to it, playing the script he was writing over and over to be sure he would know how to answer the questions that might come.

After his parents died there was a brief time before he went to his aunt, he said, when he was looked after by a guardian, an uncle, a half-uncle really, and the guardian, this half-uncle, had disappeared with all the money from his parents' estate, the little there was, and all their belongings, even his toys.

I had a few books and a few clothes and that was about it.

And this guardian, your half-uncle, he just disappeared? Sarah sounded more sympathetic than anyone ever had except his own mother.

He dropped me – he abandoned me and then my aunt took me in. He abandoned me with her. He left me there. At her door.

God, Sam, that's terrible. You poor thing. She looked wounded and tears welled up in her eyes as they flared red at the ducts. She wiped them and put her hands on his and held them as if to squeeze truth from his fingers.

He could hear the engine gunning and then feel the bump like a boulder rearing up from the earth and the black-headed gearshift in his small hand, and then the other bump that collapsed into a crunch, and another softer crunch, and then seeing the body deflated and covered in roses like water in the lights from the truck. For years he had taken pains to be sure he felt nothing about that moment and how it made everything in his life change from one state of things to another. He knew he had made the change happen even if it was an accident. There was no question it was an accident. His parents had died because of an accident. That was how everyone had explained it to him. He tried to remember who had first told him about his parents being dead – it must have been the police or Mrs Gush, the old toothless woman – but there was a gap, as if the film of his memory had been cut and entire days of footage lost and burned up in a broken projector, bubbling yellow and black into whiteness.

Accidents were always happening. He had come from a country of accidents. He tried to under-stand what this meant. It seemed to mean that no one was ever responsible for anything if only you could tell the truth and most of all if you could say you were sorry. But he had not told the truth and he was not sorry.

There was no way to explain all this so he said nothing for a moment and tried to think of an explanation that would make sense in his head. By some movement of grace he had found this woman who seemed to like him, and now that he had found her he could not imagine being without her, but to tell the truth about everything would risk too much. He could not trust that she would understand, he could not trust that she would keep his secrets. He could sense her hunger for strangeness and story, for the hidden and the scandalous, and he knew that hunger was insatiable.

It just happened, he said, shaking his head. *I don't remember how it made me feel. I missed my parents. That's what I felt.*

He could see that she wouldn't be satisfied with what he had felt. He would always need to give more, to paint a landscape of fantasy, because he was sure that she wanted for him to have come from a place she couldn't imagine. So he told her about birds she hadn't heard of – hadedas and bulbuls and loeries – and plants she had never seen – giant euphorbia and cabbage trees and wild figs – and mountains so green and soft it looked as though they'd been upholstered with velvet and dotted with specks of cotton-wool sheep. He animated grey motes of dust into troops of vervet monkeys on plateaux and mountain passes and herds of springbok grazing the plains, great bustards exploding out of the flat Karoo and families of baboons camped in the middle of highways. He told her about landmarks from his childhood, Table Mountain, Fish Hoek, Camps Bay, and spun stories of hot weather in the months that were winter in the northern hemisphere.

Yes, she said, *it sounds like an amazing place. But there are people in it, too, Sam. And I want to hear about them. I want to hear more about your parents. You've never even told me their names.*

Peter, he said, *and Ilse.*

SAM

Before we were married, I finally told Sarah what my parents really were, that they had died in an attack, but that they were the attackers, that they had killed themselves by accident, and killed others in the process – some innocent, some complicit in the institutions of apartheid.

I told her in the car on a trip to her parents' house in Virginia. I waited until we were driving, knowing that I wouldn't be able to back away from what I had to confess.

'You're saying that your parents were suicide bombers.' Her voice was so quiet it was almost inaudible above the sound of the road.

'Their deaths were accidental. As I understand it, they were going to leave the car outside the police station and phone in a warning, but there was a problem with the device. While they were waiting for the right moment, the appointed time, before they'd left the car, the bomb detonated.'

'I thought the anti-apartheid struggle was non-violent.'

I had imagined she would scream and shout in

anger. Instead, she sounded stunned, like someone struck by a sudden and incomprehensible grief.

'You have to understand it in context. It was an accident. It wasn't supposed to happen the way it did. Innocent people were not supposed to die. You can read the TRC testimony about their case. Their deaths were an error.' I remember struggling to catch my breath, feeling my throat constricting. It seemed perverse to talk about my parents in this way, as though their deaths were the equivalent of a clerical mistake: the wrong file pulled from the records, the wrong order processed, the wrong employee terminated.

For ten miles we drove in silence. I opened my mouth and felt myself beginning, almost despite my own better sense, to tell Sarah the truth about Bernard. My heart was racing to collapse but I wanted her to know. I wanted finally to tell someone what I'd done.

'I guess in the end it doesn't matter,' she said, before I could find the courage to speak. 'But I wish you'd told me in the first place.'

In the end I didn't tell her about Bernard. I still haven't. I tell myself that now it's too late, and that no good could ever come from the telling.

With no one left to ask which year I received the train set, which the red tricycle, I stew all the Christmases before my parents died into a single hot, chaotic day with a trip to the beach, a Hawaiian-themed feast, a Mexican lunch, twelve guests, two guests, grandparents, no grandparents, and my mother and father always drinking sundowners out of a plastic thermos, wearing swimming costumes and rubbing sunscreen into my skin. The first Christmas that I spent with my aunt in Beaufort West, the heat shimmered off the painted metal roofs and my arms stuck to tables, my legs to the plastic chairs on the back veranda. Friends of Ellen's came for lunch and she made five different salads and a roast chicken and there was Christmas cake with rolled icing and marzipan, bought from a woman at the church. She gave me gifts designed to comfort more than cheer: new shoes, a pair of shorts, an anthology of short stories. As I opened them I felt no happiness and struggled not to burst into tears, and then I cried anyway when I opened the photograph of my mother as a teenager, which Ellen had put in a silver frame. Whether Ellen had any gifts to open herself I can't remember.

I've managed to forget the first Christmas after my parents died, alone with Bernard in his house, surrounded by beer and beef, hot from the braai. There were no gifts that year, none that I want to remember.

I decide to believe that my parents doubted, withdrew at the last moment, considered, consulted each other, confirmed they were doing the right thing no matter the risk to themselves or what their failure would mean for me. They couldn't believe they were driving to their own deaths. They couldn't have wished to kill. I've tried to convince myself it was only supposed to be an exercise to prove the power to kill, assuming a bomb can ever just be an exercise.

The container from New York came a few days ago and I go searching for the file I've kept of transcripts and clippings relating to my parents.

★

CAPE TOWN, 29 OCTOBER 1999 – SAPC

MK COMMISSAR DESCRIBES TRAINING FOR CAPE TOWN SAPS BLAST

The TRC today heard that the 1988 bomb that killed five people outside of the Cape Town Central Police Station was a justifiable attack on a government target designed to demonstrate to the apartheid regime that they were not untouchable.

Six former members of MK, Umkhonto we Sizwe, the armed wing of the African National Congress, made applications for amnesty in relation to their involvement in this and a number of other attacks on government installations in the 1980s.

Among the applicants was Joe Speke, 52, who planned some of the attacks during his tenure as head of the ANC's Special Operations Unit, including the attack on Cape Town's Police Station. Mr Speke described how the Cape Town Central

Police Station bomber Peter Lawrence underwent training in the use of a remote-controlled device that malfunctioned, inadvertently killing both Lawrence and his wife, the reporter and ANC activist Ilse Lawrence, who was with him in the car at the time of the blast. One police officer and two civilians were also killed when the car, loaded with 10kg of explosives, prematurely detonated.

Mr Speke, who is represented by Cape Town-based lawyer and Professor of Law at UCT William Wald, was cross-examined by Carlo Du Plessis, SC, who is representing the families of the two civilians killed in the blast. The families oppose the amnesty application of Mr Speke on the grounds that the victims were civilians whose deaths could serve no political purpose. Mr Speke suggested it was possible that the Lawrences' cell had been infiltrated by the security services and the bomb sabotaged.

Mr Speke will finish his testimony on Monday.

© South African Press Corporation

★

I read a report like this and struggle not to be angry. What stupid people, I think. What stupid people to risk their lives in that way. Even if the bomb hadn't gone off prematurely, they almost certainly would have been caught and sent to prison – or if they'd managed to escape, taking me out of the country for a life in exile, as must have been their plan, then they still might have been assassinated. I know that they loved me but how much can they really have loved me if they were willing to risk my own well-being? I put the file away before I make the mistake of reading anything more unsettling. If their mission was compromised, perhaps there is a kind of solace in that, knowing that they were killed not in error, as a result of their own mistakes, but by the enemy itself, the state.

We take only a few days off for the holidays and then both go back to work. I shut myself in the office at the university and return to the recordings of my interviews with Clare, making careful transcriptions that take much longer to complete than the conversations themselves. I'm still only in the first days of the interviews, early in the process. My voice always sounds strangled, pinched and otherworldly as it comes out of the computer speakers. Clare, though, sounds just like I remember her.

'Did motherhood change the way you wrote?' I can hear the inflection in my voice, a modulation I know was intended to suggest a judgement already formed.

'You forget that I was a mother,' she drawls, clearing her throat and coughing, 'before I was ever a writer.'

'But the two unpublished novels that you dismiss

as juvenilia, those were written before you were married, so I think the question isn't unjustified.'

'Fine then. Did motherhood change the way I wrote? You mean the practice of writing or the content?' Without any audible transition, she goes from dismissive to sounding as though she's at least willing to weigh the question seriously.

'Either. However you wish to interpret "wrote" or "writing".'

'It's not a terrible question now that I think about it,' she says, pausing again, and I remember her looking out the windows at her garden, always looking, as though the plants, the trees and the flowers, perhaps even the lawns and the lap pool, held all the answers. 'Motherhood changed the practice of writing in predictable ways. My time was no longer entirely my own, though such an experience is not unique, least of all for a mother. Simply, the case is this: investing oneself in the institution of family is always about the partial annihilation of self (for the unlucky, for those who comprehensively rebel against the constraints of family because they feel no other choice but to do so, family feels like the *total* annihilation of self, the foreclosing of all possibility of individual subjectivity). For me, as a mother and wife at that historical moment in this most socially retrogressive of settler countries, it meant that I was suddenly burdened with child care, with the fundamentals of dirty nappies and hungry mouths and wailing and nap time and then, eventually, with the ferrying back and forth to school and to see friends and the dramas of adolescence, while the children see the parents, if they see them at all (if mine saw me at all), as disciplinarians and facilitators and protectors rather than actors in their own right: the child's narrative, for the child, has to eclipse that of the parent, who is a mere supporting character. So motherhood robbed me of time, and to claw back some of that time (here I'm being grotesquely confessional), I carved it out of my marriage – less time for my husband, more for the writing and the children. My son would tell you a different version, one in which, once my career took off, I was almost always absent, and he was raised by his father, nannies, au pairs, maids, and even gardeners. But it would not be an accurate version, nor, I admit, a wholly inaccurate one, and in that respect I do not feel I have to apologize for having been absent at times as my children grew up. I was there when it was important to be there. As for the content of the writing, whether the biological and chemical fact of motherhood changed my style and form and subject matter, I'll have to leave that to the critics, who will decide after my death.'

ABSOLUTION

Clare had no appetite for dinner. She pushed her food around on the plate, toying with it like a cat fondling an animal it has killed by mistake, while Mark finished one portion and helped himself to another, as if he could neither eat his fill nor be done with the meal fast enough. Eye contact between them, when it happened, was only momentary; it seemed that her son was doing everything in his power to avoid looking at her. The plate before him, the series of four geometric paintings on the walls of the dining room, and the windows with their views of the floodlit back garden, lights turning the trees and shrubs into a static menagerie and the pool into a fantasy portal of shimmering green, these were what Mark's eyes rested upon, not on the face of his mother. It was impossible to tell him how much this hurt. Clare tried not to stare at him, but she could not help it; he was all she had left in the world apart from the people whom she paid to organize and look after her. She knew that he was no longer hers to claim – that right belonged to his wife and his children, if it belonged to anyone.

'Was it only last year that I had the house invasion?' Clare asked, less because she was uncertain and more to break the silence.

'Don't you remember, Mother? It was the year before.' He said it in a way that suggested Clare was often forgetful and she felt the rebuke like a punch to the gut.

For many years before the break-in Mark had encouraged her to sell up and move somewhere more secure than the house on Canigou Avenue, and when at last she had recognized there was no other choice but to subject herself to voluntary house arrest behind high walls and gates and electric fencing, with Marie as her personal turnkey, always stalking behind, even then she had complained that it was no way to live, no way for a woman, no way for any person, let alone someone who had forever taken her freedom for granted. In retort Mark had told her South Africa was no place for a single elderly woman, or two such women, to be living without the protection of a man at home twenty-four hours a day. Go to Australia or New Zealand, he'd pleaded, or Britain or France, or even America. Any one of those would be preferable to here. Clare had asked him, thinking of his wife who had experienced several near misses on the street outside their house, if marriage or the companionship of a man guaranteed protection. No, Mark had been forced to concede, if it were possible for him to find a job elsewhere in the world, somewhere safer, a place where he could go out to the shops in the evening without worrying about what might be waiting at home when he returned, or what might happen on the way there or back when he was doing something as innocuous as picking up the dry-cleaning, then he would move the whole family, Clare included, without hesitation. He had reached the conclusion that South Africa was simply no place to be a woman of any age or any race. 'The only thing that would make these people change,' he'd said, 'is if all the women in the entire country simply left. That's what it would take: the desertion by more than half the population to demonstrate that they've had enough of being treated as less than second-class citizens, less than animals, but as property held by the community of men, open to the exploitation of men, abused and subjugated and made to act against their own interests, to be complicit in the violence that is done against them by men.'

'So you must remember the particulars of the house invasion,' Clare said, pushing aside her plate. 'The incompetence of the police, the failure to locate any viable suspects or follow any of the evidentiary leads, the fact that a great many things of obvious value – electronics and silver and the like – were ignored in preference for an object of no obvious value except perhaps to a collector of legal paraphernalia.'

'Grandpa's wig.'

'Quite.'

'And the police never solved the case.'

'It was a travesty of investigation and legal process. They accused me of being something like a criminal for living in so vulnerable a position, as though Rondebosch were Langa, and they made insinuations about my long-term safety, even my right to remain in this country as a white woman, never mind the validity of my birthright to call myself a citizen of the republic. They suggested I was a foreigner, or if not an actual foreigner, then in essence no different to one.'

'If it were a matter of all the white women leaving the country, I've begun to think that one would find a great many supporters for such a solution.'

It was not something Clare herself would have said – indeed, she thought it far from accurate, and began to see that her son's politics were not as progressive as she had once believed.

'In any case,' she continued, 'what is important about the recent events is that the wig was returned – at least, it has come back to me, and, I think, was intended to do so all along. Though it was left up to me to find it, it was hiding in plain sight, and not even hiding, but broadcasting its location in a most symbolic way.'

'I don't follow. The police solved the case after all?'

'Some months after the invasion and theft, on a particularly pleasant day, Marie suggested we go for a drive to Stellenbosch, and on the way back visit Nora and Stephan's graves in Paarl. In the cemetery, just adjacent to the eternal flame that Stephan's family had insisted on, as though he were some kind of national hero, as though, through its ongoing illumination, his ideas were worth commemorating, there was my father's wig in its box with his name stencilled on the lid in gold.'

Clare watched Mark take in the information and then, seeing that some part of him did not believe her story, she left the dining room and returned a moment later with the battered black tin box in her hands. Mark opened it, removed the wig, mounted it on the head of his left hand, and turned the hairpiece round to examine it.

'It's certainly the one,' he said. 'I was obsessed with this wig as a child.'

'Apart from photographs and books and his collection of pens it was the only thing of my father's that I truly cared about when he died. I had no idea it meant anything to you.' She shook her head back into focus. 'So: the wig is stolen, it disappears for a period, the police can find no leads, the police baulk at being asked even to investigate the theft of an item so obviously without significant value, and when next I think to visit the grave of my assassinated sister and brother-in-law I find it there, as if awaiting me, as if left as a message and reminder. Not, in fact, *as if*, but very intentionally, I believe, the wig was taken from me and removed to that symbolic place as a way for my tormentors to speak to me.'

'What on earth do you mean, Mother?'

Clare tried to remain composed, but how infuriating her son could be!

'You're saying that the thieves *knew* who you were and that Nora was your sister. So all it means is that you were *deliberately* targeted rather than being the victim of a random crime. Beyond that, I really don't understand what you're getting at.'

Clare sighed dramatically and motioned to Mark to give her the wig. She tucked a stray hair back into place, returned it to its tin box, closed and fastened the lid. 'Correct. There was nothing random about the invasion, nor were the intruders ordinary criminals – or if they were, they were acting on behalf of people who are not ordinary criminals. Who can say whether my tormentors, for that is how I think of them, are the ones who actually did the dirty work, or were nothing more than the puppets of those who wished to tell me what they knew about me in the most personally intrusive and intimidating if ultimately quite petty way. It's the kind of stunt that might be masterminded by a bureaucrat, an administrator who takes perverse delight in the meaning and value of a staple or paperclip or a tape-dispenser.'

'I still don't follow. What are you suggesting these tormentors, as you call them, actually knew about you?'

Clare took a deep breath and spread her hands. 'Here we come to the long tail of the root, clinging to its earth of history. This is information that will change how you think of your mother – information that will, I fear, batter our relationship into something lesser, a thing scarred and defeated and spooked by the revelation.'

'You make it sound as though you were the criminal instead of the people who broke in.'

'Indeed,' she said, her voice growing hoarse, her chin quivering despite herself, 'that is the very thing I am, a criminal, and not in the way the police suggested, not because I allowed myself to become a victim through my own failures of security, such as they were, but a true criminal.'

She let the confession settle between them, waiting for Mark's response. He furrowed his brow and looked as though he did not believe her.

'Or, perhaps I should put it this way. Even if the crime is not a crime as such, I do and can only regard myself as guilty of something like criminal negligence, or if not negligence, then recklessness – recklessness with the lives of others, recklessness with information that endangered those lives. During the whole circus of the Truth and Reconciliation Commission I thought of doing something symbolic and audacious – that is, applying for amnesty as a political criminal. Ultimately, however, I lacked the courage, and did not want to trivialize the much more serious crimes committed by those guilty at less than one remove, as I ostensibly am. Nonetheless, a part of me still feels that an amnesty hearing is what I most need – a judicial process, a hearing of the truth in a formal way, and a judge to pass sentence, to tell me that the thing I did was done not just out of personal spite, but for political reasons.'

Mark sat up straighter in his chair. If he did not understand the nature of his mother's crime, she hoped he might appreciate the urgency of her need. 'But the proceedings of the Amnesty Committee are finished now, and have been for some time,' he said, looking perplexed.

'I quite understand that. I know there is no real hope of actual political amnesty.'

'So what – are you thinking of turning yourself over to the police for whatever crime you imagine you've committed?'

'I have bad relations with the police as it is. They would think I was mocking them after the whole wig imbroglio. I am certain they would not take my confession seriously – they might even charge me with wasting police time. No, this is no longer a matter for the authorities.'

Clare looked at her son, his expression fixed, all good humour and affection suppressed.

'You see, the root of the tail begins with you,' she said. Mark's left eyebrow flared at its outer tip but the rest of his face remained fixed, jaws working his food. 'You were the first grandchild in the family, though Nora had been married a decade longer than I and had produced no issue. As a result, you caused considerable bad feeling between my sister and me. My pregnancy and your successful birth, your extreme, translucent beauty as a baby, these were streams of oil poured on the fire that had separated Nora from me since my own birth. Some first-born children adapt. They take well to those who follow. They are instinctive nurturers and protectors and guides, as you were with Laura – at least in your better moments. My sister had none of that nurturing sense, or if she did, it was so eclipsed by her rage at my usurping her position as the sole focus of our parents' attention that the only way she could respond to me was with resentment and hatred – resenting my coming, and hating my being. I will spare you the catalogue of her offences against me as a child: the burnings and beatings, the trickery and abuse, the destruction of my most treasured books, her attempt to undermine my happy relations with our parents. It was only on this last point that she failed, and in failing was fully exposed to them for the terrorist she had been. Not just a terrorist, but my jailer and torturer, my own nursery sadist.'

As she spoke, Clare observed Mark's face crease in disbelief.

'I know you think I exaggerate – in this, in all things – but please hear me out. It was during the winter holidays and we were spending a week with Uncle Richard and Aunt Frances on the farm to coincide with Dorothy's twelfth birthday. I had only just turned eleven myself. Frances had planned a party for the family and some of Dorothy's friends from her school in Grahamstown. With the help of my mother, who as you must remember was an excellent cook, Frances had produced a stunningly beautiful cake for the occasion. At the hour of its presentation, with all the family and friends and neighbours and even the household staff and their children assembled to watch Dorothy blow out the candles, Aunt Frances went to fetch the cake from the pantry. As we were waiting, we heard her cry out, then reappear looking pale and shocked. In her hands she held the platter on which the cake had been decorated, and on top of the cake was a large pile of dog shit, a great brown splotch. Dorothy burst into tears as Frances looked for explanation. The assembled children, and not a few of their parents, erupted with laughter. As if this weren't shocking enough, Nora stepped forward and pointed at me. In her most self-righteous voice she announced that she had seen me earlier in the back garden, collecting the dog shit with a trowel. But before I could even protest – I'd done nothing of the kind, but had been playing hide-and-seek with Dorothy and some of her friends all morning, so had no alibi for the entire period – one of the servants' children screamed that Nora was a liar, and that he had watched *her* collecting the dog shit and had watched *her* carrying it into the pantry and sneaking out again before anyone else could see. The child shouted this with such conviction that no one, I think, could have doubted the truth of what he said.

'Had it been left at that, it would have been forgotten, because to punish Nora on the word of that child would have been unthinkable, even to our egalitarian-minded parents. While the adults might have believed the boy, a part of them would have elected to disbelieve him because of his colour, and that disbelief would have won the day. But Nora could not leave the accusation alone, and at the same time was too young to know how to handle her accuser in a way that would have made her look like the innocent, wronged party – the role that I, in fact, inhabited. Having been wrongly accused, I stood through the entire drama as the truly innocent so often will: shocked and silent with my mouth agape. Nora, however, rushed at her accuser and pulled at his shirt and slapped him across the face two or three times before my father and Uncle Richard could pull her away from the boy, who was half her age and less than half her size.

'After that day, I marked a change in the way my parents handled Nora. She was no longer trusted to look after me or any other child. She was given no responsibilities at home. My parents were still warm with her, but in a more distant way, as though she had done something so outrageous that they could never see her again as they had before. The crime of putting dog shit on our cousin's twelfth-birthday cake would have been forgivable, even understandable. It was chiefly about jealousy – if not of Dorothy, then perhaps, indirectly, of me. But Nora compounded that crime first by accusing me of what *she* had done – thereby trying to undermine our parents' affection for me – and second by assaulting the only witness to the actual crime.'

'So,' Mark said, the furrows of his brow deepening, 'you're saying that the real problem, as far as your parents were concerned, was that Nora had committed a premeditated crime designed to destroy their good impression of you, the favoured child.'

'How do you conclude that I was the favoured child?'

'You must have been, or Nora must have believed you were, if she felt pushed to do what she did – if she felt so marginalized already that she could only do something to make you look bad.'

Clare observed a shift in Mark's attitude, as though his mind required a legal problem to master and direct his attention, and to make this encounter with his mother less difficult to bear.

'I had never quite considered it in that way. The greatest crime was the assault on the truth-teller – the powerless one who has nothing to lose by speaking the truth, or who has everything to lose but doesn't know what he has to lose, and therefore *must* be telling the truth.'

'What happened to the child?'

'As far as I remember, he was taken inside the

house and had cold compresses applied to his face and was given sweet tea and a piece of the reserve cake Aunt Frances had made in case there was not enough of the first. That other cake had been hidden, safe in the airing cupboard. There was plenty of the reserve, and we all rallied our spirits for Dorothy's sake. Nora, however, disappeared with my father. I cannot say whether she was beaten. I suspect she was not. My parents never punished me physically, and I have no memory that they ever did so to Nora. Rather, I suspect she was subjected to one of my father's philosophical interrogations, which were often as painful as a beating might have been for the way in which he could make one feel totally exposed, unable to hide, and diminished to something less than the ideal child one was expected to be – less than that, but not less than human. My father knew how to tread that line, to make us see our faults without destroying our sense of our own humanity. After I was married, and more particularly after you were born, things became much worse between Nora and me. The question is, did I ultimately do what I did because of all the terrors Nora inflicted on me, or because of my own sense of investment in a moral and political and democratic struggle? The political or the personal?'

'And what is it that you believe you're guilty of doing?'

Although the house was warm and the day had been hot a shudder of chill ran round Clare's shoulders. She had never spoken to anyone of what she had done, not even her husband, certainly not her parents, who would have been horrified and might never have forgiven her. Only those who had witnessed her transgression must have known, and she had long since lost touch with them; the story had come out neither in the trial of the supposed assassin, nor in the hearings of the Truth and Reconciliation Commission.

'I gave away Nora's location. I told someone who was not supposed to know where she and Stephan would be on a particular night. The information was used, and, as you know, they were murdered in their bed. For a long time I believed it was mere carelessness that made me do it, and a desire to be thought important by people I respected and feared not a little. The more time that passes the more I think that I knew exactly what I was doing – I knew how the information would be used and what the consequences would be. In retrospect it felt as much like a political decision as a personal one. Stephan was powerful and had the power to do great evil. In eliminating him, I felt as though I were striking a blow against the whole edifice of the apartheid state. Nora was collateral damage, as one now says. Her political role was negligible, and largely symbolic.'

Clare watched as Mark struggled to look at her, turning instead to gaze out on to the floodlit garden. Hoping to catch his eye in the glass if not in the flesh, Clare turned to face in the same direction. The lights in the garden and the pool were on a timer and without warning they suddenly went off, leaving the two of them staring at each other in the dark reflective surface of the dining-room windows.

CLARE

Working in my vegetable garden with Adam this morning, preparing the ground for a new sowing of lettuce seeds, I inadvertently disturb a colony of ants, which begin to rush at me like escaped prisoners, crawling up onto my sandals and biting my feet and ankles before I can get away from them. Adam turns the hose on my feet without asking permission, and the ants scatter and drown.

'I am sorry, Mrs Wald.' He looks startled, embarrassed and rather frightened by what he has just done.

'Do not be sorry, Adam, for goodness sake. You did exactly the right thing.' In truth, I am surprised by this sudden intimacy. It suggests the kind of physical rapport that Jacobus and I once had, easy and mutually understood as exactly what it was, the necessary movements and actions of a cohesive working relationship. Later, Marie administers calamine lotion and no permanent harm is done. The surviving ants will have gone back to their business and I resolve to leave the lettuce for another day.

I think about provocation. Was it possible for a white woman of privileged background, who could only be a beneficiary of this country's unjust system, to feel provoked into attack or provoked into aiding and abetting an attack?

The path you took to the work you felt you must do, Laura, is something I have no difficulty understanding. It is the work itself, if 'work' we can call it – the espionage, the bombings, the killing of innocents, even if their innocence was compromised by their participation in the architecture of apartheid, in its institutions and governing apparatus, its economies of oppression and utilities of isolation – that my mind is unable to reconcile with what I believe to be moral and ethical forms of resistance. I cringe before violence, because I know how easy it is for the culture of violence to infect even the just. I look at what our democratic country has become, at the way civic violence has been forged as its currency and coat of arms, and I wonder whether non-violent civil disobedience, notwithstanding the sluggishness of its progress, might have been the better way to win liberation. India achieved it thus; it may be an unequal society, but one can walk its streets for the most part without fear.

I knew I had raised a radical when I discovered a file marked TOP SECRET hidden between your mattress and box springs – you must have been only thirteen or fourteen. Inside the file were handwritten transcripts of conversations you had

406

overheard between your father and me and our visiting friends. Many dinner parties' worth of conversations were there, recorded in your precise hand. In brackets, you summarized aspects of our dialogue that held no interest: '(They spend twenty-two minutes discussing Alan Paton)'; '(Tedious half an hour on La Guma)'; '(Who is Rick Turner?)'; '(Dinner begins with ten minutes talking about trips to the farm)'. What concerned you, what held your interest and moved your pen to write records of adult conversation unnerving in their accuracy, were the political discussions with our friends about all that we knew to be wrong, and what we thought should be done. Your father and I were often in agreement with each other, our friends not always so, as my more radical days had passed by that time. Some phrases you underlined in red, identifying the speakers when you knew who they were. I remember how I shivered when I began to discern a pattern that betrayed a position and an ideology: 'non-violent protest is not taken seriously'; 'but you must answer force with force'; 'should we sit down or sit-in like the Americans while a holocaust is going on around us?'. The firebrands, the most outspoken amongst our closest friends, friends who were later banned, some of them forced into exile, some of them killed in detention, their words were the ones that you highlighted, not your father's or my own more temperate beliefs. We were too passive, too pacifist for you, and beneath our least courageous demurrals you drew a wavy line in yellow marker pen, marking us as cowards and wafflers. I cried when I saw those yellow waves and understood by that mark what you thought of me.

I replaced the file in your bed and never spoke about it to you or your father, hoping that you would bend your sense of injustice, and what I now begin to understand was your sense of provocation, into something creative. (Where did that file go? I never saw it again after you left home, and did not find it among your effects after your disappearance.) It sounds like vanity to say I wished you would be like me, or indeed like your father, who channelled his rage into a passionate exploration, interrogation, and explication of the law. And so I rejoiced when you became a journalist, relieved that you could be outspoken on the page, and hoping beyond reason that you would do nothing to endanger yourself. You would do good! You would reveal injustice! You would fight with words!

On the rare occasions we saw you after your return to Cape Town, I remember how quickly you grew frustrated and angry. I could see you deciding that you had no choice but to do something more direct than report the news, the little you were allowed to tell. Instead, you would throw yourself into the inferno and rage as long as you could, burn as a holy fire, a flame of purgation running across this land, charring the blond grass black.

This is how I understand it: you felt you could not make yourself heard, you believed you had no choice but to act, to cap your pen and silence the keys of your typewriter, to let the ink dry and the ribbons decay, to leave the work of truth-telling limited and curtailed by the state to other, more patient people. I understand this decision. I understand that somehow your father and I raised a woman who was not content to do what was safe, least of all to do what she was told. I understand you felt you had no choice but to act.

But we never taught you to kill.

★

Turning to your notebook today I find a page devoted, inexplicably, to facts about Rick Turner, the philosopher and activist who, after nearly five years as a banned person, was assassinated in his home, killed by a bullet fired through a window. Finding notes about him here in your hand gives me a terrible, aching chill. Turner encouraged the activism of whites and I see in a flash how, although he was killed while you were still a child, his model and call to action might have been the nudge out of complacency that you needed, hurtling you straight into the armed struggle.

I wonder, though, if it can be that simple. Your notes are more a compilation of known facts about the case, and Turner's unsolved murder, than the kinds of thoughts one takes down when inspired by a hero or martyr. It is almost as though you were preparing an in-depth investigation, as though you had discovered, at last, who Rick Turner was – not just a friend of a friend of the family, someone mentioned over dinner conversation at the time of his murder, but a man with a story of his own, a different kind of model for being white in this country than your father or I could ever manage to provide.

1999

Sam had been awake for half an hour feeling restless in bed under the winter duvet that had emerged in recent days from the closet where Sarah was making space for his few clothes. She must have been awake too because when the phone rang she caught it on the first note.

May I say who's calling? Her voice sounded throttled as it rose in pitch and she turned to him and spoke in a whisper, her brow corrugating: *It's the police. In Beaufort West. But I can't really understand what the man is saying.* The way she said *Beaufort West* made him smile. Each syllable was so clearly and roundly pronounced, Bow-Fort-West, at the same time that her voice fragmented into a series of clogged-sounding tones that were difficult to listen to. Then he realized what she was saying and he took the phone in his hands and felt as though she had passed him a weight heavier than conscience.

He did not have to ask her. She offered to come with him, to be sure he was not alone in facing what had happened. He would tell the faculty administrator that there was a serious situation at home and he would have to be away but would try to be back before the beginning of the spring semester.

A 'situation' was the safest thing to call what had happened. It meant not only the actions that had taken place but the location of those actions. It meant not just the house and the street and the town but also the region and province and country where his aunt lived and the relation of all those places to the locations around them, their state and condition, the areas further beyond them, and so on until the context became the whole world with a bright throbbing crime in a remote lower quadrant. In his mind all of it together was a specific situation and he could see it as if in a dramatic tableau masked with a scrim of suspended sand as fine as flour caught in the footlights. He knew he would see it when they approached the town from the west, the curtain of dust rising like hands from the yellow earth.

He had been looking forward to the holidays, and an escape to the heat of the southern hemisphere in the midst of the northern winter, even if that escape was only to the dry pan of the Karoo and the social torpor of Beaufort West, where days would pass in the company of his aunt and her friends, all wanting to hear news of his life abroad, eager for an escape themselves. Ellen had planned a trip to Plettenberg Bay for the New Year, and a stop in Prince Albert on the way back, because, she'd said, *It always feels like spring there, no matter what time of year.*

Lying in bed that morning, the phone still in his hand, he could feel the broken expectation of that escape raining down around him, and then he realized the rain was not just in his head but outside the window, a shower of ice that began to coat the glass, contorting their view of the traffic, the canary sludge of taxis, bleeding brake lights along West End Avenue.

SAM

It's an oppressive mid-January day in the tower of Senate House, the windows too small, the air stagnant, the buildings outside a strange blend of the post-industrial, brutalist, and a kind of retro vision of the future.

'If Cape Town is San Francisco meets Miami Beach,' Sarah has taken to telling friends in the States, 'then Johannesburg is Beverly Hills crossed with Cleveland and *Blade Runner*.'

I'm spending long hours in this office, driving back and forth each day from the house along Jan Smuts Avenue, which is always packed with cars, traffic congested by the shifting widths of the road: three lanes in one direction, to two lanes, to one lane, to two again, and sometimes it feels like five lanes in both directions, when in fact it's nothing like that big.

'I love it here,' Sarah said this morning, 'this is my idea of paradise – working in a cottage in a beautiful garden with my own swimming pool and great produce. The only drawback is the lingering fear that I might wake up with a shotgun in my face. But I guess that could happen anywhere.'

I pause at the intersection of Jan Smuts and St Andrews; a billboard ahead of me shows a domestic worker in a green uniform kicking a soccer ball under the legend A NATION UNITED. In front of the billboard are signs pointing in opposite directions: THE HEADACHE CLINIC to the right, the SOUTH AFRICAN HUMAN RIGHTS COMMISSION to the left. A British oil company has sponsored the billboard. A man approaches my car, walking through the lanes of traffic with a hand-lettered sign: WELDER/ PAINTER, his cell number scrawled underneath. There are signs like that all over the city, tacked to trees and taped to walls. When he holds it up to my window, I raise my hand in apology and wave him off.

The task of transcribing the interviews with Clare is taking longer than I expected. It makes me feel as though I'm beginning to drown in her words – and it's not just the transcripts, but the mountain of material she allowed me to copy from her archive, and the various earlier interviews I had conducted with the few reliable people who would speak about her, not to mention the entire book- shelf in the university library that holds her published works, and the further shelves containing all the books about her books. It seems not so much an impossible task as one that could take years to complete; I have only twelve months until the deadline imposed by the publisher.

I'm about to go buy a cold drink and a bag of

popcorn when the phone rings. It's Lionel Jameson.

'I was hoping you might forgive my brusqueness back in December.' His voice squeaks and hums, fast and hoarse with digital static; if I didn't know better I'd think he was on the other side of the world. 'To be honest, your visit took me completely by surprise – it was a real shock.'

'Did you think I was dead or something?'

There's a silence on the line and then, without answering my question, he blurts out: 'If the offer of dinner still stands, I'd like to accept it. I think you owe me that much at least.'

I don't know what to make of his tone, but I speak with Sarah and we agree to have him over on Friday. She goes to Angola early next week and for some reason I feel now that I'd rather not see Lionel alone.

When I phone him back with the address he says, 'Oh, very posh. Another thing, there's someone else I'd like to bring along, if that's okay?' He doesn't need to tell me it's Timothy – I know it already, as if by a premonitory nightmare.

On Friday evening, while it's still light, they arrive in a sleek black car – Timothy's not Lionel's. We watch as the gate closes and though we're reasonably secure in this miniature compound, Timothy gives a practised wave of the device that engages the central-locking mechanism.

'I know who you are,' he says, pressing a ten-year-old bottle of Kanonkop Pinotage into my hands, 'and I assume you remember who I am.'

The difference between the two men could not be more pronounced. As shabby and drawn as Lionel is, his skin climate-damaged and eyes bloodshot, face unshaven for several days, Timothy is overripe and over-processed. His nails have been manicured, his suit is more expensive than anything I'll ever be able to afford. He's rotten with success.

After I make the introductions the four of us sit by the pool, drinking sundowners until it gets dark. Timothy now works for the South African Tourist Board. He listens while the rest of us talk, staying silent in a way that unsettles me. Sarah excuses herself every few minutes to take a call or answer an e-mail, absences during which I might have expected either man to say something complimentary about her, but as soon as she leaves Lionel falls silent and both men stare at the ground, swirling their glasses, waiting for a top-up. The cheese and crackers and olives I put out disappear; Sarah and I barely touch them.

I'm about to suggest we go inside for dinner when Timothy finally speaks.

'Lionel tells me you want to know about Laura Wald.'

'Yes, though we don't have to do it now. I just

hoped you might be able to tell me something about what happened to her.'

The two men look at each other, as if to check they are still in agreement about some point decided earlier. Minutes pass and it's almost dark, the sun going down in a single rapid shuttering as a chill spreads across the lawn. A hadeda erupts from the garden next door, beaten metal wings flapping, and lets out a single monstrous cry. Timothy stares at me in a strange, assessing way.

'Listen, my friend – you don't have any idea what you're asking.'

Over dinner, the four of us chat as if there were no history between the men and me. Timothy gives us tips on what to do and see in Johannesburg, where not to go, how seriously to take the security and personal safety warnings. Lionel insists it isn't as dangerous as we've been made to believe. I struggle to concentrate on the conversation, wondering all the while what Timothy meant, catching his eye in brief moments, seeing him studying me when he thinks no one will notice, as if he might not believe I am who I claim to be.

When we finish dinner Sarah excuses herself again, explaining that she's trying to finish a story before she goes to bed – we agreed in advance that she'd give me space to talk alone with the men. There is no story to finish, no late-Friday deadline she has to meet.

Left alone, silence again overtakes us. They ask me nothing about myself, about my life in the years since I last saw them. If I don't ask questions, the men don't speak – I think of them as men in a way that I don't think of myself. There's a raw hardness and danger about them, a lack of domestication and care, as though they might break a chair or smash a glass if the fancy struck them, thinking nothing of the consequences. It's not the way I remember either of them.

'Is there nothing you can tell me about Laura?'

I'm perplexed by their hesitation and wonder if this is just a particular kind of South African awkwardness that I've forgotten – the unwillingness to speak, the filling of silence with small talk, or talking all the way around a subject without ever landing on it.

'Just what is it exactly that you think you want to know, my friend?' Timothy asks, smiling in a way that is not remotely amused.

'I'd like to know what happened to her.'

'*Ag*, no, you wouldn't, really,' he says, shaking his head rhythmically, each turn to the left or right punctuating a syllable.

Lionel shifts in his chair, fiddles with his glass, clears his throat. 'You can't just leave it at that,' he says to Timothy. 'You should tell Sam what he wants to know.'

'I don't have anyone else to ask,' I say. 'I mean, I wouldn't know who to approach or where to begin. You understand that I'm not asking so much for the sake of the book, as for my own curiosity. Laura was a friend. She was almost like a mother to me then.'

'No man, this is all ancient history,' Timothy says, waving his hands, shooing the past back into the lounge. He stands and paces round behind his chair, still shaking his head. Lionel looks embarrassed, raises his eyebrows at me and gives a pained smile as Timothy reaches over for the bottle of wine, pours himself another glass and drinks it in loud slurps. He takes a book on Johannesburg from the shelf and cracks it open. It's obvious that he knows something about Laura.

'If you're not going to tell Sam –' Lionel begins, but Timothy interrupts him.

'We've been through the resurrection of the dead already, all that poring over the past, the reading of bones. It was exhausting for all of us. It did no good, either. There's nothing more to say about it, Sam. You don't want to be asking these questions.'

'I just want to know what happened to her. You don't have to tell me anything, I accept that I can't force you to, but if you know where she ended up . . .' I'm aware of the pleading in my voice, uncomfortable because it reminds me of myself as a child, the way I pleaded with Laura, the ways I used to plead to my aunt, teachers, anyone who failed to give me what I wanted.

'You want to know something?' Timothy sighs,

replacing the book on the shelf and turning to me, pointing with his glass. 'What I can tell you is that Laura was on the wrong side of history. *That's* what I can tell you.'

I don't understand what he means. What he's suggesting seems impossible. 'You mean she was too militant?'

Timothy snorts, sips at his drink. 'God, you really have no idea, do you?'

'Come on, Tim, there's no reason he should.' Lionel edges forward on the chair as if he's about to say more, but then Timothy puts out his arm and Lionel slides back into place.

'She was on the *wrong* side, Sam.' Timothy sits again; his voice is softer now, as though he's making an effort to measure his tone against my expression. 'She was on the wrong side and someone found her out. That's all I know.'

'But nothing like that came out in the TRC –'

'The TRC was imperfect. It was incomplete. It does not represent the totality of late-apartheid history. Listen,' he says, bringing his hands together like a preacher, 'she was an embarrassment. No one wanted to talk about her – not us, and not the other side. There was, I don't know, some kind of cover-up, and that doesn't happen from the bottom. A cover-up needs a mandate, if you see what I mean. The family, thankfully, never pushed the case. If they had, who knows what would have emerged. We might actually know what happened to her.'

'Then you don't know?'

'I only know that she went away with one of the others, and she never came back. The man who took her, he died not long after, killed by a letter bomb in Mozambique. If anyone knew what happened to her, and where she ended up, where she might be buried, he did. But he can't tell us. So effectively she disappeared.'

The information comes at me like an invasion or an explosion. I feel assaulted, shattered, interfered with. I want them out of the house. It was a mistake to contact Lionel in the first place. I make sudden excuses, say that Sarah has an early morning. Lionel looks embarrassed and I hear Timothy say something under his breath like, 'I told you it would end this way.' Watching the car reverse down the driveway, all I can hope is that I won't ever see them again. I don't want to know their version of history.

Back inside, I tell Sarah what Timothy said. As I speak my hands and arms shake and I begin to lose my voice. I manage to tell her that I don't know how to understand it. She holds on to me, listens as I heave and rant. Laura was supposed to be a friend of my parents, and all that time, I choke, she was deceiving them. Sarah doesn't tell me to calm down or ask me to try to forget about it.

'Is it possible,' I say, seeing red everywhere I look, the room beating and buzzing around me, 'that she sabotaged my parents?'

Sarah shakes her head. It's a question she can't answer.

★

Monday morning. Sarah flies to Angola for the week. I take her to the airport and then barricade myself in the house where I turn to Clare's new book, which arrived today and is, perhaps ironically, the very distraction I need from thinking about Laura. I have difficulty believing what Timothy told me, and no reason to believe he'd lie. And yet it seems impossible that Laura would have been on the other side. It makes no sense, and at the same time it seems to make perfect sense – not just of her disappearance, but of the way my parents died.

I turn away from these thoughts, churning in a crazy cycle, almost sick with nausea, and hope to find solace, perhaps even insight, in Clare's words.

Absolution has a tasteful matte cover with an image of a whitewashed Cape Dutch farmhouse in summer, surrounded by trees with a mountain rearing up behind it, all of it viewed through a broken windowpane with a snail creeping over shards of glass along the sill that frames the scene. If it weren't for the distorting effect of the window, the image of the house in the landscape would almost be kitsch, a stereotype of the South African pastoral setting, a second-rate Pierneef, but I suppose that might also be intentional. With the framing device, however, it invites us to speculate on the nature and ownership of the house with the cracked window, and the person or persons who occupy it, who might be looking through the rippling broken glass, past the snail, at the elegant house in the distance. It could be a worker's cottage on a wine estate, draughty and ill-lit, poorly maintained, close enough to the big house to have a good view of it without encroaching on the idyll, the goats on the lawn, the ducks in a shaded pond, squirrels and oaks imported from England. The text itself has nothing to do with the image, or at least nothing obvious. As I read I know that I'm hoping to find something, even an oblique reference, a whisper or a silence that might refer to me.

Of course there's nothing. The book was written before I started interviewing Clare and I can't detect so much as an indirect reference to me, not even a meaningful silence. I try not to be disappointed. By the time I finish it's late evening, almost dark outside.

Standing in the kitchen, the doors and windows closed and locked though the air inside is stifling, I pour a glass of wine and hold the book at arm's length, turning it over in my hands, feeling the smoothness of its cover. On the back the publisher has categorized the volume as FICTION, in case we have any doubts. But doubts are exactly what it seems like we should be having, because here is

Clare, named in the text, and there is Marie, as well as Clare's son Mark, who can't be happy about the way his mother has represented him. The book offers what appears to be an accurate description of Clare and Marie's unusual domestic arrangement, which is too intimate, too symbiotic to be only a business matter. While they are two professionals, employer and employee, they have become inseparable and interdependent in a way that speaks more of friendship or love than of contract and remuneration. I see Marie wheeling a lunch cart into Clare's study, the silent communication between them expressed through the eyes and other body language – a barely lifted finger, the tiniest raising of the chin, a tightening of lips. It's a kind of magic that two people should be able to read each other so fluently.

Whether or not Clare suffered a robbery or house invasion I do not know – she has never spoken of one to me. In counterpoint to the book's narrative of recent trauma and upheaval, there are long discursions about her ancestors, their migration from England to South Africa in the 1820s, and the economic histories of the family, all rendered in a distant third-person voice. The balance between the two – the sometimes surreal narrative of trauma, and the rather dry historiography of family and childhood – does not seem like fiction per se. Clare tells me in a covering note that it's as close to a memoir as anything she'll ever write, but it isn't presented as one and at the same time

I can't quite see how it operates as fiction. Or maybe the real question I should be asking is: what does calling it fiction allow Clare to do?

The real shock is Clare's discussion of her sister, Nora. This is what she was getting at all along, I think – the question she expected me to ask at our last meeting in Cape Town, the trail she thought I'd caught! It is tempting to read the book as nothing more than the occasion for an elaborate confession of her complicity in a capital crime, namely that she carelessly provided information that led to the assassination of her sister and brother-in-law. The turn towards history might be construed as a way of placing her actions in a larger context, if not an actual defence or apology for what she did: look at where I came from to understand what I did, what I had to do. History deceives, she seems to be saying, it makes us vain. Of course, categorizing the book as fiction allows her to dodge any legal question of her responsibility for those deaths if it were ever to be put to her. *This is a novel,* she could say, *a version of me that bears only passing resemblance to the historical me. Do not confuse that person, the individual speaking to you now, with the person on the page. Many people wanted to kill my brother-in-law. I had no part to play.* On the copyright page is a disclaimer: *Any resemblance to real people, living or dead, is entirely coincidental, including those characters that share the same names as my son, Mark Wald, my assistant, Marie de Wet, and my ex-husband, William Wald. I use those names with the permission of the historical subjects to whom they are attached.*

I write a note thanking Clare for the book and flattering her style at the same time that I remain a little confused; the 'house invasion', which is of considerable importance at the beginning of the book, is never resolved. But there is also fatigue in its pages, beneath which courses a puzzled anger at the way the world has turned out – more specifically at what our country has become after all the initial hope, the expectation of a society that would transform itself by a collective force of goodwill and selfless love into a model for the way the world might yet be. Instead, Clare seems to say, the country has shown itself to be a cruel microcosm for the way the world really is, the war of all against all, red in tooth and claw, a waking nightmare of exploitation and corruption and hideous beauty that appears doomed never to end or to end in only one possible way. One could be forgiven for reading the book as a particular kind of Afro-pessimism, although I suspect this is not her intention.

But I say none of this in my response and tell her I look forward to seeing her in Stellenbosch in May, and to continuing our conversation. In fact, I don't need to conduct further interviews. As for the stray lingering question, the occasional need for some local clarification, it could all be done from here, over the phone or by e-mail. The truth is that I long to see her. Searching for her in the text, I flip through the book again, and suddenly see the formal dedication I missed the first time, the pages stuck together:

For my children – those I kept close, and those I denied.

I feel my throat tighten and surge into my mouth, acid rising. Perhaps, I think, she remembers me after all.

ABSOLUTION

As Mark stared at his mother's reflection in the window, Clare knew that if she stopped before the picture was clear the unresolved story would forever be rumbling around between them, causing trouble. She tore at her piece of bread and then, finding she still had no appetite, put it down on the plate.

'You were the perfect baby. You almost never cried or fussed. You smiled and laughed and had the biggest eyes of any child I'd ever seen, as though you were desperate to take in everything around you. I thought you were going to be a scientist, because you seemed to have such a natural capacity for observation. That was before we knew you were so short-sighted.' Before that, she thought, and before they knew about the other problems, the heart murmur that she had always refused to call a defect, the severe asthma that appeared in adolescence – problems that had been blessings of a sort.

Mark grinned in a way that reminded Clare of William, charming and persuasive, and put his fingers to the frames of his glasses. 'The law is a good antidote, my own pair of binoculars.'

Clare wondered if he knew how little one could see through binoculars – detail of one small object at a distance, but nothing around it or in between: the thing but not the context for the thing.

'As a baby you looked as though you'd been minted by the gods, or sent from Hollywood central casting. If there were ever a born hero, you appeared to be he.'

'You're saying Nora was jealous.'

'From the earliest days of her marriage she had tried to get herself pregnant. Eventually they did tests and nothing, she confided to my mother, was found to be wrong with her, which meant the problem was with Stephan – which meant, in those days, no option but childlessness or adoption. And Stephan was wholly against adoption. He said there was no way of knowing what might be lurking in the genes of a stranger's baby. He feared a racial throwback that would only display the telltale characteristics later in life. So imagine when your aunt's hated baby sister produced this divine-looking infant! It was the slap Nora had been bracing herself against since the day of Dorothy's birthday party. It signalled the beginning of total war between us, though for me it felt as if nothing had changed. I had always known that she regarded me as an adversary at best, if not something much less benign. For some, it is possible to be the object of hatred and continue responding with love, or if not with love then at least with indifference. And then there are people like me,' Clare said, resting her head on one hand. 'I did not want to hate my sister, truly I didn't. I wanted to be more virtuous than her, more loving. But I was not good enough. Her hatred fostered my hatred. I lacked the moral maturity to answer evil with love, to be selfless in the best possible way.'

'You say it was the start of a war, but I can't imagine what you mean,' Mark said, turning to look directly at his mother once again. 'The thing at Dorothy's party, the cake, I understand how that could affect your relationship as children. But as adults, she must have done something terrible for you to talk about her like this. I didn't have any idea you hated her.'

'This, again, is where you fit in, or not just fit, but are the keystone of the whole architecture of what I perceived – for admittedly it is my subjective view – as her plot against me. Do not scoff. Remarkable a child as you might have been, you were not old enough to be aware, certainly not to have any memory of those days. Within a month of your birth Nora was driving into town and dropping by the house on Canigou Avenue completely unannounced, at all hours, accompanied by the driver she and Stephan employed. Often she brought a camera and insisted on taking pictures of you, her "darlingest" as she put it – not her "darlingest nephew", but *her* darlingest" – as if you belonged to her and not to me. At first I was confused, surprised but also hopeful, imagining that she might let go of the old animosities and take a positive role in our lives. I was hopeful, too, that her sudden interest in you might signal a diminishing involvement in the politics of Stephan and his party. If she could drift so far from where she had begun, I thought, there was no telling what might yet become of me. We do not, as young people, know that drift and realignment are not always to be feared. Nora, however, had drifted blindly, putting herself to sea quite happy to embrace whatever port she arrived in first.'

'But the visits, and the photos of me – have I seen those photos?'

'I never saw them myself. I imagine they must have been sinister, unrepresentative of the way things were. Because she came unannounced at odd hours, she often found – and eventually I understood that she knew she would find and *expected* to find – the house in some significant disarray. No doubt she hoped to catch you gnawing on a contraband copy of *Lady Chatterley's Lover*. In those early years of our marriage your father and I lived like bohemians. We had no servants to help us keep the place clean, and I was struggling to write and to look after you and to keep house while your father did little on the domestic front apart from dandle you and coo and pronounce you the most beautiful and intelligent baby that ever was. I accept that he was busy, but it did not make things any easier.'

'So you never actually saw the photographs. You only assume they were sinister.'

'I think I have grounds to assume as much. Not long after she started visiting, my parents, who had already moved down to Fish Hoek at that point, phoned to ask if all was well. They wanted to know if your father and I were coping. I said, with not a little shock, that we were certainly coping just fine. They wondered if they could come up for a visit one day. I told them they were welcome at any time, but reminded them that I was trying to work as well as be the housekeeper and mother. I thought it would end at that.'

'But the photos – assuming there were any – didn't end with Granny and Grandpa?'

'This is the point where I became quite seriously unsettled – frightened even. I think the idea was to lay a certain kind of groundwork with your grandparents. Some weeks after they had phoned, your father's head of department called him in for a meeting and asked if all was well at home, and made noises about creating the right kind of environment to safeguard a child's welfare. He mentioned the importance of the moral as well as the physical environment, as if to suggest that in our case both might be in question. Your father assured him everything was perfectly fine at home and the next week we hired our first maid. I've forgotten her name – Pamela or Pumla. Your father built a well-camouflaged locker in the loft space above our bedroom and there I hid the risky books and papers, better than I had in the past. In a way Nora did us a favour. When the police did come knocking there was nothing for them to find. We presented an unremarkable bourgeois front that, on the surface, no one could question. We got our act together, thanks in large part to Nora's harassment.'

'But you don't have hard evidence that she said anything against you to anyone. You just assume –'

'You did not know your aunt, my dear. I must ask you to trust my version.'

'It seems highly subjective and conjectural. It doesn't sound as though you've anything apart from circumstantial evidence. Did your parents or Dad's department head mention any photos?'

'No, but –'

'So it ended with that.' Mark sounded as though he had heard more than enough. Clare wondered if he was as belligerent in the court-room as he was with her. No wonder he was so successful.

'No, it did not end there. A month after your father had the meeting with his head, a social worker of sorts came to visit me at home. She was unannounced, but everything was in order, clean, tidy, nothing amiss, a true vision of suburban perfection, achieved at great cost, mind you. The woman apologized and left after half an hour of chatting with me, playing with you, and refusing to answer my questions. A week later the police came, explaining that someone had phoned with a tip that we were endangering a child. They found nothing, bid us a rather menacing farewell, and then left us alone.'

'And you assume it was Nora.'

'It must have been.'

'Might it not have been someone with a grudge against Dad, or against you, or even against Grandpa?'

'I suppose it is possible. But Nora is the most obvious suspect. In any event, when none of these interventions had the desired effect she began trying to visit again, always dropping by at the most inconvenient times. By that point I had no reservations about refusing to let her inside, but I also became terrified that she would never stop until she had what she truly wanted.'

'Which was what?'

'Don't you see? She wanted to dispossess me of my child, to take you from me, and have you as her own. If she couldn't conceive her own child, she would have the next best thing. I began to understand that if I wanted to keep you, I was going to have to defend you at all costs. I was going to have to get rid of her. I had to make her disappear.'

As the kettle boiled Clare found a jar of instant coffee in the pantry. She had to read the instructions on the label and was uncertain what a teaspoon might be, whether it meant a formal cooking measure as her mother had once used, or an informal utensil of inexact volume that most people used. She assumed the latter and put two rounded teaspoons of the coffee granules in each cup – it was the way Adam took it, though he always wanted three sugars as well. The water boiled and she poured it, leaving room for milk in one of the cups. Her own coffee she preferred black. She searched the pantry for sugar but could find none, then thought to look in the cupboard next to the stove, but it wasn't there either. Then she remembered there were canisters on the kitchen counter, and with insulting obviousness there was one marked SUGAR next to the kettle itself. She must ask Marie to start labelling cupboards with detailed inventories of their contents. If a library has a catalogue, so should a kitchen.

Finding two coasters in the corner cabinet in the lounge, she set down the cups on the coffee table. Mark was watching the news and had failed to look at her when she entered the room.

'I hope it's all right,' she said, indicating the coffee. 'I'm rather lost in a kitchen.'

'Thank you, I'm sure it's fine.' He spoke without looking at her, his eyes on the screen. Not bothering to ask if he minded, Clare turned off the television.

'Can't you speak to me as though you were my son, and not just my interlocutor?'

Mark sighed, sipped his coffee, and put down the cup with a force that surprised Clare. 'You're expecting me to play too many parts, Mother. You seem to want me to be your confessor and judge, as well as your child. Sometimes I wonder if you even want me to be the last man in your life. I can't be all of these things at once. If it's a confessor or a judge that you most need right now, then I suppose that's what I can be. But if you want a child I can't play that part any more. You didn't raise us to be warm. Is there more to your confession about Aunt Nora? Are there further horrors you feel you have to tell me?'

'If you can bring yourself to listen to this old woman, there is yet only a little more, if you will hear it,' Clare said, her voice brittle and off-key in her own ears.

'Of course I can, Mother. That isn't what I meant. I'm tired, and I'm sorry if I sounded brusque. It wasn't my intention.'

'What remains of the Nora saga is the exact circumstance of my betrayal, if it is possible to betray one who is already objectively one's enemy. After her campaign against me –'

'Such as you saw it.'

'Fine, my *sense* of her campaign against me, or what felt like her attempt to have me declared an unfit mother – after that there was a change of events in my favour. As you know, Stephan was more than a rising star in the Party, but something like its hoped-for Messiah, and he was appointed to a diplomatic post that took him and Nora to Washington, DC. I cannot express how relieved I was to see them leave the country. *At last*, I thought, *she is out of my life!* Almost a year passed in great peace and then one day I heard from Nora herself that she and Stephan were returning, and would be in Cape Town for only a few nights before moving to Pretoria. Stephan was being promoted to a senior position in the executive, and all signs pointed to him being tipped for elected office, she told me. As you might guess, the prospect of Nora's return, and of Stephan's promotion, filled me with dread. I had visions of her doing whatever it took to remove you from my care, and as soon as I hung up the phone began planning for our own emigration, assuming that would be the only way to keep you safe from her.'

'And did you see them when they returned to Cape Town?'

'In a manner of speaking,' Clare said, the image of Nora and Stephan's faces as she had last seen them flashing up out of her memory. 'The day before their return I went to a meeting of one of the groups with which I had begun to affiliate myself. I believed it was mostly a talking shop for like-minded radicals. We had no formal affiliation, no name for what we were. I knew little about the other members except that they were young men and women who were united by their abhorrence of oppression. There were rumours that one of the group, a man who seldom spoke, might have connections with MK, or was even an MK cadre himself. I don't remember his name, might never have known it, so I can't be more specific. Everyone knew that Nora was my sister and somehow Stephan came up in the course of the conversation. Here was a chance, I thought, to prove myself interesting to these people I respected, and in the case of the man who seldom spoke, who may or may not have been part of the liberation movement's armed struggle, perhaps even to prove myself useful. I announced that my sister and brother-in-law were returning home, that Stephan had been recalled, and that they would arrive in Cape Town the following day for a stay of a few nights. The man who seldom spoke suddenly looked more alert and asked if they would be staying with me. I told him no, they would be staying at a guest house in Constantia. I gave him the name, knowing as I did that it was quite possible I was putting my sister's life in jeopardy. Nora had intimated on the phone that their return was not public knowledge, and that the place they would be staying was also secret as Stephan had received death threats. There had been stories about Stephan and his activities in Washington in the national press, stories about the money he was winning from international investors and the IMF – it had all been widely reported, critically by those who had the courage to criticize, in celebration by the mouthpieces of the Establishment. I knew that in giving away not only their itinerary but also their location in Cape Town I might be endangering both of them. And rather than feeling remorse, what I felt was this torrent of excitement, and even a kind of ecstatic terror, that I had shown myself to be not just a faculty wife and mother, not just a writer who had published very little, but someone with information and knowledge who knew when that knowledge might be useful and was not afraid to act. The man who seldom spoke thanked me for the interesting information, and we moved on to other matters.'

'And in the following days . . .?'

'Two days later they were dead. The police woke me in the middle of the night and took me to identify the bodies. Their faces had been disfigured. Their supposed assassin, John Dlamini, was a man I had never met at any of the gatherings I attended, certainly not the man who seldom spoke and was rumoured to be involved with MK. Dlamini, as you know, was arrested shortly thereafter and, unlike other assassins and would-be assassins in this country – Tsafendas and Pratt, for instance – Dlamini was not found to be insane and unbalanced, but was promptly sentenced to death. He did not protest his innocence or claim to be controlled by a foreign body (human or animal or national), but insisted he was working alone and wished only to destroy the quintessence of the apartheid state, or something to that effect. He died in custody before the execution could be carried out.'

'Is that the end of your story?'

The coldness of Mark's voice, the abrupt thwack of his speech in the room, pulled Clare out of her own narrative. She looked down at her lap to find that her hands were shaking. 'I suppose it is. Will you cross-examine me? Will you call other witnesses?'

'There can't be a trial where no crime has been committed. If anything you're merely a gossip, and your gossiping resulted in the deaths of two people, at least one of whom was wholly innocent.'

'You mean your Aunt Nora.'

Clare watched as Mark wove his fingers together and frowned. She knew what he must think of her, that she was a monster, that he could never love her again, assuming he ever had. He sighed once more and she wondered whether, in his meetings with clients, with the unambiguously criminal, he showed his frustration and impatience so openly. She hoped for the sake of the innocent that he did not.

At last, his eyes blinking with what looked like fury, he spoke. 'Nora didn't do anything wrong apart from trying to intervene in your life and make trouble. I don't see that she had a political function. If we started killing off everyone who made ordinary mischief, we'd soon depopulate half the planet. But it's my guess you wouldn't think that such a bad thing.'

CLARE

The vision of you caged and naked, under the beating sun, tethered to the shore and waiting for the sea to take you, for the predators to consume you, is nothing but a vision. If you had been captured I have to hope your fate would have been more prosaic. They would have taken you to the women's jail in Johannesburg, and after spending time in the block for prisoners awaiting trial, and then submitting to the trial itself, you would have passed the term of your sentence, assuming you were not sentenced to death, in one of the few small but comparatively comfortable white-washed rooms.

I went there again not so long ago, to that prison which is now a museum. I tried to imagine you into that space, to see your lean and limber body testing itself against its confinement. At least there, in prison, you would have been reachable. If arrested and detained, I might have found a way to aid your defence, might yet have had correspondence with you, seen you again, come to know you better, to repair all that I failed to do, to make you love me again. I would have made amends,

442

repented to you, sought your absolution for my failures against you.

During my visit to the museum I found it difficult to be moved by the cells once reserved for white women, or by their stories. Compared to the women of colour, who were detained in conditions unsuitable for dogs, conditions that would have tested even the mettle of rats, the white women lived in relative comfort.

I looked for your name in the histories of dissent in the museum's displays but could find no reference. Your name has not been rehabilitated. You have not been made over into a hero. The saints of the struggle are those whom we know were murdered, or who survived to turn themselves into holy orators.

But perhaps my nightmare vision is not so fanciful. There are secrets that remain buried in the history of this country, people who were kidnapped and never recovered, remains buried in unmarked graves whose locations have been forgotten or suppressed, lives never accounted for, disappearances unexplained. Perhaps you did escape, into Lesotho or Zimbabwe or Mozambique, or slipped over into Swaziland or even the Transkei, and from one of those places were kidnapped and brought back into the country, or killed on the spot.

I see you in a bay on the northern Natal coast, in one of the old covert facilities, your pale skin burned and ravaged, your head immersed, your body wracked by electric shock, your arms dislocated from hanging, lacerations at your wrists and ankles. Your torturers no longer saw you as human, not even as animal, but as a thing outside of nature, a monster who had stolen life to animate herself. They killed not just out of indifference, those men, and not only out of hate – but out of fear.

★

Unlike in your final notebook, detailing your journey with Sam in the days leading up to your disappearance, this earlier one offers no sustained narrative. It is, instead, a collection of fragments: notes about your work, the stories you were writing for the paper, and telegraphic diary entries about your life. If you had a lover, you say nothing about him.

The work at the *Cape Record* kept you ever busier as the weeks and months progressed. You had no particular 'beat', such as crime or education or labour, the kinds of topics where the real news was happening. Instead, your editors held you down in the pool of general news reporters, assigned in large part to cover what the press has always called 'human interest stories': a housewife's award-winning roses grown in memory of her husband; a blanket-drive for the poor and homeless ahead of the winter storms; the first-hand account of a teenage girl who was the sole survivor of a boating accident off Noordhoek.

Most days you stayed late to finish stories and

arrived before dawn on others. You began to work weekends and holidays when the news editor bullied you into doing more than you should have, made leering comments about you and said he thought of you like a daughter. You stayed late not because of him but because of the work, hoping that if you proved your ability you would be allowed to cover more interesting news.

When you did have time off you saw Peter and Ilse. Sometimes you went to their house for dinner, or else you invited them to your apartment where, as inept a cook as your mother, you made eggs and toast smothered with chutney and melted cheese. You had no other friends apart from someone you only identify as 'X', to whom you spoke on the phone at least once a week. I assume this must have been a lover from university, someone still in Grahamstown, perhaps even a professor, a man like your father who could not keep his hands off his students.

'X' suggested you start jogging as a way of relaxing and building your strength. In the evenings, at least three days a week, you ran through residential streets in Observatory and Rondebosch. One night a drunk who might have stumbled down from the mountain forests tackled you against the dark side of a building just around the corner from your apartment. He was large but so intoxicated that you easily repelled him, kneeing him in the groin and pulling the fingers back on his left hand until they broke, crushing the digits into a lumpy

445

pulp that you squeezed like an orange. You ran home as he shouted for the police, as if the law should have been protecting him instead of you.

Though you marvelled at your own strength, after the encounter with the drunk you only ran during the day, in the mornings before going to work. You did push-ups and sit-ups and kept a log of how many each day. You maintained a meticulous record of everything you ate, as though you were training for the Olympics. You bought a scale and weighed yourself each morning.

One evening you helped Peter distribute stacks of pamphlets throughout the city, hoping that you would not be caught. If the security police had discovered this notebook the scant details you sketched of that single evening might have been the only clue that you were involved in anything illicit. Your words are so circumspect that at times I question whether they are yours and not the work of someone else, copying your hand, using you as his puppet.

All these things you never told us when they were happening, knowing we would have implored you to be careful, to look after yourself, not to do anything foolish. We could never come up with the words that you wanted to hear. I remember a Sunday in the autumn of that year when you condescended to come home for lunch. It was the first time I had seen you since your move back to the city. When I asked if I could come to your apartment you made excuses – it was a mess, you said, and it was not the kind of place I would be comfortable. By then Mark was living in Johannesburg, so the three of us sat in the dining room, eating. Your father asked if you had made many friends at the paper.

'I met one of your old students, Ilse. She's a freelancer.'

William, I remember, tried to look unfazed. 'Oh, yes? How is she?' he asked, looking at his plate.

'Married,' you said. I knew what it meant and wondered at the time if you did as well. I hastened the end of the meal, and sent you on your way.

I wonder, after all, if I hate you for every secret you kept from me.

★

While some of your colleagues were detained and arrested, held without trial, charged with offences both preposterous and petty, you remained as untouched by the chaos as most of us were, safe in our white streets. You never moved beyond the general reporting of the 'human interest story', the inconsequential, while others threw themselves into clouds of tear gas, struggling to tell as much truth as they could report under the ever more stringent restrictions and regulations imposed by the government against the press. Some were fined, others spent months and even years in detention, a few died. Others still were lucky to escape with vandalism of their property and anonymous threats against their lives. Your editors, whose own lives and families were threatened, rewrote stories so that they obscured more than they revealed. Those of us who read such news were left having to put together the pieces, to discern through the silences and obfuscations (the surreal avowals that, for instance, the details and purpose of a gathering could not be disclosed even though one had nonetheless occurred) that a peaceful demonstration had taken place on Adderley Street and been met with the force of police bullets.

And yet you, Laura, went on writing your stories about high-achieving child prodigies and exceptional housewives. *Perhaps*, you wrote in the notebook, *they will eventually trust me to do something more important.*

Yet no promotion, no greater freedom ever came. You met with Peter and Ilse and their circle of friends and associates. In private, you compiled further notes on Rick Turner, and when you had exhausted that topic, finding no answers and not knowing where else to turn in search of the truth, expanded your scope. I read it with horror: *Unsolved deaths. Robert Smit. Rick Turner. Stephan Pretorius. Nora Boyce Pretorius.* From an individual you shifted to a theme, became obsessed with the dead, whatever side they might be on.

But unlike Smit or Turner, whose deaths have remained, objectively, unsolved and unexplained, the deaths of your aunt and uncle had their day in court. A man confessed and was found guilty.

Nonetheless, something about the resolution did not satisfy you, as if you intuited that the story of their deaths was only a cover, obscuring the real story, the one beneath and behind the cover story.

On the phone, you spoke with 'X' about your frustrations at the paper.

'I want to do something more significant. They give me no latitude. If I come up with an idea, I have to get their approval first. Mostly they give my ideas to other reporters and leave me with news that doesn't matter. I told them I wanted to write an in-depth investigative piece on the Turner murder and they laughed. It was old news, ancient history no one wanted to hear. I haven't made them trust me.'

'If it's not working out perhaps you should quit,' said 'X'. 'Find a more direct way to be involved. Go to work for one of the alternative papers. Get Ilse to make an introduction, to *Grassroots* or the *New Nation* or *South*. Perhaps the *Record* is too tame. We should have known they wouldn't give someone like you a long enough lead.'

The following week you turned in your resignation to the *Record*, as if you had been waiting for the permission of that man, that former lover, a consent for you to slip from the back rows of safe respectability and slide into the orchestra pit, to take up your sticks and play.

Not knowing where else to turn, you went to Peter and Ilse and told them, 'I'm ready. I want to do something more.' Ilse took you in her arms

449

and though you were still unsure of her, still felt that tickle of anger at the freedom with which she lived her life, expecting other people to clean up her messes, you believed that together the two of them pointed to the road you were destined to follow.

*

Dear Sam,

Thank you for your generous message about *Absolution*. I am glad you think it – rather politely, I fear – a not wholly uninteresting foray into that well-charted country of life writing that I claimed to revile and mistrust. You see how unreliable I am.

Regarding the speaking events in May. Either such things are now beyond one's power to police, or I am simply too fatigued to fight in the way I once could. My woman of business says it is the only way for one to operate these days – by this she means that no one but those regarded as the truly exceptional, the recluses (all of them male, I note, most of them dying or dead), can get away with saying no.

For the Winelands Festival we shall spend two nights at a hotel in Stellenbosch, as the organizers have roped me into a reading, a book signing, a panel discussion, a pantomime as well for all I know, spread over the course of three days. My woman of business wanted me to go to America but I demurred. I am too old and too frail, I said, and this she seemed to accept. Such excuses don't wash at home. The truth is I hate travel, and all the administrative bumf (nasty word for nasty things) that inevitably goes with it these days: travel is, more and more, paper chasing paper. In a moment of weakness, thinking I was being too difficult, too precious about my health, I looked at the visa application to visit your adopted country and discovered its demand that I provide my tribal name. I was minded to invent one and submit the form for sport, then thought better of it, fearing it might get me arrested or detained or rendered to a secret base.

As busy as the Festival is bound to be, I shall nonetheless have ample time for you, please do not fear (I have this hunch that you spend a great deal of your life in states of fear; is that unfair?). What I mean is, almost the only thing about the trip I look forward to is the promise of seeing you again.

Yours,
    Clare

1999

Because their flight arrived after dark and they'd been warned that the road into the city was unsafe at night, they stayed over at the airport hotel. The room was small but serviceable and the bellhop put down their suitcases with a flourish that felt out of place in the utilitarian setting. Sarah tipped the man a hundred rand and all at once he looked grateful and astounded but also suspicious, as if the money must be some kind of trap. Sam gave him a confidential nod to indicate it was okay, he should take it. Never mind that five or ten rand would have been plenty.

They watched the news and Sarah was surprised that she could understand what was being said. *I thought it would all be more foreign.*

Wait till the Xhosa news, Sam said, poking her in the ribs. *You won't understand a word of that.*

She tried to sound out words in Afrikaans on signs in the room and he couldn't help laughing at her mispronunciation, so endearingly wrong with its hard consonants and rounded, musical vowels. *Flat*, he told her, *the vowels should be flatter, and the 'g' is a 'ch' like in 'Bach' or 'loch'.*

Bahk, she said. *Lock*. He was surprised that she couldn't hear the difference.

The next morning he watched her at the buffet in the lobby. There was juice in plastic containers, stale croissants, individual boxes of American cereal brands, eggs that looked as though they had been cooked the day before and reheated and then forgotten about and fried in grease to reheat them again. The coffee tasted like it had been two hours on the boil by 8 a.m. A fresh fruit salad was the only truly local thing available, but at least it was good. Sam felt embarrassed by the meal while Sarah ate without complaint, giving no sign that she thought anything was lacking.

This is not representative, he said. *South Africans are usually good with food. This is pretty dreadful.*

It's fine, Sam. I feel like I'm back home.

He thought of the breakfasts his mother and aunt had once made, the habitual parade of courses: first juice and cereal (porridge in winter), then fruit, followed by an egg and sausage and sometimes slices of fried brinjal, ending with toast and home-made preserves and a pot of strong tea. The hotel breakfast was a poor introduction; he wanted Sarah to love his country even though the point of the trip had nothing to do with entertainment or amusement or being a tourist falling for a new place. There was nothing amusing about what had happened, and as he thought about it he felt more on edge, recalibrating his reactions, expecting threat rather than hoping all would be well. A victim was complacent, a survivor vigilant. He had grown up in something like a state of war, and it was difficult to remember that was no longer the case. The potential for danger was everywhere. At school in Port Elizabeth he had been taught how to identify limpet mines and that knowledge and the reflex attached to it had never gone away. Every time he approached a vehicle or entered a building, a part of his brain did an automatic scan for the telltale outline. For the sake of survival and self-preservation, one had to retune the dial, pay attention to the emergency frequencies, receive all incoming communications, and ignore nothing that might tip one off to the presence of danger. Pay attention to the Morse code, the signal fires, the sounds of distant voices and the thunder of feet, and one stood a better chance of staying alive.

There was traffic getting out of Cape Town and a backup in the Huguenot Tunnel. In the Hex River Valley a jack-knifed truck that had swerved to miss a herd of goats was blocking the road. In avoiding the animals the truck had hit their owner, who lay dead in the eastbound lane. With the delays it took them most of the day to drive the 450 kilometres to Beaufort West, the place that had never felt like home, but in which, according to the law, Sam now owned a house. Just before the turn-off to the Karoo National Park he took over the driving again, inching into town.

One kilometre over the limit and they'll stop you,

he said. *If we're going to get stopped I'd rather it was me.*

The house looked just as it had a year earlier. Flocks of white pelargonium were blooming and the lawn had been recently mowed. Only the dust on the path, more dust and dead bougainvillea leaves on the veranda, and a film of dust on the windows and shutters betrayed less than a week of inattention. Sam ran his finger along the frame of the door and it came back with a yellow-brown mask of powder. Nature would take over with breathless speed. One had to be vigilant in all kinds of ways.

Opening the front door, the smell worked its way into his nostrils by degrees and then, once it had a firm grip, took hold of his entire body and squeezed in an awful embrace. *Wait here*, he said, panting and leaving Sarah in the front hall. It was the smell of blood overheated, faeces and urine and dust, gunpowder and drawers emptied out. At first he saw only components of disarray in Ellen's bedroom, with a Rorschach stain of twin baying goats at the centre, marking the site of an explosion. If the police had come to take evidence there was no way of telling. All was disorder, objects shaken and mixed towards higher levels of entropy, chaos irreversible. He remembered the way his own house had looked after the police had disembowelled it.

He couldn't help but see the situation through one of Clare's recent books, in which a farmer returns home from a weekend away at an agricultural show to discover his wife's dismembered body laid out on their bed, the limbs arranged in a question mark.

The Rorschach suddenly shifted, revealing itself as a three-headed dog in a lane between two houses. A window had been left open and the breeze was blowing dust and movement into the space. He picked his way across the room, put his hands on the burglar bars that were covered with a layer of grit, and looked out at the garden. The window closed with a sound like a stack of books falling to the floor as the dust along the sill shuddered and rearranged itself. Looking back at the stain he took a shallow breath and felt a twist of nausea. It would have to wait until the next day. He closed the door behind him. *There's no one here,* he called to Sarah, and realized what a stupid thing it was to say.

Sam and Sarah's number had been on a slip of paper taped to the refrigerator, the first on a list of emergency contacts, followed by Ellen Leroux's doctor, colleagues at her school, a few friends, and women from the church. It was a short list. Sam was her only family, and as he looked at the other names, most of which meant little to him, he realized he was now completely alone in the world. There was no longer anyone to phone in the middle of the night, no one to go home to, no one who could be compelled under force of filiation if not of law to acknowledge a responsibility to him. Home had become a place he owned, emptied of people. The blood beat in his eardrums; to be without a home again filled Sam with a new kind of terror.

Why are there locks on the fridge and cupboards? Sarah stood in the middle of the kitchen looking hungry and scared. In his backpack Sam found a pouch containing half a dozen keys.

I don't know which is which, he said. *You'll have to try them all. I think it's the gold one for the fridge. Each of the cupboards has a different skeleton key.*

They're open, Sam. I just don't understand why there are locks.

To keep your domestic from stealing food. It's not unusual. I guess the locks on the cupboards are a little unusual, but you'd struggle to buy a fridge or freezer in this country without built-in locks on its doors. It's just the way things are.

Was your aunt a racist?

Ellen Catharina Leroux, who only locked the refrigerator and freezer and cupboards when she went on holiday, who had a pillow in the lounge embroidered with a line of dancing Sambo figures, who had never employed a domestic because she thought it was demeaning to everyone concerned, who had started a programme tutoring township children on the weekends, would have been horrified by the suggestion that she was a racist.

On the kitchen counter were three red tins of Christmas cookies. There was a turkey in the freezer, and the pantry glowed with jars of home-made *konfyt*, palegreen jewels of melon rind suspended in syrup. Sam's bedroom was already made up and in the closet he found wrapped gifts for him, as well as two small parcels for Sarah, left undisturbed by his aunt's attackers. His grandmother's jewellery box was still in its hiding place, the few small pieces untouched.

Sarah had a shower to cool off and Sam sat on his bed swallowing down the sobs as they came. When he heard Sarah getting out of the shower he went to the kitchen, splashed his face with cold water and dried it with a tea towel.

Even the shower door has locks inside, Sarah said, shivering now that the sun had gone down.

I never noticed.

Why would you want to lock yourself inside your shower?

In case someone breaks in. In case they get into the bathroom while you're in the shower and you don't know what else to do but lock yourself into an even smaller space and hope that whoever it is will just give up and go away. I don't know. I don't have all the answers, Sarah.

Are you okay?

I was just washing my face. I'll make us some dinner. Sit down. Wouldn't you like to get us a drink? There's wine in the pantry, and whisky, unless they've taken it. Glasses are in the cupboard next to the sink.

Although Ellen had a panic button in the kitchen, she did not have one in her bedroom. All the locks in the world hadn't saved her. Whoever did it had forced the back door, shot her in her bed, taken her television, stereo, microwave oven, and a watch with no significant value, fleeing before the police or the security company's guards could arrive. On Sam's direction the company had replaced the door before he and Sarah arrived.

The police had assured Sam they were following up leads, but he was not hopeful; it was a town with a reputation for corruption and administrative sloth and there was little expectation that the culprit or culprits would ever be caught.

She wasn't raped, he told Sarah the next day, after coming back from identifying the body. *At least there's that. Her face is terrible. She was probably pleading for her life and then he just got tired of it and shot her.*

While Sam was away, Sarah had stripped Ellen's bed, bundling the sheets into a plastic bag whose seams strained under the pressure. *What about the mattress?* she asked. *I don't think the stain will come out.*

The women from the church will know what to do. If you find me the number I'll phone them.

Sarah was better than he could have imagined. She made tea and cooked meals that comforted him with their simplicity: macaroni and cheese, spaghetti and meatballs, stew with kudu meat, an omelette and biscuits. She placed phone calls and came through with money when the accounts were not immediately transferrable to Sam. She ordered flowers for the funeral, helped choose the music, and charmed the women of the church where Ellen, although rarely a churchgoer in recent years, was still a member. She sampled food that was new to her and tried to make Sam happy without ever diminishing the solemnity of the situation. With the help of the Women's Federation she arranged a brunch following the memorial service and helped Sam set up a fund to pay for a scholarship in Ellen's name at the school where she'd taught. She phoned her father's lawyers whose firm had a branch in Cape Town and within days the red tape was cleared, the accounts were in Sam's name, and the property his to do with as he liked. Everything she did was perfectly pitched – efficient and businesslike without being unfeeling. It was a way that reminded Sam, not for the first time, of Laura.

Though grateful for everything she'd done, almost despite himself he began to resent the part Sarah was playing so effortlessly – the American saviour with a golden touch. Without thinking, he began to do little things that might alienate her, forcing her to reveal some hidden selfishness. But when he wanted to sleep alone for a night in the room that had been his since he first came to live with Ellen, Sarah made up the couch in the living room and slept there without complaint.

The police assured Sam they would follow up leads.

SAM

I spend the rest of the summer, the sweltering days of February and the cooler days of early autumn – March, April – trying to forget what Timothy told me, and what Lionel did not deny. Perhaps, I begin to feel now, my Aunt Ellen was right: it is better to forget and move on from the past and its people; we're mistaken in thinking we know them.

During the days I spend in my cell of a university office, I'm either working on the book or preparing for teaching, though the two are symbiotic, one feeding the other. I only have two classes this term, one an honours-level course on contemporary South African literature, the other a Masters course devoted in its entirety to Clare's books. The students work hard, they're engaged, they tease me about my Americanized vowels and ask, as the term progresses, whether I'm getting enough sleep. They express concern for my well-being in a way that both touches and alarms me. I go to bed earlier and get up later each morning. I stop resisting the attempts by the domestic worker to do things like launder and iron my clothes. This is what we are paying her to do. It makes no sense for us to do it ourselves.

On weekends Sarah and I go to the malls, out to dinner in Illovo, on a day trip to Pretoria to see the Voortrekker Monument and the Union Buildings. One Saturday, as we're about to leave the glitzy mall at Sandton, we overhear a child plead with her parents, 'Do we have to go back to South Africa?', as if the mall were not just a different kind of social space, but a separate political entity – the post-apartheid version of an independent homeland for the elite, whatever their colour.

Sarah and I cautiously explore the city centre with one of her fellow correspondents, a reporter for one of the wire services, and while nothing happens, we manage to frighten ourselves back to the northern suburbs. When I tell my colleagues that even the much-lauded Newtown Cultural Precinct felt too edgy for me, most of them laugh. 'You've been in America too long,' one says, slapping me on the shoulder, trying to be good-natured, I think, but also sounding a little resentful.

Despite these dissonances, I settle back into life in my country. Johannesburg grows on me in a way that I didn't expect it would. The mania about security mutates into a feeling closer to instinct and reflex. To spend all of one's life behind one kind of locked door or another, as many locked doors as possible, is simply the way things are, or at least the way Sarah and I choose to live while we're here. I know my colleagues and my students – perhaps even Greg – would insist there are other ways, perhaps riskier but more alive, more engaged. It's not a mode I'm capable of embracing.

By early April, as autumn begins to arrive, I finish transcribing my interviews with Clare. I settle on a form and a voice for the book – a rhythm that alternates between the historical account of her life and critical analysis of the novels, unfolding in a voice as closely approximating her own – the cool tone and sometimes angry formality, the dry tease and dismissal – as I find it possible to write. I finish a draft of the first two chapters, one about the English settler ancestors on both sides of her family, and the other about her first novel, *Landing*. I have always thought of *Landing* simply as a book about a woman who checks out of her stultifying Lower Albany farm life to live alone in a series of caves on the Tsitsikamma coast – a feminist refusal of gender norms and expectations, of the husband who forces himself on her, and an embrace of the natural world. Rereading it, I see the book is only superficially about these things. It is, more profoundly, about a refusal to be complicit in the privilege that apartheid bestowed upon and codified for whites. The heroine, Larena, instead embraces an outlaw position, living outside and beyond the reach of the law, invisible to the state, governable only by her own idiosyncratic sense of ethics and morals. I read it again and imagine

Laura poring over those words as a young woman, finding a forward echo of herself, discovering in its pages a map for the route she might follow.

★

May. Sarah has managed to convince her editors that the Festival is worth a feature, so she accompanies me to Stellenbosch (in fact, having heard me talk endlessly about Clare for years, Sarah's eager to meet her). The events last from Friday through Sunday and I've arranged to see Clare in private on Saturday. We fly to Cape Town on Thursday afternoon. The plane is packed with a sports team from a girls' school in Johannesburg. All of the girls are in the same T-shirts, and most of them act as if they've never been on a plane before: they run around the cabin, talk loudly, begin singing what must be a team song. The adult chaperones and the flight attendants do nothing to control them. I complain to one of the chaperones who tells me that I should just calm down and go to sleep. As we begin the descent to Cape Town, the girls all mass on one side of the plane to get views of the mountain and the city. It feels as though the aircraft might not be able to take it, that the poor distribution of weight will be too much and we'll fall into a tailspin, crashing into my old neighbourhood.

We pick up a car at the airport and drive through to Stellenbosch; after the sprawl and modernity of

Johannesburg, the old town appears like an oasis out of historical fantasy, the Disneyland version of the eighteenth-century Cape, with its whitewashed restaurants and cafés and wine bars. I try to relax over dinner, but feel the tension wrapping itself around inside me. This is the chance, I know, to lay everything out with Clare, to put our mutual past on the table, and decide what it means.

Friday. Clare is one of three writers on the bill at tonight's event, held in an austere modern lecture theatre in the university's Arts Faculty building. Of the other two writers, one is an Australian now resident in San Francisco, the other a Zimbabwean who lives in Cape Town. Clare is the last to read and she's chosen a long passage from near the beginning of *Absolution*.

It's a strange thing to watch, Clare talking about herself, or some fictional self, in the third person, but I begin to see again the woman I met in Amsterdam, and through the process of reading she becomes someone other than the woman I came to know in Cape Town. Both selves, and the self who is described in the book, if that self is separate, all seem to exist simultaneously. In flashes I think I can see each one of them move across her face, take primacy for a moment, and then recede in deference to one of the others. There's a dark humour in her reading that I didn't find in the book when I read it myself. As I listen, I can't help wondering if she knows the truth about

465

Laura. There are moments towards the end of *Absolution* when she seems almost to suggest, to hint, that Laura was not what she appeared to be.

The audience is attentive if a little bemused by Clare, as if they aren't sure what to make of the reading. Some have already managed to get a copy of the book and a man further down our row is following along in the text itself, occasionally shaking his head as though the words Clare is speaking don't match the words on the page.

She reads for nearly forty minutes, longer than either of the others. At the end the applause isn't as enthusiastic as it was for the Australian, who condescended to take questions from the Zimbabwean while Clare sat apart to one side, waiting for her turn. She stands on her own at the end and the evening finishes with the MC reminding us that all three authors will be signing books in the lobby, where there is a reception with wine donated by one of the local estates.

By the time Sarah and I make our way out of the auditorium the lines are already twenty-minutes deep and stretch outside to the street – the longest for the Australian, the next longest for Clare. The Zimbabwean has only a few dedicated admirers, alternative student types with Lenin hats and Peruvian cloth bags. Sarah has brought along a first edition of *Changed to Trees* that she acquired as a student.

As we reach the head of the line Clare sees us and stands. Marie, sitting back to one side, nods at me without smiling, but in a way that looks almost confidential, as if we share a secret. I introduce Sarah to Clare, who is more gracious than I expect her to be.

'Would you mind signing my book?' Sarah asks, sounding star-struck. 'I don't want to trouble you.'

'It's no trouble. After all, it's why I'm here, holding this pen.' Clare frowns for a moment, turning her face down to the book, but by the time she puts her name to the page and looks up again the frown is gone. 'And you, Sam, I shall see you tomorrow at one o'clock sharp,' she says, giving nothing away. 'So much more to talk about.'

Saturday. After a morning of attending more readings and book signings with other writers, Sarah goes off to conduct interviews with the Festival organizers. Before we part for the day, she kisses me and takes my hand.

'Try, if you can, to ask her about the past,' Sarah says. I know she understands how difficult it is. 'Try to put it to rest, for your own sake. If she doesn't remember you, she doesn't, but this uncertainty is going to drive you crazy.'

When I arrive at the guest house where Clare is staying, she orders coffee for us and sends Marie into town to buy a book the Australian writer recommended last night. 'One of his own,' Clare explains, rolling her eyes. 'I told him I was troubled by the Orientalism I detected in his last novel. He retorted by pointing out that all the black characters in *Absolution* are maids or gardeners, and said I should read his previous book, because it would make sense of the one that disturbed me, although they are not sequels "in any obvious sense", according to him. I call that impudence.'

A young woman arrives with the coffee and Clare asks me to pour. The table is so low I have to kneel.

'It's been a long time since I've had a man down on his knee before me.'

At times it feels like she must have a secret twin, and the two of them trade off, taking over the role of Clare Wald for as long as one can stand it, and then passing the part on to the other, one playing Clare as a brittle authoritarian, the other as a solicitous and gossipy flirt.

'When we last met,' I begin, taking out my notebook and audio recorder, 'we were talking about your work as an advisory reader for the censors.'

'Yes, what I suspect you regard as my complicity in the workings of a brutally unjust and philistine regime. That was the idea, was it not, behind your little *coup de théâtre*: the presentation of my censor's report?'

'I have to admit, when I first saw the report on *Cape Town Nights* I thought I had found something extraordinary, because it seemed to run counter to every belief you've ever espoused publicly. But the idea that you worked to censor one of your own books – I still don't know what to make of it,' I say, thinking all the while of what is really on

468

my mind. Sarah is right. I drive myself mad with hesitation, my inability to be direct and say what I actually think. But the fear of causing offence is so great that it cancels out every other intention.

'Does it make me less interesting to you?'

'Not at all. If you had acted to silence another writer, someone you did or didn't know, then that could have been explained away as necessary if regrettable pragmatism – you feeling forced to do what you did not wish to do. Or even as a momentary lapse, a kind of madness. But to think of all the effort required to produce a text that you knew would in all likelihood be banned, and then to be faced with recommending the banning of your own work, that's –'

'Another kind of madness,' she says, arranging a pillow behind her back and propping herself in the corner of the couch. 'To be honest, I had no guarantee that the book I wrote as Charles Holz would be sent to me for review. It was, in that case, pure chance, but then pure chance is responsible for many of the most peculiar weirdnesses of history. Poor Charles – I conjured him only as a sacrifice. He was as much a character as all my others, but the fiction of his being was only apparent to me, and was in many ways my most successful creation, until you came along. He has his own bureaucratic life. You can find the entry for the banning of his book in the *Government Gazette*. His name even appears in a handful of history books and critical studies. One academic has gone so far as to dig up a stray copy of the novel – even banned books found a home in university libraries, as curiosities safe only for academic study – and mentioned it in passing in a larger survey of censored books under the apartheid regime. It makes for entertaining reading, although only, I'm certain, to me. Anyone else could not be very interested in the book. Described as it is – a tale of interracial romance and violence, blasphemy against all three Abrahamic religions, a celebration of Communism, and a sensationalist account of the workings of the ANC and MK – it has only very limited appeal these days. When I embarked on this project of yours it never occurred to me that Charles and his *Cape Town Nights* would even come up. I thought it was all buried, truly. Now I am toying with the idea of republishing it. I have the manuscript, of course, and a copy of the first – the *only* – edition. Who, I wonder, sent you the report? As far as I knew, I was the only one who still had a copy of it.'

'I haven't found out.'

'Nor shall we, I suspect,' Clare says, looking preoccupied. 'I suppose I could have denied knowing who Charles was or where he might be, but there seemed no point in lying to you. You, I think, would have dug up the truth no matter what I might have said.'

'But would you acknowledge that it was also self-serving, in a way, to admit it was you?'

'Oh yes. If I reveal that I was the writer whose

470

work I advocated banning then I inoculate myself against criticism. I do see that entirely. But it's the truth, and even though it should immunize me there's also something damning about *that*, isn't there? As if I had planned it from the beginning – a way to indemnify myself against ever being called to account for my work as a censor. *See*, I would be able to say, *I may have banned a book, but it was only one of my own.* I fear I did not think quite so tactically at that age. If anything, it was an experiment. And the experiment failed, in a way, when the book was delivered to me for review. Some other censor might have read it and decided it should pass, though I cannot imagine that would have happened. Or they might have read it and said, *This is indisputably the work of Clare Wald.* Though that is even more unlikely, because the book was nothing like anything else I'd ever written, and not least because at the time Clare Wald did not have an unmistakable style or trademark. My first few books were so different from one another. At the time, Clare Wald was too young to be known or even recognizable. There, you have trapped me into talking about myself in the third person,' she says, holding out her cup for me to refill. She smiles in a way that looks almost compassionate, but I've learned not to trust my readings of her expressions. The face says one thing and she'll be thinking something else altogether.

The afternoon progresses and while I try to

concentrate on the task at hand, returning to points we've covered in the past and clarifying a few areas that still seem fuzzy, the whole time I'm thinking of Laura, of what I've learned about her, and of standing on Clare's porch at her old house. I look at Clare and I see her younger face, behind the mesh of screen, and I see her daughter's face, too, as I last saw it in the hills above Beaufort West. In moments of silence between us I try to understand what Laura's care for me means in light of Timothy's revelation, but I can't reach any conclusions. All I know with certainty is what I experienced and what I observed. In the absence of evidence, everything else is hearsay and conjecture.

Clare's face gradually falls into the look of disappointment I've come to know so well. I'm letting her down, but if she wants me to ask about my own place in her life, the place that almost was, I still can't bring myself to do it. The dread of hearing her answer is enough to keep me mute on that point. If only she would give me some concrete sign that she remembers that day on her doorstep.

'You might have guessed that the other thing I have to ask about is Nora.'

'Yes, I thought you would come to that.'

'*Absolution* is fiction –'

'I didn't want to call it that. The publishers insisted. It's easier to sell a novel than a weird hybrid of essay and fiction and family and national history, although it's really the latter – both fiction and something that is not quite fiction but less than proper history or memoir. That is why I said I didn't think it would usurp the position of your own book.'

'So the confession about your role in Nora's assassination is which of those? Fiction or non-fiction?'

'I leave that to you to decide, Samuel. You know I am loath to explicate my own texts. All I will say is that there is no evidence to support either conclusion – that the historical Clare Wald did or did not make herself complicit in the assassinations of the historical Nora and Stephan Pretorius, as distinct from the fictional analogues for all three of those individuals, which is how I would urge anyone to read the characters in that book.'

'And the wig? Was the house invasion real?'

'It was real. The wig was stolen, and recovered more or less as the book suggests. But it remains, like so many crimes in our country, unsolved.'

'But –'

'No, Samuel. Really. I've said as much as I dare.'

One half of Clare's mouth turns up in a smile and she looks like she might want to say more, but it's clear that I can push her no further. Just then Marie returns having taken much longer than necessary to buy the Australian writer's book. Clare tells her we've almost finished, explaining to me that she has a dinner appointment with the Festival organizers.

'I have a great many commitments over these few days. More and more people are scavenging for a shred of my time. The university wished for me to spend a month with them and did what such institutions are capable of doing, dangling bewitching amounts of money in an attempt to convince me I should be resident on campus and give a whole series of readings and lectures. "Really, I do not need the money," I told the very nice woman who approached me. "But think of your children, and your estate," she said. "One of my children has long been missing and presumed dead," I told her, "and the other is quite rich." "Then give it all to a deserving charity and think what good it would do," she said. "*I have a better idea*," I suggested. "Why don't *you* give it directly to a deserving charity of *my* choice and we can leave it at that?" "I'm afraid it doesn't work that way," said the woman, explaining in her terribly nice way that it was money in payment for services, as though I were some kind of working woman and the university the wealthiest of possible tricks. That is unkind of me. In fact I think nothing of the sort, but it is not quite my idea of what a writer's life is supposed to be, all that punditry, puffery, public intellectual posturing and – I'll avoid the most obvious word since we both know what it is. In the end I told her no and begged her give the money to one of a list of charities I thought worthy of support. She said she would do what she could, but suspected it would not be possible. Would I at least give a lecture? she asked. I submitted to that. So I must also come back here next week. It is exhausting even thinking about it. You will have to forgive me, Samuel, if I must say goodbye for now. Others make demands on me and I lack the strength to fight off all of them.'

Though she looks sympathetic I can't help wondering if it's a performance of sympathy and she's just a very good actress, playing the role the situation demands. I gather my recorder and note-book and stuff them into my satchel. Before I leave the hotel room, she stops me, a hand on my arm.

'This you may take away,' she says, passing me a thick envelope that she's pulled from the drawer of an end table, her hands shaking, lower lip finding its way in between her teeth. 'It is for you. I mean, you may keep it. It's something I need you to read. Wait until you get back to wherever you're staying. Do not read it now. Do not read it in front of me. Please do not read it in the lobby downstairs and come racing back. Read it and think. I shall wait to hear from you.'

I can't help being intrigued, but I promise to wait. I walk back into town and then turn south, towards the river, stopping at a café on Ryneveld when I can't contain my curiosity any longer. Inside the envelope there's a letter and a thin typescript.

Dear Samuel,
There are questions you came to Cape Town to
ask that you did not ask. There are questions
I should like to ask you as well. But in the
absence of either of us having the courage to
ask the questions for which we most want
answers – the answers without which the entire
process seems to me pointless – I offer you the
enclosed text. I thought I knew how to frame
the questions, but I did not. I also thought I
should find the courage to ask you, and I did
not, still have not. The text I offer is for you,
not for the book. It is for you and for my
daughter and for me, not for publication. The
only way I know how to ask the questions is
to write around them, to interpose my own
imagination into the events as parties neces-
sarily invested with their own versions of history
have related them to me. What I want from
you, if you feel able to offer it, is an indication
of where I have gone wrong in this imagining.
I am asking in the only way I know how, for
you to tell me what you know.
  Love,
  Clare

At first I am simply confused, and unsure what it
is I'm reading.

You come out, across the plateau, running
close to the ground, find the hole in the

fence you cut on entry, scamper down to the road, peel out of the black jacket, the black slacks, shorts and T-shirt underneath; you are a backpacker, a student, a young woman hitchhiking, a tourist, perhaps with a fake accent. Soon it will be dawn. But no, I fear this isn't right. Perhaps it wasn't there, not that town – not the one on the plateau, but the one further along the coast at the base of the mountains . . .

She must have made a mistake. She never would have intended for me to see this. It is far too personal. And then I turn a page and find myself in the text and begin to feel dizzy. But the versions of me and of Bernard that I find in her words are people I don't recognize, and the events she recounts are not the events as they occurred. She knows and she doesn't know. As dinnertime approaches, and I'm due to meet Sarah back at our hotel, I come to the end:

> You wanted him to throw out his arms and cling to you, cry out not to be abandoned, force you into doing what you could not.
> But he had nothing to say.
> Of course I remembered him at once. Not just here. I knew him immediately in Amsterdam. And finding him suddenly before me, it was like being faced with my own assassin. I wondered if he had come

to exact his pound of flesh. But he has only ever been charming. *What does he want? I ask. Why can he not say what he has come to say?*

On the final page, in the long lines of her shaky hand, is a brief postscript:

Come back tomorrow afternoon and say what you failed to say in Cape Town. Let us say what we both know is between us. C.

ABSOLUTION

Though still shaken by Mark's abrupt dismissal of her confession, the next morning Clare made an attempt to return to her usual routine. She woke early and swam before her son was up. Adam arrived as she was drying off and she buzzed him in through the front gate. After a long period of negotiation and renegotiation, she and Adam had settled into a routine that suited Clare and that she hoped also suited him. He had accepted her small patch of exotic plants, the vegetables and herbs and flowers, while she had accepted that as far as growing conditions and soil amendments and the indigenous species were concerned, Adam would have to be treated as the authority, and that beyond the imposition of her kitchen parterre, the structure of the garden should remain unchanged, at least for the present.

With Adam's agreement, Clare ordered two hundred Queen of the Night bulbs, which she had decided should go across the pale front of the house in an unbroken mass, providing a sombre and elegant ribbon of contrast in the spring. 'We will have to replant them every autumn,' she told him. 'Queen of the Night is a fussy, unpredictable tulip, not very robust. If you can make them bloom from year to year, I should be impressed. Would your brother approve of them, do you think?'

'He did not like tulips so much,' Adam said, 'because he thought they are the Dutchman's flower. But these black tulips, I think he never saw these ones. I think they will make a nice memory.'

'A memorial. Yes, I think it is a very nice way to think of them,' Clare said. 'One fitting for a gardener, always needing renewal.'

When Clare returned indoors, she found Mark in the kitchen, drinking his milky coffee and reading the *Mail & Guardian*.

'Have you had time to consider?' Clare asked. 'Have you reached a decision, or can you only offer absolution from the instance?'

'No pleasantries this morning, Mother?'

'You leave me to sleep on my confession and refuse to pass sentence. I have not slept. I could not sleep, in expectation of what you might say. I have been swimming to try to do something with my nervous energy and my anxiety of anticipation. Don't make me wait any longer. Tell me if what I did deserves amnesty, if it truly had political motivation, or if you think I did it out of nothing more than personal spite. That is all I am asking, for your opinion.'

Mark closed the newspaper and folded it in half, so that the masthead remained visible. The front-page story was an investigation of government corruption, of backroom deals and nepotism and fraud in the ruling party, of police payoffs and arms deals and trafficking and the silencing of dissent. Smoke and fire, Clare thought, there is far too much smoke. She sat across from Mark at the breakfast table and tried to draw his eyes to hers as he looked down at the paper, at his coffee cup and pale hands, avoiding her gaze. He drank, slurping his coffee, exhaling and inhaling, and exhaling again so loudly that the exhalation could only be called a sigh. He had condescended to play Clare's game; it struck her as unfair that he should now begrudge fulfilling his role, which would see the process to its necessary conclusion.

'You want to know my opinion. This is only the verdict of this court, as you clearly like to imagine it. I don't say that I'm the final authority or that I have any particular *moral* authority in this case. I feel, perhaps, that I should recuse myself because of my involvement with you, the defendant, and with the victims, although I have no memory of the latter and nothing that I recognize as strong feeling for them. Possibly, though, a small part of me even now wishes that I had been given the chance to know them, and wishes that they had also been given the chance to change, to show themselves more than and less than what you and others thought of them. Change, as you would yourself admit, Mother, is not impossible. The crime you committed – betraying the location of two people whose lives held a symbolic value in this country at the time – is not clear to me. That is to say, it is not clear to me that there is a definite connection between what you said and what happened. We would have to prove that someone – perhaps the man you suspected of being an MK cadre – had reported the information to someone else, perhaps Mr Dlamini, the man who was found guilty and sentenced to death for carrying out the assassinations. Without being able to determine that, I cannot reach a verdict. Let us assume, though, for the sake of this artificial process, that you were responsible in some way, directly or indirectly, which leaves the question of whether your motivation was political or personal – the one being excusable, under the rubric of amnesty that briefly held sway in this country, the other being merely criminal. What I must decide is whether you've proved that your motivation was political. My immediate feeling is that you have not. You were not a member of the ANC or the Communist Party, and certainly not of MK,' he snorted. 'You couldn't even bring yourself to become a member of the Black Sash. You were taking orders from no one, so I fail to see how your action was political.'

'I was a member of the Progressive Party. Give me that at least.'

'Fine. You belonged to a political party that was a small voice of opposition, but your primary concern, as you yourself have made clear, was personal. You feared I would be taken away from you. Your secondary motivation was even more personal: the selfish wish to appear useful to people you respected and feared. Perhaps you now rationalize this as political intent, but in truth it was not. You sat behind your desk and removed yourself from conflict and gossiped with friends and fellow travellers. You might have attended meetings in the early Sixties, but by the second half of the decade you were retreating ever further into your work and your teaching. Don't deny it.'

'I suppose I cannot, if you put it that way.'

'So if your crime was not political, then amnesty is not possible. Assuming you are guilty of what you suspect, you are a mere criminal in the eyes of the law, and should be treated as such.'

'And what does that mean?'

'It means nothing. Because you are guilty of nothing. Loose lips sink ships. You spoke when you should have had better sense, but you didn't pull the trigger. You did not plan the killings. You are not even an accomplice. You have overplayed your role in history, Mother, and I suggest you do nothing else but get over it. I should find you in contempt for wasting the court's time and let them put you in irons and send you down. Perhaps a little punishment would silence your mind.'

'You make me out to be just some cloistered housewife, peddling words. Nothing but a paper tiger in a paper cage.'

'You've sentenced yourself to your own imprisonment, Mother.' Mark stuffed the newspaper in his attaché and clicked it shut, scrambled the twin combination locks on the case, and straightened his tie. 'You never needed me in the first place.'

Clare spent the rest of the morning trying to read but found it easier to plot other plantings of tulips with Adam than to focus her mind on words. Words were too prone to suggest other words, and in reading an innocuous sentence like 'the fish leapt from the lake and turned in mid-air, catching the light as the gemsbok charged into the water', Clare's mind could drift to memories of herself as a child, and her sister as a teenager, and, once again, the cake emerging from the pantry, crowned with shit, the accusation that followed, the whole history of their lives as sisters. Tulips and weeding, the silence of garden work with a man she had come to understand a little and trust a bit more – it was an easier way to make the day pass as she waited for her son's inevitable return.

At least, she assumed it was inevitable. She checked the guest room and found his suitcase was still there, his clothes in the closet. He had left the house after breakfast, and she expected he would be coming back for dinner, although he had given no indication of his plans. But for the suit-case, she might have assumed he had already returned to Johannesburg, to the wife who disliked Clare and the grandchildren she never saw.

As evening came, and still with no word from Mark, she put her defrosted dinner in the oven

484

and watched the news while the nut loaf baked. Taxi drivers, irate that their monopoly should be challenged, had opened fire with automatic weapons on a city bus full of morning commuters coming from the townships; three were dead, scores injured. This was not what was supposed to happen, not how things were intended to work out after all the decades of darkness, but Clare could no longer force herself to feign surprise. Surprise and outrage were taxing emotions. It was easier and less exhausting to resign oneself to the state of things and hope to live out the full span of one's natural life as little disturbed by the world as might be possible.

Following the news were the soaps and, after discovering that Zinzi and Frikkie were going to be married against the protestations of their two families, Clare began to feel herself nodding off. She made a cup of coffee and lowered the blinds in the kitchen, so that Donald Thacker, his kitchen windows open and lights on next door, could not look in on her. He had taken to waving from his own windows when he caught sight of Clare in hers. It was an intrusion too far, to be hailed like that as one went about one's evening.

Perked up by the caffeine, she decided to watch a locally made espionage thriller about a mercenary who had been involved in every 'low-intensity conflict' of the second half of the twentieth century – the Congo, Angola, Nicaragua, etc. – and specialized in infiltrating liberation movements believed to have Communist backing. In the film, the man finally meets his match in the head of a special MK unit planning the Church Street bombings in 1983. Over the course of the film the mercenary infiltrates the unit, but begins to find himself sympathizing with the very ANC agents he is attempting to undermine, and whose bombs he has been ordered to sabotage, in hopes that they will blow up themselves instead of the South African Air Force headquarters.

Clare fell asleep before she could discover what happened to the mercenary – whether he became a turncoat and helped the ANC, or proceeded with the sabotage. She could not remember the details of the actual case, but seemed to recall that things had not gone strictly as planned. She assumed, though, that the film was fiction, that no mercenary mole working on behalf of the apartheid government had been involved, at least not in that particular case.

She opened her eyes to find the test pattern humming on the television screen, and above that the insistent buzzing of the intercom. It was ten past midnight.

'Who is that? Mark?' she shouted, squinting at the intercom's video monitor and turning on the floodlights to illuminate the front gate.

'I've lost your clicker, Mother,' he said, leaning out the window of his hire car. 'You don't need to shout. It's not a transatlantic link.'

'Are you alone?'

'Yes, I'm alone. It's perfectly safe for heaven's sake. Just hurry up before someone does come along.'

Clare pushed the button to open the gate and watched on the monitor as Mark's car lurched up the drive. She waited until the gate had closed, certain that no one had followed him in, before opening the front door. Perhaps Marie's idea for a double set of gates was not so ludicrous. It was possible to imagine how one might be followed or ambushed. It drove Clare mad that her own country could make her think in this damnable way, make her lose all trust and belief in the best nature of her fellow citizens.

'What are you still doing up?' gesturing at Clare's creased day clothes, her shirt stained with red wine and a glob of drying gravy.

'What else did you expect me to do? You didn't call, you didn't let me know when to expect you.'

'I thought I said –' stammering, unknotting his tie, out of breath and still holding his attaché case in one hand '– I thought I explained that I had an all-day meeting with clients, and dinner with colleagues this evening.'

'You charged out of the house without saying a word to me. Perhaps you mentioned it yesterday.'

'I was feeling distracted this morning and not in the best of moods. I apologize unreservedly. Honestly, Mother, I've had a guilty conscience about you all day, after what I said to you this morning.' He paced around at the entrance to the lounge, still working his tie with one hand, until it came loose and he was able to whip it off and throw it over a chair. It was unlike him to shed something in this way, to be anything less than fastidious.

She picked up their earlier conversation as though there had been no lapse. 'Perhaps I have held an inflated sense of my own importance, but I hoped you might understand why this should be so. There is nothing to prove that Nora and Stephan's deaths were *not* the result of my carelessness, Mark, just as there is, admittedly, nothing concrete to say that they were. But I cannot help feeling what I do. Harsh words or the suggestion of draconian punishment, those do not help in a case like mine. I do not respond well to threats of punishment. When I raised the matter with you, what I wished for was an open engagement. I spoke of it only because I respect your mind, and your sense of justice, not because I wished to burden you. I want you to understand what haunts me, what increasingly and quite literally keeps me awake at night. If I cannot tell you, then whom can I tell?'

He shook his head and rolled his eyes. 'If it helps you to forgive my brusqueness, then try to understand that part of my response this morning was total exasperation with the role you had assigned me. I didn't want to play it. I didn't like the choice of dialogue. I wanted to write my own response, but felt I couldn't. I said what I believed you wanted me to say, in the way that you wanted to hear it. If you love me then give me the chance to speak my own words and not yours. Stop playing ventrilo –'

'Then speak! Say what you have to say.'

'Then don't interrupt me!' he shouted, his face reddening. They stood in silence for a moment and then the phone rang. Clare wanted to ignore it but feared it might be Marie.

'Mrs Wald?'

'Yes? Who is this?'

'It's your neighbour, Donald Thacker.'

'What do you want?'

'I saw that your lights were all on, and that a car had come in. I wanted to be sure there was nothing the matter.'

'Nothing in the least. Thank you for your concern. I must say goodnight now. I have a guest,' she said, and put down the phone. 'My neighbour,' she said to Mark. 'A busybody English widower.'

Mark dropped into a chair, flinging his attaché case onto the carpet. He took an inhaler from his jacket pocket and administered himself a dose.

'Please go ahead. I shall remain silent,' Clare said. 'For a change, I shall be the one to listen.'

Mark looked exhausted and glanced at Clare in a way that made her feel she was expecting far too much of him. She did not want to cause him further sadness or pain, or to force him to shoulder a duty that was by rights only hers to bear.

'You gave me your confession,' he said, his breath

coming more steadily. 'Now I wonder if you'd be willing to hear mine? Like yours, it's not a confession of a crime per se. I think we can agree that you've committed no crime. Equally, mine isn't a confession of sin, since sin is something I don't believe in, and I suspect you don't either, though I realize we've never had that conversation. So it's a secular confession of – I don't know what to call it. Let's call it a secular confession of shortcoming, as yours was something like a secular confession of carelessness. These are confessions that we can only make to each other. Maybe, I don't know, I might be able to say this to Dad, though he and I don't speak about things like this. It's not easy for me, as the person who listens to other people's grievances and failures and who's always looking for flaws and shortcomings in my professional life, to describe my own, or even to admit that I have any.'

He paused, and as he was about to speak again the phone rang.

'Blast that man,' Clare said, and picked up the phone. 'What do you want?'

'Mrs Wald? It's Donald Thacker again. I'm sorry to bother you but I noticed that the lights were still on and I wondered if perhaps something *was* wrong only you couldn't say because you would be overheard. If there *is* something wrong, why don't you say to me "Yes, I would be very happy to join your bridge party," and then I should know that I ought to phone the police.'

'Really, Mr Thacker, I must go now. I am busy with my guest,' she said, and put down the phone. 'A most insistent man. Please continue.'

'The year that Laura disappeared, she came to see me in Jo'burg. I was single, working all the time, putting money aside. If things got worse I thought I might emigrate. I've never told you this, have I? I was on the verge of packing it in and going abroad – I was also afraid that my medical exemption would no longer be enough to keep me safe from the army, that things were getting so desperate they'd force even the likes of me to shoulder a gun, or at least press me into serving in some more bureaucratic capacity. In any case, the time I'd spent at Oxford convinced me I could live in England if I had to. And if not there, then Australia or New Zealand, or even the Netherlands. So I was saving up in expectation of leaving. I knew it would take everything I could scrape together to do it comfortably, which was the only way I was prepared to do it. I didn't want to suffer. Laura came to me the spring before she disappeared. It was a strange meeting. She spoke almost in gibberish. I wondered if she was on drugs of some kind. I knew what she was involved in and even having her in my flat terrified me. The last thing I wanted was her activity attaching itself to me and ruining my own chances of getting out of the country. But what I remember most from that last meeting was how frightened she seemed.'

'Did she say what she was afraid of?'

'It was obvious that she believed in what she was doing, but that she was having second thoughts and was worried about her own safety. She said she was being selfish but she needed to get out. So she asked me for help. What she wanted was a loan, to start over somewhere else. That's what she asked me to give her. She spent two hours that evening asking in about a hundred different ways, promising me that nothing bad would happen if I helped her, that I would pay no price. In the end, I didn't believe her story. I thought she was lying. I thought she wanted the money for other things.'

'For her associates.'

'Yes. I thought it was a ruse. And I didn't want to be involved in any of that. I was keeping my hands clean. I was afraid that if I gave her anything, and if something happened and the money could be traced back to me, then that would be the end of my career and the end of my chances to get out. So I refused to help. And what was so horrible about the whole thing was that she acted like it was the very answer she'd been expecting. She tried to change my mind even though I think she knew it was impossible. I was so stubborn. When she disappeared I realized that I'd made the wrong decision. She'd never given me any reason to disbelieve her. She was the most truthful person I've ever known. Who was I to think she would deceive me?'

He covered his eyes with his left hand and his

mouth with the right. It was no longer apparent to Clare what she should do or how she should behave, if it would be wrong to cross the room and hold her son, or if that was the very thing he wanted. They sat in silence for ten minutes and then he removed his hands from his face and looked at her. As he was about to speak the intercom at the front gate buzzed.

'If this is my neighbour I shall phone the police to charge him with harassment. Yes?' Clare barked, pushing the intercom button as the screen flickered into an image of the driveway. 'Oh God what do you want?'

'Mrs Wald? It's Donald Thacker again.'

'I can see that.'

'I know that something is wrong there. I know you're being held hostage. If your attackers can hear me, then they should know that I have a gun and that I've phoned the police. The police are on their way and everything is going to be fine.'

'Mr Thacker, you have made a fool of yourself. There is no one here but my son.'

The little black-and-white image of Donald Thacker looked stunned, and then Clare could hear the police sirens and the different pitch of her own security company's sirens. It took a further half hour to sort out the confusion. Clare consented to the police and security company undertaking a search of the house to be certain there were no intruders hiding in wait until the authorities had left. The police were not amused and warned Mr

Thacker he could be charged with wasting police time.

'Truly, I thought there was something amiss,' he said, blustering the night with his hands. 'I thought I was being a good neighbour and a good citizen.'

Thacker looked so pitiful and frightened that Clare asked the police not to charge him and finally everyone left except Thacker himself.

'I am sorry,' he said, 'but your lights are almost never on at night, and I thought you were alone.'

'Thank you for your concern,' Clare said, shaking his hand as cordially as she could. 'We must go to bed now. My son has an early morning.'

Clare clicked Thacker in and out of her gate and went back inside to find Mark almost in the same position as before the interruption.

'Will you forgive me?' he asked.

'For Laura? Oh, Mark, no. I cannot do that. It is not for me to forgive or to judge. You did what you felt you had to do. If you wish forgiveness, you must ask Laura for forgiveness. I am not Laura,' she said, realizing that she was angrier with her son than she had ever been before. Not only was Clare the wrong person from whom to ask forgiveness, she also lacked the capacity to forgive what Mark had done.

'But Laura is dead.'

'Even still,' she cried, trying to make her face immobile where it convulsed into spasm. 'That shouldn't prevent us from asking Laura to forgive our failures against her.'

'And if she had asked you for money?'

'She did not ask me. But yes, if she had asked me, I would have given it. I wouldn't have thought twice, just as I would give it if you asked. But my relationship with each of you is – was – different from your relationship with each other. I cannot say that you did the wrong thing. You believed you were doing what you had to do at the time. You regret it now. You wish my forgiveness, but from my perspective there is nothing to forgive. I don't hold you accountable for Laura's actions, for what she did, and what became of her, whatever that might have been. She was only accountable to herself. I could have been a different kind of mother to her, and that might have changed everything. We cannot say that one moment or series of moments determined what Laura became. She was an adult. She made her own decisions. I think we dishonour her by assuming we could have changed her mind so easily.'

It was not yet light the next morning and there was already breaking news of another commuter bus being fired on by masked gunmen. Six passengers were reported dead, dozens injured. Nurses striking over a pay deal were barricading hospital entrances so that patients and ambulances and even the doctors themselves could not enter. Hospital workers were toyi-toying in operating theatres, dancing in protest around anaesthetized patients. Injured people were dying on the pavements outside. A woman gave birth in a car park. Abandoned by ward nurses, mental patients rioted for food. The military had been called in to restore order and provide emergency medical assistance, but they were also threatening to strike. Meanwhile, the Health Minister had been indicted for siphoning millions into an offshore account. Clare turned off the television, went to shower and dress, and had the coffee made by the time Mark emerged from his bedroom.

'I've been called back home, Mother. I'm afraid I have to leave this morning.'

'I would say it has been nice to see you but I fear it hasn't been nice for you. It hasn't been entirely nice for me, but that's not what I mean. I am glad you came and I hope you will come to stay again soon. I shall promise not to burden you with further confessions. It is clear that the only answer to my problem is one I must find myself. Short of the dead granting me forgiveness, I have little hope of absolution, and thus of being freed from these memories.'

'There's one thing I don't think I understand,' Mark said, sweeping his tie over his shoulder as he sat down to his coffee. 'The wig. Do you truly believe that Uncle Stephan's relatives are the ones who broke into the old house?'

'If not his relatives then his friends or associates, or even people hired by them.'

'But what does it mean, if that's what actually happened?'

'I took it as a warning – that they knew the role I had played, and they knew that justice had not been done, so far as my involvement was concerned. Perhaps it was not their plan. After all, Marie and her little handgun interrupted them. Perhaps they had other spoils in mind than symbolic ones.'

'Or they were nothing more than ordinary thieves who were interrupted and took the first thing to hand as they fled the house.'

'But then why return the wig to the monument? Your version does not make sense if you think about its return – it requires that they would have been knowledgeable thieves, thieves with a sense of remorse about what they had taken, who returned it to a place where I *might* find it, but not to the house itself.'

'You'd moved out. And it's possible that they *did* know who you were and were only targeting someone they thought might have money. Not all thieves are idiots. I've met my share of knowledge-able ones . . . and remorseful ones, too.'

Clare shook her head and moved around the kitchen, putting bread in the toaster, refilling her son's coffee cup.

'It's not completely impossible, what you say, but I prefer my version. It was a symbolic act – perhaps not the act the robbers intended. Possibly they intended nothing symbolic at all, but some-thing brutal: a reckoning of the flesh. We will not know. I think I no longer fear them. There is little to fear from the living but pain, and pain is, in the end, transitory. I could survive pain, or if not survive it then transcend it.'

Together they ate breakfast in silence. When they were finished, Mark pulled his belongings together, put his suitcase at the door, and the two of them moved through the house without speaking. There was no one else to mediate them, no employee to give them occasion to speak about something other than themselves. Clare finally stopped herself from searching out new reasons to be absent or preoccupied and stood waiting at the door while Mark moved between the guest room and the bathroom and the kitchen and the back porch. It was as though he were delaying departure but could not tell her he wished to stay longer.

When it was almost nine and he had only half an hour to get to the airport he put his arms on Clare's shoulders and leaned close to kiss her once on each cheek. She inhaled him and caught the scent that he would never realize was the smell of his mother and father in equal parts, a hybrid of the two: a fecund spiciness on one hand, a formal, feathery mustiness on the other. Clare put her arms around his back and brought him close and said, though she hoped it was unnecessary, 'You know everything there is to know about me. I have no more secrets. Everything will be archived. It will not be yours, but it will be yours to read. I trust you not to contest my wishes or my final actions.'

'You speak as though you were about to die.'

'Most nights now I feel I am already with the dead.'

He looked at her and put his forehead against hers. It was a thing he had not done since he was a small boy, staring her down at closest range. They held each other's gaze for a moment and then he broke away.

'Before I go I have a request,' he said, taking her hands in his.

'Anything I'm able to do, you know that I shall.'

'I beg of you, please, not to put any of this in one of your books. What we've said to each other is just for you and me. It's not for other people to read. I don't want anyone reading it, in whatever way you might try to disguise it. Don't make up a character that did something similar to what I did to Laura, not even remotely like it. Don't record my confession to you in your diaries or journals for people to read once you're dead. Don't take my story or my words. These are my words.'

'I understand entirely,' Clare said, opening the door.

It was time for him to go.

CLARE

I wake in this hotel in the middle of a night that is never quite night, the old green street-lights flickering outside my window, students shouting below on the street, crying out in ecstasy and relief and yearning, and even here you come to me, Laura, at the foot of my bed, waking this old woman who might as well be dead, my hair grown iron-strong and stringy, eyes dropping into the sinkholes of my skull. You fondle my feet and tickle my toes, the cold burn of your spirit raising welts on my soles. What must I do to make you leave me alone?

I take myself back to that day, to the porch and the men and the boy before me. What sign did you give that I should know Sam's importance? I remember chiefly my terror of the men. It was obvious to me, thinking back on it, that they could not have been strangers you met on the road. They could only be your associates. I knew you would never have consigned your notebooks to people you were not certain you could trust. And I knew the type: the frozen eyes, the determined watchful-ness, alert and jackal-wary, lion-fierce. I knew they came with news of you, and if not with news then in search of you – that was my fear, what they might do to find you, the measures they might take to extract information from me, alone in the house, interrupted and surprised and caught with my guard down. They would take what they wanted, take me as well, to find you. Now I know these fears were unfounded, or if not baseless then perhaps exaggerated, heightened beyond reason.

But not only that, I feared those men might not be what they claimed to be, that it was all a ruse to get themselves inside, to take what was not theirs, that they were no friends of yours. I feared petty criminals, robbers, and invaders. I feared violation. I feared my sister's adopted family, feared that these men had come to visit revenge upon me for the crime I committed in my own younger days. At least that fear was not misplaced, I have to believe, only premature. They would come later, with greater stealth and silent menace.

I wish you could have appreciated how alike we were.

Understand that you were the braver. I always knew this was so.

Your colleagues, from whom I had nothing to fear, presented you to me in text and image, in the form of notebooks and your final letter, and the photographs they had taken, as if to prove their intimacy with you, and you with the boy. I imagined you had slept with the men, perhaps all three of you together, crammed into tight beds, flung out across the floor, rolling round campfires in the bush. A mother will imagine this despite herself, the complications of her children's lives, the constellations of their bodies, fear for their safety and their hearts and the wounds they will bear. I feared you had not been a willing partner, but could only choose to succumb to them, to be a trapdoor in the night into which they crawled, battering you open but leaving you half-intact, frame splintered and hinges sprung, but recognizable for all that. I feared what they could do to me, these associates of yours who might batter in the night. At first I believed I could smell you on the notebooks, feel your sweat and secretions through the bindings, taste your breath in the odours that came off the men. When they left I pressed your letter to my nose and searched for you there.

After presenting your texts, the only thing that now remains of you, they pushed the boy forward, assuming he was mine, and in that movement of two small feet it all became more complicated. Logic said I had no responsibility. No one could make him mine but you, and you were there only on the page, elusive and indirect. You did not tell me to take him, and if you did not tell me, there was no way for me to know your wishes. I needed you to say, 'Take this child, Mother, and keep him close.' I needed direction. I waited for command.

I know that waiting is a form of cowardice.

Understand that I did not know, did not allow myself to know. I was too scared and too selfish to know what to do, and to make myself see what should have been obvious, to piece together the picture you presented, in the smell of connection that remained on those pages.

I can only ask you to forgive me. I have asked you countless times and will ask you again. Tell me what I must do, the penance I must offer. Show me how to make you go away.

In the weeks and months after you left the *Record*, smaller units of time that stretched to larger ones until years passed, our infrequent meetings became ever more rare. And when you did condescend to visit us at the old house on Canigou Avenue, you almost never spoke to me. I would find you in the garden with your father, and as I approached, a tray of drinks in hand, you would fall silent. After such meetings I would ask William what you said, and he always replied, 'Next to nothing. I did all the talking, asking questions, imploring her to be careful. She didn't ask for money but I gave her some anyway. You don't mind?'

'Don't be ridiculous. You know I don't mind,' I would say, wishing you'd had the courage and grace to ask me, or to ask both of us together. I would have given it then, given whatever you asked. If we did not know with certainty what you were doing then we suspected. The law-abiding are not so cagy, so circumspect. We imagined the danger you must have been in and the imagining drove us mad, until, tormented by our worries about you we would find ourselves lying together at night, both awake, unable to sleep because every slipping into unconsciousness was a fall into nightmare visions of you come to grief. What did I fail to do to make you understand that I loved you more than anyone else, would have done anything for you? Why did you set me up as your adversary when all I ever wanted was to be your champion?

Looking at your other notebooks for that period, I see now that your entries become ever more cryptic. On the rare occasions when you record what people say in conversation, you no longer provide named attribution. In place of names are, at first, single initial letters. Later, in the absence of initials there are different colours of ink: red, black, blue, green – a code legible only to you, for which you alone held the key, now lost. Who was black? Who green? Were you yourself red, the most prominent colour, a blaze running across the field of white pages?

In the end even snatches of conversation go. In their place are only dates and times, written in one colour or another. Instead of people, the colours seem to represent locations. It is only in the final notebook that you return to the fluidity of prose, telling the story of your last days, knowing, I now feel certain, that you were not walking merely to some indistinct sense of your own fate. You knew you were crossing the frontier – not to freedom, but to your death.

As the holidays approached, Sam knew that Sarah would want to be with her parents. *You don't have to stay*, he said. *You should go home now. I'll come back as soon as I can.*

He promised he would see her again in January, and everything would go on as before. He asked Sarah if he could send a few boxes of Ellen's things to her apartment – photographs and mementoes, the books by Clare Wald that had given him a map to his own self as a boy, all the things he wanted to keep. Ellen's house was already on the market, the furniture would be sold or donated, the life he had known dispersed once again.

You don't have to ask, Sarah said, *send anything you want to keep.*

He knew what this meant, that everything he owned in the world would be with Sarah, in a country that was not his own.

The police continued to assure Sam they were following up leads and would notify him if there were any developments. They promised they were doing all they could. They suggested there was no reason for him to delay his return to New York since he had not been present at the crime and therefore could provide no evidence that might help their investigation.

On Christmas morning he woke alone in his aunt's house. There was no television to watch and no radio to listen to. He had donated the food in the freezer to the church, which had promised it would be distributed to a needy family. One of the members from the Women's Federation had brought him a plastic bag full of pastries, half of which he ate for breakfast, listening to the silence and the bells pealing across town and the shriek of eagles shredding the air.

He made a salad for lunch and spent the rest of the day sorting through closets and boxes and files, putting those things he was going to throw away in Ellen's bedroom, and all that he wanted to keep in his own. No one had been to view the house, but he felt he should begin to put the place in order.

Late in the afternoon there was a knock and when he answered, dragging open the heavy front door and looking through the bars of the wrought-iron gate that was supposed to protect the house from burglars, there was a stranger standing ten centimetres from him.

What do you want? Sam barked. The man stepped back, looking as though he'd been hit in the chest, and Sam immediately regretted his tone. The man would only want food or money, and would have a long story about his family and his hunger and it being an expensive time of year.

Are you Mister Leroux? the man asked. He had a thin moustache and shook when he spoke. Sam realized he was only a teenager in a man's body.

Do you have some business with Ms Leroux? If you do I'm afraid she's dead.

Are you not Miss Leroux's son?

I'm her nephew. What is this about? Say whatever it is you want, Sam thought, just tell me what you need so I can tell you *no* and send you out of my life.

I'm very sorry to disturb you, sir, the young man said, reaching into his back pocket and retrieving an envelope whose corners were bent. He handed it to Sam, who took it as if it were alive. *I was one of Miss Leroux's students. I was still at university when there was the funeral, and I wanted to say I was sorry to hear that she died. I wanted to offer her family my condolences.*

I'm her only family.

Then I offer you my condolences, sir. She was a very good teacher and a very good person. She wrote me references. I was so sorry –

The young man shook his head and turned his back to Sam. Across the street a neighbour was at her window, watching them, a phone in her hand.

Thank you for the card, Sam said. Despite what he felt rationally, he could not bring himself to trust the man. It was possible he was lying, was himself the perpetrator, the murderer with the gun that produced ghastly red inkblots, come to see if there were any other women to rob or rich relatives to fleece. Or he was an emissary of the perpetrators, a scout sent to see if the case was likely to go away or be hounded to conclusion by the survivors.

But no, Sam thought, this man is innocent. If he wanted to do right by the man, whose card – Sam ripped it open – was sincere and elegantly phrased, he should invite him in and give him tea, and perhaps even a token by which to remember his teacher. That's what Ellen would have wanted. Indeed, Sam was sure that's what Ellen herself would have done, and she would have done it with far less hesitation. *That's very kind of you. Thank you again for the card.*

I'm so very sorry, the young man said. *Thank you for your time, sir. I would wish you a happy Christmas but I cannot imagine that it is a happy day for you. So instead I'll just wish you peace*, he said, putting his hands together.

Sam wondered why this kind of exchange, which should have been so natural and appropriate, was something he could not bring himself to do properly. If the man had been white he would not have thought twice about letting him in. He could not think of himself as a racist, he was sure he was not, but one had to be careful. Everyone must understand that one had to be careful.

The house was his although he knew he could never again call it home. He could not live in this town or inhabit these rooms. Let someone else have it. He didn't know where he belonged. He was not even sure he could live in this country again.

The house sold faster than he'd expected it would, to a young couple expecting a baby. Like his aunt the woman was a teacher. The man had just been hired at the prison. Looking at the scrub-bare hills to the north and listening to the grinding of trucks on the route between Johannesburg and Cape Town that passed through the middle of town, Sam couldn't imagine wanting to start anything there, let alone a family. It was impossible to drive from one end of Beaufort West to the other without passing the pale walls of the prison built in the middle of the roundabout on the national route. Sam knew what kind of place put a prison at its heart. He notified the neighbours and the church that the house had sold and he would not be coming back. It hadn't been his choice to come here in the first place, and if he belonged anywhere in the world it was not in the middle of these plains, yawning wide their hunger for more lives.

He thought of trying to find the place in the hills where Laura had taken him. He remembered the graves dug and the bodies going into the ground. The country was caught in a spasm of memory. Perhaps others would find the graves, and among the bodies they would find the crushed remains of Bernard. And the truck? What had happened to Bernard's truck? He could think of nothing that would connect him to the crime other than the truck.

He knew there had been hearings about his parents but at the time he had made the decision not to come forward. It was his choice and no one could force him to testify if he did not wish to do so. Silence was his territory.

Maps revealed nothing. Maps were a tracery of lies. The place where he thought the farm should have been was in the middle of the Karoo National Park, which had been founded nearly a decade before the events he remembered. Impossibility layered on impossibility. One afternoon he drove high up into the Nuweveld, but could find nothing that resembled what he remembered. There were no buildings, only acacia and a troop of baboons that rained down the cliffs, a shower of cinders. In places the dirt road looked as he remembered it should, and then he would round a curve to see a new vantage that failed to fit his memory of the place. If the gravesite were ever to be found, he would not be the one to find it.

He'd made a room in his mind where such information could live. Bernard lived there, and now his aunt did too. Parts of Sam lived there as well.

Home was a place he wanted to be and one where he knew he could no longer stay. The sun was too close, the earth too dry, the land itself all too familiar, a terrain telling stories he did not want to remember, stories about himself, and his past, and the life he might have led.

He would tell Sarah everything about his past and his parents. He would hide nothing so there could be nothing to hide. He would tell her about Bernard, everything about him, what he had done and how it had felt.

It would be impossible to tell her anything.

One day he would tell her everything.

SAM

Sunday. When I arrive at her guest house Clare is waiting outside on the yellow front porch, leaning against one of the white pillars. The sun is flashing off the pale green paint of the metal roof. She looks younger, almost as she did twenty years ago on the porch of her old house.

'Since it's a nice day, I was hoping we might go for a walk,' she says, stepping down into the gravelled parking area at the front and taking my hand as if I were a beau picking her up for a date. 'What we need to say is not for note-taking and audio recording. Do you agree?'

'Yes. Today is not for the book.'

We head west, back into town past the university. Clare moves with surprising agility and at times I struggle to keep pace. At Ryneveld we turn south, as I did yesterday, and Clare pauses in a café for a coffee and pastry. 'I am learning to indulge myself,' she says. 'I think indulgence is not such a bad thing at my age. My son says I am too thin and should eat more. He did not stipulate what I should eat.'

As we approach the intersection with Dorp Street, standing for a moment outside an old whitewashed house with a single elegant gable over the door, I thank her for the text she gave me yesterday. I don't know what else to call it, so I refer to it as the letter, her letter to Laura.

'Letter, yes,' Clare says, 'it's a letter of sorts. More like one half of a diary I've been keeping since you arrived last August. Your coming occasioned it.'

'Of course, Laura must be dead. You say as much in the book, after all.'

'Logic would say so. No contact, no word, no sign – at least, no *natural* sign. There is another me, one afflicted by nightmares, who is not so convinced – the me who is suspicious of certainties, who still clings to the hope of mysterious things in heaven and earth. Miracles and resurrections and hauntings. But we are dodging the main point of the letter. Were you not surprised that I remembered you all this time?'

'In all our meetings you've never given any indication that you knew who I was. For ages you acted as though you didn't even recognize that I was South African. So yes, I was very surprised.'

'Cruel of me, I know. But then you have played a kind of game as well, keeping your cards hidden, or at least you thought they were hidden. Little did you know that I had dealt the deck.'

'I can't help feeling that everything might have

been easier if one of us had said something in the first place.'

'Or it might all have fallen apart. I might have snapped, or you might have taken flight. Listen, I know I am not an easy person to deal with. Truth be told I have cultivated my difficult persona. But then *easy* is not necessarily *good*, as any philosopher will tell you. Part of me felt you needed to earn that recognition. And also, there was a significant part that feared what you might do if I admitted to remembering you. I was afraid of your anger.'

Stopping to finish her coffee, she puts the empty cup in a bin with great attentiveness, as though wanting to credit the cup and its disposal with as much significance as our conversation. She brushes crumbs from her fingers and takes my hand as if picking up a small bird. 'Did you think you got this job on the basis of your intellect alone, on supreme good luck, the quality of your work, and the references of a few scrappy scholars who think themselves gods?'

'I supposed that I had. I thought it was chance that brought me back to you. And my own talent.'

'A flattering rationale, but no. I chose you. I commanded your presence. I said to my editor, "If you're going to insist on this project, for the sake of book sales after my death, then I get to choose my biographer." And I chose you, which pleased me a great deal more than my editor, who had half a dozen much higher-profile writers just waiting to do the job. Seeing you in Amsterdam was terrifying but also something like a gift. You were the answer to my problem. I knew immediately who you were: the boy at the door.'

'I never saw so much as a flicker of recognition.'

She raises a hand in modesty. 'We're dealing with two matters here. The first matter is the project at hand, the biography. If it serves to create new interest in my work, and prevents it falling out of print when I am dead, then that will make my son happy, no matter how he protests, and it will make my publishers very happy indeed. The second matter is: why you? I chose you not because I respect your work more than anyone else's. I have read more insightful scholarship, more theoretically sophisticated engagements, and better written ones, too. You're here because of who you are, because of your place in my family, or the place that I denied you in my family. You're here also because I hoped you might know something more about my daughter in the days before she disappeared. Let us be honest about that at least.'

I feel my legs begin to wobble as she smiles her child's smile, pursing her lips. Standing here with her now, I know I can never tell her what I've learned from Timothy and Lionel. Whatever she may or may not guess about Laura, to tell her what I now believe to be the truth would, I fear, destroy her. Despite whatever lingering resentment I may feel about the past, the last thing I want to do is hurt her.

516

'I have never forgotten you, Sam. How could I? That day, I saw you before you knocked. Lionel, Timothy, and you, all three emerged from a bright little car and stared at my house, consulting a piece of paper, a slip with an address, I presume, then crossed the street and knocked. My husband was at a conference in Johannesburg and I was alone in the house. Suddenly here were these two strange men and a boy on my doorstep, so it was not a good beginning because I was already on guard. Lionel and Timothy introduced themselves and Timothy presented an envelope from my daughter, and her notebooks, and Lionel's photographs. One of them asked if I had heard from Laura. I said no, and pointed at you, and asked who you were. Timothy spoke. He said, "This boy was with your daughter. It seems she was taking him to his aunt in Beaufort West. But then we were in Beaufort West some days ago and we found Sam on the street, running around like a stray. He says his aunt couldn't take him in. She did at first, to please your daughter, but as soon as Laura left, his aunt kicked him out onto the street, in a town where he doesn't know anyone. We just found him in the street." I asked them where Laura was now and they said they could not tell me because they did not know themselves. Is this the way you remember it?'

'More or less,' I say. 'But you don't know the whole story. They were making it up. At that point I hadn't even been to see my aunt. '

517

'We'll come to that. For now, what is important is what *I* remember of that day. I asked them why they had brought you to *me*, of all people in the world. Timothy spoke again. He explained that because you were with my daughter, they thought perhaps I might be some relation of yours. "At first," said Timothy, "we actually thought Sam was Laura's son, but she told us that wasn't so. But maybe a cousin, we thought, a nephew or cousin. And since she'd asked us to bring these papers to you when we could, we thought maybe you'd know what to do with Sam." I looked at you, sternly I think now, and knew that you were no relation of mine. You were not the son of my son, not the child of my cousins or my cousins' children. You stared so blankly at me, Sam, with those dead eyes that I see even now in moments when your mind is elsewhere, and when you think no one is looking. There were bruises on your gangly arms. Your hair was long, fraying at the ends, and even though it was obvious that you'd just been washed, you looked like someone who had been filthy for a long time before that, like a tramp, or a stray. Dusty and ashen.'

'Do you remember what you said next?'

'Yes. And I have regretted it since. It is but one in the long catalogue of my regrets. I said, "I'm sorry, I don't know this boy. He is not one of my relatives. Do you know me, child?" You shook your head, holding tightly, so tightly to Lionel's hand. And Timothy asked, as if he couldn't believe my cold-heartedness, "He isn't one of your family? You have no obligation?" '

'And you said, "I'm afraid he isn't. I don't. He's nothing to do with me. I don't know him. I can't explain how he came to be with my daughter. Child, can you tell us how you came to be with my daughter?" That's what you said.'

'I don't remember the words quite in that way,' Clare says, touching my arm, 'but never mind. Our versions are close enough. And you, when I asked you that hard question, you only shook your head. You had nothing to say. Tell me now, if you can. Tell me what you know.'

I can't let the challenge pass. I did have things to say, and I still do. So I tell Clare the truth about what happened, about my idealistic parents, their friendship with Laura, their deaths, their memorial service, seeing Clare and her husband there, the promise he made, the promise Laura herself made, that if I ever needed anything, all I had to do was to come ask. As I tell her all of this, Clare's face drops, scrambles in confusion, becomes a wet red grid.

'You can't be Peter and Ilse's son? You can't. Oh God,' she cries, ignoring my hand and turning away from me. She finds a bench and collapses on it. 'I didn't realize. I thought you were just a stray of my daughter's. I felt badly enough about *that*, you see. And now. Oh God!' she shouts. A man across the street turns to see if something is the matter, but Clare is oblivious. 'I didn't understand that you were important. But how could I? There were two boys in my memory – the filthy boy at the door with the men, and the clean-scrubbed boy at the funeral, Peter and Ilse's child. I always wondered what happened to the boy at the funeral, but I paid so little attention to my husband's life. A dead student was a tragedy, but – I never thought. I was so consumed in my own life and work. I should have remembered your face but perhaps – is it possible I didn't see you properly at the funeral?'

'It is possible. I saw you, but I don't remember if you saw me.'

'You must understand that my husband's life was my husband's. I played the faculty spouse when I had to, but I paid no attention to details. I had my own career, my own students. What's more, there were many things about my husband's life – I mean to say, we did not have an uncomplicated marriage. There was a great deal I tried quite hard to ignore, to not know about. But –' Her fingers search her face and after a moment she turns to look at me in a way she hasn't before. 'I should have seen it long ago. Of course you're Ilse's child,' she says, leaning over and kissing my cheek. 'I never even *told* my husband about you and the men. You must believe that – you must understand, he didn't know you'd ever come. It isn't his fault. You see I knew what Laura must have done and I was so furious with her. All I wanted was to hear from her, but *directly* from her.

And to receive those notebooks and her letter made me so panicked, so very angry. I had to believe that she really might still be alive, and to be faced with you, this responsibility that she had shouldered, it somehow compounded my anger. But this is awful. You knew her, didn't you? You must have known her for years.'

I think of all I might now say, how I could, in one way, write the end of Laura's story for Clare. But it's not for me to do. I know that the end I could provide would only be the beginning of another volume, the reading of which Clare might not survive. Instead, I tell her that Laura appeared like a saviour when I most needed one.

'How do you mean? A saviour, what, in the way I imagined?'

'Not quite.'

I replay the scene of that day in my head, the remote site where Bernard and I stopped, the falling light, the fury that had broken out inside me as I looked at him there, tight with his own kind of wrath, asleep on the ground with a magazine covering his face. I see my hand turn the key, feel the click of the ignition. My father had put me on the seat in front of him a few times, so I knew how to move the gearshift, how to put my foot on the clutch, to shift the balance from the clutch to the accelerator. The idea was to give Bernard a fright, or perhaps just to drive away. I could say that the accelerator stuck. I could say that the truck went faster than I expected it would and I lost control. I could say that my foot didn't find the brake in time. But now, as I play back the scene, a different version begins to piece itself together.

Bernard is asleep on the ground and I have been left alone in the cab of the truck. As with all the versions I remember I'm almost delirious from dehydration. But in this version, Bernard is still alive when Laura arrives. She comes stealing out of the bush, sees Bernard, and runs in a crouch to the truck. In this version she understands everything. She's been searching for me, tracking me down, trying to save me from the man on the ground. She climbs over me to the driver's side and tells me to be quiet and close my eyes. I put my hand on the gearshift but she removes it, puts it down on the seat. I hear the key turn in the ignition; she depresses the clutch, puts the truck into gear, and accelerates. The bump is the same, and the crunch that comes after. We reverse and stop, we go forward again. With each repetition there's less resistance. The smell of Laura comes back to me, a smell like myself. I realize, in this moment with Clare, that I finally know the truth of that night. We did it together, Laura and I.

Across the street a parade of children in winter school uniforms moves past, teachers at either end keeping them in line. A boy steps out to look at a poster on the wall of a building and with a single word one of the teachers shouts him back into place. That it could be so simple, to know where to step, how to walk, to be told when one has fallen out of line, to be reminded when one has erred and told how to correct oneself. I can see that it's cost the boy something to obey. He wants to run back to the poster, he wants to cross the street to a shop, he does not want to go where all of his classmates are going. Clare is watching him, too.

'A goat midst the sheep,' she says, nodding towards the boy. 'He's the one who'll make a mark, for better or for worse.'

Words begin to pile up in my mouth. I edit and reorder them. 'Because you've trusted me with so much, there's something I feel I'd like to trust you with,' I say, knowing the story I'm about to tell is no longer the truth.

'A secret?'

'Assuming Laura is dead, it's a secret that no one else knows, not even my wife. I still don't have the courage to tell her. It's a secret that should change the way you think about your daughter. It seems fitting that you should be the only other person who knows. In telling you, I'm putting everything in your hands – my freedom and my life.' The story is for Clare's sake, not for mine, and for the sake of Laura's memory.

Clare nods as the parade of children passes around the corner. I assemble the version I want her to know, the feeling of doing it, *my* foot on the accelerator and *my* hand on the wheel and gearshift. It runs like a film on a loop that lives inside me and which I live inside.

'Laura was mysterious, a fighter and a force of nature, but she wasn't a murderer, not a killer in cold blood, not as you imagined her in your diary. She didn't kill my uncle.'

As Clare's face clears and she turns her body to look at me more closely, I know this is the right thing to say.

'Are you telling me what I think you are?'

'Yes. But you were right about the truck.' The words come out in a croak, my voice breaking.

'It was what she wrote in her notebook, that she ran him over with his own truck. But somehow, ultimately, I could not believe she would be so indirect. A truck makes more sense if the driver is a child.'

'What does that make me?'

'It makes you little different from me, but as a child – at least as a white child in those days – you almost certainly would not have been held account-able. What I did to put my sister and brother-in-law in jeopardy was worse in a way, because it was careless and selfish. It is a crime that has haunted me in a very real sense. Writing this last book was my attempt at self-exorcism, a casting out of my demons and my sense of complicity in their deaths, as well as my sense of great failure in not being a better mother to my daughter – and not only my daughter, but to my son as well.'

'There's more,' I say, and struggle to tell her the rest, about the bodies in the truck, about the grave and Bernard's burial, as I remember it. I tell her about once trying to find the place again in the hills above Beaufort West and now not knowing whether to believe what I remember. Clare listens, looking at me even when I can't bear to look at her.

'The historical record would suggest you are mistaken,' Clare says, her voice cool, analytical. 'As far as I am aware, there have been no discoveries of mass graves. There are two things to say about that. First, that history is not always correct, because it cannot tell all the stories that have been, cannot account for everything that happened. If it could, historians would be out of work, because there would be nothing left to do with the past but to interpret what is known. Second, that the record of memory, even a flawed memory, has its own kind of truth. Perhaps the literal truth is not what you have remembered, but the truth of memory is no less accurate in its way. Our whole country has been a mass grave, whether the bodies are in one location or in many, whether killed in one day or over the course of decades. There is still a further thing to consider. It is possible, through a sense of vanity, either conscious or unconscious, to attribute crimes wholly to oneself in which one has had only a partial hand. Do I know with certainty that the people to whom I spoke were responsible for transmitting the information I revealed about my sister and brother-in-law to the person or persons responsible for their assassination? No. There is only a temporal link. I spoke carelessly and the result, it seemed to me, was their deaths. But I have no incontrovertible proof of my own involvement apart from my *sense* of my own involvement. That is why, as Dostoevsky says in his quotation of Heine, *that a true autobiography is almost an impossibility*, because it is in the nature of humans to lie about themselves. You look confused, Samuel. I am not suggesting that what you have told me is a lie. But to remember yourself as, in a very real sense, the agent of your own emancipation, that is a kind of vanity. Let us assume that you did kill Bernard, that you were also complicit in the transport of the bodies of people killed in apartheid atrocities. Without wishing to excuse the killing of your uncle, it is possible to explain it as the result of both historical circumstance and your own highly personal experience of trauma. In the same passage, Dostoevsky says that everyone remembers things he would only confide to his friends, and other things that he would only reveal to himself, under the cloak of privacy. *But there are other things which a man is afraid to tell even to himself.* The question I think you have not asked is why you hated Bernard such that your rage had no choice but to express itself – or, seen another way, that you had no choice but to defend yourself. There are gaps in your narrative. Perhaps you did not tell me the whole story. You need to ask yourself what Bernard himself must have done to make you act as you did.'

'Some might call that moral relativism.'

'Indeed. Should you have killed Bernard?' she asks in a matter of fact way, as if weighing the options. 'No. Objectively you should not because that kind of killing is an evil act. But if you wanted to survive, did you have any choice to act except as you did? Again, I suspect the answer is no. You killed in self-protection. And if we want to satisfy the rigid moralists, we might say that, young as you were, you did not appreciate the consequences of your actions.'

I open my mouth to disagree but she raises a hand to silence me.

'In fact it doesn't matter. What matters, I think, is that there are still things you are hiding, and that are hidden from you. I have felt this since the moment you walked in the door last August. Here, I thought, is a young man who does not yet know himself. I look at you now and I know there are things you are not yet telling me, that you may never tell me.'

★

Monday. While I see Clare again Sarah finishes her story on the Festival. On Sunday afternoon the Australian author got drunk with a group of students and punched a former fan who had accused him of selling out.

Setting aside the more recent past, Clare fleshes out the details of her time in Europe as a young woman, her return to South Africa, her marriage,

527

the births of Mark and Laura, and the beginning of her work as a censor. We speak once again of Laura and she shows me her daughter's notebooks and final letter, in which Laura takes responsibility for Bernard's death. My false confession, I realize, made no difference whatsoever.

'I have no further use for these,' Clare says. 'And anyway, I have kept photocopies for myself. The originals are yours to keep. Marie will confirm that I am compos mentis and witness the gift, lest my son should ever dispute it. Perhaps one day you will get something else as well, something like what you truly deserve.' She takes a breath as if about to say more, but then shakes her head. 'I myself cannot wholly make up for the way you were denied – denied by myself, and also perhaps by others. What different lives we might have led if I'd had the courage and generosity to take you in, a second son. Will you tell your wife, now that you have told me? Will you tell her everything about your past?'

'I don't know. I'm not sure it's something I can bear for her to know.'

Clare holds my hand, gripping it in a way that my mother used to, holding it so hard it hurts. 'I understand that reluctance. Perhaps you are right. Some things are better left hidden. But if you want my opinion, I think you should trust her. Give her a chance.' She draws herself up to her full height and takes my other hand. 'So, we must say goodbye, but only goodbye *for now*, because

I have no doubt I will see you again, perhaps even in Johannesburg. I trust you will be as honest as you feel able to be, and write me as you remember me. Let others judge. But perhaps I may be allowed an afterword.'

CLARE

The garden is closing into winter, the tomato plants have been pulled up and the Cape gooseberries and lemons are beginning to ripen. Everywhere there is the smell of wood smoke, which rises off the Cape Flats and suspends itself in a band that half obscures the mountains above Stellenbosch. On the worst days the outline of the sun is distinct to the naked eye, a flat red disc.

Inside the house there is no dust on any surface, no fingerprints on the cupboards or appliances in the kitchen. Every cushion and rug in the lounge is square.

Nosipho is too conscientious to be lax even when this old cat goes out prowling. The silver has been polished and the crystal treated in some magical way that makes it appear newly cut. I open the tin containing my father's wig and find that it also looks refreshed, as though rewoven with the hair of a pony.

'You have outdone yourself,' I tell her, and she smiles, showing a gap in her teeth that was not there before.

'What has happened to your tooth?'

'It had to come out.'

'We must get it fixed. Tell Marie I say it must be fixed. She will make you an appointment with my dentist.'

Call it penance of a kind. It is too little, I know – too little sent in the right direction and the wrong direction at the same time. I have made a resolution to find Stephan's family, whoever may remain, and make my confession to them. The dead cannot offer absolution.

The time away seems to have done me good. The insomnia is gone, even if you are not, Laura. I know now that you will never entirely go, that I must accept your comings and goings and trust they will be unpredictable and that I can always rely on them.

★

During an appearance at the Book Lounge the other day a man asked me how you had died, since *Absolution* refers to your death in the context of your activities, which I allude to in only vague terms. I told him I did not know how you had died because your remains had never been recovered, but death had to be assumed. I told him I had no death certificate and that none of your colleagues, apart from two men who themselves came looking for you, had ever been in contact with me, even to express condolences or thank me for the sacrifice that you made. During the obligatory book signing the man came up to me and, in the way of a surprising number of young men today, was so overcome by emotion that he put his arms around my shoulders without asking permission. At first I was shocked, and then found myself comforted as I could not have expected to be. 'You're so brave,' said the man, 'so very, very brave.'

'It's only fiction after all,' I told him, turning over the book to point at the label on the back, just above the barcode. Language makes the world around us, and all that we encounter. If I call it fiction, then fiction it is.

The man looked at me quizzically and said, 'But that's not fiction, is it? The stuff about your daughter, that's not all fiction? All of the family stuff, that has to be real,' he said, very determined that I should agree. He was right of course.

'No, that is not fiction. Most of it isn't,' I said, 'but some of it is. According to the book itself, it is nothing but fiction, even the family histories, and even my dead daughter.' The man shook his head and, looking as though he might cry, walked away. I had not given him what he wanted. I had nothing to give but what I gave. It cannot be one thing or the other, black or white. It is both and neither and something else, something in between.

The book, whatever its life in the world may yet prove to be, has been an important personal achievement for me, no less than this diary. It and the diary have been my exorcism, my casting out of demons, and at last I feel that I may stop mourning for my failure to mourn properly all these years over my unburied dead. I mourn for you now, Laura, for the loss of you. Not only for you, but for my parents, and for Nora, too, all the parts of you four that remain abroad in the world, clinging to the living.

★

I go to Johannesburg to facilitate the series of lectures about literature and the law arranged in conjunction with the Constitutional Court, with no minor assistance from Mark, who has been more generous than most would imagine in allowing me to use his identity and his own history in the way I have. Before seeing Sam again, I phone your father to ask him if he remembers Sam's parents, Peter and Ilse. Oh yes, he remembers them, all three of them, and wants to know how to contact Sam. I ask him to wait, not to do it yet, to give it time, until the biography is finished and off to press.

Even less than my own book, Sam's will not, I fear, please Mark, but there is little he can do to stop it. He knows better than to cross me. While there is nothing libellous in the draft Sam has shown me, he does say things I wish might have remained hidden, although as more time passes I know that revelation should rather come while one is alive and able to rebut any unwarranted claims. Sam makes no such claims, but, reading what he reveals, others will leap to conclusions I may yet wish to police, or even deny. At least he has given me the chance to offer my perspective. Others will say what they wish.

★

I saw Sam several times in Johannesburg over the course of that week, and in those days I stopped seeing him through your words, Laura, as he appeared in your final notebook, and stopped seeing him even through the distortion of my own memory: as a child on my doorstep, a child younger than he was, a stray with no voice or energy, no family and no history, nothing to give and everything to take, a mere husk. I knew I had to stop seeing him as a vessel that you and I were intent to fill with our words and ideas, our own narrative of who he was. At last, without any distractions, indeed after having surrendered your notebooks to him, as only seemed right, I felt I could begin to see him as he actually is, or at least as he actually was with me, remembering the truism that each of us shows different aspects of ourselves to different people. I do not see him as he is when alone with his wife, or with his students. Perhaps he is with me as he is with senior colleagues. Or perhaps he behaves with me as he behaves with no one else in the world. It would

534

please me to think that our relationship is unique for us both. In those few days I tried to treat him as I would ideally have treated you, Laura, or your brother, but never managed to.

We kept meeting at the university, shivering in the winter sun, pacing around in front of the main building, going to gape and laugh at the murals in the Cullen Library, eating ice cream despite the cold. I went to dinner at his house, enjoyed the company of his charming wife. I did everything I swore I would never do. He offered to introduce me to his new colleagues but I demurred. I was no longer interested in business or books. Rather, those days felt like an ideal version of the reunion between the adopted child and his birth mother, brought together after years of searching for each other. We both recognized that our relationship was at once less profound and more complex than that metaphor suggests. If there is a biological connection it is through the soil of our country: the dust underfoot, rich with life, and the dirt of decay that sticks to us all.

What astonished me more than anything was that I began to see you in Sam, in his hardness and determination and watchfulness: the predator who knows what it is to be wounded, and hunts with the knowledge that he may yet be the hunted. His eyes are your eyes, his smell part of the same blend that pulsed from your pores and still flows from the pores of your brother.

I told him I felt that he had been stalking me

all these years, and at last, when the strength was leaving me, and his own was just beginning to wane, he'd chased me to ground. He laughed and said he'd been feeling the same way. I do not think he was lying.

There is no guile about him. And that, I know, is the quality of the greatest of liars. I am prepared for the biography, when it finally appears, to bear no resemblance to the drafts he shows me. I hope that will not be so, but as much as I have – almost despite myself – come to love him and believe all that he tells me, to want to keep him close and put him in the place where you once stood, I do not trust him, and never shall.